Indiscreet Journeys

Stories of Women on the Road

Indiscreet Journeys

Stories of Women on the Road

EDITED BY
Lisa St Aubin de Terán

faber and faber
BOSTON • LONDON

First published in the United States in 1990 by Faber and
Faber, Inc., 50 Cross Street, Winchester, MA 01890. Orig-
inally published in the United Kingdom in 1989 by Virago
Press Limited, 20-23 Mandela Street, Camden Town,
London NW1 0HQ.

Library of Congress Cataloging-in-Publication Data
Indiscreet journeys : stories of women on the road / edited
by Lisa St Aubin de Terán.
   p.   cm.
   ISBN 0-571-12941-2
   1. Women travelers—Fiction. 2. Short stories—Women
authors.
   I. St Aubin de Terán. Lisa. 1953-
PN6120.95.W7215   1990
808.83' 1—dc20   89-48496

Printed in the United States of America

For Alexandra Pringle

𝒯

Contents

✑

Acknowledgements

Permission to reproduce stories by the following authors is gratefully acknowledged: Louise Erdrich: to Henry Holt & Co., Inc. for 'The Beet Queen'. Copyright © 1986 Louise Erdrich; Sylvia Townsend Warner: to the Executors of the author's Estate for 'But at the Stroke of Midnight' from *Selected Stories* (Chatto & Windus/The Hogarth Press, 1988); Box-Car Bertha: to Harper & Row Publishers, Inc. for the extract from *Sister of the Road*; Edna O'Brien: to the author, Jonathan Cape Ltd and Lescher & Lescher Ltd for 'The Outing' from *The Love Object*; Willa Cather: to University of Nebraska Press for 'A Wagner Matinée' from *Willa Cather's Collected Short Fiction, 1892–1912*, edited by Virginia Faulkner, introduction by Mildred R. Bennett. Copyright © 1965, 1970 University of Nebraska Press; Jean Rhys: to André Deutsch Ltd for 'The Insect World' from *Sleep It Off Lady*; Jessie Kesson: to Chatto & Windus/The Hogarth Press Ltd and the author for extracts from *The White Bird Passes*; Isabelle Eberhardt: to Nina de Voogd, Virago and Beacon Press for extracts from *The Passionate Nomad*; Anna Maria Ortese: to Grandi & Vitali Sri for 'Thunder in Naples'. Translation copyright © Judith Landry 1989; Elizabeth Taylor: to the Estate of Elizabeth Taylor for 'The Excursion to the Source' from *The Devastating Boys*; Dorothy Parker: to Duckworth & Co. Ltd and Viking Penguin, Inc. for 'Here We Are' from *The Portable Dorothy Parker*. Copyright © 1931, 1959 Dorothy Parker. All rights reserved; Colette: to Farrar, Straus & Giroux, Inc. and Martin Secker & Warburg Ltd for 'Journey's End' from *The Collected Stories of Colette*. Translation copyright © 1957, 1966, 1983 Farrar, Straus & Giroux, Inc.; Jeanette Winterson: to A. D. Peters & Co. Ltd for 'The Lives of Saints'; Beryl Markham: to Century Hutchinson Ltd and J. A. Belcher Ltd for 'Something I Remember'; Elizabeth Bowen: to Jonathan Cape Ltd, the author's Estate, and Alfred A. Knopf, Inc. for 'Love' from *The Collected Stories of Elizabeth Bowen*. Copyright © 1981 Curtis Brown Ltd, Literary Executors of the Estate of Elizabeth Bowen; Malachi Whitaker: to Carcanet Press Ltd for 'Landlord of the Crystal Fountain' from *The Crystal Fountain and Other Stories*; Katherine Mansfield: to Alfred A. Knopf, Inc. for 'An Indiscreet Journey'. Copyright © 1924 Alfred A. Knopf; © 1952 John Middleton Murry; Miles Franklin: to Angus & Robertson (UK) Publishers for extracts from *My Brilliant Career*. Copyright © 1901, 1954 Estate of Miles

Introduction

When I first thought of collecting together ideas and stories about women on the road, I was drawn to the theme by my admiration for the great women travellers of the eighteenth and nineteenth centuries – a love that took me endlessly to second-hand bookshops in search of the memoirs of middle-aged ladies in tweeds and galoshes, who had nursed their parents, or housekept for their brothers, and then emerged from their chrysalis of the put-upon spinster into exotic moths and butterflies. Their hovering aura of respectability never quite left them. Among nomads, cannibals and wild Indian tribes, the possibility of a mackintosh square or a slice of Madeira cake or a sniff of sal volatile seemed to travel with them. Their mixture of magic and common sense must have saved them many times in situations where any other, less incongruous attitude must surely have meant their death.

However, the more I considered that genre of explorer, the more I realized that the same spirit of adventure was to be found not only in the parson's daughters who got away and walked around Africa or Egypt, but also in the ones who stayed at home. Gradually my theme broadened to include any sort of journey, like that in Edna O'Brien's story 'The Outing', where Mrs Farley, our anxiously romantic heroine, rides on a bus and falls in love with a bargain, a three-piece suite in a junk shop, and then shapes her life around it. Pieces such as 'Journey's End' by Colette found their niche through expressing so succinctly the idea that the quality, not the quantity, of travel was what mattered. Colette's actress has walked the boards for years, touring as far afield as Saigon, where she sang in an operetta, 'in a theatre lit by eight hundred oil lamps'.

Ill-health and starvation wages have reduced her to a sorry state, but a surprise bus ride home from Mantes to Pigalle is what sticks in her memory as her one great journey.

The road I chose became very much the road of life, and the ultimate qualification for inclusion was merely to have set foot on it. It is not easy to define the word 'journey'; its metaphors have the cobweb quality of gut-spun silk. At times there seemed to be so many roads for inclusion that the possibilities fanned out indefinitely and became as zany as the Hope and Crosby films. No anthology of this nature can ever be complete, but it would be, I believe, inexcusably lacking if it did not contain something by or about those 'women of the streets' who have earned their living by marketing their charms ever since the concept of commerce was invented. I have chosen Harriette Wilson, one of my earliest heroines, to represent her tribe. In the eighteenth century she was one of England's most successful courtesans. Her salon was a centre of wit and fashion, and her horizontal career was often matched by her sisters'. 'Many called us the Three Graces', she wrote.

After years of passionate and notorious entanglements, financial need drove her to write her *Memoirs*, which she offered to suppress in return for a stipend from the – by then ancient – Duke of Wellington. 'Publish and be damned' was his famous reply to the woman he had once loved. *The Memoirs of Harriette Wilson* were published, and they proved so popular that the bookseller had to erect a barricade to protect himself from her eager public. Her book is a poignant and witty account of one of life's great romantics. She turned from the path of virtue, as she relates, by following the bad example of her eldest sister, Amy:

We were all virtuous girls, when Amy, one fine afternoon left her father's house and sallied forth, like Don Quixote, in quest of adventures. The first person who addressed her was one Mr Trench, a certain short-sighted pedantic man . . . when Fanny and I discovered her abode, we went to visit her, and when we asked her what on earth had induced her to throw herself away on an entire stranger . . . ? Her answer was, 'I refused him the whole first day; had I done so the second, he would have been in a fever.'

Amy was really very funny, however spitefully disposed towards me. To be brief with her history: Trench put her to school again, from motives of virtue and economy. From that school she eloped with General Maddan.

Amy's virtue was something like the nine lives of a cat.

Harriette herself took up the quixotic quest and she never looked back, except to gaze honestly at the world she knew and loved.

All the characters in this collection have dreamt of, or set out for, or found, the mythical drinking well of life. A few of them – such as the young bride in Dorothy Parker's 'Here We Are' – one feels, will never get there. Her honeymoon journey manages to be alternately static and retrogressive. From its starting point of a newly wed couple on a train, the story moves relentlessly forward as though uphill through molasses. The distance between the couple grows in direct relation to their nearness to their goal: the honeymoon hotel which will seal their sentence. Written with Dorothy Parker's inimitable deadpan wit, it gives a flip-side view of the conventional romantic version of brides and trains.

As a means of travel and a way of escape (however temporary) the railways provide a vast network of potential adventure. In the surreal sequence of events related in 'The Beet Queen', a child of 'only eleven years old, but already [she was] so short and ordinary that it was obvious she would be this way all her life', jumps out of a box-car of a train in Argus, USA, and the world distils into suspended emotion around her. Louise Erdrich's 'The Beet Queen' is one of America's great short stories, but the queen of her railroads is undoubtedly the extraordinary Box-Car Bertha, hobo extraordinaire. The old blues song says: 'When a woman gets the blues/She hangs her head and cries/But when a man gets the blues/He flags a freight train and rides.' 'Box-Car Bertha' is the autobiography of a hobo who broke that stereotype.

Hundreds of women have lived lives as dangerous and adventurous as the intrepid Bertha's, but only a few have written them down. One of the bands that seems most intriguing are the soldiers who have been fighting in male disguise for as long as their men have gone to war. Some of these, like the Edwardian Valerie Arkell-Smith, who masqueraded as Captain Leslie Ivor, did it for fun. Others, like Hannah Snell, served in the East Indies for financial reasons. After five years she retired herself from the navy. In a pub, celebrating with her mess-mates, she announced to the sailor who had shared her bed, 'Had you known, Master Moody, who you had between a pair of sheets with you, you would have come to closer quarters ... I am as much a woman as my mother ever was, and my real name is Hannah Snell.' Most of them went out of love for a man and stayed out of love of the exhilaration they found in travel and combat.

There are many different kinds of courage, and many different kinds of rebellion. Another of my own heroines was a West Indian slave from the island of Guadeloupe. After the slave rebellion there was quashed by the same French Revolutionary government that had first incited it, there was a spate of exemplary executions in which all the ringleaders were killed. Most mourned of these was a woman called Solitude, a yellow-eyed commander who was hanged immediately after giving birth to a new slave. According to contemporary reports, her group of condemned prisoners were paraded through the streets from the prison to the gibbet outside town. It was a long walk under a tropical sun, eased only by a drinking well placed by the way to refresh prisoners *en route* to their death. It was the custom to allow a rest there at the watering place. Of all the condemned, Solitude alone refused to drink and was whipped for it. Her last words were 'It seems that no one is allowed to say "from this well I shall not drink".'

Women have been drawing water from wells since time began. They are the pitcher-carriers. The road to the well has always been theirs. Often, it was the only road they would ever walk, so it is little wonder that it became a way of escape and an injection of excitement into the prevailing drudgery. It was a place of love and intrigue and emotional release. Taps and plumbing have done away with the need to carry water in most countries, but the well of life still will not be refused. The need to wander has remained like a poppy seed lying fallow until the right moment strikes. This moment that triggers a woman into motion can be either momentous or trivial. It will often be the latter. Regardless of what drives them there, women have for ever been avoiding, having, or seeking indiscreet journeys. Be they explorers or courtesans, camp followers or commuters, entertainers or bolters, they all share the instinctive curiosity of women about each other and an impulsive affinity with their surroundings. Some, like Marianne Evans, the nineteenth-century travelling botanical painter, funnelled their experience into science by culling colour and detail with a passion bordering on zeal. Some of the women in this collection travelled through a love of restlessness itself, while others were restless through love. Some women are driven by necessity, others through boredom. Some sought success and some secrecy, or even just a client for the night.

A few – most notably, here, Beryl Markham – actually flew. Nurtured on the freedom available to a neglected white child in Kenya at the turn of the century, Beryl Markham ran wild. In her teens she trained racehorses. At twenty-three she trained the winner of the Kenya St Leger. She married three times and fell in love with – among others – an English prince. While still very young she became a commercial pilot. She was the first person to fly from England to America. Her true loves were riding and flying; her writing was a secondary affair.

Novelists like Elizabeth Taylor and Jessie Kesson clearly have writing near the centre of their lives. In her autobiographical novel *The White Bird Passes*, Jessie Kesson describes the life of a child growing up in Elgin, Scotland, and then being taken away to an orphanage by 'the cruelty man'. Her keen sense of observation, inspired grasp of place and speech, and rare sense of humour give her pride of place among her peers. Few writers can have travelled as infrequently as Jessie Kesson, even within their own community, yet her imagination is universal, her flying hours are clocked up in her mind. This has been the case with some of the greatest women writers, many of whom never really travelled at all. As Elizabeth Taylor says in her novel *At Mrs Lippincote's*, 'Men are not forced to turn their desolation to advantage as women are. It's easier for them to dissipate their passion, quell their restlessness in other ways. The Brontë girls just couldn't slip down to the pub. So they had to take to writing.'

In a position of social weakness and emotional strength, the female imagination has been commuting for centuries from the mundane to the miraculous. Travel does not necessarily make people great, but it can be a short cut to understanding human nature. I believe that a real understanding of other people is one of the requisites for greatness. By going abroad, whether to another country or just another street, a person is forced to observe a little more closely what they might otherwise ignore around them. Because of social taboos and the physical vulnerability of women, it has always been harder for them to travel, particularly alone. Perhaps that is why their feats seem the more admirable once achieved. This book is about the women who went to the drinking well and the wishing well, and about the ones who quelled their restlessness in writing, and also about the ones who just slipped down to the pub.

Lisa St Aubin de Terán, Venice, 1989

LOUISE ERDRICH

ℐ

The Beet Queen

Long before they planted beets in Argus and built the highways, there was a railroad. Along the track, which crossed the Dakota–Minnesota border and stretched on east to Minneapolis, everything that made the town arrived. All that diminished the town departed by that route too. On a cold spring morning in 1932 the train brought both an addition and a subtraction. They came by freight. By the time they reached Argus their lips were violet and their feet were so numb that, when they jumped out of the box-car, they stumbled and scraped their palms and knees through the cinders.

The boy was a tall fourteen, hunched with his sudden growth and very pale. His mouth was sweetly curved, his skin fine and girlish. His sister was only eleven years old, but already she was so short and ordinary that it was obvious she would be this way all her life. Her name was as square and practical as the rest of her: Mary. She brushed her coat off and stood in the watery wind. Between the buildings there was only more bare horizon for her to see, and from time to time men crossing it. Wheat was the big crop then, and this topsoil was so newly tilled that it hadn't all blown off yet, the way it had in Kansas. In fact, times were generally much better in eastern North Dakota than in most places, which is why Karl and Mary Lavelle had come there on the train. Their mother's sister, Fritzie, lived on the eastern edge of town. She ran a butcher shop with her husband.

The two Lavelles put their hands up their sleeves and started walking. Once they began to move they felt warmer although they'd been traveling all night and the chill had reached in deep.

1

They walked east, down the dirt and planking of the broad main street, reading the signs on each false-front clapboard store they passed, even reading the gilt letters in the window of the brick bank. None of these places was a butcher shop. Abruptly, the stores stopped and a string of houses, weathered gray or peeling gray, with dogs tied to their porch railings, began.

Small trees were planted in the yards of a few of these houses and one tree, weak, a scratch of light against the gray of everything else, tossed in a film of blossoms. Mary trudged solidly forward, hardly glancing at it, but Karl stopped. The tree drew him with its delicate perfume. His cheeks were pink, he stretched his arms out like a sleepwalker, and in one long transfixed motion he floated to the tree and buried his face in the white petals.

Turning to look for Karl, Mary was frightened by how far back he had fallen and how still he was, his face pressed in the flowers. She shouted, but he did not seem to hear her and only stood, strange and stock-still, among the branches. He did not move even when the dog in the yard lunged against its rope and bawled. He did not notice when the door to the house opened and a woman scrambled out. She shouted at Karl too, but he paid her no mind and so she untied her dog. Large and anxious, it flew forward in great bounds. And then, either to protect himself or to seize the blooms, Karl reached out and tore a branch from the tree.

It was such a large branch, from such a small tree, that blight would attack the scar where it was pulled off. The leaves would fall away later that summer and the sap would sink into the roots. The next spring, when Mary passed it on some errand, she saw that it bore no blossoms and remembered how, when the dog jumped for Karl, he struck out with the branch and the petals dropped around the dog's fierce outstretched body in a sudden snow. Then he yelled, 'Run!' and Mary ran east, toward Aunt Fritzie. But Karl ran back to the box-car and the train.

So that's how I came to Argus. I was the girl in the stiff coat. After I ran blind and came to a halt, shocked not to find Karl behind me, I looked up to watch for him and heard the train whistle long and shrill. That was when I realized Karl had jumped back on the same box-car and was now hunched in straw, watching out the opened door. The only difference would be the fragrant stick blooming in his hand. I saw the train pulled like a string of black beads over the horizon, as I have seen it so many times since. When it was out of sight, I stared down at my feet. I was afraid. It was not that with Karl gone I had no one to protect me, but just the opposite. With no one to protect and look out for, I was weak. Karl was taller than me but spindly, older of course, but fearful. He suffered from fevers that kept him in a stuporous dream state and was sensitive to loud sounds, harsh lights. My mother called him delicate, but I was the opposite. I was the one who begged rotten apples from the grocery store and stole whey from the back stoop of the creamery in Minneapolis, where we were living the winter after my father died.

This story starts then, because before that and without the year 1929, our family would probably have gone on living comfortably and even have prospered on the Minnesota land that Theodor Lavelle broke and plowed and where he brought his bride, Adelaide, to live. But because that farm was lost, bankrupt like so many around it, our family was scattered to chance. After the foreclosure, my father worked as day labor on other farms in Minnesota. I don't even remember where we were living the day that word came. I only remember that my mother's hair was plaited in two red crooked braids and that she fell, full length, across the floor at the news. It was a common grain-loading accident, and Theodor Lavelle had smothered in oats. After that we moved to a rooming house in the Cities, where my mother thought that, with her figure and good looks, she could find work in a fashionable store. She didn't know, when we moved, that she was pregnant. In a surprisingly short amount of time we were desperate.

I didn't know how badly off we were until my mother stole six heavy, elaborately molded silver spoons from our landlady, who was kind or at least harbored no grudge against us, and whom my mother counted as a friend. Adelaide gave no explanation for the spoons, but she probably did not know I had discovered them in her pocket. Days later, they were gone and Karl and I owned thick overcoats. Also, our shelf was loaded with green bananas. For several weeks we drank quarts of buttermilk and ate buttered toast with thick jam. It was not long after that, I believe, that the baby was ready to be born.

One afternoon my mother sent us downstairs to the landlady.

This woman was stout and so dull that I've forgotten her name although I recall vivid details of all else that happened at that time. It was a cold late-winter afternoon. We stared into the glass-faced cabinet where the silver stirrup cups and painted plates were locked after the theft. The outlines of our faces stared back at us like ghosts. From time to time Karl and I heard someone groan upstairs. It was our mother, of course, but we never let on as much. Once something heavy hit the floor directly above our heads. Both of us looked up at the ceiling and threw out our arms involuntarily, as if to catch it. I don't know what went through Karl's mind, but I thought it was the baby, born heavy as lead, dropping straight through the clouds and my mother's body. Because Adelaide insisted that the child would come from heaven although it was obviously growing inside of her, I had a confused idea of the process of birth. At any rate, no explanation I could dream up accounted for the groans, or for the long scream that tore through the air, turned Karl's face white, and caused him to slump forward in the chair.

I had given up on reviving Karl each time he fainted. By that time I trusted that he'd come to by himself, and he always did, looking soft and dazed and somehow refreshed. The most I ever did was support his head until his eyes blinked open. 'It's born,' he said when he came around, 'let's go upstairs.'

But as if I knew already that our disaster had been accomplished in that cry, I would not budge. Karl argued and made a case for at least going up the stairs, if not through the actual door, but I sat firm and he had all but given up when the landlady came back downstairs and told us, first, that we now had a baby brother, and, second, that she had found one of her grandmother's silver spoons under the mattress and that she wasn't going to ask how it got there, but would only say we had two weeks to get out.

The woman probably had a good enough heart. She fed us before she sent us upstairs. I suppose she wasn't rich herself, could not be bothered with our problems, and besides that, she felt betrayed by Adelaide. Still, I blame the landlady in some measure for what my mother said that night, in her sleep.

I was sitting in a chair beside Adelaide's bed, in lamp light, holding the baby in a light wool blanket. Karl was curled in a spidery ball at Adelaide's feet. She was sleeping hard, her hair spread wild and bright across the pillows. Her face was sallow and ancient with what she had been through, but after she spoke I had no pity.

'We should let it die,' she mumbled. Her lips were pale, frozen in a dream. I would have shaken her awake but the baby was nestled hard against me.

She quieted momentarily, then she turned on her side and gave me a long earnest look.

'We could bury it out back in the lot,' she whispered, 'that weedy place.'

'Mama, wake up,' I urged, but she kept speaking.

'I won't have any milk. I'm too thin.'

I stopped listening. I looked down at the baby. His face was round, bruised blue, and his eyelids were swollen almost shut. He looked frail, but when he stirred I put my little finger in his mouth, as I had seen women do to quiet their babies, and his suck was eager.

'He's hungry,' I said urgently, 'wake up and feed him.'

But Adelaide rolled over and turned her face to the wall.

Milk came flooding into Adelaide's breasts, more than the baby could drink at first. She had to feed him. Milk leaked out in dark patches on her pale-blue shirtwaists. She moved heavily, burdened by the ache. She did not completely ignore the baby. She cut her skirts up for diapers, sewed a layette from her nightgown, but at the same time she only grudgingly cared for his basic needs, and often left him to howl. Sometimes he cried such a long time that the landlady came puffing upstairs to see what was wrong. I think she was troubled to see us in such desperation, because she silently brought up food left by the boarders who paid for meals. Nevertheless, she did not change her decision. When the two weeks were up, we still had to move.

Spring was faintly in the air the day we went out looking for a new place. The clouds were high and warm. All of the everyday clothes Adelaide owned had been cut up for the baby, so she had nothing but her fine things, lace and silk, good cashmere. She wore a black coat, a pale green dress trimmed in cream lace, and delicate string gloves. Her beautiful hair was pinned back in a strict knot. We walked down the brick sidewalks looking for signs in

5

windows, for rooming houses of the cheapest kind, barracks, or hotels. We found nothing, and finally sat down to rest on a bench bolted to the side of a store. In those times, the streets of towns were much kindlier. No one minded the destitute gathering strength, taking a load off, discussing their downfall in the world.

'We can't go back to Fritzie,' Adelaide said, 'I couldn't bear to live with Pete.'

'We have nowhere else,' I sensibly told her, 'unless you sell your heirlooms.'

Adelaide gave me a warning look and put her hand to the brooch at her throat. I stopped. She was attached to the few precious treasures she often showed us – the complicated garnet necklace, the onyx mourning brooch, the ring with the good yellow diamond. I supposed that she wouldn't sell them even to save us. Our hardship had beaten her and she was weak, but in her weakness she was also stubborn. We sat on the store's bench for perhaps half an hour, then Karl noticed something like music in the air.

'Mama,' he begged, 'Mama, can we go? It's a fair!'

As always with Karl, she began by saying no, but that was just a formality and both of them knew it. In no time, he had wheedled and charmed her into going.

The Orphan's Picnic, a fair held to benefit the orphans of Saint Jerome's after the long winter, was taking place just a few streets over at the city fairground. We saw the banner blazing cheerful red, stretched across the entrance, bearing the seal of the patron saint of loneliness. Plank booths were set up in the long, brown winter grass. Cowled nuns switched busily between the scapular and holy medal counters, or stood poised behind racks of rosaries, shoe-boxes full of holy cards, tiny carved statuettes of saints, and common toys. We swept into the excitement, looked over the grab bags, games of chance, displays of candy and religious wares. Adelaide stopped at a secular booth that sold jingling hardware, and pulled a whole dollar from her purse.

'I'll take that,' she said to the vendor, pointing. He lifted a pearl-handled jackknife from his case and Mama gave it to Karl. Then she pointed at a bead necklace, silver and gold.

'I don't want it,' I said to Adelaide.

Her face reddened, but after a slight hesitation she bought the necklace anyway. Then she had Karl fasten it around her throat. She put the baby in my arms.

'Here, Miss Damp Blanket,' she said.

Karl laughed and took her hand. Meandering from booth to booth, we finally came to the grandstand, and at once Karl began to pull her toward the seats, drawn by the excitement. I had to stumble along behind him. Bills littered the ground. Posters were pasted up the sides of trees and the splintery walls. Adelaide picked up one of the smaller papers.

THE GREAT OMAR, it said, AERONAUT EXTRAORDINAIRE. APPEARING HERE AT NOON. Below the words there was a picture of a man – sleek, mustachioed, yellow scarf whipping in a breeze.

'Please,' Karl said, 'please!'

And so we joined the gaping crowd.

The plane dipped, rolled, buzzed, glided above us and I was no more impressed than if it had been some sort of insect. I did not crane my neck or gasp, thrilled, like the rest of them. I looked down at the baby and watched his face. He was just emerging from the newborn's endless sleep and from time to time now he stared fathomlessly into my eyes. I stared back. Looking into his face that day, I found a different arrangement of myself – bolder, quick as light, ill-tempered. He frowned at me, unafraid, unaware that he was helpless, only troubled at the loud drone of the biplane as it landed and taxied toward us on the field.

Thinking back now, I can't believe that I had no premonition of what power The Great Omar had over us. I hardly glanced when he jumped from the plane and I did not applaud his sweeping bows and pronouncements. I hardly knew when he offered rides to those who dared. I believe he charged a dollar or two for the privilege. I did not notice. I was hardly prepared for what came next.

'Here!' my mother called, holding her purse up in the sun.

Then without a backward look, without a word, with no warning and no hesitation, she elbowed through the crowd collected at the base of the grandstand and stepped into the cleared space around the pilot. That was when I looked at The Great Omar for the first time, but, as I was so astonished at my mother, I can hardly recall any detail of his appearance. The general impression he gave was dashing, like his posters. The yellow scarf whipped out and certainly he had some sort of moustache. I believe he wore a grease-stained white sweater, perhaps a loose coverall. He was slender and dark, much smaller in relation to his plane than the poster showed, and older. After he helped my mother into the passenger's cockpit and jumped in behind the controls, he pulled a pair of green goggles down over his face. And then there was a startling, endless moment, as they prepared for the takeoff.

'Clear prop!'

The propeller made a wind. The plane lurched forward, lifted over the low trees, gained height. The Great Omar circled the field in a low swoop and I saw my mother's long red crinkly hair spring from its tight knot and float free in an arc that seemed to reach out and tangle around his shoulders.

Karl stared in stricken fascination at the sky, and said nothing as The Great Omar began his stunts and droning passes. I did not watch. Again, I fixed my gaze on the face of my little brother and concentrated on his features, blind to the possibilities of Adelaide's sudden liftoff. I only wanted her to come back down before the plane smashed.

The crowd thinned. People drifted away, but I did not notice. By the time I looked into the sky, The Great Omar was flying steadily away from the fairgrounds with my mother. Soon the plane was only a white dot, then it blended into the pale blue sky and vanished.

I shook Karl's arm but he pulled away from me and vaulted to the edge of the grandstand. 'Take me!' he screamed, leaning over the rail. He stared at the sky, poised as if he'd throw himself into it.

Satisfaction. That was the first thing I felt after Adelaide flew off. For once she had played no favorites between Karl and me, but left us both. So there was some compensation in what she did. Karl threw his head in his hands and began to sob into his heavy wool sleeves. Only then did I feel frightened.

Below the grandstand, the crowd moved in patternless waves. Over us the clouds spread into a thin sheet that covered the sky like muslin. We watched the dusk collect in the corners of the field. Nuns began to pack away their rosaries and prayer books. Colored lights went on in the little nonreligious booths. Karl slapped his arms, stamped his feet, blew on his fingers. He was more sensitive to cold than I. Huddling around the baby kept me warm.

The baby woke, very hungry, and I was helpless to comfort him.

10

He sucked so hard that my finger was white and puckered, and then he screamed. People gathered around us there. Women held out their arms, but I did not give the baby to any of them. I did not trust them. I did not trust the man who sat down beside me, either, and spoke softly. What I remember most about him was the sadness. He wanted to take the baby back to his wife so she could feed him. She had a new baby of her own, he said, and enough milk for two.

'I am waiting,' I said, 'for our own mother.'

'When is she coming back?' asked the young man.

I could not answer. The sad man waited with open arms. Karl sat mute on one side of me, gazing into the dark sky. Behind and before, large interfering ladies counseled and conferred.

'Give him the baby, dear.'

'Don't be stubborn.'

'Let him take the baby home.'

'No,' I said to every order and suggestion. I even kicked hard when one woman tried to take my brother from my arms. They grew discouraged, or simply indifferent after a time, and went off. It was not the ladies who convinced me, finally, but the baby himself. He did not let up screaming. The longer he cried, the longer the sad man sat beside me, the weaker my resistance was, until finally I could barely hold my own tears back.

'I'm coming with you then,' I told the young man. 'I'll bring the baby back here when he's fed.'

'No,' cried Karl, coming out of his stupor suddenly, 'you can't leave me alone!'

He grabbed my arm so fervently that the baby slipped, and then the young man caught me, as if to help, but instead he scooped the baby to himself.

'I'll take care of him,' he said, and turned away.

I tried to wrench from Karl's grip, but like my mother he was strongest when he was weak, and I could not break free. I saw the man walk into the shadows. I heard the baby's wail fade. I finally sat down beside Karl and let the cold sink into me.

One hour passed. Another hour. When the colored lights went out and the moon came up, diffused behind the sheets of clouds, I knew the young man wasn't coming back. And yet, because he looked too sad to do any harm to anyone, I was more afraid for

Karl and myself. We were the ones who were thoroughly lost. I stood up. Karl stood with me. Without a word we walked down the empty streets to our old rooming house. We had no key but Karl displayed one unexpected talent. He took the thin-bladed knife that Adelaide had given him, and picked the lock.

Once we stood in the cold room, the sudden presence of our mother's clothing dismayed us. The room was filled with the faint perfume of the dried flowers that she scattered in her trunk, the rich scent of the clove-studded orange she hung in the closet and the lavender oil she rubbed into her skin at night. The sweetness of her breath seemed to linger, the rustle of her silk underskirt, the quick sound of her heels. Our longing buried us. We sank down on her bed and cried, wrapped in her quilt, clutching each other. When that was done, however, I acquired a brain of ice.

I washed my face in the basin, then I roused Karl and told him we were going to Aunt Fritzie's. He acquiesced, suffering again in a dumb lethargy. We ate all there was to eat in the room, two cold pancakes, and packed what we owned in a small cardboard suitcase. Karl carried that. I carried the quilt. The last thing I did was reach far back in my mother's drawer and pull out her small round keepsake box. It was covered in blue velvet and tightly locked.

'We might need to sell these things,' I told Karl. He hesitated but then, with a hard look, he took the box.

We slipped out before sunrise and walked to the train station. In the weedy yards there were men who knew each box-car's destination. We found the car we wanted and climbed in. There was hay in one corner. We spread the quilt over it and rolled up together, curled tight, with our heads on the suitcase and Adelaide's blue velvet box between us in Karl's breast pocket. We clung to the thought of the treasures inside of it.

We spent a day and a night on that train while it switched and braked and rumbled on an agonizingly complex route to Argus. We did not dare jump off for a drink of water or to scavenge food. The one time we did try this the train started up so quickly that we were hardly able to catch the side rungs again. We lost our suitcase and the quilt because we took the wrong car, farther back, and that night we did not sleep at all for the cold. Karl was too miserable even to argue with me when I told him it was my turn to hold

Adelaide's box. I put it in the bodice of my jumper. It did not keep me warm, but even so, the sparkle of the diamond when I shut my eyes, the patterns of garnets that whirled in the dark air, gave me something. My mind hardened, faceted and gleaming like a magic stone, and I saw my mother clearly.

She was still in the plane, flying close to the pulsing stars, when suddenly Omar noticed that the fuel was getting low. He did not love Adelaide at first sight, or even care what happened to her. He had to save himself. Somehow he had to lighten his load. So he set his controls. He stood up in his cockpit. Then in one sudden motion he plucked my mother out of her seat like a doll and dropped her overboard.

All night she fell through the awful cold. Her coat flapped open and her pale green dress wrapped tightly around her legs. Her red hair flowed straight upward like a flame. She was a candle that gave no warmth. My heart froze. I had no love for her. That is why, by morning, I allowed her to hit the earth.

By the time we saw the sign on the brick station, I was dull again, a block of sullen cold. Still, it hurt when I jumped, scraping my cold knees and the heels of my hands. The pain sharpened me enough to read signs in windows and rack my mind for just where Aunt Fritzie's shop was. It had been years since we visited.

Karl was older, and I probably should not hold myself accountable for losing him too. But I didn't call him. I didn't run after him. I couldn't stand how his face glowed in the blossoms' reflected light, pink and radiant, so like the way he sat beneath our mother's stroking hand.

When I stopped running, I realized I was alone and now more truly lost than any of my family, since all I had done from the first was to try and hold them close while death, panic, chance, and ardor each took them their separate ways.

Hot tears came up suddenly behind my eyes and my ears burned. I ached to cry, hard, but I knew that was useless and so I walked. I walked carefully, looking at everything around me, and it was lucky I did this because I'd run past the butcher shop and, suddenly, there it was, set back from the road down a short dirt drive. A white pig was painted on the side, and inside the pig, the lettering 'Kozka's Meats'. I walked toward it between rows of tiny fir trees. The place looked both shabby and prosperous, as though

11

Fritzie and Pete were too busy with customers to care for outward appearances. I stood on the broad front stoop and noticed everything I could, the way a beggar does. A rack of elk horns was nailed overhead. I walked beneath them.

The entryway was dark, my heart was in my throat. And then, what I saw was quite natural, understandable, although it was not real.

Again, the dog leapt toward Karl and blossoms from his stick fell. Except that they fell around me in the entrance to the store. I smelled the petals melting on my coat, tasted their thin sweetness in my mouth. I had no time to wonder how this could be happening because they disappeared as suddenly as they'd come when I told my name to the man behind the glass counter.

This man, tall and fat with a pale brown moustache and an old blue denim cap on his head, was Uncle Pete. His eyes were round, mild, exactly the same light brown as his hair. His smile was slow, sweet for a butcher, and always hopeful. He did not recognize me even after I told him who I was. Finally his eyes widened and he called out for Fritzie.

'Your sister's girl! She's here!' he shouted down the hall.

I told him I was alone, that I had come in on the box-car, and he lifted me up in his arms. He carried me back to the kitchen where Aunt Fritzie was frying a sausage for my cousin, the beautiful Sita, who sat at the table and stared at me with narrowed eyes while I tried to tell Fritzie and Pete just how I'd come to walk into their front door out of nowhere.

They stared at me with friendly suspicion, thinking that I'd run away. But when I told them about The Great Omar, and how Adelaide held up her purse, and how Omar helped her into the plane, their faces turned grim.

'Sita, go polish the glass out front,' said Aunt Fritzie. Sita slid unwillingly out of her chair. 'Now,' Fritzie said. Uncle Pete sat down heavily. The ends of his moustache went into his mouth, he pressed his thumbs together under his chin, and turned to me. 'Go on, tell the rest,' he said, and so I told all of the rest, and when I had finished I saw that I had also drunk a glass of milk and eaten a sausage. By then I could hardly sit upright. Uncle Pete took me in his strong arms and I remember sagging against him, then nothing. I slept that day and all night and did not wake until the next morning. Sleep robbed me as profoundly as being awake had, for when I finally woke I had no memory of where I was and how I'd got there. I lay still for what seemed like a long while, trying to place the objects in the room.

This was the room where I would sleep for the rest of my childhood, or what passed for childhood anyway, since after that train journey I was not a child. It was a pleasant room, and before me it belonged entirely to cousin Sita. The paneling was warm-stained pine. Most of the space was taken up by a tall oak dresser with fancy curlicues and many drawers. A small sheet of polished tin hung on the door and served as a mirror. Through that door, as I was trying to understand my surroundings, walked Sita herself, tall and perfect with a blond braid that reached to her waist.

'So you're finally awake.' She sat down on the edge of my trundle bed and folded her arms over her small new breasts. She was a year older than me. Since I'd seen her last, she had grown suddenly, like Karl, but her growth had not thinned her into an awkward bony creature. She was now a slim female of utter grace.

I realized I was staring too long at her, and then the whole series of events came flooding back and I turned away. Sita grinned. She looked down at me, her strong white teeth shining, and she stroked the blond braid that hung down over one shoulder.

'Where's Auntie Adelaide?' she asked.

I did not answer.

'Where's Auntie Adelaide?' she asked, again. 'How come you came here? Where'd she go? Where's Karl?'

'I don't know.'

I suppose I thought the misery of my answer would quiet Sita but that was before I knew her. It only fueled more questions.

'How come Auntie left you alone? Where's Karl? What's this?'

She took the blue velvet box from my pile of clothes and shook it casually next to her ear.

'What's in it?'

For the moment at least, I bested her by snatching the box with an angry swiftness she did not expect. I rolled from the bed, bundled my clothes into my arms, and walked out of the room.

The one door open in the hallway was the bathroom, a large smoky room of many uses that soon became my haven since it was the only door I could bolt against my cousin.

Every day for weeks after I arrived in Argus, I woke up thinking I was back on the farm with my mother and father and that none of this had happened. I always managed to believe this until I opened my eyes. Then I saw the dark swirls in the pine and Sita's arm hanging off the bed above me. I smelled the air, peppery and warm from the sausage makers. I heard the rhythmical whine of meat saws, slicers, the rippling beat of fans. Aunt Fritzie was smoking her sharp Viceroys in the bathroom. Uncle Pete was outside feeding the big white German shepherd that was kept in the shop at night to guard the canvas bags of money.

Every morning I got up, put on one of Sita's hand-me-down pink dresses, and went out to the kitchen to wait for Uncle Pete. I cooked breakfast. That I made fried eggs and a good cup of coffee at age eleven was a source of wonder to my aunt and uncle, and an outrage to Sita. That's why I did it every morning, with a finesse that got more casual until it became a habit to have me there.

From the first I made myself essential. I did this because I had to, because I had nothing else to offer. The day after I arrived in Argus and woke up to Sita's calculating smile I also tried to offer what I thought was treasure, the blue velvet box that held Adelaide's heirlooms.

I did it in as grand a manner as I could, with Sita for a witness and with Pete and Fritzie sitting at the kitchen table. That morning, I walked in with my hair combed wet and laid the box between the two of them. I looked at Sita as I spoke.

'This should pay my way.'

Fritzie looked at me. She had my mother's features sharpened one notch past beauty. Her skin was rough and her short curled hair was yellow, bleached pale, not golden. Fritzie's eyes were a swimming, crazy shade of blue that startled customers. She ate heartily, but her constant smoking kept her string-bean thin and sallow.

'You don't have to pay us,' said Fritzie, 'Pete, tell her. She doesn't have to pay us. Sit down, shut up, and eat.'

Fritzie spoke like that, joking and blunt. Pete was slower.

14

'Come. Sit down and forget about the money,' he said. 'You never know about your mother...' he added in an earnest voice that trailed away when he looked at Aunt Fritzie. Things had a way of evaporating under her eyes, vanishing, getting sucked up into the blue heat of her stare. Even Sita had nothing to say.

'I want to give you this,' I said. 'I insist.'

'She insists,' exclaimed Aunt Fritzie. Her smile had a rakish flourish because one tooth was chipped in front. 'Don't insist,' she said. 'Eat.'

But I would not sit down. I took a knife from the butter plate and started to pry the lock up.

'Here now,' said Fritzie. 'Pete, help her.'

So Pete got up slowly and fetched a screwdriver from the top of the icebox and sat down and jammed the end underneath the lock.

'Let her open it,' said Fritzie, when the lock popped up. So Pete pushed the little round box across the table.

'I bet it's empty,' Sita said. She took a big chance saying that, but it paid off in spades and aces between us growing up, because I lifted the lid a moment later and what she said was true. There was nothing of value in the box.

Stick pins. A few thick metal buttons off a coat. And a ticket describing the necklace of tiny garnets, pawned for practically nothing in Minneapolis.

There was silence. Even Fritzie was at a loss. Sita nearly buzzed off her chair in triumph but held her tongue, that is until later, when she would crow. Pete put his hand on his head in deep vexation. I stood quietly, stunned.

What is dark is light and bad news brings slow gain, I told myself. I could see a pattern to all of what happened, a pattern that suggested completion in years to come. The baby was lifted up while my mother was dashed to earth. Karl rode west and I ran east. It is opposites that finally meet.

ISABELLA BIRD

from
A Lady's Life in the Rocky Mountains

DEER VALLEY, *November*
Tonight I am in a beautiful place like a Dutch farm – large, warm, bright, clean, with abundance of clean food, and a clean, cold little bedroom to myself. But it is very hard to write, for two free-tongued, noisy Irishwomen, who keep a miners' boarding-house in South Park, and are going to winter quarters in a freight-waggon, are telling the most fearful stories of violence, vigilance commit-tees, Lynch law, and 'stringing', that I ever heard. It turns one's blood cold only to think that where I travel in perfect security, only a short time ago men were being shot like skunks. At the mining towns up above this nobody is thought anything of who has not killed a man – i.e. in a certain set. These women had a boarder, only fifteen, who thought he could not be anything till he had shot somebody, and they gave an absurd account of the lad dodging about with a revolver, and not getting up courage enough to insult anyone, till at last he hid himself in the stable and shot the first Chinaman who entered. Things up there are just in that initial state which desperadoes love. A man accidentally shoves another in a saloon, or says a rough word at meals, and the challenge, 'first finger on the trigger', warrants either in shooting the other at any subsequent time without the formality of a duel. Nearly all the shooting affrays arise from the most trivial causes in saloons and bar-rooms. The deeper quarrels, arising from jealousy or revenge, are few, and are usually about some woman not worth fighting for. At Alma and Fairplay vigilance committees have been lately formed, and when men act outrageously and make themselves generally obnoxious they receive a letter with a drawing of a tree, a

16

man hanging from it, and a coffin below, on which is written 'Forewarned'. They 'git' in a few hours. When I said I spent last night at Hall's Gulch, there was quite a chorus of exclamations. My host there, they all said, would be 'strung' before long. Did I know that a man was 'strung' there yesterday? Had I not seen him hanging? He was on the big tree by the house, they said. Certainly, had I known what a ghastly burden that tree bore, I would have encountered the ice and gloom of the gulch rather than have slept there. They then told me a horrid tale of crime and violence. This man had even shocked the morals of the Alma crowd, and had a notice served on him by the vigilants, which had the desired effect, and he migrated to Hall's Gulch. As the tale runs, the Hall's Gulch miners were resolved either not to have a groggery or to limit the number of such places, and when this ruffian set one up he was 'forewarned'. It seems, however, to have been merely a pretext for getting rid of him, for it was hardly a crime of which even Lynch law could take cognizance. He was overpowered by numbers, and, with circumstances of great horror, was tried and strung on that tree within an hour.[1]

I left the place this morning at ten, and have had a very pleasant day, for the hills shut out the hot sun. I only rode twenty-two miles, for the difficulty of riding on ice was great, and there is no blacksmith within thirty-five miles of Hall's Gulch. I met two freighters just after I left, who gave me the unwelcome news that there were thirty miles of ice between that and Denver. 'You'll have a tough trip,' they said. The road runs up and down hill, walled in along with a rushing river by high mountains. The scenery is very grand, but I hate being shut into these deep gorges, and always expect to see some startling object moving among the trees. I met no one the whole day after passing the teams except two men with a 'pack-jack'. Birdie hates jacks, and rears and shies as soon as she sees one. It was a bad road, one shelving sheet of ice, and awfully lonely, and between the peril of the mare breaking her leg on the ice and that of being crushed by windfalls of timber, I had to look out all day. Towards sunset I came to a cabin where they 'keep travellers', but the woman looked so vinegar-faced that I preferred to ride four miles farther, up a beautiful road winding along a sunny gulch filled with silver spruce, bluer and more silvery than any I have yet seen, and then crossed a divide, from which the view in all the ecstasy of sunset colour was perfectly glorious. It was enjoyment also in itself to get out of the deep chasm in which I had been immured all day. There is a train of twelve freight-waggons here, each waggon with six horses, but the teamsters carry their own camping blankets and sleep either in their waggons or on the floor, so the house is not crowded. It is a pleasant two-storey log-house, not only chinked but lined with planed timber. Each room has a great open chimney with logs burning in it; there are pretty engravings on the walls, and baskets full of creepers hanging from the ceiling. This is the first settler's house I have been in in which the ornamental has had any place. There is a door to each room, the oak chairs are bright with rubbing, and the floor, though unplaned, is so clean that one might eat off it. The table is clean and abundant, and the mother and daughters, though they do all the work, look as trim as if they did none, and actually laugh heartily. The ranchman neither allows drink to be brought into the house nor to be drunk outside, and on this condition only he 'keeps travellers'. The freighters come in to supper quite well washed, and though twelve of them slept in the kitchen, by nine o'clock there was not a sound. This freighting business is most profitable. I think that the charge is three cents per pound from Denver to South Park, and there much of the freight is transferred to 'pack-jacks' and carried up to the mines. A railroad, however, is contemplated. I breakfasted with the family after the freight train left, and instead of sitting down to gobble up the remains of a meal, they had a fresh tablecloth and hot food. The buckets are all polished oak, with polished brass bands; the kitchen utensils are bright as rubbing can make them; and, more wonderful still, the girls black their boots. Blacking usually is an unused luxury, and frequently is not kept in houses. My boots have only been blacked once during the last two months.

[1] Public opinion approved this execution, regarding it as a fitting retribution for a series of crimes.

SYLVIA TOWNSEND WARNER

☞

But at the Stroke of Midnight

She was last seen by Mrs Barker, the charwoman. At ten minutes to eleven (Mrs Ridpath was always punctual, you could set your watch by her) she came into the kitchen, put on the electric kettle, got out the coffee-pot, the milk, the sugar, the two pink cups and saucers, the spoons, the coffee canister. She took the raisin cake out of the cake tin, cut two good slices, laid them on the pink plates that went with the two cups, though not a match. The kettle boiled, the coffee was made. At the hour precisely the two women sat down to their elevenses. It was all just as usual. If there had been anything not just as usual with Mrs Ridpath, Mrs Barker would certainly have noticed it. Such a thing would be quite out of the common; it would force itself on your notice. Mrs Ridpath was never much of a talker, though an easy lady to talk to. She asked after Mrs Barker's Diane and David. She remarked that people in the country would soon be hearing the first cuckoo. Mrs Barker said she understood that the Council were poisoning the poor pigeons again, and together they agreed that London was no longer what it was. Mrs Barker could remember when Pimlico was a pleasure to live in – and look at it now, nothing but barracks and supermarkets where they treated you with no more consideration than if you were a packet of lentils yourself. And at eleven-fifteen she said she must be getting on with her work. Later, while she was polishing the bath, she saw Mrs Ridpath come out of the bedroom and go to the front door. She was wearing her grey and had a scarf over her head. Mrs Barker advised her to put on a mac, for it looked like rain. Mrs Ridpath did so, picked up her handbag, and went out. Mrs Barker heard the lift come up and go down, and that was the

19

last she knew. It was Saturday, the day when she was paid her week's money, and she hung about a bit. But Mrs Ridpath didn't come back, and at a quarter past one she left. Her credit was good, thank God! She could manage her weekend shopping all right, and Mrs Ridpath would pay her on Monday.

On Monday she let herself in. The flat was empty. The Aga cooker was stone-cold, the kitchen was all anyhow; the milk bottles hadn't been rinsed, let alone put out. The telephone rang, and it was Mr Ridpath, saying that Mrs Ridpath was away for the weekend.

By then, Aston Ridpath was so determined that this must be so that when Mrs Barker answered him he waited for a moment, allowing time for her to say that Mrs Ridpath had just come in.

For naturally, when he got home from his office on Saturday (the alternate Saturday when he worked during the afternoon), he expected to find Lucy in the flat, probably in the kitchen. There was no Lucy. There was no smell of cooking. In the refrigerator there was a ham loaf, some potato salad, and the remains of the apple mousse they had had on Friday. It was unlike Lucy not to be there. He turned on the wireless for the six o'clock news and sat down to wait. By degrees an uneasiness and then a slight sense of guilt stole into his mind. Had Lucy told him she would not be back till after six? He had had a busy day; it might well have slipped his memory. It was even possible that she had told him and that he had not attended. It was easy not to attend to Lucy. She had a soft voice, and a habit of speaking as if she did not expect to be attended to. Probably she had told him she was going out to tea, or something of that sort. She sometimes went to picture galleries. But surely, if she had told him she would not be back in time to get dinner, he would have noticed it? By eight o'clock it became obvious that she must have told him she would not be back in time for dinner. No doubt she had told him about the ham loaf, too. She was thoughtful about such matters – which was one reason why her conversation was so seldom arresting. It would not do to seem inattentive, so he would eat and if there was time before she got back, he would also wash up.

He ate. He washed up. He hung the dishcloth on the rail. In some ways he was a born bachelor.

The telephone rang. As he expected, it was Golding, who had

said he might come round that evening with the stamp album he had inherited from an uncle who had gone in for philately. He didn't know if there was anything in it worth having; Ridpath would know. Golding was one of those calm, tractable bores who appear to have been left over from ampler days. Every Sunday he walked from Earls Court to St Paul's to attend matins. Now he arrived carrying a large brown paper parcel and a bunch of violets. 'Lucy's out,' said Aston, seeing Golding look round for somewhere to dispose of the flowers. 'She's gone out to dinner. Have a whisky?'

'Well, yes. That would be very pleasant.'

The album turned out to be unexpectedly interesting. It was after eleven when Golding began to wrap it up. His eye fell on the violets.

'I don't suppose I shall see Mrs Ridpath. I think you said she was dining out.'

'She's dining with some friends.'

'Rather a long dinner,' said Golding.

'You know what women are like when they get together,' said Aston. 'Talk, talk, talk.'

Golding said sympathetically, 'Well, I like talking too.'

Golding was gone. As Aston picked up his violets, which would have to be put into some sort of vase, he realized with painful actuality that if Lucy wasn't back by midnight he would have to do something about it – ring up hospitals, ring up the police. It would be necessary to describe her. When one has been happily married to a woman for nearly twenty-five years it is too much to be expected to describe her. Tall. Thin. Knock-kneed. Walks with a stoop. Brown eyes, brown hair – probably safer to say grizzled. Wearing – How the hell was he to know what Lucy would be wearing if she had gone out to dinner? If he were to say what occurred to him, it would be tweeds.

Suppose she had not gone out to dinner? Suppose – for fiction is after all based on real life – suppose she had gone off, leaving that traditional note on her pincushion? If she had a pincushion. He walked into their bedroom. There was a pincushion, a very old and wilted one, but there was no note on it. He could see no note anywhere. There were some letters on her desk. He read them. They were from shops, or from friends, recounting what the friends had been doing.

If only he had listened! If only she had not got into this unfortunate trick of mumbling! For she would certainly have told him whom she was going out to, 'Aston, I'm having dinner with...' It seemed as if he could almost recapture the words. 'Aston, I'm going...' Could she have continued, 'away for the weekend'? For that would explain everything. It was perfectly possible. There were all those friends who wrote to her about flying in hovercrafts to the Isle of Wight, visiting Leningrad, coming back from cruises to the West Indies. Why shouldn't she be spending the weekend with one or other of these Sibyls or Sophies? It was April, a season when it is natural to spend weekends in the country – if you like that sort of thing. Only a few weeks ago he had remarked that she was looking tired and would be the better for country air. An invitation had come; mindful of his encouragement she had accepted it. He could now almost swear he had heard the words 'Aston, I am going away for the weekend.' No doubt she had also told him where. He had failed to remember it, but one cannot remember everything.

He ate some biscuits, went to bed with a clear conscience, and was asleep in five minutes.

In the morning his first conscious thought was that Lucy was away for the weekend. The conviction was so strong that presently he was able to imagine her being brought breakfast in bed – brown-bread toast, honey, piping-hot coffee; he could positively see the tray. There she would lie, listening to the birds. If it had not been for that unlucky moment of inattention, he would have been able to construct some approximation of the surrounding landscape. London is surrounded by the Home Counties. Somewhere in the Home Counties – for if she had told him she was going to Yorkshire or Cape Wrath he would surely have registered the fact – Lucy was having breakfast in bed. He was glad of it. It would do her good. Thinking affectionately of Lucy, he lay in bed for some while longer, then got up and made his breakfast. The bacon took a long time to cook. He had omitted to riddle the stove overnight; the fire had choked and was almost out. He looked about conscientiously to see if Lucy had left any food he ought to heat up. He did not want to be found with any kind of provisions uneaten. When Lucy went to visit her cousin Aurelia in Suffolk, she always left, he remembered, quantities of soup. This time she had left nothing. No doubt she had said, at that moment when he wasn't attending, that he had better eat out.

Accordingly, Aston ate out. His mind was at rest. Wherever Lucy might be, she could not be with Aurelia and would return from wherever it might have been his own normal Lucy. During those Suffolk absences all he could be sure of was that Aurelia was leading Lucy, whether up a windmill or to Paris, by the nose, and that what he received back would be Aurelia's Lucy: talking in Aurelia's voice, asserting Aurelia's opinions, aping Aurelia's flightiness, flushed, overexcited, and giggling like a schoolgirl. Thoroughly unsettled, in short, and needing several days to become herself again. Family affection is all very well, but it was absurd that visits to a country cousin – a withered virgin and impecunious at that – should be so intoxicating that Lucy returned from them as from an assignation, and acknowledged them as such by leaving him with such quantities of soup. Even when she went to Aurelia's funeral she provided it; and came home saying in Aurelia's voice that cremations would be all right if they weren't so respectful. But now there was no soup and his mind continued to be at rest till he was in the bathroom brushing his teeth before going to bed and noticed Lucy's sponge. It was a new sponge; he had given it to her for Christmas. There was no excuse for leaving it behind. Apparently she had not taken anything – not her hand lotion, not her dusting powder. Examining Lucy's dressing-table, he saw that she had taken nothing from that either. In a moment of blind panic he fell on his knees and looked for her body under the bed.

This was probably due to Wordsworth's tiresome trick of staying about in one's memory. If Lucy had been christened Angelina, he would not have been under the same compulsion to suppose she was dead. Lucy (his Lucy) kept Wordsworth beside her bed. He looked up the poem and found that on this occasion Wordsworth was mistaken, though in the following lyrics he had lost her and it made a great difference to him. Then he remembered that Samuel Butler had wickedly put it about that Wordsworth, aided by Southey and Coleridge, had murdered Lucy. This meant returning to the sitting-room for Butler. Half an hour with Butler recalled him to reason. Lucy must have forgotten to pack her sponge and had bought a new hairbrush.

But the sponge and the hairbrush had shaken him. He did not sleep so well that night, and when he got up to a cold, companionless Monday morning the reality of Lucy's absence was stronger than the ideality of her breakfast tray floating somewhere in the Home Counties, and he hoped very much she would soon be back – by which time Mrs Barker would have put things straight, so that there would be nothing to impede him from saying, 'And now tell me all about it.' For that was the form of words he had decided on.

When he came back that evening everything had been put straight. But still there was no Lucy.

Anxiety hardens the heart. Addressing the absent Lucy, Aston said, 'I shall ring up Vere.' Vere was his sister – a successful widow. He did not like her very much and Lucy did not like her at all. She lived in Hampstead. He rang up Vere, who cut short his explanations by saying she would come at once and grapple.

She came with a suitcase and again cut short his explanations.

'I suppose you have told the police.'

'Told the police, Vere? Why the hell should I tell the police? It's no business of theirs. Nothing would induce me to tell the police.'

'If Lucy doesn't reappear and you haven't told the police, you'll probably be suspected of murder.'

As Aurelia walked towards the Tate Gallery she noticed that she was wearing a wedding ring. Her first impulse – for she was a flighty creature – was to drop it into a pillar-box. Then some streak of latent prudence persuaded her that it would be more practical to sell it. She pulled it off – it was too large for her and revolved easily on her finger – and dropped it into her bag. She remembered that there had been a second-hand jewellery shop a little farther along. She had sometimes looked in through its wire-meshed windows at coral earrings and mosaic brooches of the Colosseum, St Peter's, and other large celebrities. Once, long ago, she had bought herself an unset moss agate there. It was only a simulacrum of moss, but the best that then presented itself. The shop was still in its old place. She went in and presented the ring. The jeweller looked with compassion at the sad middle-aged woman in a mackintosh with a wisp of greying hair plastered to her forehead by the rain. To judge by the ring, she must have known better days. It was both broad and heavy, and he could give her a good sum for it. 'I'm afraid I must ask for the name,' he said. 'It's a formality.'

'Aurelia Lefanu, Shilling Street, Lavenham.' She smiled as she gave the address.

Well, at any rate, the poor thing loved her home.

The same unaccountable streak of prudence now told Aurelia she must do some shopping. Stockings, for instance. It was raining harder, and her feet felt wet already. One need suggested another, and impressed by her own efficiency she bought some under-clothes. Finally, as it was now raining extremely hard and she had collected several paper parcels, she bought a tartan grip. The Tate would be full of people who had gone in to shelter from the rain; but they wouldn't be looking at the Turners. Joseph Mallord William Turner, staring from under his sooty chimney-pot hat, sucking in colour as if from a fruit, making and remaking his world like some unendingly ambitious Jehovah and, like a Jehovah, peopling it with rather unsuccessful specimens of the human race, was hers and hers alone for the next hour. When she left the gallery, Joseph Mallord William Turner had got there before her. The rain had stopped. A glittering light thrust from beneath the arch of cloud and painted the river with slashing strokes of primrose and violet. The tide was at the full, and a procession of Thames shipping rode on it in blackness and majesty.

'Oh!'

In her excitement she seized the elbow of the man beside her; for he too was looking, he too, no doubt, was transfixed. Touched by her extreme emotion and her extreme wetness, he said, 'I'm hoping to catch a taxi. Can I give you a lift? It's going to pelt again in a moment, you know.'

'I've forgotten to take out my bag. Could you wait an instant?'

Seeing its cheapness – indeed, he could read the price, for the tag was still hanging from it – he supposed she was some perpetual student who would be much the better for a good square tea. She had a pretty voice.

The light grew dazzling. In another minute a heavier rain would descend; if he could not secure the taxi that had just drawn up to discharge its passenger, there would be no hope of another. He hauled her down the steps, signalling with her tartan bag, and pushed her in.

'Where can I take you?'

'Where? . . . I really don't know. Where would be suitable?' And gazing out of the window at the last defiance of the light, she murmured, '"Whither will I not go with gentle Ithamore?"'

He gave his own address to the driver. The taxi drove off.

Turning to him, she said, 'Marlowe, not me, I'm afraid it may have sounded rather forward.'

'I've never been called Ithamore in all my life. It's a pretty name. What's yours?'

'Mine's a pretty name, too. Aurelia.'

So it was in London that she breakfasted in bed, that Sunday morning, wearing white silk pyjamas with black froggings – for however cleverly one goes shopping one cannot remember everything, and she had forgotten to buy a nightdress. In all his life he had never been called Ithamore. In all his life he had never met anything like Aurelia. She was middle-aged, plain, badly kept, untravelled – and she had the aplomb of a *poule de luxe*. Till quite recently she must have worn a wedding ring, for the dent was on her finger; but she bore no other mark of matrimony. She knew how to look at pictures, and from her ease in nakedness he might have supposed her a model – but her movements never set into a pose. He could only account for her by supposing she had escaped from a lunatic asylum.

She must be saved from any more of that. He must get her out of England as soon as possible. This would involve getting him out of England, too, which would be inconvenient for Jerome and Marmor, Art Publishers, but the firm could survive his absence for a few weeks. It would not be longer than that. Once settled at Saint-Rémy de Provence, with Laure and Dominique to keep an eye on her, and with a polite subsidy, she would do very well for herself – set up an easel, maybe; study astronomy. She would feel no need for him. It was he who would feel need, be consumed with an expert's curiosity.

She had spoken of how Cézanne painted trees in slats, so he drove her through the beechwoods round Stokenchurch and along a canal to a hotel that concealed its very good cooking behind a rustic Edwardian face. Here she said she was tired of eating cooked food, she would prefer fruit. She was as frank as a nymph about it, or a kinkajou. This frankness was part of her savour. It touched him because it was so totally devoid of calculation or self-consciousness. It would have been remarkable even in a very young girl; in a middle-aged woman showing such marks of wear and tear it was resplendent. It was touching, too, though rather difficult to take, that she should be so unappreciative of his tact. He had led her to a prospect of Provence; he had intimated that he sometimes went there himself; that he might have to go there quite soon; that he hoped it might be almost immediately, in order to catch the nightingales and the wisteria . . .

'Will you take me, too?' she inquired. To keep his feet on the ground, he asked if she had a passport.

On Monday morning he rang up Jerome and Marmor to say he had a cold and would not be coming in for a few days; and would Miss Simpson bring him a passport-application form, please. The form was brought. He left Aurelia to fill it in while he went to his bank. As this was a first application, someone would have to vouch for her, and he would ask Dawkins to do it. Dawkins was closeted with a customer. He had to wait. When he got at him, Dawkins was so concerned to show that the slight illegality of vouching for someone he had never set eyes on meant nothing to him that he launched into conversation and told funny stories about Treasury officials for the next fifteen minutes.

'Aurelia! I'm sorry to have left you for so long . . . Aurelia?'

Standing in the emptied room he continued to say, 'Aurelia'. The application form lay on the table. With a feeling of indecency, he read it. 'AURELIA LEFANU. Born: Burford, Oxon. 11th May 1923 Height: 5 ft. 10. Eyes: Brown. Hair: Grey.' The neat printing persisted without a waver. But at the Signature of Applicant something must have happened. She had begun to write – it seemed to be a name beginning with 'L' – and had violently, scrawlingly erased it.

She had packed her miserable few belongings and was gone. For several weeks he haunted the Tate Gallery and waited to read an unimportant paragraph saying that the body of a woman, aged about forty-five, had been recovered from the Thames.

'If you haven't told the police –' The thought of being suspected of murdering Lucy left Aston speechless. The aspersion was outrageous; the notion was ridiculous. Twenty years and more had passed since they were on murdering terms. But the police were capable of believing anything, and Vere's anxiety to establish his innocence was already a rope round his neck. Vere was at the telephone, saying that Mr Ridpath wished to see an officer immediately. There appeared to be some demurring at the other end, but she overcame it. While they waited, she filled in the time by cross-examining him. When did Lucy tell him she was going away for the weekend? How did she look when telling him? If he wasn't quite sure that she had done so, what made him think she had? Had she been going away for other weekends? Had he noticed any change in her? Was she restless at night? Flushed? Hysterical? Had her speech thickened? If not, why did he say she mumbled? Had he looked in all her drawers? Her wardrobe? The wastepaper baskets? Why not? Had she drawn out money from her post-office savings? Had she been growing morbid? Had she been buying cosmetics, new clothes, neglecting the house, reading poetry, losing her temper? Why hadn't he noticed any of this? Were they growing apart? Did she talk in her sleep? Why did she never come to Hampstead? And why had he waited till Monday evening before saying a word of all this?

When the police officer came, she transferred the cross-examination to him. He was a large, calm man in need of sleep, and resolutely addressed himself to Aston. Aston began to feel better.

'And you were the last person to see Mrs Ridpath?'

Interrupting Vere's florid confirmation, Aston had the pleasure of saying 'No', and the further pleasure of saving her face. 'My sister has forgotten about our charwoman. Mrs Barker must have seen her after I did. She came up in the lift just as I was leaving for work.'

The police officer made a note of Mrs Barker and went away, saying that every endeavour would be made. 'But if the lady should be suffering from a loss of memory, it may not be so easy to find her.'

'Why?' said Vere. 'I should have thought –'

'When persons lose their memory, in a manner of speaking they lose themselves. They aren't themselves. It would surprise you how unrecognizable they become.'

When he had gone, Vere exclaimed, 'Stuff and nonsense! I'm sure I could recognize Lucy a mile off. And she hasn't much to be recognized by, except her stoop.'

Bereft of male companionship, Aston sat down with his head in his hands. Vere began to unpack.

She was in the kitchen, routing through the store-cupboard, when Mrs Barker arrived on Tuesday morning. She said, 'Well, I suppose you know about Mrs Ridpath?'

Mrs Barker put down her bag, took off her hat and coat, opened the bag, drew out an apron and tied it on. Then, folding her hands on her stomach, she replied, 'No, Madam. Not that I know of.' Her heart sank; but a strong dislike is a strong support.

'Well, she's gone. And Mr Ridpath has put it in the hands of the police.'

'Indeed, Madam.'

'Not that that will be much use. You know what the police are like.'

'No, Madam. I have had no dealings with them.'

'They bungle everything. Now, why three packets of prunes? It does seem extraordinary. She was the last person in the world one would expect to do anything unexpected. Did she ever talk to you about going away? By herself, I mean?'

'No, Madam. Never.'

Mrs Barker had no doubt as to where Lucy had gone. She had gone to the South of France – to a pale landscape full of cemetery trees, as in the picture postcard, not sent by anyone, which she kept stuck in her dressing glass and said was the South of France. Remarking that she must get on with her work, Mrs Barker went smoothly to the bedroom, removed the postcard, and tucked it into her bosom.

Loath as she was to admit that her sister-in-law could have a lover, Vere was sure that she had eloped. (Men are so helpless, their feelings so easily played on.) She was sure that Lucy's detestable charwoman knew her whereabouts and had been heavily bribed. A joint elevenses was when she'd catch the woman and trip her into the truth.

This was forestalled by Mrs Barker bringing her a tray for one at ten-fifty, remarking that Madam might be glad of it, seeing how busy she was with her writing: and quitting the room with an aggressively hushed tread. Vere believed in leaving no stone unturned. Though she was sure that Lucy had eloped, this didn't seem to have occurred to Aston yet. A series of confidential letters to Lucy's friends might produce evidence that would calm his mind. Not one of the tiresome women had signed with more than a given name, so the envelopes would have to be directed to 'Sibyl', 'Sophie', 'Peg', and 'Lalla'; but a 'Dear Madam' would redress that. The rest would be easy: a preliminary announcement that she was Aston's sister and was writing to say that Lucy had left home for no apparent reason since she and Aston had always seemed such a happy couple; and that if Lalla, Peg, Sophie, or Sibyl could throw any light on this, of course in strictest confidence, it would be an inexpressible relief. More she would not say; she did not want to prejudice anyone against Lucy.

All this took time. The friends might know each other and get together; it would not do if her letters to them were identical. It would suggest a circular. Her four letters done – for she did not propose to write to people like the linendraper in Northern Ireland who regretted he could no longer supply huckaback roller towels – she would get to work on Mrs Barker; differently, this time, and appealing to her feelings.

It was in vain. However, she managed to get the woman's address from her, so she rang up the police station and stated her conviction that Mrs Barker knew what she wouldn't say and should be questioned and, if need be, watched. As Vere was one of those people who are obeyed – on the fallacious hypothesis that it tends to keep them quiet – an inspector called that afternoon on Mrs Barker. He could not have been pleasanter, but the harm had been done; everybody in the street would know she had been visited by the police. Both the children knew it when they got in – David from school, Diane from her job at the fruiterer's. 'Mum! Whatever's happened?' 'Mum! Is anything wrong?'

The sight of them turned the sword in her heart. But she did not waver. Go back to those Ridpaths she would not; nor demean herself by asking for the money she was owed, though it might mean that the payments on David's bicycle and the triple mirror in Diane's bedroom could not be kept up. Pinch, pawn, go on the streets or the Public Assistance – but grovel for her lawful money to that two-faced crocodile who set the police on her she would not. She drew on her savings; and comforted herself with the thought of the two-faced crocodile down on her knees and doing her own scrubbing. The picture was visionary. Vere was on a committee – among other committees – of a Training Home for Endangered Girls, and whistled up an endangered mental deficient in no time.

'Now, now.' Aurelia adjured herself, gathering her belongings together. 'Now, now. Quickly does it. Don't lose your head.' Going down in the lift she was accompanied by the man in Dante – the decapitated man who held his head in front of him like a lantern and said through its lips, 'Woe's me.' But fortunately he got stuck in the swing door. She was alone in the street and knew that she must find a bus. A taxi would not do, it must be a bus; for a bus asks you nothing, it substitutes its speed and direction for yours, it takes you away from your private life. You sit in it, released, unknown, an anonymous destiny, and look out of the window or read the advertisements. A bus that had gone by at speed slowed as a van came out of a side street. She ran, caught up with it just as it moved again, clambered in, and sat down next to a stout man who said to her, 'You had to run for it, my girl.' She smiled, too breathless to speak. Her smile betrayed her. He saw she was not so young as he took her for. She spent the day travelling about London in buses, with a bun now and then to keep her strength up. In the evening she attended a free lecture on town and country planning, given under the auspices of the London County Council. This was in Clerkenwell. During the lecture she noticed that her hands had left off shaking and that for a second time she had yawned quite naturally. Whatever it had been she had so desperately escaped from, she had escaped it. Like the lecture, she was free. It had been rather an expensive day. She atoned for this by walking to King's Cross and spending the night in the ladies' waiting room. It was warm, lofty, impartial – preferable, really, to any bedroom. The dutiful trains arrived and departed – demonstrations of a world in which all was controlled and orderly and would get on very nicely without her. Tomorrow she would go to some quiet place – Highgate Cemetery would do admirably – and decide where to go next.

It was in Highgate Cemetery, studying a headstone which said 'I will dwell in the house of the Lord for ever', that Aurelia remembered hostels. The lecturer in Clerkenwell had enlarged on youth hostels. But there were middle-aged hostels, too – quiet

31

establishments, scenes of unlicensed sobriety; and as youth hostels are scattered in wild landscapes for the active who enjoyed rock-climbing and rambling (he had dwelt on rambling and the provision of ramblers' routes), middle-aged hostels are clustered round devotional landmarks for the sedentary who enjoyed going to compline. She had enough money to dwell in a middle-aged hostel for a week. A week was quite far enough to plan for. Probably the best person to consult would be a clergyman. There was bound to be a funeral before long. She would hang on its outskirts and buttonhole the man afterwards. 'Excuse me,' she would begin. 'I am a stranger . . .'

'Excuse me,' she began, laying hold of him by the surplice. He had a sad, unappreciated face. 'I am a stranger.'

Thinking about her afterwards – and she was to haunt his mind for the rest of his life – Lancelot Fogg acknowledged a saving mercy. His Maker, whom he had come to despair of, an ear that never heard, a name that he was incessantly obliged to take in vain, had done a marvel and shown him a spiritual woman. His life was full of women: good women, pious women, energetic, forceful women, blighted women, women abounding in good works, women learned in liturgies, women with tragedies, scruples, fallen arches – not to mention women he was compelled to classify as bad women: bullies, slanderers, backbiters, schemers, organizers, women abounding in wrath; there were even a few kind women. But never a spiritual woman till now. So tall and so thin, so innocently frank, it was as if she had come down from the west front of Chartres into a world where she was a stranger.

There was nothing remarkable in what she had to say. She wanted to find a hostel somewhere away from London – but not far, because of paying for the ticket – where she could be quiet and go to compline and do some washing. He understood about washing, for being poor he sometimes tried to do his own. But her spirituality shone through her words; it was as if a lily were speaking of cleanliness. Spirituality shone even more clearly through her silences. While he was searching his mind for addresses, she looked at him with tranquil interest, unconcerned trust, as though she had never in her life known care or frustration – whereas from the lines in her face it was obvious she had known both. She was so exceedingly tranquil and trustful, in fact, that she gave an impression of impermanence – as if at any moment some bidding might twitch her away. Non-attachment, he remembered, was the word. The spiritual become non-attached.

'Would Bedfordshire be too far?'

'I don't think so. I should only be there a week.'

He had remembered one of the women in his life who had been kind and who now kept a guest-house near a Benedictine monastery. He gave her the address. She thanked him and was gone. So was the funeral party. The grave was being filled in with increasing briskness. That afternoon, he must preside at the quarterly meeting of St Agatha's Guild.

The mistake, thought Aurelia, had been to dwell on compline. Doing so she had given a false impression of herself. The recommended Miss Larke of St Hilda's Guest-house had no sooner let her in than she was exclaiming, 'Just in time, just in time! Reverend Fogg rang up to say you were coming – the silly man forgot to mention your name, but you are the lady he met, aren't you? – and that you would be going to compline. I'm afraid we've finished supper. But I'll keep some soup hot for you for when you get back. And here is Mrs Bouverie who will show you the way. She's waited on purpose.'

'How do you do? How kind of you. My name is Lefanu. Is the abbey far away?'

'If we start now we'll make it,' said Mrs Bouverie.

They started. Mrs Bouverie was short and stout and she had a short stout manner of speech. Presently she inquired, 'RC or AC?'

Aurelia was at a loss. The question suggested electricity or taps.

'Roman or Anglo?'

Aurelia replied, 'Anglo.' It seemed safer, though it was difficult to be sure in the dark.

'Mrs or Miss?'

Aurelia replied, 'Miss.'

She had felt so sure that she would be fed on arrival that this day, too, she had relied on buns, resisting those jellied eels which looked so interesting in the narrow street that twisted down to the river – for instead of going straight to the guest-house she had spent an hour or so exploring the town to see if she'd like it. She did like it. But she had never eaten jellied eels.

She had never been to compline, either. This made it impossible to guess how long it would go on, or exactly what was going on, except that people were invisibly singing or reciting in leisured tones. If she had not been so hungry, Aurelia decided, she could have understood why compline should exercise this charm on people. There was a total lack of obligation about it which was very agreeable. And when it had mysteriously become over, and they were walking back, and Mrs Bouverie remarked how beautifully it ended a day, didn't it, Aurelia agreed – while looking forward to the soup. The soup was lentil. It was hot and thick, and she felt her being fasten on it. The room was full of chairs, the chairs were full of people, the television was on. She sat clasping the mug where the soup had been. But it wilted in her grasp. She knew that at all costs she must not faint. 'Smelling salts!' she exclaimed. A flask of vinegar was pressed to her nose, her head was bowed between her knees. When she had been taken off to be put to bed with a hot-water bottle, Mrs Bouverie announced, 'She's Anglo.'

'Naturally. They are always so absurdly emotional,' said a lady who was Roman.

Miss Larke returned, reporting that the poor thing was touchingly grateful and had forgotten to bring a nightdress.

In the morning Aurelia woke hungry but without a vestige of gratitude. The sun shone, a thrush was singing in the garden, it was a perfect drying day.

Aurelia, the replacement of Lucy, was a nova – a new appearance in the firmament, the explosion of an ageing star. A nova is seen where no star was and is seen as a portent, a promise of what is variously desired: a victory, a pestilence, the birth of a hero, a rise in the price of corn. To the man never before called Ithamore she was at last an object of art he could not account for. To Lancelot Fogg she was at last a spiritual woman. To the denizens of St Hilda's Guest-house she was something new to talk about – arresting but harmless. At least, she was harmless till the evening she brought in that wretched tomcat and insisted on keeping it as a pet. If Lancelot Fogg had not recommended her so fervently, Aurelia with that misnamed pet of hers would have been directed to lodgings else-where. It was bad enough to adopt a most unhealthy-looking tomcat, but to call the animal Lucy made it so much worse; it seemed a deliberate flout, a device to call attention to the creature's already too obvious sex.

34

'But why Lucy, Miss Lefanu? Surely it's inappropriate?'

'It's a family name,' she replied.

Lucy developed on Aurelia's fourth evening at the guest-house. She was again accompanying Mrs Bouverie to compline when a distant braying caught her ear. Looking in the direction of the braying, she saw a livid glow and exclaimed, 'A circus!'

'It's that dreadful fair,' Mrs Bouverie replied. 'As I was telling you, my brother-in-law who had that delightful place in Hampshire, not far from Basingstoke, such rhododendrons! I've never seen such a blaze of colour as when they were out . . .'

When she had seen Mrs Bouverie safely down on her knees, Aurelia stole away and went off to find the fair. Fairs, of course, are not what they used to be, but they are still what they are, and Aurelia enjoyed herself a great deal till two haunted young men in frock coats and ringlets attached themselves to her, saying at intervals, 'Spare us a reefer, beautiful. Have a heart.' For they, too, had seen her as a nova. At last she managed to give them the slip and hurried away through the loud entrails of a Lunar Flight. This brought her to the outskirts of the fair, and it was there she saw the cat lying on the muddied grass under the bonnet of a lorry. Its eyes were shut, its ears laid back. It had gone under the lorry bonnet for warmth, and was paying the price.

When she came back with a hot dog, it had rearranged itself. In its new attitude she could see how thin it was and how despairingly shabby. She knelt down and addressed it from a distance. It heard her, for it turned its head away. The smell of the hot dog was more persuasive. It began to thresh its tail. 'You'll eat when I'm gone,' she said, with fellow-feeling, and scattered bits of hot dog under the bonnet and began to walk away – knowing that its precarious balance between mistrust and self-preservation could be overset by a glance. She had left the fairground and was turning into a street full of warehouses when she saw that the cat, limping and cringing, was following her. She stopped, and it came on till it was beside her. Then it sat down and raised its face towards her. Its expression was completely mute – and familiar. The cat was exactly like her cousin Lucy.

When she picked it up it relaxed in her arms, rubbed its head against her shoulder, and purred. The cat took it absolutely for granted that it should be carried off by a deity. Still throned in her arms, it blinked serenely at the mortals in the guest-house, sure that they soon would be disposed of.

There were a great many things to be done for Lucy. His suppurating paw had to be dressed, his ears had to be cleaned and his coat brushed, food had to be bought for him, and four times a day he had to be exercised in the garden. In the intervals of this, his fleas had to be dealt with. Using a fine-tooth comb she searched them out, pounced on them, dropped them in a bowl of soapy water, resumed the search. It was a dreamlike occupation: it put her in touch with the infinite. Twenty. Thirty. Forty-seven. Fifty-two. From time to time she looked sharply at the bowl of soapy water and pushed back any wretches that had struggled to the rim.

The total of fleas went up in bounds. The money in her purse decreased. Even using the utmost economy, stealing whenever she conveniently could, having sardines put down to Miss Larke, she would not be left with enough to pay for a second week at the guest-house. Lucy's paw healed slowly; it would be some while yet before he could provide for himself. She noticed that Lucy's paw was increasingly asked about; that suggestions for his welfare multiplied.

'I wonder why you don't put an advertisement in the local paper, saying "Found". All this time his real owners may be hunting for him, longing to get him back.'

Aurelia looked deeply at the speaker. It might be worth trying. There is no harm in blackmail, since no one is obliged to give in to it. On the other hand, it is no good unless they do.

She composed two letters: 'Unless you send me fifty pounds in notes, I shan't be able to come back.' 'Unless you send me fifty pounds in notes, I shall be forced to return.'

Combing out fleas to a new rhythm of 'he loves me, he loves me not', she weighed these alternatives. The second would probably have the stronger appeal to Aston's heart. Poor Aston, she had defrauded him too long of the calm expansion of widowerhood. But the stomach is a practical organ; the first alternative might be the more compelling. She did not, of course, mean to return, in either case. Since her adoption of Lucy, she had become so unshakably Aurelia that she could contemplate being Lucy, too, so far as being Lucy would further Aurelia's designs. But Lucy, the former Lucy, must be Aurelia's property. There must be no little escapades into identity, no endorsing of cheques, no more slidings into Lucy Ridpath. That was why the money must come in notes. Even so, who was it to be addressed to?

It was time for Lucy to scratch in the garden. For the first time, he tried to scratch with both hind legs Everything became easy. Whichever the chosen form of the letter demanding money with menaces, Aurelia, signing with a capital L., would ask for the money to be directed to Miss Lefanu, *poste restante*. Lucy had been Lefanu when Aston married her. He could not have forgotten this; it might even touch his heart and dispose him to add another five pounds. All that remained was to decide which letter to send, and to post it from Bedford, which was nearby and non-committal. The envelope had been posted before she realized that both letters were enclosed.

'Lucy's handwriting,' said Aston. 'She's alive. What an infinite relief!'

'I never supposed she wasn't,' said Vere. 'Still, if it's a relief to you to see her handwriting – it doesn't seem such a niggle as usual, but that's her 'L' – I'm sure I'm glad.'

'But Vere, on Monday evening, on *Monday evening*, you said I must ring up the police or I should be suspected of murdering her.'

'So you would have been. They always jump to conclusions. Well, what does Lucy say?'

The letters had been folded up together. The first alternative was uppermost.

'She seems to have got into some sort of trouble. She says she can't come home unless I send her fifty pounds.'

'Fifty pounds? Where is she, then, California?'

'The postmark is Bedford. She's gone back to her maiden name.'

'Fifty pounds to get back from Bedford. Fifty pounds! She must have got herself mixed up in something pretty fishy. Yes. I heard only the other day that Bedford is an absolute hotbed of the drug traffic. That's what she wants the money for. Poor silly Lucy, she'd be wax in their hands. Aston! You'll have to think very carefully, apart from this absurd demand for money, about having her back. If she were here alone all day with no one to keep an eye on her – What does she say on the second sheet?'

'Is there a second sheet? I hadn't noticed. She says – Vere, I can't make this out. She says, "Unless you send me fifty pounds in notes I shall be forced to return."'

'Nonsense, Aston! You're misreading it. She just made a fair copy and then put them both in.'

'But Vere, she says unless I send her the money she will be forced to return.'

'She must be raving. Why on earth should she expect you to pay her to keep away? Let me see.'

After a pause, she said, 'My poor Aston.'

Her voice was heavy with commiseration. It fell on Aston like a wet sponge. His brief guilty dazzle of relief (for as long as Lucy wasn't dead he really didn't want to live with her again; what he wanted was manly solitude, and he had already taken the first steps towards getting shot of Vere) sizzled out.

'Poor Lucy! I must send her something, I suppose.'

'Yes, you ought to. But not too much. Ten pounds would be ample. What's Bedford? No way at all.'

When Aurelia called at the post office, the clerk handed her two letters. She opened Aston's first.

Dear Lucy,

I will not try to persuade you. The heart has its reasons. But if a time ever comes when you want to come back, remember there will always be a door on the latch and a light in the window.

I will say nothing of the anxiety your leaving without a word has caused me.

– Aston

Four five-pound notes were enclosed.

The other letter was from Vere. It ran:

Aston is now recovering. I will thankfully pay you to keep away.

This letter was accompanied by ten ten-pound notes.

Aurelia bought Lucy some tinned salmon and a handsome travelling basket. But for the greater part of that afternoon's journey, Lucy sat erect on her knee looking out of the window and held like a diviner's twig by his two front legs. She relied on Lucy to know at a snuff which station to get out at, just as he had known how to succeed in blackmailing – for while she was debating which of the two letters to send he had leaped on to the table, laid his head on her hand, and rolled with such ardour and abandonment that she forgot all else, so that both letters went off in the one envelope. Relying on Lucy, she had chosen a stopping train. It joggled through a green unemphatic landscape with many willow trees and an occasional broached spire. Lucy remained unmoved. She began to wonder if his tastes ran to the romantic, if high mountains were to him a feeling – in which case she had brought him to quite the wrong part of England. In the opposite corner sat a man with leather patches on his elbows, paying them no attention. Then at a station called Peckover Junction two ladies got in, and resumed (they were travelling together) a conversation about their grand-children. From their grandchildren they turned to the ruin of the countryside – new towns, overspill, and holiday camps.

'Look at those caravans! They've got here, now.'

'Don't speak to me of caravans,' said the other lady.

Disregarding this, the first lady asked if there were as many as ever.

'More! Such hideosities at poor Betcombe ... and the children! Swarming everywhere. I shall never find a tenant now. Besides, all these new people have such grand ideas. They must have this, they must have that. They don't appreciate the past. For me, that's its charm. If it weren't for the caravans, I'd be at Betcombe still, glorying in my beams and my pump. Do you know, it was eighteenth century, my pump?'

'Would you like me as a tenant?' said Aurelia. 'I can't give you any references just now, but I'd pay ten shillings a week. No, darling!' This last remark was addressed to Lucy, who had driven his claws into her thigh.

'Ten shillings a week – for my lovely little cottage?'

'A pound a week.'

'Really, this is so sudden, so unusual. No references ... and I suppose you'd be bringing that cat. I'm a bird-lover. No, I'm afraid it's out of the question. Come, Mary, we get out here.'

For the train was coming to a halt. Both ladies gathered their belongings and got out. From the window Aurelia saw them get in again, a few carriages farther up.

'You're well out of that,' observed the man with leather patches. 'I know her place. It's a hovel. No room to swing a cat in, begging your cat's pardon.'

Lucy rounded himself like a poultice above his scratch. Aurelia said she expected she had been silly. The train went on. An atmosphere of acquaintance established itself. Presently the man asked if she had any particular place in mind.

'No. Not exactly. I'm a stranger.'

'Because I happen to know of something that might suit you – if you don't object to it being a bit out of the way. It's a bungalow, and it's modern. If you're agreeable, I'll take you to see it.'

It was impossible not to be agreeable, because he was so plainly a shy man and surprised at finding himself intervening. So when he got out she got out with him, and he took her to a Railway Arms where she and Lucy would be comfortable, and said he would call for her at ten the next morning.

He was exactly punctual. When she had assured him how comfortable she and Lucy had been, there seemed to be nothing more to say. Fortunately, he was one of those drivers who give their whole mind to driving. They drove in his van. It was lettered 'George Bastable, Builder and Plumber', and among the things in the back was a bathtub wrapped in cellophane. They drove eastward, through the same uneventful landscape. He turned the van into a track that ran uphill – only slightly uphill, but in that flat landscape it seemed considerable. 'There it is.'

A spinney of mixed trees ran along the top of the ridge. Smoke was rising through the boughs. So she would have a neighbour. She had not reckoned on that.

But the smoke was rising from the chimney of a bungalow, and there was no other building there.

He must have got up very early, for the fire was well established, the room was warm and felt inhabited. The kitchen floor was newly washed and a newspaper path was spread across it.

'You'd find it comfortable,' he said.

'Oh, yes,' she said, looking at the two massive armchairs that faced each other across a hideous hearth mat.

'It hasn't been lived in for three years, though I come out from time to time to give a look to it. But no damp anywhere – that'll show how sound it is.'

'No. It feels wonderfully dry,' she said, looking at a flight of blue pottery birds on the wall.

Lucy was shaking his basket.

'May I let your cat out? He'd like a run, and I daresay he'd pick up a breakfast, bird's-nesting.'

Before she could answer, he had unfastened the lid and Lucy had bounded over the threshold. How was she to answer this man who had taken so much trouble and was so proud of his bungalow?

'Did you build it yourself?'

'I did. That's why I know it's a good one. I built it for my young lady. When I saw you in the train, you put me in mind of her, somehow. So when you said you wanted somewhere to live –' He stared at her, standing politely at a distance trying to recapture the appearance of his nova in this half-hearted lady, no longer young.

The house had stood empty for three years. She had died. Poor Mr Bastable! Aurelia's face assumed the right expression.

'She left,' he said.

'How *could* she?' exclaimed Aurelia.

This time, there was no need to put on the right expression. She was wholeheartedly shocked at the behaviour of Mr Bastable's young lady – and if the young lady had come in just then she would have boxed the ungrateful minx's ears. Instead, it was Lucy who trotted in, looking smug, with fragments of eggshell plastered to his chops, sat down in front of the fire, and began cleaning himself. Mr Bastable remarked that Lucy had found a robin's nest. He was grateful for Aurelia's indignation but shy of saying so. He suspected he had gone too far. Somewhat to his surprise he learned that Aurelia would like to move into his lovely bungalow immediately. He drove her to the village to do her shopping, came back to show her where the coal was kept, gave her the key. Watching him drive away she suddenly became aware of the landscape she would soon be taking for granted. It sparkled with crisscrossing drains and ditches; a river wound through it. A herd of caravans was peacefully grazing in the distance.

Happiness is an immunity. In a matter of days Aurelia was unaffected by the flight of blue pottery birds, sat in armchairs so massive she could not move them and felt no wish to move them, slept deliciously between pink nylon sheets. With immunity she watched Lucy sharpening his claws on the massive armchairs. She had a naturally happy disposition and preferred to live in the present. Happiness immunized her from the past – for why look back for what has slipped from one's possession? – and from the future, which may never even be possessed. Perhaps never in the past, perhaps never in the future, had she been, could she be, so happy as she was now. The cuckoo woke her; she fell asleep to Lucy's purr. In the mornings he had usually left a dent beside her and gone out for his sunrising. Whatever one may say about bungalows, they are ideal for cats. She hunted his fleas on Sundays and Thursdays. He was now so strong and splendid that for the rest of the week he could perfectly well deal with them himself. She lived with carefree economy, seldom using more than a single plate, drinking water to save rinsing the teapot, and as far as possible eating raw foods, which entailed the minimum of washing up. Every Saturday she bought seven new-laid eggs, hard-boiled them, and spaced them out during the week – a trick she had learned from Vasari's *Lives of the Artists*. It was not an adequate diet for anyone leading an active life, but her life was calculatedly inactive – as though she were convalescing from some forgotten illness.

On Saturday evenings Mr Bastable called to collect the rent and to see if anything needed doing – a nail knocked in or a tap tightened up. He always brought some sort of present: a couple of pigeons, the first tomatoes from his greenhouse, breakfast radishes. As the summer deepened, the presents enlarged into basketloads of green peas, bunches of roses, strawberries, sleek dessert gooseberries. But as the summer deepened and in spite of all the presents and economies Aurelia's wealth of one hundred and twenty pounds lessened, and she knew she must turn her mind to doing something about this. She could not dig; there was no one but Mr Bastable to beg from. The times were gone when one could take in plain sewing. Surveying the landscape she had come to take for granted, she saw the caravans in a new light – no longer peacefully grazing but fermenting with ambitions and cultural unrest.

By now they must have bought all the picture postcards at the shop. She had always wanted to paint. For all she knew, she might turn out to be quite good at it. Willows would be easy – think of all the artists who painted them. By now the caravaners must be tired of looking at real willows and would welcome a change to representational art. She took the bus to Wisbech, found an arts-and-crafts shop, bought paper, brushes, gouache paints, and a small easel. That same evening she did two pictures of willows –

one tranquil, one storm-tossed. Three days later, she set up the easel on the outskirts of the caravan site and began a caravan from life. It was harder than willows – there were no precursors to inspire her – but when she had complied with a few suggestions from the caravan's owner she made her sale and received two further commissions. By the beginning of August she was rich enough to go on to oils – which was more fun and on the whole easier. It was remarkable how easily she painted, and with what assurance. The demand was chiefly for caravans. She varied them, as Monet varied his haystacks. Caravan with buckets. Caravan with sunset. Pink caravan. One patron wanted a group of cows – though his children were cold towards them. She evaded portraits, but yielded to a request for an abstract. This was the only commission that really taxed her. Do as she might, it kept on coming out like a draper's window display. But she mastered it in the end, and signed it A. Lefanu like the rest.

By the end of September she had made enough to keep her in idleness till Christmas – when she would have thought of something else.

Winter would bring a new variety of happiness – slower, more conscious, and with more strategy in it. The gales of the equinox blowing across the flats struck at the spinney along the ridge, blew down one tree, and shook deadwood out of others. Here was an honest occupation. She set herself to build up a store of fuel against the winter. It was heavy work dragging the larger branches over the rough ground clogged with brambles and tall grass, but Lucy lightened it by flirting round her as she worked, darting after the tail of the branches, ambushing them and leaping on them as they rustled by. She was collecting fuel, Lucy was growing a thick new coat; both of them were preparing their defences against the wintry months ahead. Mr Bastable said that by all the signs it would be a hard winter, preceded by much rain and wind. He advised her to get her wood in before the rain fell and made the ground too soggy to shift it. If she manages the first winter, he thought, she will settle. Though she was an ungrateful tenant, or at any rate an inattentive receiver, he wanted her to settle; it delighted him to see her making these preparations. Later on, he would complete them by chopping the heavier pieces into nice little logs. Taking Mr Bastable's advice, Aurelia decided to get the wood in, working on till the dusk was scythed by the headlights of passing cars, till Lucy vanished into a different existence of being a thing audible – a sudden plop or a scuffling. She never had to call him when she went indoors. By the time she was on the threshold he was there, rubbing against her, raising his feet in a ritual exaggeration. He was orderly in his ways, a timekeeper. He took himself in and out, but rarely strayed. When she came back from selling those unprincipled canvases, he was always waiting about for her, curled up on the lid of the water butt, drowsing under the elder, sitting primly on the sill of the window left open for him. He was happy enough out of her sight, but he liked to have her within his.

So she told herself, later on, that foggy, motionless November evening when he had not come in at his usual time. She had kindled a fire, not that it was cold – indeed, it was oddly warm and fusty; but the fog made it cheerless. It was a night to pull the curtains closer, listen to the snap and crackle of a brief fire, go early to bed. She had left the curtains unclosed, however. If Lucy saw that a fire had been kindled, he would be drawn from whatever busied him. He was a very chimney-corner cat, although he was a tom. Twice the brief fire died down, twice she made it up again. She went to the door, peered uselessly into the fog, called him. It was frightening to call into that silent, immediate obscurity.

'Lucy. Lucy.'

She waited. No Lucy. She must resign herself to it. Tonight Lucy was engaged in being a tom. As she stood there, resigning herself to it and straining her ears, she felt the damp of the foggy air pricked with a fine drizzling rain. A minute later, the rain was falling steadily; not hard but steadily. She had not the courage to go on calling. The pitch of her voice had frightened her; it sounded so anxious. She went indoors and sat down to wait. On a different night she would have left the window open and gone to bed. And in the morning Lucy would have been there, too, and in her sleep her arm would have gone out and round him.

With the rain, it had become colder. She added coal to the fire. It blazed up but did not warm her. She counted the blue pottery birds and listened. She listened for so long that finally she became incapable of listening, and when there was a sound which was not the interminable close patter of rain she did not hear it, only knew that she had heard something. A dragging sound . . . the sound of something being dragged along the path to the door. It had ceased. It began again. Ceased.

When she snatched the door open, she could see nothing but the rain, a curtain of flashing arrows lit by her lighted room. A noise directed her – a tremulous yowl. He struck at her feebly when she stooped to pick him up, then dragged himself on into the light of the doorway. She fell on her knees. This sodden shapeless thing was Lucy. He looked at her with one eye; the other sagged on his cheek. His jaw dangled. One side of his head had been smashed in; his front leg was broken. When she touched him he shrank from her and yowled beseechingly. Slowly, distortedly, he hitched himself over the threshold, across the room, tried to sit up before the fire, fell over, and lay twitching and gasping for breath. When at last she dared touch him, his racing heartbeats were like a machine fastened in him. She talked to him and stroked his uninjured paw. He did not shrink from her now, and perhaps her voice lulled him as the plumpness of his muscular soft paw lulled her, for he relaxed and curled his tail round his flank as though he were preparing to fall asleep. Long after he seemed to be dead, the implacable machine beat on. Then it faltered, stumbled, began again at a slower rate, fluttered. A leaden tint suffused his eye and his lolling tongue. His breathing stopped. He flattened. It was inconceivable that he could ever have been loved, handsome, alive.

'Lucy!'

The cry broke from her. It unloosed another.

'Aurelia!'

She could not call back the one or the other. She was Lucy Ridpath, looking at a dead cat who had never known her.

The agony of dislocation was prosaic. She endured it because it was there. It admitted no hope, so she endured it without the support of resentment.

The rain had gone on all the time and was still going on.

Lucy Ridpath's mackintosh was hanging in the closet, ready to meet it. Mrs Barker had advised her to put it on and she had done so. Tomorrow she would put it on again when she went out to dig a hole in the sodden ground for the cat's burial. It is proper to bury the dead; it is a mark of respect. Lucy would bury Lucy, and then there would be one Lucy left over.

She sat in the lighted room long after the light of day came into it. Then she put on the mackintosh and took up the body and carried it out. The air was full of a strange roar and tumult, a hollow booming that came from everywhere at once. The level landscape was gone. The hollow booming rose from a vast expanse and confusion of floodwater. Swirling, jostling, traversed with darker streaks, splintering into flashes of light where it contested with an obstacle, it drove towards the river. Small rivulets were flowing down from the ridge to join it, the track to the road was a running stream. In all that water there must be somewhere a place to drown.

With both hands holding the cat clasped to her bosom, she walked slowly down the track. When she came to the road, the water was halfway to her knees. A little farther along the road there was a footbridge over the roadside ditch. It was under water but the handrail showed. She waded across it. The water rose to her knees. With the next few steps she was in water up to her thighs. It leaned its ice-cold indifferent weight against her. When a twig was carried bobbing past her, she felt a wild impulse to clutch it. But her arms were closed about the cat's body, and she pressed it more closely to her and staggered on. All sense of direction was gone; sometimes she saw light, sometimes she saw darkness. The hollow booming hung in the air. Below it was an incessant hissing and seething. The ground rose under her feet; the level of water had fallen to her knees. Tricked and impatient, she waded faster, took longer strides. The last stride plunged her forward. She was out of her depth, face down in the channel of a stream. She rose to the surface. The current bowed her, arched itself above her, swept her onward, cracked her skull against the concrete buttress of a revetment, whirled the cat out of her grasp.

BOX-CAR BERTHA

✐

from
Sister of the Road

I am thirty years old as I write this, and have been a hobo for fifteen years, a sister of the road, one of that strange and motley sorority which has increased its membership so greatly during the depression. I have always known strange people, vagrants, hoboes, both males and females. I don't remember when I didn't know about wanderers, prostitutes, revolutionists. My first playhouse was a box-car. Conductors in freight yards used to let me ride in their cabooses. Before I was twelve I had ridden in a box-car to the next division and back.

Police and pinches, jails, bughouses, and joints seem to have been always a part of my life. When I knew that a man was stealing, or a woman hustling, or some poor girl going nutty, or that a guy was on the lam, or learned that a pimp was living with four women – it all seemed natural to me, an attitude given me by my mother, to whom nothing was ever terrible, vulgar, or nasty. Our family never had any hard luck, because nothing seemed hard luck to it, nor was it ever disgraced, for there was nothing which it would acknowledge as disgrace. When my mother changed her 'husband', I simply took it for granted. When I was pinched the first time for riding in a box-car, it didn't seem unusual to me. Many of the men and women I knew had been arrested for the same thing. In my world somebody was always getting arrested. My mother was arrested when I was a baby because she wouldn't marry my father. As I grew up, if we missed a meal or two now and then, or a half-dozen meals, it wasn't anything to get excited about. All my life I have lived with hungry and lonely people.

My mother wasn't what the world would call a good woman.

47

She never said she was. And many people, including the police, said she was a bad woman. But she never agreed with them, and she had a way of lifting up her head when she talked back to them that made me know she was right. I loved her deeply from the first day I can remember until she died. I love to think of her. Her example and influence and sacrifice (she always denied that she ever made sacrifices for her children) proved that she loved us and that she was a woman of rare courage and of fine principles all her own. I remember her first when she was cooking in a railroad camp for a section gang not far from Deadwood, South Dakota. The man whom I called 'Father' was the foreman of the gang laying the tracks of the Northwestern. I was the oldest of mother's four children. Each of us had a different father.

'Hobo, hobo, where did you come from?' is the earliest chant I learned. There were always wandering men, and even then a few women traveling on the railroad and on the highway. I read an article the other day saying that now women hoboes and tramps have so increased that one out of every twenty persons on the road is a woman. I don't know what the percentage was when I grew up, but I remember some of these women very vividly, probably because there were so few of them then.

I heard Harry Hopkins, relief administrator, speak this year. He says that now we have 6,800 transient women in the country. This count is taken from the government shelters and transient bureaus. There must be twice that many actually unattached and hitch-hiking and riding freights and walking about the country. That would make 13,600 women, 'sisters of the road', as the men call us. No wonder people are writing books about us!

My childhood was completely free and always mixed up with the men and women on the road. There weren't many dolls or toys in my life but plenty of excitement. We were set down on side tracks in the midst of vast hills and ravines. We used the river for swimming and washing. I learned my first spelling from the names on the box-cars. What early geography I knew I learned by asking the men about the towns and cities, the names of which were chalked on the cars. I learned numbers by counting the cars on long freights.

I don't ever remember anyone telling me a real fairy story in my whole childhood, but the tales of the gandy dancers, and of the bundle stiffs, of their jobs in the wheatfields of Minnesota and the rides on the blinds to and from them, and the breathtaking yarns of mushing in Alaska, or getting pinched in San Francisco, or of drunken brawls in New Orleans' dives were thrillers I remember to this day.

Some of the men in the gang had their families with them. Half the kids boasted that their cradles had been handcars. We took for playthings all the grand miscellany to be found in a railroad yard. We built houses of railroad ties so big that it took four of us to lift one of them in place. We invented games that made us walk the tracks. We crossed pins on the main tracks and let the big engines crash over them and leave tiny pairs of scissors for us. We played with the men's shovels and picks and learned to use them. And we lined up to wave with ceremony to the passenger trains that thundered by.

We girls dressed just like the boys, mostly in hand-me-down overalls. No one paid much attention to us. They saw to it that we had something to eat and a place to sleep at night. And they saw to it that we did our simple chores. But the men never thought of changing their conversation in front of us. The men worked hard and the women worked harder. Mother was always busy cooking and serving meals and cleaning, and she taught me and the other girls how to cook and clean and to wash men's clothes.

'Bertha,' she would say, 'as long as you can keep men clean and well fed and love them a little, they'll be perfectly satisfied. They're all babies. They need to be looked after. Teach them to depend upon you. But never let them make a slave of you.'

Mother was a handsome blonde, straight-shouldered, deep-breasted, with penetrating steel-grey eyes, and with a sort of glow about her that attracted everyone, especially when she talked. She was the kind of woman who looks after everyone, and everybody called her 'Mother Thompson' even when she was so young that all the tramps (as well as all the others) tried to make love to her.

Her father, Moses Thompson, was a Kansas pioneer, who spent his whole life trying to right the wrong of the oppressed. He was an abolitionist. When he was yet in his teens he worked with John Brown and he served in the Civil War. Later he was one of the earliest workers for the emancipation of women, and published, at Valley Forge, Kansas, a little paper, *The Women's Emancipator*, advocating votes for women and freedom from marriage. He was one of the committee that in the eighties organized the famous free-love convention at Worcester, Massachusetts. He served three terms in jail, two for sending birth control information through the mail (the federal authorities called it obscene), and one for admitting that he advised his daughter, my mother, against marrying the father of her child.

When Mother was twenty, Grandfather was living on the farm and publishing his little paper. Walker C. Smith, an active free-thought and eugenist propagandist, a man of forty, stopped in while making a tour of the west. He had corresponded with Grandfather. He stayed at the farm and became Mother's lover the first week. Grandfather knew it. He urged her not to marry. During the last months of her pregnancy, the neighbors began to talk, and five days after I was born, the village parson, the sheriff, and three good citizens came and asked bluntly whether Mother was married or intended to marry.

'No, my daughter is not married,' Grandfather told them, 'and, what is more, she is not going to be married. She and Smith love one another and they have a child because they wanted one. They are both intelligent and healthy, and that's all a child needs in its parents.'

Someone swore out a warrant for the whole family, and two weeks later they were tried at the county seat. Mother and Father were sentenced to six months in jail. Grandfather was fined a hundred dollars and costs, which he promptly refused to pay. So he was sent to jail too. All of them enjoyed their stay there. Grandfather wrote a series of articles which were published in the New York and London liberal papers. Father caught up on his back reading. Mother did the jail cooking and sewing, nursed me, and studied Esperanto and socialism.

'When we all got out of jail, the liberals and the radicals in Kansas City gave us a great mass meeting,' Mother said. 'There had been a lot of publicity. You made your first public appearance there, in my arms, held high for all those people to see.'

My father did not go back to the farm with Mother and Grandfather.

In the spring of 1906 Grandfather died, and Mother, for no particular reason (and against her better judgment, she said)

50

married a young tow-headed farmer, Toby Miller, and moved to a large farm near Bismarck. During the next two years my sister, Ena, and brother Frank were born. But only Ena was Toby's child. Frank was the son of a traveling physician named A. H. Wright. Mother met him at a carnival. Her husband, Toby, made the best of it. He knew of the relationship, and later that Frank was not his child, but he treated the little fellow, as he did me, like his own.

When I was five, again without any good reason that Mother could ever remember or of which I have any recollection, she hitched up a team, took us three children and a valise of clothes and drove into Bismarck. Before nightfall she had found a job as cook in a nearby construction camp, and within a month was living with the foreman of the gang, who always referred to us as 'my wife and children'. Eleven months later my sister, Margaret, was born.

Mike Blake, our new father, was a husky silent man, heavy-handed with the men, but having for my mother a respect and devotion, and for all of us a rough tenderness. He gave us children as much care as if we had been his own. He worked hard and drank hard. Drunk or sober, he was good to Mother. And if he was ever jealous – and he had much cause – he was most successful in hiding it.

This period with Mike left an impression on me. There was security in the rough way he bossed the men and Mother and us. Mother seemed to take a fierce delight in the heaviest kind of work for him. By watching her there I learned the urge I now know so well, for serving men who work and drink and talk. Across our box-car threshold came many men, those of the gang who missed womenfolk and who had talk to offer, and various dirty, footsore, gay and bedraggled hoboes, all of them bringing in to us the world of careless living detached from the rest of the world.

There were few women hoboes those days. The only two I remember seemed to have about them something of my own mother's way of raising up her head proudly with an idea and of telling a funny story or in talking without embarrassment about hustling and living with men and leaving them.

I saw one (in dusty black sweater and striped overalls) flip a freight that had stopped at our switch to take on an empty, and ride the rods right out of our camp, waving to Mother in our doorway and to the gang who held up their shovels in astonishment. I had seen her bundle her things together on Mother's table a few minutes before. She had a book along. She had been in Detroit. She spoke of a child in Memphis. She was going to talk at an IWW meeting on the coast. She and Mother laughed together because the men wouldn't be able to get at her on the rods. I knew that she had spent a couple of nights over in the men's shacks. Mother knew it. We didn't think anything about it. But the look on her face as she talked about going on west, and the sureness with which she swung under the freight car, set my childish mind in a fever. The world was easy, like that. Even to women. It had never occurred to me before.

One other woman I remember, older and more battered looking, who traveled with a whole gang of men, and rolled out of an empty with them one day when a freight slowed up around our curve. One of the men had had a meal of Mother's on a trip the other way a few months before. These men treated the woman with them as if she were a man. She wore skirts, though. She carried her own water and washed out her underwear and some of their shirts, borrowing soap from Mother. She smoked, rolling her own. I was interested in this. Mother never had.

This woman was going off somewhere to some man, or away from some man, I don't remember which. It seemed natural to me that she should be going to a man or away from a man. And not important. Far more important to her, and to the men hoboes she was with, was food, and a place to wash, and the hills they had come through, or an idea someone had given them in another camp.

Much as I liked our life along the railroad, I don't remember being upset at all or wondering about it when, at the time I was eight, Mother left Mike and the box-cars and took us to Aberdeen and opened a boarding-house. The boarders were mostly railroad men, show and carnival people, and the kind of folks who don't like to stay at hotels. We always got labor people and strikers and radicals. Practically all the hoboes who passed through Aberdeen stopped at our house for a meal and a wash-up. Often they slept in the big barn. When a hobo would knock at Mother's back door and begin, 'Lady, will you –' she always snapped back, 'You're a professional bum. Only the professionals on the road call me "lady".'

But she always fed them and talked to them.

These and the railroad hands and the IWW men filled up our boarding-house. Every night there would be a discussion about sex and strikes and socialism. All the agitators stayed there. I learned afterward that 'Mother Thompson' became known that year from coast to coast among the radicals and the hoboes.

We had a woman hobo now and then, but they were still few enough in those days to cause a little stir, even among the men hoboes. They were almost always alone. Once in a while they traveled in pairs, but very seldom with men. Some of them were hitch-hiking. There weren't very many automobiles then, and they always told of wild and exciting rides with strangers across the long stretches of prairies. They explained that alone they could get rides from men in cars easier than if they were with men, and that food and shelter and a little money now and then came easier that way.

Most of the women on the road in those days were agitators, it seems to me. They wore their hair bobbed, long. They talked excitedly and got the men hoboes all roused up to go on to San Francisco or wherever they were going for some meeting. Now and then one of them seemed to be just hoboing without purpose, as hundreds of women are doing now, having no place in view except some city they had heard about or liked on a previous trip. Mother accepted them all.

Since then I have thought a lot about why women leave home and go on the road. I've decided that the most frequent reason they leave is economic and that they usually come from broken or from poverty-stricken homes. They want to escape from reality, to get away from misery and unpleasant surroundings. Others are driven out by inability to find expression at home, or maybe because of parental discipline. Some hobo their way about to faraway relatives, or go to seek romance. The dullness of a small town or a farm, made worse by long spells of the same kind of weather, may start them off. Or some want better clothes. But others are just seized with wanderlust. The rich can become globe-trotters, but those who have no money become hoboes. Some of the women I knew way back there in Aberdeen fell into this class, I guess. And I did, too, when I first took the road, wanting freedom and adventure such as they had, with maybe a few of the other things thrown in. But I never wanted to leave home because home wasn't exciting.

Ena and I went to public school a little over two years in Aberdeen. I don't remember much about it. We also went to Sunday School and to every revival and to any kind of meeting that came to town. We played with a lot of kids who ran around as we did. Mother took us to hear everybody, quoting Grandfather, 'The more you hear, the more you learn, the better you will be to judge for yourself.'

Aberdeen had 'a line', a row of houses of prostitution just outside the city limits. There were fifteen girls working in there. They were not allowed to visit generally in the town. They were not even permitted to shop. They had to go direct from the depot to the joints. The police watched them closely. But they let them come to our house. They would come in for a meal. Sometimes their lovers and their pimps would stay as paying boarders. Sometimes the girls would take me to their joints for a visit. I was fascinated. Quickly I learned how they conducted their business. I suppose you will be horrified when I say that it did not disgust me. It seemed like any other business to me.

Mother did not seem to have any objection to having me visit these girls. She did not seem to mind their talk in front of me. She accepted it as she did the stories other women and men brought in of labor meetings in Birmingham and of hoboing across the country for Idaho apple picking. It may seem unkind and undaughterly and disloyal of me to relate these things about my mother, but if I am to tell an honest story of my life and the influences that moulded it, I must begin it, as I have, by telling about my mother.

EDNA O'BRIEN

An Outing

Mrs Farley was sitting in a bus when she first saw it. She spotted the price as the bus swerved round the corner and she wondered if it could be possible. A three-piece suite for nine pounds! Perhaps it was nineteen? Or ninety? All day she thought about it.

Next morning she walked there on her way to work. Nine pounds it was. Quite a good three-piece suite covered in dark green tapestry. Second-hand of course but not so shabby that you'd know. After all, it could be one that she'd had in her house for years, ever since she married. She'd buy it.

Luckily she had a pound in her bag which served as a deposit. While the man wrote out a receipt she sat on the armchairs, then on the couch, moving along the seat to make sure it was thoroughly sprung. How well it would fit into her front room. In the evenings, she and Mr Farley would have an armchair each. In May when Mr Farley went on the boiler-maker's outing she and her friend would share the couch. It would be perfect. May . . . the sun through the windows shining on the castor-oil plant, and the couch a darker shade of green with antimacassars to protect it from sun and greasy hair. There would be a cushion for behind his back, and with a bit of luck some things would be in bloom, disguising the creosote-soaked fence. He would see what a good gardener she was.

'Certainly, madam,' the shop assistant was saying in answer to her question about delivery. They would deliver anything; she could pay as and when she liked.

'Have a look around at other things,' he said. They sold new as well as second-hand furniture.

'I'd love one of those.' She pointed to a display of cut-glass vases that were on a glass-topped table. Even in winter light the chips of cut glass revealed the colours of a rainbow. Wisteria would go lovely in a tall vase like that. Weepy wisteria. Her favourite flower. A watery blue, faded, rather like a garment that has had repeated washings.

'When I win the pools,' she said, and went off to work smiling to herself.

It was a shocking day. The snow had been on the ground now for eight whole weeks. When it first fell, and at each new fall, it was downy white, but in between it was the colour of Mr Farley's chamber pot as she picked it up for emptying each morning. No fresh vegetables either. Talk of coal and paraffin oil being rationed. London was never able to cope with crises, no planning.

She was doing two houses that morning. In all, she cleaned six houses a week; two on Mondays, Wednesdays and Fridays. She devoted the other days to her own home and consequently it was a little palace. Even her husband admitted it. He saw a lot of houses because he installed boilers. He knew how dirty the average London house was: soot on the window sashes, wainscotings never wiped, television knobs never dusted.

'Well I got a bargain at last,' she said to Mrs Captain Hagerty, her first employer, that morning. Mrs Captain Hagerty was on the telephone complaining about a blanket which she'd bought and which had shrunk.

'It's my lucky year,' Mrs Farley said, taking off her coat, her outside cardigan and her boots. There was no doubt, Mrs Captain Hagerty thought, but that Mrs Farley was more spry. She was still plump, but her face was different: the lines softer, the look in her eye not so heartlessly blue. Could Mrs Farley have found another man? Mrs Captain Hagerty thought not, but she was wrong. Mrs Farley had indeed found a man in her forty-sixth year. They had known each other slightly for years – he lived nearby – had chatted at bus stops on and off, and once he let her take his turn in the butcher's. Just before Christmas she realized that she had not seen him for weeks, and for several more weeks she searched for him. She would think of his face, especially at night, when she was tired – his thin, disappointed face and his eye sockets riddled with crow's feet. He worked in a furniture factory, and probably had to keep his eyes constantly screwed up so as not to get sawdust in them. That was the thing about hard work, it showed on your hands, or face, or some part of you.

She'd given up hope of ever seeing him again when in fact they met in a snowfall one day and she rushed to shake hands with him. He'd got thinner but the crow's feet were less pronounced. He'd been sick. Nearly died he said. Suddenly, before she knew what she was doing, she had a hand out saying, 'Don't die on me,' and then they pulled off gloves and gripped hands like two people who had a desperate need to grip. They went for a walk down a side street.

'I saw something about a snowflake on television,' she said to him. 'It's a perfect crystal.'

'I saw that, too,' he said, and squeezed her hand tighter. The snow brushed her cheeks but softly, like petals, and warm tears filled her eyes. They were both in the same predicament, married to people they didn't care for, working all day, home at night, television, bed, alarm clock set for six. She thought it a coincidence that they should both be bordering on forty-six and be keen gardeners. Before a half hour was spent they were in love, and like all clandestine lovers they were already conscious of their risks. It was her dry eyes, he said, that first drew her to him, that day in the butchers. She admitted that she'd had plenty of occasion to cry, in her time.

'Even now,' he said. Through the film of tears she saw him smile at her and she told him how happy they were going to be.

'Yes, I've had a lot of good fortune lately,' she said to Mrs Captain Hagerty as she mopped up the pool of water under the radiator, which her boots had caused.

Mrs Captain Hagerty was saying in her splendidly authoritative voice into the telephone:

'Is that the manager? Well, this is Mrs Captain Hagerty, yes, it *is* a blanket, strawberry-coloured, it shrunk shockingly. I can't tell you, I mean it's hardly fit for a single bed now . . .' Then she listened for a second or two, smiled at the mouthpiece, and in a changed voice said, 'Oh, but how kind, how terribly kind, and you'll collect it . . . thank *you*.'

Mrs Captain Hagerty had had her way. A van was on its way to collect the fated blanket which she had boiled by mistake in the copper. She was even willing to listen to Mrs Farley's troubles for a few seconds, although she couldn't tolerate any sordid stories about the change.

'It's a lovely shop,' Mrs Farley was saying. 'It's on the 93 bus route, right at the corner. I spotted this bargain yesterday, off the bus . . .'

Mrs Captain Hagerty decided that they might as well have coffee. If she had to listen to some story it was as well to be comfortable. Mrs Farley could make up the time later.

'Green matches everything,' Mrs Captain Hagerty said as she stirred saccharine into her coffee. One had to say something to these people.

'And lovely vases,' Mrs Farley went on. 'Lovely, cut-glass ones, that shimmer.'

Mrs Farley was getting quite lyrical. She hadn't mentioned her womb for weeks.

'And they had ever such a funny card on the counter in front of the vases,' Mrs Farley said, and then blushed as she recited it, the way a child would recite!

> 'Lovely to look at,
> Delightful to hold,
> But if you break me
> Consider me sold.'

'Quite,' Mrs Captain Hagerty said. Enough was enough. She stood up to make some more telephone calls. Mrs Farley had to drink down the last of her coffee hurriedly.

That night, in her small front room, Mrs Farley looked at her husband's face in the faint, blue glow from the television screen and decided she would ask him when he wakened up. Even in dim light her husband was plain: fat, with round, pug-like cheeks and a paunch. Awake or asleep he tried to disguise the paunch by placing folded hands across it, and as far as she was concerned, merely drew attention to it. Yes, she'd ask him. She'd done everything to please him all evening. He'd had steak and kidney pie, a pint of director's bitter from the pub, and the right television channel going. He only tolerated the channel which carried advertisements, insisting that the other lot were socialists. It seemed foolish because he slept through it anyhow, but he was a stubborn man and had to have his way.

'Dan,' she said when she saw him stir. 'D'you know what I was just thinking about? D'you remember the winter of the big freeze and you found a lump of coal on the road and brought it home and it turned out to be ice that was black with soot?'

'I remember it,' he said. It was the only memory they ever resorted to. The ice had melted in the grate, ruining the chopped sticks which Mrs Farley had put there. In the end they'd gone out to a pub to get warm. It was nineteen forty-seven, the year of her first miscarriage. They often went to pubs then and had beer and salt-beef sandwiches.

'Yes, I was just thinking about it,' she said, 'when I was looking at you there asleep. Funny how you think of things for no reason.'

'I remember it,' he said. 'It was in Hartfield Road, just beyond the railway bridge . . . I was coming along, very cold it was . . .'

From a distance she heard his voice receding into the story and she lowered the television.

'Dan,' she said when he had finished. 'I did something reckless today. I couldn't help it.'

'What reckless?' He was wide awake now, his tongue dampening the corners of his mouth.

'I put a pound down on a three-piece suite.'

'We have all the furniture we need,' he said. 'Still paying for those damn beds, I am.'

A year before Mrs Farley had implored him to get single, divan beds. She wasn't well, she said, and would be happier in a single bed. She needed privacy. It inconvenienced him no end.

'A three-piece suite for only four pounds,' she said. 'It is a most beautiful, olive green.'

'It must be worm-eaten, you wouldn't get anything for four pounds.'

'I beat him down,' she said. 'They were asking nine, but I beat him down. I think it was my eyes that did it.' The sleepy salesman hadn't even noticed her.

'I'm not buying it,' he said. 'You can take that for definite.'

'You remember,' she said, 'that you said you might get me an umbrella for my birthday, well, if you're getting me anything, I'd rather have the money.'

If he gave her three pounds and if she did an hour extra for Mrs Captain Hagerty, and skimped on the food for herself, she might have the eight pounds balance by May the 10th, which was the day Mr Farley was going on the outing to Brighton. She'd invited her friend in. They had nowhere to meet, except on the street, and they couldn't do much there except each take off a glove and walk hand-in-hand down a road, and up again. Once or twice they took a bus ride and had a cup of coffee a few miles away in Chelsea, but it didn't feel natural.

They met on Saturdays and by coincidence Mr Farley's outing was planned for a Saturday too. Her friend had promised to spend the whole afternoon with her, and for once he would defy his wife and say he was going to a football match. If she had the three-piece suite by then they could sit next to each other on the couch.

'I made no promises about birthdays or anything else,' Mr Farley was saying. Sulky old pig.

'Oh, forget it,' she said, turning up the television sound. 'If being married for seventeen years means nothing to you I can't help it. I can only feel that there's something the matter some- where . . .' She clattered off towards the kitchen in her old bedroom slippers, mumbling.

'Just a minute now . . .' he called, but she went into the kitchen and worked her temper out by tidying the cutlery drawer.

That night when he asked for his rights, Mrs Farley was gratified to be able to say no.

'You look well,' her friend said, when they met the following Saturday. Each time she looked younger. Her cheeks were seas- oned like an apple and her eyes shone. There was no telling, of course, about her figure because in winter clothes she was shapeless like everyone else.

'It's my hair,' she said. She'd given herself a home perm and put a little peroxide in the water. If Mr Farley knew he'd kill her, so she had to sit well out of the light.

'Yes,' she said. 'I've been told I have hair the texture of a baby's.'

He touched the permed ends with his finger, and asked how her week had been.

'I love you more than ever.'

'I love *you* more than ever,' he said.

'How's your wife?' she asked.

His wife was attending a National Health psychiatrist, learning after seventeen years of marriage how to be a married woman.

'Not that it matters now to me,' he said, squeezing Mrs Farley's fingers. Her hands were coarse from all the washing and scrubbing but she'd bought rubber gloves and was taking more care.

'Is she nice-looking?' Mrs Farley asked.

'Not as nice as you,' he said. 'She's nothing to you.'

His wife had been a nurse and Mrs Farley reckoned that she would look down on her, who did for people. At least they'd never meet.

'She's bitter,' he said. 'You know, bitter . . . always getting a rub at you.'

Mrs Farley knew it well. Mr Farley did that too.

'Don't remind me of her,' he said. They had arrived at the brick arch under the railway bridge, and she stood with her back to the wall waiting for him to kiss her. The thick, jagged icicles which hung from one corner of the arch were dripping down the wall and underneath the pool of water was refreezing. She'd taken off one of her jerseys so as not to be too bulky for him.

'I've decided what we'll have the day you come in,' she said as she kissed his cold nose. The poor man had bad circulation.

'What?' he said.

'Pork chops and apple sauce,' she said. 'And bread-and-butter pudding to follow.'

'That will be lovely.'

'You'll see the garden,' she said. She heard herself describe the garden as it would be, wisteria on the fence, peonies in the heart-shaped bed, lily of the valley in the deep grass under the gooseberry bush. And then as he opened her coat and put his arms around her she heard herself describe her own front room and in it the olive green three-piece suite figured prominently.

There was nothing he said he liked better than a house-proud woman. His wife wouldn't even transfer tea from the packet into a biscuit tin which they used as a caddy. Mrs Farley said a woman like that didn't deserve a home.

'It's time,' he said, kissing her mouth, then her chin, then her neck which had got crepe with the years.

They began to walk, her hand in his pocket. Sometimes their hips touched. His body was very thin. His hip-bone stuck out.

'We'll have the time of our lives,' she said. She didn't know quite what would happen the day he visited her, but it would be the deciding one in their lives.

'You'll give me pork chops,' he said.

'Two for you and one for me.'

'And a cuddle?' he said.

'I might,' she said. She felt glowy all over, even her toes were no longer numb.

'Oh.' She put out her hand to make sure. It had begun to snow again. Her perm would be ruined.

'Just a minute,' he said, and ran into a paper shop. He came back with something for her head.

'A new paper,' she said. 'That we haven't even read.'

He held it over her as they walked along, keeping step.

'We're extravagant,' she said. They stopped and kissed, using the paper as a shield to dismiss the world. That's what being in love meant.

Three days before Mr Farley's summer outing Mrs Farley celebrated her forty-seventh birthday. A day like any other, she cleaned two houses and hurried home to put on the dinner. Mr Farley hadn't mentioned the birthday that morning, but then he was unbearable in the mornings. She bought a cake just to make the meal resemble a happy occasion. The antimacassars were made, she had paid five pounds on the three-piece suite and if he gave her money instead of an umbrella she could pay the balance by Saturday. She would have it delivered that day and when he came home from his outing he would be too tired to complain. There was one thing she would have to be careful about: her friend's pipe. Mr Farley had a sensitive nose, as he didn't smoke himself. She'd have to get her friend out of the house by five and prop the door back as well as opening the window.

'Is that you, Dad?' She was upstairs when she heard him come in. The 'Dad' was an affectionate word since one of the three times when Mr Farley was almost a father.

'It's me,' he said. She came down in a flowered summer dress, her face newly freckled, because she'd done a bit of gardening while the dinner was cooking. Afterwards she undressed upstairs, and had a good look at herself in the mirror. If the neighbours knew they would have the Welfare Officer on her.

'Dinner's ready,' she said to Mr Farley, as she got his slippers from under the stairs. He put them on, then walked across to the laid table and put three pound notes on her side plate.

'What's that for?' she asked.

'Well, I got enough hints,' he said.

'No you didn't,' she said, 'and not even a card with it.' She sulked a bit. If she looked too happy he might take the money back. Happiness was the one thing he could not abide.

'What use is a card?' he said.

'I may be sentimental, but don't forget I'm a woman,' she said. The three-piece suite was hers and she could hardly contain herself with excitement.

After dinner he went out and got a card which had 'To my dear wife' on the outside.

'I suppose I have a lot of the schoolgirl in me,' she said, putting it on the mantelshelf. She was doing everything to humour him. They discussed what shirt he'd wear on the outing and she said she'd make sandwiches in case he got peckish on the journey. They were having lunch, of course, in Brighton.

'Don't fall for any young girl in a bathing-suit,' she said.

'Is that what you think I'll be doing?' he said.

'Well, who knows? A handsome man, fancy free.'

That pleased him. He offered to share some of his beer. That night she couldn't very well refuse him his rights, but it was her friend's body she imagined that circumferenced her own.

Next day when Mrs Captain Hagerty was shopping, Mrs Farley took the opportunity to telephone the furniture shop. She arranged to call in Saturday to pay the balance on the suite and asked if they could deliver it the same morning. The man – she recognized him as the one who took her money each week – said certainly.

On the Friday night she slept badly. For one thing Mr Farley had to be up early to catch the coach at Victoria Station. Also she was in a tremor over her friend's visit. Would he like the lounge? Would the pork chops be a little greasy? What would she wear? She'd offer him a sherry when he first arrived, to break the ice. She thought of the doorbell ringing, of a kiss in the hallway, then walking ahead into the room where the three-piece suite would instantly catch his eye. And thinking of these things she fell fast asleep.

'No, no, no.' She wakened from a nightmare with tears streaming down her face. She'd been dreaming that she met him at a bus stop and his face was more wretched than ever. He couldn't come, he said. His wife had found out and threatened to kill herself. He had to promise never to see Mrs Farley again. In the dream Mrs Farley said she would go to his wife and beg her to show some mercy. She ran to his house although he called after her not to.

His wife turned out to have the long, coarse face of one of the women Mrs Farley worked for.

'If you let me see your husband every Saturday for an hour, I'll scrub your house from top to bottom,' Mrs Farley said. The coarse-faced woman seated on a chair nodded to this and from nowhere a bucket of water and a scrubbing-brush appeared. Mrs Farley knelt in that small room and began to scrub the linoleum, which had some sort of pattern. She scrubbed with all her might, knowing that it was bringing her back to her friend. Just when she scrubbed the last corner, a wall receded and the room grew larger, and the more she scrubbed the greater the room became, until finally she was scrubbing a limitless area with no walls in sight. She turned to protest, but the coarse-faced woman had vanished and all she heard was the echo of her own voice cursing and sobbing and begging to be let out. She knew that her friend was at the bus stop waiting for her to come back, and greater than the pain of losing him was the injustice. He would think she had betrayed him. It was then she cried 'No, no, no' in her dream and wakened to find herself in a sweat. She got up and took an aspirin. At least it was a relief to know it was a dream. Her legs quaked as she stood at the window and looked out at the garden that was grey in the oncoming dawn. Sometimes she turned to glance at Mr Farley in case he should be awake. The sheet rose and fell over his paunch – he had thrown off the blanket. He was snoring slightly. Tomorrow he was going away, far away to the seaside, on an outing with thirty other men. Thirty other wives would have a day alone. And it came to her again, the conviction that he would die in exactly four years when he was sixty-six. A man in the flat downstairs had died at sixty-six, and because he too had been fat, and grumpy, and had a paunch, Mrs Farley believed that a similar fate awaited her husband. She would be fifty, not young, but not too old. The widow downstairs had bloomed in the last few months and begun to wear loud colours and sing when she was tidying her kitchen. Guiltily Mrs Farley got back into bed and prayed for sleep. Without sleep her face would look pinched and tomorrow she would need to look nice. She shook. That dream had really unnerved her.

By morning she had composed herself. She cooked a big breakfast for Mr Farley and stood at the gate while he walked out of sight towards the main road. Then she dashed back into the house, washed up, dusted the lounge, made a shopping list. By nine o'clock she was at the furniture shop. The assistant smiled as she came forward with the money. When she had paid he murmured something about not being sure whether they could deliver on a Saturday.

'But you promised, you promised,' she said. 'You've got to deliver it, where's the manager?'

Being easily intimidated, the assistant fled to find the manager. She walked back and forth, hit her clenched fists together and finally to distract herself she went across to look at the cut-glass vases. Her face in the mirror of the display table was purple. Bad temper played havoc with her circulation. She held a vase in her hand and with her thumb felt the sharp, cut edges. Her eyes were fixed on the door through which he'd disappeared – if only he'd hurry. The vase she held in her hand cost nine pounds and shivering she put it down. 'Lovely to look at, delightful to hold, but if you break me, consider me sold.' An accident like that could wreck her plans for weeks, to think that the vase cost the same as the three-piece suite, to think there were people who could buy such a thing and run the risk of breaking it.

'Madam, I'm very sorry but I'm afraid we can't.' A sly, unaccommodating person he was.

'You can't,' she said. 'You can't let me down.'

'It's not me, madam, I'd be only too glad. The manager has got on to them now and they say they simply can't.'

'Where is he?' Mrs Farley said, and instinctively she went towards his office door. She'd get that suite delivered if she had to carry it on her back.

The manager met her halfway across the shop. He wore thick, blue-tinted spectacles and she could not be sure what his attitude was, but he sounded sorry enough.

'Is it very urgent, madam?'

'It's my whole life,' she said, not knowing why she said such a rash thing, and then heard herself telling him an elaborate lie about how her son was graduating as a doctor that day and how his friends were coming in to tea and she wanted something for them to sit on. As a father himself the manager said he understood how she felt, and he would have to do something. Another customer stared, as if Mrs Farley had admitted to some terrible crime, then, when she caught his eye, he slunk away, embarrassed; maybe he thought he might be drawn into an argument or asked to contribute money.

'We can't disappoint your boy on a day like this, can we?' the manager said. Mrs Farley thought it the saddest thing anyone had ever said to her. If Mr Farley was listening, or her friend, she'd die!

The upshot was that the manager got another van from a removal firm who were willing to deliver the stuff. There was an extra charge of a pound. Mrs Farley protested. The manager said she could either wait until Monday and have it delivered free, in the shop van, or settle for the removers. She gave in of course.

The movers arrived in an enormous pantechnicon, and she was worried that some of the neighbours might mention it to Mr Farley and ask if he was moving house or something. That was why, when they pulled up, she asked them could they move their van down the street a little, as it was blocking a motorcar entrance. They were very nice about it.

The men put the three pieces of furniture where she told them and then, half-heartedly she offered them a cup of tea. That delayed her another twenty minutes. When they were gone she went into the front room to reaffirm what she already knew. The three-piece suite was not a success; it did nothing for the room. It was dark and drab. Mr Farley would be right in thinking that it was a mistake. Frayed threads, dimmed stains, a leftover from someone else's life. What had she been thinking of the day she chose it? Of him, her friend, the man she was going to see in a couple of hours. She got a clothes brush and began to brush the couch carefully, hoping that when she'd done it it would look plush. She came on a ludo button that was stuck down in one of the corners and for a minute she thought it was a shilling. After she had done it carefully with the clothes brush she got out the vacuum cleaner and cleaned it thoroughly all over.

Just in case anything went wrong, Mrs Farley and her friend had previously arranged to meet outside the pub. When he saw her come towards him he knew there was something amiss. She held her head down and wore her flat, canvas shoes.

'Hello.' He came forward to greet her.

'He didn't go,' she said. 'He got suspicious at the last minute.'

For the two hours Mrs Farley had debated what she should say to her friend. One thing was sure: she dare not have him in the front room because he would catch her out in her boasting. Always when she described that room she described the three-piece suite. What he would see was a drab piece of furniture in a drab room where brown paint prevailed. Mr Farley did his own decorating and insisted on brown because it did not have to be renewed so often. She could not let him see it. He would say she was no better than his wife and she did not want that.

'Don't worry,' he said. 'Come and have a drink.'

'You're all dressed up,' she said. He wore a dark suit, a white shirt and a lovely striped tie. He looked wealthy. He looked like the sort of man who would have a wallet full of fivers and a home with easy chairs, and a piano.

'I'm sorry,' she was saying to his disappointed face.

'We'll have a nice day anyhow,' he told her. He worried if the pound he had would see them through. He had not banked on spending any money other than the drink in the pub when they met and a small bottle of liqueur as a little gift to her.

'What will you have?' He'd brought her into the lounge bar and sat her on a high upholstered couch that circled the wall.

'Anything,' she said. He got her a sherry.

'Cheers,' he said, and pushed her cheeks upwards with his hand until she appeared to be smiling.

'I dreamt about you last night,' she said.

'A nice dream?' He smiled so gently.

'A lovely dream.' She couldn't disappoint him any more.

Mrs Farley insisted on buying lunch. They ate in the restaurant that adjoined the pub and they talked in whispers. It was a lovely place with embossed wallpaper and candlesticks on the tables. Everywhere she looked she saw wall couches and easy, comfortable chairs. He wondered if they put candles into the candlesticks at night and she said they probably didn't because there wasn't a trace of candlegrease. Under the table they gripped hands every few minutes and looked into each other's eyes, desperate to say something.

The lunch cost over a pound, the amount she had set aside anyhow to get the pork chops and sherry and things. While she was in the ladies' room, he debated whether he should propose pictures, or a bus ride around London, or a short boat trip up the Thames. With his money, it had to be just one of those.

They settled on the pictures. They were both thinking that they could snuggle down and have a taste of the comfort they might have had in Mrs Farley's front room.

The picture turned out to be an English comedy about crooks, and though the handful of people in the cinema laughed, neither Mrs Farley nor her friend found it funny at all. It bore no relation to their own lives, it had nothing to do with their predicament. They said, when they came out, that it was a pity they'd stayed inside so long as the day was scorching.

'Do I look a show?' she asked. Her mouth was swollen from kisses.

'You look lovely.'

What to do next?

'Let's have a walk by the river, and then tea,' he said. He knew a cheap café up that way.

'Are you superstitious?' she asked. He said not very. She said she'd broken something that day and was afraid she'd break two other things. A splinter from a kitchen cup was in her finger.

'I'd like that black one,' he said. He'd been admiring boats that were moored to the riverside. He'd rather have a boat than a car, he told her.

They'd sail away under arched bridges, over locks, out to a changeless blue sea.

'Is it true that the blue lagoon isn't blue?' she asked.

'We'll go there and see when I get my boat,' he said.

She would wear trousers and a raincoat on the boat, but when they came ashore at Monte Carlo and places she would have flowered dresses.

'You never asked me what I broke,' she said.

'Oh, tell me.'

'A cup.'

'A cup.'

Possibly he thought it was silly but it worried her.

'I'll tell you,' he said. 'Get a couple of old cracked ones and break them and then you won't have anything to worry about.'

The cups reminded them both of home and duty. He would have to go shortly.

By five-thirty they had talked and walked for an hour. But they had said nothing. He apologized for the bad picture, she said she was sorry she couldn't bring him in.

'Still, we had a grand time,' she said.

'No, we hadn't,' he said. 'I should have thought of something special.'

'What do other people do?' she asked.

'Oh, they go to the seaside, they go to hotels, they go to places,' he said. She was sorry now that she hadn't risked it and told him. He would have understood; it might have brought them closer together. She looked at him with regret, with love, she looked intently to keep his image more distinctly in her mind. She might not see him dressed up again for ages.

They kissed and made their arrangements for the following Saturday, at their usual place.

As she walked away she did not turn round to wave, in case he might expect a smile. Anyhow he was occupying himself, with taking off his tie and rolling it up neatly. His wife had not seen him go out with it on.

She walked, deep in thought. She'd lost her chance. Her husband would live for ever. She and her friend were fated to walk up and down streets towards the railway bridge, and in the end they would grow tired of walking, and they would return, each to a makeshift home.

HARRIETTE WILSON

✒

from
Harriette Wilson's Memoirs
of herself and others

I shall not say why and how I became, at the age of fifteen, the mistress of the Earl of Craven. Whether it was love, or the severity of my father, the depravity of my own heart, or the winning arts of the noble Lord, which induced me to leave my paternal roof and place myself under his protection, does not now much signify: or if it does, I am not in the humour to gratify curiosity in this matter.

I resided on the Marine Parade, at Brighton; and I remember that Lord Craven used to draw cocoa trees, and his fellows, as he called them, on the best vellum paper, for my amusement. Here stood the enemy, he would say; and here, my love, are my fellows: there the cocoa trees, etc. It was, in fact, a dead bore. All these cocoa trees and fellows, at past eleven o'clock at night, could have no peculiar interest for a child like myself, so lately in the habit of retiring early to rest. One night, I recollect, I fell asleep; and, as I often dream, I said, yawning, and half awake, Oh, Lord! oh, Lord! Craven has got me into the West Indies again. In short, I soon found that I had made but a bad speculation by going from my father to Lord Craven. I was even more afraid of the latter than I had been of the former; not that there was any particular harm in the man, beyond his cocoa trees; but we never suited nor understood each other.

I was not depraved enough to determine immediately on a new choice, and yet I often thought about it. How, indeed, could I do otherwise, when the Honourable Frederick Lamb was my constant visitor, and talked to me of nothing else? However, in justice to myself, I must declare that the idea of the possibility of deceiving Lord Craven, while I was under his roof, never once entered my head. Frederick was then very handsome; and certainly tried, with all his soul and with all his strength, to convince me that constancy to Lord Craven was the greatest nonsense in the world. I firmly believe that Frederick Lamb sincerely loved me, and deeply regretted that he had no fortune to invite me to share with him.

Lord Melbourne, his father, was a good man. Not one of your stiff-laced moralizing fathers, who preach chastity and forbearance to their children. Quite the contrary; he congratulated his son on the lucky circumstance of his friend Craven having such a fine girl with him. 'No such thing,' answered Frederick Lamb; 'I am unsuccessful there. Harriette will have nothing to do with me.' – 'Nonsense!' rejoined Melbourne, in great surprise; 'I never heard anything half so ridiculous in all my life. The girl must be mad! She looks mad: I thought so the other day, when I met her galloping about, with her feathers blowing and her thick dark hair about her ears.'

'I'll speak to Harriette for you,' added His Lordship, after a long pause; and then continued repeating to himself, in an undertone, 'Not have my son, indeed! six feet high! a fine, straight, handsome, noble young fellow! I wonder what she would have!'

In truth, I scarcely knew myself; but something I determined on: so miserably tired was I of Craven, and his cocoa trees, and his sailing boats, and his ugly cotton nightcap. Surely, I would say, all men do not wear those shocking cotton nightcaps; else all women's illusions had been destroyed on the first night of their marriage!

I wonder, thought I, what sort of a nightcap the Prince of Wales wears? Then I went on to wonder whether the Prince of Wales would think me so beautiful as Frederick Lamb did? Next I reflected that Frederick Lamb was younger than the Prince; but then, again, a Prince of Wales!!!

I was undecided: my heart began to soften. I thought of my dear mother, and wished I had never left her. It was too late, however, now. My father would not suffer me to return; and as to passing my life, or any more of it, with Craven, cotton nightcap and all, it was death! He never once made me laugh, nor said nor did anything to please me.

Thus musing, I listlessly turned over my writing-book, half in the humour to address the Prince of Wales. A sheet of paper, covered with Lord Craven's cocoa trees, decided me; and I wrote the following letter, which I addressed to the Prince.

BRIGHTON.

I am told that I am very beautiful, so, perhaps, you would like to see me; and I wish that, since so many are disposed to love me, one, for in the humility of my heart I should be quite satisfied with one, would be at the pains to make me love him. In the mean time, this is all very dull work, Sir, and worse even than being at home with my father: so, if you pity me, and believe you could make me in love with you, write to me, and direct to the post-office here.

By return of post, I received an answer nearly to this effect: I believe, from Colonel Thomas.

Miss Wilson's letter has been received by the noble individual to whom it was addressed. If Miss Wilson will come to town, she may have an interview, by directing her letter as before.

I answered this note directly, addressing my letter to the Prince of Wales.

SIR,

To travel fifty-two miles, this bad weather, merely to see a man, with only the given number of legs, arms, fingers, etc., would, you must admit, be madness, in a girl like myself, surrounded by humble admirers, who are ever ready to travel any distance for the honour of kissing the tip of her little finger; but if you can prove to me that you are one bit better than any man who may be ready to attend my bidding, I'll e'en start for London directly. So, if you can do anything better, in the way of pleasing a lady, than ordinary men, write directly: if not, adieu, Monsieur le Prince.

I won't say Yours,
By day or night, or any kind of light;
Because you are too impudent.

It was necessary to put this letter into the post office myself, as Lord Craven's black footman would have been somewhat surprised at its address. Crossing the Steyne, I met Lord Melbourne, who joined me immediately.

'Where is Craven?' said His Lordship, shaking hands with me.

'Attending to his military duties at Lewes, my Lord.'

'And where's my son Fred?' asked His Lordship.

'I am not your son's keeper, my Lord,' said I.

'No! By the bye,' inquired His Lordship, 'how is this? I wanted to call upon you about it. I never heard of such a thing, in the whole course of my life! What the Devil can you possibly have to say against my son Fred?'

'Good heavens! my Lord, you frighten me! I never recollect to have said a single word against your son, as long as I have lived. Why should I?'

'Why, indeed!' said Lord Melbourne. 'And since there is nothing to be said against him, what excuse can you make for using him so ill?'

'I don't understand you one bit, my Lord.' (The very idea of a father put me in a tremble.)

'Why,' said Lord Melbourne, 'did you not turn the poor boy out of your house, as soon as it was dark; although Craven was in town, and there was not the shadow of an excuse for such treatment?'

At this moment, and before I could recover from my surprise at the tenderness of some parents, Frederick Lamb, who was almost my shadow, joined us.

'Fred, my boy,' said Lord Melbourne, 'I'll leave you two together; and I fancy you'll find Miss Wilson more reasonable.' He touched his hat to me, as he entered the little gate of the Pavilion, where we had remained stationary from the moment His Lordship had accosted me.

Frederick Lamb laughed long, loud, and heartily at his father's interference. So did I, the moment he was safely out of sight; and then I told him of my answer to the Prince's letter, at which he laughed still more. He was charmed with me for refusing His Royal Highness. 'Not,' said Frederick, 'that he is not as handsome and graceful a man as any in England; but I hate the weakness of a woman who knows not how to refuse a prince, merely because he is a prince.' – 'It is something, too, to be of royal blood,' answered I frankly; 'and something more to be so accomplished: but this posting after a man! I wonder what he could mean by it!!'

Frederick Lamb now began to plead his own cause. 'I must soon join my regiment in Yorkshire,' said he (he was, at that time, aide-de-camp to General Mackenzie); 'God knows when we may meet again! I am sure you will not long continue with Lord Craven. I foresee what will happen, and yet, when it does, I think I shall go mad!'

For my part, I felt flattered and obliged by the affection Frederick Lamb evinced towards me; but I was still not in love with him.

At length the time arrived when poor Frederick Lamb could delay his departure from Brighton no longer. On the eve of it, he begged to be allowed to introduce his brother William to me.

'What for?' said I.

'That he may let me know how you behave,' answered Frederick Lamb.

'And if I fall in love with him?' I inquired.

'I am sure you won't,' replied Fred. 'Not because my brother William is not likeable; on the contrary, William is much handsomer than I am; but he will not love you as I have done, and do still; and you are too good to forget me entirely.'

Our parting scene was rather tender. For the last ten days, Lord Craven being absent, we had scarcely been separated an hour during the whole day. I had begun to feel the force of habit; and Frederick Lamb really respected me, for the perseverance with which I had resisted his urgent wishes, when he would have had me deceive Lord Craven. He had ceased to torment me with such wild fits of passion as had, at first, frightened me; and by these means he had obtained much more of my confidence.

Two days after his departure for Hull, in Yorkshire, Lord Craven returned to Brighton, where he was immediately informed, by some spiteful enemy of mine, that I had been, during the whole of his absence, openly intriguing with Frederick Lamb. In consequence of this information, one evening, when I expected his return, his servant brought me the following letter, dated Lewes:

A friend of mine has informed me of what has been going on at Brighton. This information, added to what I have seen with my own eyes, of your intimacy with Frederick Lamb, obliges me to declare that we must separate. Let me add, Harriette, that you might have done anything with me, with only a little more conduct. As it is, allow me to wish you happy; and further, pray inform me, if, in any way, *à la distance*, I can promote your welfare.

CRAVEN.

This letter completed my dislike of Lord Craven. I answered it immediately, as follows:

MY LORD,

Had I ever wished to deceive you, I have the wit to have done it successfully; but you are old enough to be a better judge of human nature than to have suspected me of guile or deception. In the plenitude of your condescension, you are pleased to add, that I 'might have done anything with you, with only a little more conduct', now I say, and from my heart, the Lord defend me from ever doing any thing with you again! Adieu.

HARRIETTE.

My present situation was rather melancholy and embarrassing, and yet I felt my heart the lighter for my release from the cocoa trees, without its being my own act and deed. It is my fate! thought I; for I never wronged this man. I hate his fine carriage, and his money, and everything belonging to, or connected with him. I shall hate cocoa as long as I live; and, I am sure, I will never enter a boat again, if I can help it. This is what one gets by acting with principle.

The next morning, while I was considering what was to become of me, I received a very affectionate letter from Frederick Lamb, dated Hull. He dared not, he said, be selfish enough to ask me to share his poverty, and yet he had a kind of presentiment, that he should not lose me.

My case was desperate; for I had taken a vow not to remain another night under Lord Craven's roof. John, therefore, the black, whom Craven had, I suppose, imported, with his cocoa trees from the West Indies, was desired to secure me a place in the mail for Hull.

It is impossible to do justice to the joy and rapture which brightened Frederick's countenance, when he flew to receive me, and conducted me to his house, where I was shortly visited by his worthy general, Mackenzie, who assured me of his earnest desire to make my stay in Hull as comfortable as possible.

We continued here for about three months, and then came to London. Fred Lamb's passion increased daily; but I discovered, on our arrival in London, that he was a voluptuary, somewhat worldly and selfish. My comforts were not considered. I lived in extreme poverty, while he contrived to enjoy all the luxuries of life; and suffered me to pass my dreary evenings alone, while he frequented balls, masquerades, etc. Secure of my constancy, he was satisfied – so was not I! I felt that I deserved better from him.

I asked Frederick, one day, if the Marquis of Lorne was as handsome as he had been represented to me. 'The finest fellow on earth,' said Frederick Lamb, 'all the women adore him'; and then he went on to relate various anecdotes of His Lordship, which strongly excited my curiosity.

Soon after this, he quitted town for a few weeks, and I was left alone in London, without money, or, at any rate, with very little; and Frederick Lamb, who had intruded himself on me at Brighton, and thus become the cause of my separation from Lord Craven, made himself happy; because he believed me faithful, and cared not for my distresses.

This idea disgusted me; and, in a fit of anger, I wrote to the Marquis of Lorne, merely to say that, if he would walk up to Duke's Row, Somerstown, he would meet a most lovely girl.

This was his answer:

If you are but half as lovely as you think yourself, you must be well worth knowing; but how is that to be managed? not in the street! But come to No. 39, Portland-street, and ask for me.

L.

My reply was this:

No! our first meeting must be on the high road, in order that I may have room to run away, in case I don't like you.

HARRIETTE.

The Marquis rejoined:

Well, then, fair lady, tomorrow, at four, near the turnpike, look for me on horseback; and then, you know, I can gallop away.

L.

We met. The Duke (he has since succeeded to the title) did not gallop away; and, for my part, I had never seen a countenance I had thought half so beautifully expressive. I was afraid to look at it, lest a closer examination might destroy all the new and delightful sensations his first glance had inspired in my breast. His manner was most gracefully soft and polished. We walked together for about two hours.

'I never saw such a sunny, happy countenance as yours in my whole life,' said Argyle to me.

'Oh, but I am happier than usual today,' answered I, very naturally.

Before we parted, the Duke knew as much of me and my adventures as I knew myself. He was very anxious to be allowed to call on me.

'And how will your particular friend, Frederick Lamb, like that?' inquired I.

The Duke laughed.

'Well, then,' said His Grace, 'do me the honour, some day, to come and dine or sup with me at Argyle House.'

'I shall not be able to run away, if I go there,' I answered, laughingly, in allusion to my last note.

'Shall you want to run away from me?' said Argyle; and there was something unusually beautiful and eloquent in his countenance, which brought a deep blush into my cheek.

'When we know each other better?' added Argyle, beseechingly. '*En attendant*, will you walk with me tomorrow?' I assented, and we parted.

I returned to my home in unusual spirits; they were a little damped, however, by the reflection that I had been doing wrong. I cannot, I reasoned with myself, I cannot, I fear, become what the world calls a steady, prudent, virtuous woman. That time is past, even if I was ever fit for it. Still I must distinguish myself from those in the like unfortunate situations, by strict probity and love of truth. I will never become vile. I will always adhere to good faith, as long as anything like kindness or honourable principle is shown towards me; and, when I am ill-used, I will leave my lover rather than deceive him. Frederick Lamb relies in perfect confidence on my honour. True, that confidence is the effect of vanity. He believes that a woman who could resist him, as I did at Brighton, is the safest woman on earth! He leaves me alone, and without sufficient money for common necessaries. No matter, I must tell him tonight, as soon as he arrives from the country, that I have written to, and walked with Lorne. My dear mother would never forgive me, if I became artful.

So mused, and thus reasoned I, till I was interrupted by Frederick Lamb's loud knock at my door. He will be in a fine passion, said I to myself, in excessive trepidation; and I was in such a hurry to have it over, that I related all immediately. To my equal joy and astonishment, Frederick Lamb was not a bit angry. From his manner, I could not help guessing that his friend Lorne had often been found a very powerful rival.

I could see through the delight he experienced, at the idea of possessing a woman whom, his vanity persuaded him, Argyle would sigh for in vain; and, attacking me on my weak point, he kissed me, and said, 'I have the most perfect esteem for my dearest little wife, whom I can, I know, as safely trust with Argyle as Craven trusted her with me.'

'Are you quite sure?' asked I, merely to ease my conscience. 'Were it not wiser to advise me not to walk about with him?'

'No, no,' said Frederick Lamb; 'it is such good fun! bring him up every day to Somerstown and the Jew's Harp House, there to swallow cyder and sentiment. Make him walk up here as many times as you can, dear little Harry, for the honour of your sex, and to punish him for declaring, as he always does, that no woman who will not love him at once is worth his pursuit.'

'I am sorry he is such a coxcomb,' said I.

'What is that to you, you little fool?'

'True,' I replied. And, at that moment, I made a sort of determination not to let the beautiful and voluptuous expression of Argyle's dark blue eyes take possession of my fancy.

'You are a neater figure than the Marquis of Lorne,' said I to Frederick, wishing to think so.

'Lorne is growing fat,' answered Frederick Lamb; 'but he is the most active creature possible, and appears lighter than any man of his weight I ever saw; and then he is, without any exception, the highest-bred man in England.'

'And you desire and permit me to walk about the country with him?'

'Yes; do trot him often up here. I want to have a laugh against Lorne.'

'And you are not jealous?'

'Not at all,' said Frederick Lamb, 'for I am secure of your affections.'

I must not deceive this man, thought I, and the idea began to make me a little melancholy. My only chance, or rather my only excuse, will be his leaving me without the means of existence. This appeared likely; for I was too shy and too proud to ask for money; and Frederick Lamb encouraged me in this amiable forbearance!

The next morning, with my heart beating very unusually high, I attended my appointment with Argyle. I hoped, nay, almost expected, to find him there before me. I paraded near the turnpike five minutes, then grew angry; in five more, I became wretched; in five more, downright indignant; and, in five more, wretched again – and so I returned home.

This, thought I, shall be a lesson to me hereafter, never to meet a man: it is unnatural; and yet I had felt it perfectly natural to return to the person whose society had made me so happy! No matter, reasoned I, we females must not suffer love or pleasure to glow in our eyes until we are quite sure of a return. We must be dignified! Alas! I can only be and seem what I am. No doubt my sunny face of joy and happiness, which he talked to me about, was understood, and it has disgusted him. He thought me bold, and yet I am sure I never blushed so much in any man's society before.

I now began to consider myself with feelings of the most painful humility. Suddenly I flew to my writing-desk; he shall not have the cut all on his side neither, thought I, with the pride of a child. I will soon convince him I am not accustomed to be slighted; and then I wrote to His Grace, as follows:

It was very wrong and very bold of me, to have sought your acquaintance, in the way I did, my Lord; and I entreat you to forgive and forget my childish folly, as completely as I have forgotten the occasion of it.

So far, so good, thought I, pausing; but then suppose he should, from this dry note, really believe me so cold and stupid as not to have felt his pleasing qualities? Suppose now it were possible that he liked me after all? Then hastily, and half ashamed of myself, I added these few lines:

I have not quite deserved this contempt from you, and, in that consolatory reflection, I take my leave – not in anger, my Lord, but only with the steady determination so to profit by the humiliating lesson you have given me, as never to expose myself to the like contempt again.

Your most obedient servant,
HARRIETTE WILSON.

Having put my letter into the post, I passed a restless night; and, the next morning, heard the knock of the twopenny postman, in extreme agitation. He brought me, as I suspected, an answer from Argyle, which is subjoined.

You are not half vain enough, dear Harriette. You ought to have been quite certain that any man who had once met you, could fail in a second appointment, but from unavoidable accident – and, if you were only half as pleased with Thursday morning as I was, you will meet me tomorrow, in the same place, at four. Pray, pray, come.

LORNE.

I kissed the letter, and put it into my bosom, grateful for the weight it had taken off my heart. Not that I was so far gone in love, as my readers may imagine, but I had suffered severely from wounded pride, and, in fact, I was very much *tête montée*.

The sensations which Argyle had inspired me with, were the warmest, nay, the first of the same nature I had ever experienced. Nevertheless, I could not forgive him quite so easily as this, neither. I recollected what Frederick Lamb had said about his vanity. No doubt, thought I, he thinks it was nothing to have paraded me up and down that stupid turnpike road, in the vain hope of seeing him. It shall now be his turn: and I gloried in the idea of revenge.

The hour of Argyle's appointment drew nigh, arrived, and passed away, without my leaving my house. To Frederick Lamb I related everything – presented him with Argyle's letter, and acquainted him with my determination not to meet His Grace.

'How good!' said Frederick Lamb, quite delighted. 'We dine together today, at Lady Holland's; and I mean to ask him, before everybody at table, what he thinks of the air about the turnpike on Somerstown.'

The next day I was surprised by a letter, not, as I anticipated, from Argyle, but from the late Tom Sheridan, only son of Richard Brinsley Sheridan. I had, by mere accident, become acquainted with that very interesting young man, when quite a child, from the circumstances of his having paid great attention to one of my elder sisters.

He requested me to allow him to speak a few words to me,

80

wherever I pleased. Frederick Lamb having gone to Brocket Hall, in Hertfordshire, I desired him to call on me.

'I am come from my friend Lorne,' said Tom Sheridan. 'I would not have intruded on you, but that, poor fellow, he is really annoyed; and he has commissioned me to acquaint you with the accident which obliged him to break his appointment, because I can best vouch for the truth of it, having, upon my honour, heard the Prince of Wales invite Lord Lorne to Carlton House, with my own ears, at the very moment when he was about to meet you in Somerstown. Lorne,' continued Tom Sheridan, 'desires me to say, that he is not coxcomb enough to imagine you cared for him; but, in justice, he wants to stand exactly where he did in your opinion, before he broke his appointment: he was so perfectly innocent on that subject. I would write to her, said he, again and again; but that, in all probability, my letters would be shown to Frederick Lamb, and be laughed at by them both. I would call on her, in spite of the devil, but that I know not where she lives.

'I asked Argyle,' Tom Sheridan proceeded, 'how he had addressed his last letters to you? To the post office, in Somerstown, was his answer, and thence they were forwarded to Harriette. He had tried to bribe the old woman there, to obtain my address, but she abused him, and turned him out of her shop. It is very hard,' continued Tom, repeating the words of his noble friend, 'to lose the goodwill of one of the nicest, cleverest girls I ever met with in my life, who was, I am certain, civilly, if not kindly disposed towards me, by such a mere accident. Therefore,' continued Tom Sheridan, smiling, 'you'll make it up with Lorne, won't you?'

'There is nothing to forgive,' said I, 'if no slight was meant. In short, you are making too much of me, and spoiling me, by all this explanation; for, indeed, I had, at first, been less indignant; but that I fancied His Grace neglected me, because –' and I hesitated, while I could feel myself blush deeply.

'Because what?' asked Tom Sheridan.

'Nothing,' I replied, looking at my shoes.

'What a pretty girl you are,' observed Sheridan, 'particularly when you blush.'

'Fiddlestick!' said I, laughing; 'you know you always preferred my sister Fanny.'

'Well,' replied Tom, 'there I plead guilty. Fanny is the sweetest

81

creature on earth; but you are all a race of finished coquettes, who delight in making fools of people. Now can anything come up to your vanity in writing to Lorne, that you are the most beautiful creature on earth?'

'Never mind,' said I, 'you set all that to rights. I was never vain in your society, in my life.'

'I would give the world for a kiss at this moment,' said Tom; 'because you look so humble, and so amiable; but' – recollecting himself – 'this is not exactly the embassy I came upon. Have you a mind to give Lorne an agreeable surprise?'

'I don't know.'

'Upon my honour I believe he is downright in love with you.'

'Well?'

'Come into a hackney coach with me, and we will drive down to the Tennis Court, in the Haymarket.'

'Is the Duke there?'

'Yes.'

'But – at all events, I will not trust myself in a hackney coach with you.'

'There was a time,' said poor Tom Sheridan, with much drollery of expression, 'there was a time when the very motion of a carriage would – but now!' – and he shook his handsome head with comic gravity – 'but now! you may drive with me, from here to St Paul's, in the most perfect safety. I will tell you a secret,' added he, and he fixed his fine dark eye on my face while he spoke, in a tone, half merry, half desponding, 'I am dying; but nobody knows it yet!'

I was very much affected by his manner of saying this.

'My dear Mr Sheridan,' said I, with earnest warmth, 'you have accused me of being vain of the little beauty God has given me. Now I would give it all, or, upon my word, I think I would, to obtain the certainty that you would, from this hour, refrain from such excesses as are destroying you.'

'Did you see me play the Methodist parson, in a tub, at Mrs Beaumont's masquerade, last Thursday?' said Tom, with affected levity.

'You may laugh as you please,' said I, 'at a little fool like me pretending to preach to you; yet I am sensible enough to admire you, and quite feeling enough to regret your time so misspent, your brilliant talents so misapplied.'

'Bravo! Bravo!' Tom reiterated, 'what a funny little girl you are! Pray, Miss, how is your time spent?'

'Not in drinking brandy,' I replied.

'And how might your talent be applied, Ma'am?'

'Have not I just given you a specimen, in the shape of a handsome quotation?'

'My good little girl – it is in the blood, and I can't help it, – and, if I could, it is too late now. I'm dying, I tell you. I know not if my poor father's physician was as eloquent as you are; but he did his best to turn him from drinking. Among other things, he declared to him one day, that the brandy, Arquebusade, and eau de Cologne he swallowed, would burn off the coat of his stomach. Then, said my father, my stomach must digest in its waistcoat; for I cannot help it.'

'Indeed, I am very sorry for you,' I replied; and I hope he believed me; for he pressed my hand hastily, and I think I saw a tear glisten in his bright, dark eye.

'Shall I tell Lorne,' said poor Tom, with an effort to recover his usual gaiety, 'that you will write to him, or will you come to the Tennis Court?'

'Neither,' answered I; 'but you may tell His Lordship that, of course, I am not angry, since I am led to believe he had no intention to humble nor make a fool of me.'

'Nothing more?' inquired Tom.

'Nothing,' I replied, 'for His Lordship.'

'And what for me?' said Tom.

'You! what do you want?'

'A kiss!' he said.

'Not I, indeed!'

'Be it so, then; and yet you and I may never meet again on this earth, and just now I thought you felt some interest about me'; and he was going away.

'So I do, dear Tom Sheridan!' said I, detaining him; for I saw death had fixed his stamp on poor Sheridan's handsome face. 'You know I have a very warm and feeling heart, and taste enough to admire and like you; but why is this to be our last meeting?'

'I must go to the Mediterranean,' poor Sheridan continued, putting his hand to his chest, and coughing.

To die! thought I, as I looked on his sunk, but still very expressive dark eyes.

'Then God bless you!' said I, first kissing his hand, and then, though somewhat timidly, leaning my face towards him. He parted my hair, and kissed my forehead, my eyes, and my lips.

'If I do come back,' said he, forcing a languid smile, 'mind let me find you married, and rich enough to lend me an occasional hundred pounds or two.' He then kissed his hand gracefully, and was out of sight in an instant.

I never saw him again.

The next morning my maid brought me a little note from Argyle, to say that he had been waiting about my door an hour, having learned my address from poor Sheridan; and that, seeing the servant in the street, he could not help making an attempt to induce me to go out and walk with him. I looked out of the window, saw Argyle, ran for my hat and cloak, and joined him in an instant.

'Am I forgiven?' said Argyle, with gentle eagerness.

'Oh yes,' returned I, 'long ago; but that will do you no good, for I really am treating Frederick Lamb very ill, and therefore must not walk with you again.'

'Why not?' Argyle inquired. '*Apropos*,' he added, 'you told Frederick that I walked about the turnpike looking for you, and that, no doubt, to make him laugh at me?'

'No, not for that; but I never could deceive any man. I have told him the whole story of our becoming acquainted, and he allows me to walk with you. It is I who think it wrong, not Frederick.'

'That is to say, you think me a bore,' said Argyle, reddening with pique and disappointment.

'And suppose I loved you?' I asked, 'still I am engaged to Frederick Lamb, who trusts me, and – '

'If', interrupted Argyle, 'it were possible you did love me, Frederick Lamb would be forgotten: but, though you did not love me, you must promise to try and do so, some day or other. You don't know how much I have fixed my heart on it.'

These sentimental walks continued more than a month. One evening we walked rather later than usual. It grew dark. In a moment of ungovernable passion, Argyle's ardour frightened me. Not that I was insensible to it: so much the contrary, that I felt certain another meeting must decide my fate. Still, I was offended at what, I conceived, shewed such a want of respect. The Duke became humble. There is a charm in the humility of a lover who has offended. The charm is so great that we like to prolong it. In spite of all he could say, I left him in anger. The next morning I received the following note:

> If you see me waiting about your door, tomorrow morning, do you not fancy I am looking for you; but for your pretty housemaid.

I did see him from a sly corner of my window; but I resisted all my desires, and remained concealed. I dare not see him again, thought I, for I cannot be so very profligate, knowing and feeling, as I do, how impossible it will be to refuse him anything, if we meet again. I cannot treat Fred Lamb in that manner! besides, I should be afraid to tell him of it: he would, perhaps, kill me.

But then, poor dear Lorne! to return his kisses, as I did last night, and afterwards be so very severe on him, for a passion which it seemed so out of his power to control!

Nevertheless we must part, now or never; so I'll write and take my leave of him kindly. This was my letter:

> At the first, I was afraid I should love you, and, but for Fred Lamb having requested me to get you up to Somerstown, after I had declined meeting you, I had been happy: now the idea makes me miserable. Still it must be so. I am naturally affection-ate. Habit attaches me to Fred Lamb. I cannot deceive him or acquaint him with what will cause him to cut me, in anger and for ever. We may not then meet again, Lorne, as hitherto: for now we could not be merely friends: lovers we must be, hereafter, or nothing. I have never loved any man in my life before, and yet, dear Lorne, you see we must part. I venture to send you the inclosed thick lock of my hair; because you have been good enough to admire it. I do not care how I have disfigured my head, since you are not to see it again.
>
> God bless you, Lorne. Do not quite forget last night directly, and believe me, as in truth I am,
>
> Most devotedly yours,
> HARRIETTE.

This was his answer, written, I suppose, in some pique.

> True, you have given me many sweet kisses, and a lock of your beautiful hair. All this does not convince me you are one bit in

love with me. I am the last man on earth to desire you to do violence to your feelings, by leaving a man as dear to you as Frederick Lamb is; so farewell, Harriette. I shall not intrude to offend you again.

LORNE.

Poor Lorne is unhappy; and, what is worse, thought I, he will soon hate me. The idea made me wretched. However, I will do myself the justice to say, that I have seldom, in the whole course of my life, been tempted by my passions or my fancies, to what my heart and conscience told me was wrong. I am afraid my conscience has been a very easy one; but, certainly, I have followed its dictates. There was a want of heart and delicacy, I always thought, in leaving any man, without full and very sufficient reasons for it. At the same time, my dear mother's marriage had proved to me so forcibly, the miseries of two people of contrary opinions and character, torturing each other to the end of their natural lives, that, before I was ten years old, I decided, in my own mind, to live free as air from any restraint but that of my conscience.

Frederick Lamb's love was now increasing, as all men's do, from gratified vanity. He sometimes passed an hour in reading to me. Till then, I had no idea of the gratification to be derived from books. In my convent in France, I had read only sacred dramas; at home, my father's mathematical books, *Buchan's Medicine, Gil Blas,* and the *Vicar of Wakefield,* formed our whole library. The two latter I had long known by heart, and could repeat at this moment.

My sisters used to subscribe to little circulating libraries, in the neighbourhood, for the common novels of the day; but I always hated these. Fred Lamb's choice was happy – Milton, Shakespeare, Byron, the Rambler, Virgil, etc. I must know all about these Greeks and Romans, said I to myself. Some day I will go into the country quite alone, and study like mad. I am too young now.

In the meantime, I was absolutely charmed with Shakespeare. Music, I always had a natural talent for. I played well on the pianoforte; that is, with taste and execution, though almost without study.

There was a very elegant-looking woman, residing in my neighbourhood, in a beautiful little cottage, who had long excited my curiosity. She appeared to be the mother of five extremely beautiful children. These were always to be seen with their nurse, walking out, most fancifully dressed. Every one used to stop to admire them. Their mother seemed to live in the most complete retirement. I never saw her with anybody besides her children.

One day our eyes met: she smiled, and I half bowed. The next day we met again, and the lady wished me a good morning. We soon got into conversation. I asked her, if she did not lead a very solitary life? 'You are the first female I have spoken to for four years,' said the lady, 'with the exception of my own servants; but', added she, 'some day we may know each other better. In the meantime will you trust yourself to come and dine with me today?' – 'With great pleasure,' I replied, 'if you think me worthy of that honour.' We then separated to dress for dinner.

When I entered her drawing-room, at the hour she had appointed, I was struck with the elegant taste, more than with the richness of the furniture. A beautiful harp, drawings of a somewhat voluptuous cast, elegant needlework, Moore's poems, and a fine pianoforte, formed a part of it. She is not a bad woman – and she is not a good woman, said I to myself. What can she be?

The lady now entered the room, and welcomed me with an appearance of real pleasure. 'I am not quite sure', said she, 'whether I can have the pleasure of introducing you to Mr Johnstone today, or not. We will not wait dinner for him, if he does not arrive in time.' This was the first word I had heard about a Mr Johnstone, although I knew the lady was called by that name.

Just as we were sitting down to dinner, Mr Johnstone arrived, and was introduced to me. He was a particularly elegant handsome man, about forty years of age. His manner of addressing Mrs Johnstone was more that of a humble romantic lover than of a husband; yet Julia, for so he called her, could be no common woman. I could not endure all this mystery, and, when he left us in the evening, I frankly asked Julia, for so we will call her in future, why she invited a strange madcap girl like me to dinner with her?

'Consider the melancholy life I lead,' said Julia.

'Thank you for the compliment,' answered I.

'But do you believe', interrupted Julia, 'that I should have asked you to dine with me, if I had not been particularly struck and pleased with you? I had, as I passed your window, heard you touch the pianoforte with a very masterly hand, and therefore I conceived that you were not uneducated, and I knew that you led almost as retired a life as myself. *Au reste,*' continued Julia, 'some day, perhaps soon, you shall know all about me.'

I did not press the matter further at that moment, believing it would be indelicate.

'Shall we go to the nursery?' asked Julia.

I was delighted; and, romping with her lovely children, dressing their dolls, and teaching them to skip, I forgot my love for Argyle, as much as if that excellent man had never been born.

Indeed I am not quite sure that it would have occurred to me even when I went home, but that Fred Lamb, who was just at this period showing Argyle up all over the town as my amorous shepherd, had a new story to relate of His Grace.

Horace Beckford and two other fashionable men, who had heard from Frederick of my cruelty, as he termed it, and the Duke's daily romantic walks to the Jew's Harp House, had come upon him, by accident, in a body, as they were galloping through Somerstown. Lorne was sitting, in a very pastoral fashion, on a gate near my door, whistling. They saluted him with a loud laugh. No man could, generally speaking, parry a joke better than Argyle: for few knew the world better: but this was no joke. He had been severely wounded and annoyed by my cutting his acquaintance altogether, at the very moment when he had reason to believe that the passion he really felt for me was returned. It was almost the first instance of the kind he had ever met with. He was bored and vexed with himself, for the time he had lost, and yet he found himself continually in my neighbourhood, almost before he was aware of it. He wanted, as he has told me since, to meet me once more by accident, and then he declared he would give me up.

'What a set of consummate asses you are,' said Argyle to Beckford and his party; and then quietly continued on the gate, whistling as before.

'But r-e-a-l-l-y, r-e-a-l-l-y, ca-ca-cannot Tom She-She-She-Sheridan assist you, Marquis?' said the handsome Horace Beckford, in his usual stammering way.

'A very good joke for Fred Lamb, as the case stands now,' replied the Duke, laughing; for a man of the world must laugh in these cases, though he should burst with the effort.

'Why don't she come?' said Sir John Shelley, who was one of the party.

An odd mad-looking Frenchman, in a white coat and a white hat, well known about Somerstown, passed at this moment, and observed His Grace, whom he knew well by sight, from the other side of the way. He had, a short time before, attempted to address me, when he met me walking alone, and inquired of me, when I had last seen the Marquis of Lorne, with whom he had often observed me walking? I made him no answer. In a fit of frolic, as if everybody combined at this moment against the poor, dear, handsome Argyle, the Frenchman called, as loud as he could scream, from the other side of the way, '*Ah! ah! oh! oh! vous voilà, Monsieur le Comte Dromedaire* (alluding thus to the Duke's family name, as pronounced Camel), *Mais où est donc Madame la Comtesse?*'

'D—d impudent rascal!' said Argyle, delighted to vent his growing rage on somebody, and started across the road after the poor thin old Frenchman, who might have now said his prayers, had not his spider-legs served him better than his courage.

Fred Lamb was very angry with me for not laughing at this story; but the only feeling it excited in me, was unmixed gratitude towards the Duke, for remembering me still, and for having borne all this ridicule for my sake.

The next day Julia returned my visit; and, before we parted, she had learned, from my usual frankness, every particular of my life, without leaving me one atom the wiser as to what related to herself. I disliked mystery so much that, but that I saw Julia's proceeded from the natural extreme shyness of her disposition, I had, by this time, declined continuing her acquaintance. I decided, however, to try her another month, in order to give her time to become acquainted with me. She was certainly one of the best mannered women in England, not excepting even those of the very highest rank. Her handwriting, and her style, were both beautiful. She had the most delicately fair skin, and the prettiest arms, hands, and feet, and the most graceful form, which could well be imagined; but her features were not regular, nor their expression particularly good. She struck me as a woman of very violent passions, combined with an extremely shy and reserved disposition.

Mr Johnstone seldom made his appearance oftener than twice a week. He came across a retired field to her house, though he might have got there more conveniently by the roadway. I sometimes accompanied her, and we sat on a gate to watch his approach to this field. Their meetings were full of rapturous and romantic delight. In his absence, she never received a single visitor, male or female, except myself; yet she always, when quite alone, dressed in the most studied and fashionable style.

There was something dramatic about Julia. I often surprised her, hanging over her harp so very gracefully, the room so perfumed, the rays of her lamp so soft, that I could scarcely believe this *tout ensemble* to be the effect of chance or habit. It appeared arranged for the purpose, like a scene in a play. Yet who was it to affect? Julia never either received or expected company!

Everything went on as usual for another month or two; during which time Julia and I met every day, and she promised shortly to make me acquainted with her whole history. My finances were now sinking very low. Everything Lord Craven had given me, whether in money or valuables, I had freely parted with for my support. Fred Lamb, I thought, must know that these resources cannot last for ever; therefore I am determined not to speak to him on the subject.

I was lodging with a comical old widow, who had formerly been my sister Fanny's nurse when she was quite a child. This good lady, I believe, really did like me, and had already given me all the credit for board and lodging she could possibly afford. She now entered my room, and acquainted me that she actually had not another shilling, either to provide my dinner or her own.

Necessity hath no law, thought I, my eyes brightening, and my determination being fixed in an instant. In ten minutes more, the following letter was in the post office, directed to the Marquis of Lorne.

If you still desire my society, I will sup with you tomorrow evening in your own house.

Yours, ever affectionately,
HARRIETTE.

I knew perfectly well that on the evening I mentioned to His Grace, Fred Lamb would be at his father's country house, Brockett Hall.

The Duke's answer was brought to me by his groom, as soon as he had received my letter; it ran thus:

Are you really serious? I dare not believe it. Say, by my servant, that you will see me, at the turnpike, directly, for five minutes, only to put me out of suspense. I will not believe anything you write on this subject. I want to look at your eyes, while I hear you say yes.

Yours, most devotedly and impatiently,
LORNE.

I went to our place of rendezvous to meet the Duke. How different, and how much more amiable, was his reception than that of Fred Lamb in Hull! The latter, all wild passion; the former, gentle, voluptuous, fearful of shocking or offending me, or frightening away my growing passion. In short, while the Duke's manner was almost as timid as my own, the expression of his eyes and the very soft tone of his voice, troubled my imagination, and made me fancy something of bliss beyond all reality.

We agreed that he should bring a carriage to the old turnpike, and thence conduct me to his house. 'If you should change your mind!' said the Duke, returning a few steps after we had taken leave: '*mais tu viendras, mon ange? Tu ne seras pas si cruelle?*' Argyle is the best Frenchman I ever met with in England, and poor Tom Sheridan was the second best.

'And you,' said I to Argyle, 'suppose you were to break your appointment tonight?'

'Would you regret it?' Argyle inquired. 'I won't have your answer while you are looking at those pretty little feet,' he continued. 'Tell me, dear Harriette, should you be sorry?'

'Yes,' said I, softly, and our eyes met, only for an instant. Lorne's gratitude was expressed merely by pressing my hand.

'*A ce soir, donc,*' said he, mounting his horse; and, waving his hand to me, he was soon out of sight.

WILLA CATHER

✑

A Wagner Matinée

I received one morning a letter, written in pale ink on glassy, blue-lined notepaper, and bearing the postmark of a little Nebraska village. This communication, worn and rubbed, looking as though it had been carried for some days in a coat pocket that was none too clean, was from my uncle Howard and informed me that his wife had been left a small legacy by a bachelor relative who had recently died, and that it would be necessary for her to go to Boston to attend to the settling of the estate. He requested me to meet her at the station and render her whatever services might be necessary. On examining the date indicated as that of her arrival, I found it no later than tomorrow. He had characteristically delayed writing until, had I been away from home for a day, I must have missed the good woman altogether.

The name of my Aunt Georgiana called up not alone her own figure, at once pathetic and grotesque, but opened before my feet a gulf of recollection so wide and deep that, as the letter dropped from my hand, I felt suddenly a stranger to all the present conditions of my existence, wholly at ease and out of place amid the familiar surroundings of my study. I became, in short, the gangling farmer-boy my aunt had known, scourged with chilblains and bashfulness, my hands cracked and sore from the corn husking. I felt the knuckles of my thumb tentatively, as though they were raw again. I sat again before her parlour organ, fumbling the scales with my stiff, red hands, while she, beside me, made canvas mittens for the huskers.

The next morning, after preparing my landlady somewhat, I set out for the station. When the train arrived I had some difficulty in finding my aunt. She was the last of the passengers to alight, and it was not until I got her into the carriage that she seemed really to recognize me. She had come all the way in a day coach; her linen duster had become black with soot and her black bonnet grey with dust during the journey. When we arrived at my boarding-house the landlady put her to bed at once and I did not see her again until the next morning.

Whatever shock Mrs Springer experienced at my aunt's appearance, she considerately concealed. As for myself, I saw my aunt's misshapen figure with that feeling of awe and respect with which we behold explorers who have left their ears and fingers north of Franz Josef Land, or their health somewhere along the Upper Congo. My Aunt Georgiana had been a music teacher at the Boston Conservatory, somewhere back in the latter sixties. One summer, while visiting in the little village among the Green Mountains where her ancestors had dwelt for generations, she had kindled the callow fancy of the most idle and shiftless of all the village lads, and had conceived for this Howard Carpenter one of those extravagant passions which a handsome country boy of twenty-one sometimes inspires in an angular, spectacled woman of thirty. When she returned to her duties in Boston, Howard followed her, and the upshot of this inexplicable infatuation was that she eloped with him, eluding the reproaches of her family and the criticisms of her friends by going with him to the Nebraska frontier. Carpenter, who, of course, had no money, had taken a homestead in Red Willow County, fifty miles from the railroad. There they had measured off their quarter section themselves by driving across the prairie in a wagon, to the wheel of which they had tied a red cotton handkerchief, and counting off its revolutions. They built a dugout in the red hillside, one of those cave dwellings whose inmates so often reverted to primitive conditions. Their water they got from the lagoons where the buffalo drank, and their slender stock of provisions was always at the mercy of bands of roving Indians. For thirty years my aunt had not been farther than fifty miles from the homestead.

But Mrs Springer knew nothing of all this, and must have been considerably shocked at what was left of my kinswoman. Beneath the soiled linen duster which, on her arrival, was the most conspicuous feature of her costume, she wore a black stuff dress, whose ornamentation showed that she had surrendered herself unquestioningly into the hands of a country dressmaker. My poor aunt's figure, however, would have presented astonishing difficulties to any dressmaker. Originally stooped, her shoulders were now almost bent together over her sunken chest. She wore no stays, and her gown, which trailed unevenly behind, rose in a sort of peak over her abdomen. She wore ill-fitting false teeth, and her skin was as yellow as a Mongolian's from constant exposure to a pitiless wind and to the alkaline water which hardens the most transparent cuticle into a sort of flexible leather.

I owed to this woman most of the good that ever came my way in my boyhood, and had a reverential affection for her. During the years when I was riding herd for my uncle, my aunt, after cooking the three meals – the first of which was ready at six o'clock in the morning – and putting the six children to bed, would often stand until midnight at her ironing-board, with me at the kitchen table beside her, hearing me recite Latin declensions and conjugations, gently shaking me when my drowsy head sank down over a page of irregular verbs. It was to her, at her ironing or mending, that I read my first Shakespeare, and her old textbook on mythology was the first that ever came into my empty hands. She taught me my scales and exercises, too – on the little parlour organ which her husband had bought her after fifteen years, during which she had not so much as seen any instrument, but an accordion that belonged to one of the Norwegian farm-hands. She would sit beside me by the hour, darning and counting, while I struggled with the 'Joyous Farmer', but she seldom talked to me about music, and I understood why. She was a pious woman; she had the consolations of religion and, to her at least, her martyrdom was not wholly sordid. Once when I had been doggedly beating out some easy passages from an old score of *Euryanthe* I had found among her music books, she came up to me and, putting her hands over my eyes, gently drew my head back upon her shoulder, saying tremulously, 'Don't love it so well, Clark, or it may be taken from you. Oh! dear boy, pray that whatever your sacrifice may be, it be not that.'

When my aunt appeared on the morning after her arrival, she

was still in a semi-somnambulant state. She seemed not to realize that she was in the city where she had spent her youth, the place longed for hungrily half a lifetime. She had been so wretchedly train-sick throughout the journey that she had no recollection of anything but her discomfort, and, to all intents and purposes, there were but a few hours of nightmare between the farm in Red Willow County and my study on Newbury Street. I had planned a little pleasure for her that afternoon, to repay her for some of the glorious moments she had given me when we used to milk together in the straw-thatched cowshed and she, because I was more than usually tired, or because her husband had spoken sharply to me, would tell me of the splendid performance of the *Huguenots* she had seen in Paris, in her youth. At two o'clock the Symphony Orchestra was to give a Wagner programme, and I intended to take my aunt; though, as I conversed with her, I grew doubtful about her enjoyment of it. Indeed, for her own sake, I could only wish her taste for such things quite dead, and the long struggle mercifully ended at last. I suggested our visiting the Conservatory and the Common before lunch, but she seemed altogether too timid to wish to venture out. She questioned me absently about various changes in the city, but she was chiefly concerned that she had forgotten to leave instructions about feeding half-skimmed milk to a certain weakling calf, 'old Maggie's calf, you know, Clark', she explained, evidently having forgotten how long I had been away. She was further troubled because she had neglected to tell her daughter about the freshly opened kit of mackerel in the cellar, which would spoil if it were not used directly.

I asked her whether she had ever heard any of the Wagnerian operas, and found that she had not, though she was perfectly familiar with their respective situations, and had once possessed the piano score of *The Flying Dutchman*. I began to think it would have been best to get her back to Red Willow County without waking her, and regretted having suggested the concert.

From the time we entered the concert hall, however, she was a trifle less passive and inert, and for the first time seemed to perceive her surroundings. I had felt some trepidation lest she might become aware of the absurdities of her attire, or might experience some painful embarrassment at stepping suddenly into the world to which she had been dead for more than a quarter of a century. But, again, I found how superficially I had judged her. She sat looking about her with eyes as impersonal, almost as stony, as those with which the granite Rameses in a museum watches the froth and fret that ebbs and flows about his pedestal – separated from it by the lonely stretch of centuries. I have seen this same aloofness in old miners who drift into the Brown Hotel at Denver, their pockets full of bullion, their linen soiled, their haggard faces unshaven; standing in the thronged corridors as solitary as though they were still in a frozen camp on the Yukon, conscious that certain experiences have isolated them from their fellows by a gulf no haberdasher could bridge.

We sat at the extreme left of the first balcony, facing the arc of our own and the balcony above us, veritable hanging gardens, brilliant as tulip beds. The matinée audience was made up chiefly of women. One lost the contour of faces and figures, indeed any effect of line whatever, and there was only the colour of bodices past counting, the shimmer of fabrics soft and firm, silky and sheer; red, mauve, pink, blue, lilac, purple, ecru, rose, yellow, cream, and white, all the colours that an Impressionist finds in a sunlit landscape, with here and there the dead shadow of a frock coat. My Aunt Georgiana regarded them as though they had been so many daubs of tube-paint on a palette.

When the musicians came out and took their places, she gave a little stir of anticipation, and looked with quickening interest down over the rail at that invariable grouping, perhaps the first wholly familiar thing that had greeted her eye since she had left old Maggie and her weakling calf. I could feel how all those details sank into her soul, for I had not forgotten how they had sunk into mine when I came fresh from ploughing forever and forever between green aisles of corn, where, as in a treadmill, one might walk from daybreak to dusk without perceiving a shadow of change. The clean profiles of the musicians, the gloss of their linen, the dull black of their coats, the beloved shapes of the instruments, the patches of yellow light thrown by the green shaded lamps on the smooth, varnished bellies of the 'cellos and the bass viols in the rear, the restless, wind-tossed forest of fiddle necks and bows – I recalled how, in the first orchestra I had ever heard, those long bow strokes seemed to draw the heart out of me, as a conjurer's stick reels out yards of paper ribbon from a hat.

The first number was the *Tannhäuser* overture. When the horns drew out the first strain of the Pilgrim's chorus, my Aunt Georgiana clutched my coat sleeve. Then it was I first realized that for her this broke a silence of thirty years; the inconceivable silence of the plains. With the battle between the two motives, with the frenzy of the Venusberg theme and its ripping of strings, there came to me an overwhelming sense of the waste and wear we are so powerless to combat; and I saw again the tall, naked house on the prairie, black and grim as a wooden fortress; the black pond where I had learned to swim, its margin pitted with sun-dried cattle tracks; the rain gullied clay banks about the naked house, the four dwarf ash seedlings where the dishcloths were always hung to dry before the kitchen door. The world there was the flat world of the ancients; to the east, a cornfield that stretched to daybreak; to the west, a corral that reached to sunset; between, the conquests of peace, dearer bought than those of war.

The overture closed, my aunt released my coat sleeve, but she said nothing. She sat staring at the orchestra through a dullness of thirty years, through the films made little by little by each of the three hundred and sixty-five days in every one of them. What, I wondered, did she get from it? She had been a good pianist in her day I knew, and her musical education had been broader than that of most music teachers of a quarter of a century ago. She had often told me of Mozart's operas and Meyerbeer's, and I could remember hearing her sing, years ago, certain melodies of Verdi's. When I had fallen ill with a fever in her house she used to sit by my cot in the evening – when the cool, night wind blew in through the faded mosquito netting tacked over the window and I lay watching a certain bright star that burned red above the cornfield – and sing 'Home to our mountains, O, let us return!' in a way fit to break the heart of a Vermont boy near dead of homesickness already.

I watched her closely through the prelude to *Tristan and Isolde*, trying vainly to conjecture what that seething turmoil of strings and winds might mean to her, but she sat mutely staring at the violin bows that drove obliquely downward, like the pelting streaks of rain in a summer shower. Had this music any message for her? Had she enough left to at all comprehend this power which had kindled the world since she had left it? I was in a fever of curiosity, but Aunt Georgiana sat silent upon her peak in Darien. She preserved this utter immobility throughout the number from *The Flying Dutchman*, though her fingers worked mechanically upon her black dress, as though, of themselves, they were recalling the piano score they had once played. Poor old hands! They had been stretched and twisted into mere tentacles to hold and lift and knead with; the palm unduly swollen, the fingers bent and knotted – on one of them a thin, worn band that had once been a wedding ring. As I pressed and gently quieted one of those groping hands, I remembered with quivering eyelids their services for me in other days.

Soon after the tenor began the 'Prize Song', I heard a quick-drawn breath and turned to my aunt. Her eyes were closed, but the tears were glistening on her cheeks, and I think, in a moment more, they were in my eyes as well. It never really died, then – the soul that can suffer so excruciatingly and so interminably; it withers to the outward eye only; like that strange moss which can lie on a dusty shelf half a century and yet, if placed in water, grows green again. She wept so throughout the development and elaboration of the melody.

During the intermission before the second half of the concert, I questioned my aunt and found that the 'Prize Song' was not new to her. Some years before there had drifted to the farm in Red Willow County a young German, a tramp cow-puncher, who had sung in the chorus at Bayreuth, when he was a boy, along with the other peasant boys and girls. Of a Sunday morning he used to sit on his gingham-sheeted bed in the hands' bedroom which opened off the kitchen, cleaning the leather of his boots and saddle, singing the 'Prize Song', while my aunt went about her work in the kitchen. She had hovered about him until she had prevailed upon him to join the country church, though his sole fitness for this step, in so far as I could gather, lay in his boyish face and his possession of this divine melody. Shortly afterward he had gone to town on the Fourth of July, been drunk for several days, lost his money at a faro table, ridden a saddled Texas steer on a bet, and disappeared with a fractured collarbone. All this my aunt told me huskily, wanderingly, as though she were talking in the weak lapses of illness.

'Well, we have come to better things than the old *Trovatore* at any rate, Aunt Georgie?' I queried, with a well-meant effort at jocularity.

Her lip quivered and she hastily put her handkerchief up to her mouth. From behind it she murmured, 'And you have been hearing this ever since you left me, Clark?' Her question was the gentlest and saddest of reproaches.

The second half of the programme consisted of four numbers from the *Ring*, and closed with Siegfried's funeral march. My aunt wept quietly, but almost continuously, as a shallow vessel overflows in a rainstorm. From time to time her dim eyes looked up at the lights which studded the ceiling, burning softly under their dull glass globes; doubtless they were stars in truth to her. I was still perplexed as to what measure of musical comprehension was left to her, she who had heard nothing but the singing of Gospel hymns at Methodist services in the square frame schoolhouse on Section Thirteen for so many years. I was wholly unable to gauge how much of it had been dissolved in soapsuds, or worked into bread, or milked into the bottom of a pail.

The deluge of sound poured on and on; I never knew what she found in the shining current of it; I never knew how far it bore her, or past what happy islands. From the trembling of her face I could well believe that before the last numbers she had been carried out where the myriad graves are, into the grey, nameless burying grounds of the sea; or into some world of death vaster yet, where, from the beginning of the world, hope has lain down with hope and dream with dream and, renouncing, slept.

The concert was over; the people filed out of the hall chattering and laughing, glad to relax and find the living level again, but my kinswoman made no effort to rise. The harpist slipped its green felt cover over his instrument; the flute-players shook the water from their mouthpieces; the men of the orchestra went out one by one, leaving the stage to the chairs and music stands, empty as a winter cornfield.

I spoke to my aunt. She burst into tears and sobbed pleadingly. 'I don't want to go, Clark, I don't want to go!'

99

I understood. For her, just outside the door of the concert hall, lay the black pond with the cattle-tracked bluffs; the tall, unpainted house, with weather-curled boards; naked as a tower, the crook-backed ash seedlings where the dishcloths hung to dry; the gaunt, moulting turkeys picking up refuse about the kitchen door.

JEAN RHYS

𝒮

The Insect World

Audrey began to read. Her book was called *Nothing So Blue*. It was set in the tropics. She started at the paragraph which described the habits of an insect called the jigger.

Almost any book was better than life, Audrey thought. Or rather, life as she was living it. Of course, life would soon change, open out, become quite different. You couldn't go on if you didn't hope that, could you? But for the time being there was no doubt that it was pleasant to get away from it. And books could take her away.

She could give herself up to the written word as naturally as a good dancer to music or a fine swimmer to water. The only difficulty was that after finishing the last sentence she was left with a feeling at once hollow and uncomfortably full. Exactly like indigestion. It was perhaps for this reason that she never forgot that books were one thing and that life was another.

When it came to life Audrey was practical. She accepted all she was told to accept. And there had been quite a lot of it. She had been in London for the last five years but for one short holiday. There had been the big blitz, then the uneasy lull, then the little blitz, now the fly bombs. But she still accepted all she was told to accept, tried to remember all she was told to remember. The trouble was that she could not always forget all she was told to forget. She could not forget, for instance, that on her next birthday she would be twenty-nine years of age. Not a Girl any longer. Not really. The war had already gobbled up several years and who knew how long it would go on. Audrey dreaded growing old. She disliked and avoided old people and thought with horror of herself

101

as old. She had never told anyone her real and especial reason for loathing the war. She had never spoken of it – even to her friend Monica.

Monica, who was an optimist five years younger than Audrey, was sure that the war would end soon.

'People always think that wars will end soon. But they don't,' said Audrey. 'Why, one lasted for a hundred years. What about that?'

Monica said: 'But that was centuries ago and quite different. Nothing to do with Now.'

But Audrey wasn't at all sure that it was so very different.

'It's as if I'm twins,' she had said to Monica one day in an attempt to explain herself. 'Do you ever feel like that?' But it seemed that Monica never did feel like that or if she did she didn't want to talk about it.

Yet there it was. Only one of the twins accepted. The other felt lost, betrayed, forsaken, a wanderer in a very dark wood. The other told her that all she accepted so meekly was quite mad, potty. And here even books let her down, for no book – at least no book that Audrey had ever read – even hinted at this essential wrongness or pottiness.

Only yesterday, for instance, she had come across it in *Nothing So Blue*. *Nothing So Blue* belonged to her, for she often bought books – most of them Penguins, but some from second-hand shops. She always wrote her name on the flyleaf and tried to blot out any signs of previous ownership. But this book had been very difficult. It had taken her more than an hour to rub out the pencil marks that had been found all through it. They began harmlessly, 'Read and enjoyed by Charles Edwin Roofe in this Year of our Salvation MCMXLII, which being interpreted is Thank You Very Much', continued 'Blue? Rather pink, I think', and, throughout the whole of the book, the word 'blue' – which of course often occurred – was underlined and in the margin there would be a question mark, a note of exclamation, or 'Ha, ha'. 'Nauseating', he had written on the page which began 'I looked her over and decided she would do'. Then came the real love affair with the beautiful English girl who smelt of daffodils and Mr Roofe had relapsed into 'Ha, ha – sez you!' But it was on page 166 that Audrey had a shock. He had written 'Women are an unspeakable abomination' with such force that the pencil had driven through the paper. She had torn the page out and thrown it into the fireplace. Fancy that! There was no fire, of course, so she was able to pick it up, smooth it out and stick it back.

'Why should I spoil my book?' she had thought. All the same she felt terribly down for some reason. And yet, she told herself, 'I bet if you met that man he would be awfully ordinary, just like everybody else.' It was something about his small, neat, precise handwriting that made her think so. But it was always the most ordinary things that suddenly turned round and showed you another face, a terrifying face. That was the hidden horror, the horror everybody pretended did not exist, the horror that was responsible for all the other horrors.

The book was not so cheering either. It was about damp, moist heat, birds that did not sing, flowers that had no scent. Then there was this horrible girl whom the hero simply had to make love to, though he didn't really want to, and when the lovely, cool English girl heard about it she turned him down.

The natives were surly. They always seemed to be jeering behind your back. And they were stupid. They believed everything they were told, so that they could be easily worked up against somebody. Then they became cruel – so horribly cruel, you wouldn't believe . . .

And the insects. Not only the rats, snakes and poisonous spiders, scorpions, centipedes, millions of termites in their earth-coloured nests from which branched out yards of elaborately built communication lines leading sometimes to a smaller nest, sometimes to an untouched part of the tree on which they were feeding, while sometimes they just petered out, empty. It was no use poking at a nest with a stick. It seemed vulnerable, but the insects would swarm, whitely horrible, to its defence, and would rebuild it in a night. The only thing was to smoke them out. Burn them alive-oh. And even then some would escape and at once start building somewhere else.

Finally, there were the minute crawling unseen things that got at you as you walked along harmlessly. Most horrible of all these was the jigger.

Audrey stopped reading. She had a headache. Perhaps that was because she had not had anything to eat all day; unless you can count a cup of tea at eight in the morning as something to eat. But she did not often get a weekday off and when she did not a moment must be wasted. So from ten to two, regardless of sirens wailing, she went shopping in Oxford Street, and she skipped lunch. She bought stockings, a nightgown and a dress. It was buying the dress that had taken it out of her. The assistant had tried to sell her a print dress a size too big and, when she did not want it, had implied that it was unpatriotic to make so much fuss about what she wore. 'But the colours are so glaring and it doesn't fit. It's much too short,' Audrey said.

'You could easily let it down.'

Audrey said: 'But there's nothing to let down. I'd like to try on that dress over there.'

'It's a very small size.'

'Well, I'm thin enough,' said Audrey defiantly. 'How much thinner d'you want me to be?'

'But that's a dress for a girl,' the assistant said.

And suddenly, what with the pain in her back and everything, Audrey had wanted to cry. She nearly said 'I work just as hard as you', but she was too dignified.

'The grey one looks a pretty shape,' she said. 'Not so drear. Drear,' she repeated, because that was a good word and if the assistant knew anything she would place her by it. But the woman, not at all impressed, stared over her head.

'The dresses on that rail aren't your size. You can try one on if you like but it wouldn't be any use. You could easily let down the print one,' she repeated maddeningly.

Audrey had felt like a wet rag after her defeat by the shop assistant, for she had ended up buying the print dress. It would not be enough to go and spruce up in the Ladies' Room on the fifth floor – which would be milling full of Old Things – so she had gone home again, back to the flat she shared with Monica. There had not been time to eat anything, but she had put on the new dress and it looked even worse than it had looked in the shop. From the neck to the waist it was enormous, or shapeless. The skirt, on the other hand, was very short and skimpy and two buttons came off in her hand; she had to wait and sew them on again.

It had all made her very tired. And she would be late for tea at Roberta's . . .

'I wish I lived here,' she thought when she came out of the Tube station. But she often thought that when she went to a different part of London. 'It's nicer here,' she'd think, 'I might be happier here.'

Her friend Roberta's house was painted green and had a small garden. Audrey felt envious as she pressed the bell. And still more envious when Roberta came to the door wearing a flowered housecoat, led the way into a pretty sitting-room and collapsed on to her sofa in a film-star attitude. Audrey's immediate thought was 'What right has a woman got to be lolling about like that in wartime, even if she is going to have a baby?' But when she noticed Roberta's deep-circled eyes, her huge, pathetic stomach, her spoilt hands, her broken nails, and realized that her housecoat had been made out of a pair of old curtains ('not half so pretty as she was. Looks much older') she said the usual things, warmly and sincerely.

But she hoped that, although it was nearly six by the silver clock, Roberta would offer her some tea and cake. Even a plain slice of bread – she could have wolfed that down.

'Why are you so late?' Roberta asked. 'I suppose you've had tea,' and hurried on before Audrey could open her mouth. 'Have a chocolate biscuit.'

So Audrey ate a biscuit slowly. She felt she did not know Roberta well enough to say 'I'm ravenous. I must have something to eat.' Besides, that was the funny thing. The more ravenous you grew, the more impossible it became to say 'I'm ravenous!'

'Is that a good book?' Roberta asked.

'I brought it to read on the Tube. It isn't bad.'

Roberta flicked through the pages of *Nothing So Blue* without much interest. And she said, 'English people always mix up tropical places. My dear, I met a girl the other day who thought Moscow was the capital of India! Really, I think it's dangerous to be as ignorant as that, don't you?'

Roberta often talked about 'English' people in that way. She had acquired the habit, Audrey thought, when she was out of England for two years before the war. She had lived for six months in New York. Then she had been to Miami, Trinidad, Bermuda – all those places – and no expense spared, or so she said. She had brought back all sorts of big ideas. Much too big. Gadgets for the kitchen.

An extensive wardrobe. Expensive make-up. Having her hair and nails looked after every week at the hairdresser's. There was no end to it. Anyway, there was one good thing about the war. It had taken all that right off. Right off.

'Read what he says about jiggers,' Audrey said.

'My dear,' said Roberta, 'he *is* piling it on.'

'Do you mean that there aren't such things as jiggers?'

'Of course there are such things,' Roberta said, 'but they're only sand fleas. It's better not to go barefoot if you're frightened of them.'

She explained about jiggers. They had nasty ways – the man wasn't so far wrong. She talked about tropical insects for some time after that; she seemed to remember them more vividly than anything else. Then she read out bits of *Nothing So Blue*, laughing at it.

'If you must read all the time, you needn't believe everything you read.'

'I don't,' said Audrey. 'If you knew how little I really believe you'd be surprised. Perhaps he doesn't see it the way you do. It all depends on how people see things. If someone wanted to write a horrible book about London, couldn't he write a horrible book? I wish somebody would. I'd buy it.'

'You dope!' said Roberta affectionately.

When the time came to go Audrey walked back to the Tube station in a daze, and in a daze sat in the train until a jerk of the brain warned her that she had passed Leicester Square and now had to change at King's Cross. She felt very bad when she got out, as if she could flop any minute. There were so many people pushing, you got bewildered.

She tried to think about Monica, about the end of the journey, above all about food – warm, lovely food – but something had happened inside her head and she couldn't concentrate. She kept remembering the termites. Termites running along one of the covered ways that peter out and lead to nothing. When she came to the escalator she hesitated, afraid to get on it. The people clinging to the sides looked very like large insects. No, they didn't *look* like large insects: they were insects.

She got on to the escalator and stood staidly on the right-hand side. No running up for her tonight. She pressed her arm against her side and felt the book. That started her thinking about jiggers again. Jiggers got in under your skin when you didn't know it and laid eggs inside you. Just walking along, as you might be walking along the street to a Tube station, you caught a jigger as easily as you bought a newspaper or turned on the radio. And there you were – infected – and not knowing a thing about it.

In front of her stood an elderly woman with dank hair and mean-looking clothes. It was funny how she hated women like that. It was funny how she hated most women anyway. Elderly women ought to stay at home. They oughtn't to walk about. Depressing people! Jutting out, that was what the woman was doing. Standing right in the middle, instead of in line. So that you could hardly blame the service girl, galloping up in a hurry, for giving her a good shove and saying under her breath, 'Oh get out of the way!' But she must have shoved too hard, for the old thing tottered. She was going to fall. Audrey's heart jumped sickeningly into her mouth as she shut her eyes. She didn't want to see what it would look like, didn't want to hear the scream.

But no scream came and when Audrey opened her eyes she saw that the old woman had astonishingly saved herself. She had only stumbled down a couple of steps and clutched the rail again. She even managed to laugh and say, 'Now I know where all the beef goes to!' Her face, though, was very white. So was Audrey's. Perhaps her heart kept turning over. So did Audrey's.

Even when she got out of the Tube the nightmare was not over. On the way home she had to walk up a little street which she hated and it was getting dark now. It was one of those streets which are nearly always empty. It had been badly blitzed and Audrey was sure that it was haunted. Weeds and wild-looking flowers were growing over the skeleton houses, over the piles of rubble. There were front doorsteps which looked as though they were hanging by a thread, and near one of them lived a black cat with green eyes. She liked cats but not this one, not this one. She was sure it wasn't a cat really.

Supposing the siren went? 'If the siren goes when I'm in this street it'll mean that it's all U.P. with me.' Supposing a man with a strange blank face and no eyebrows – like that one who got into the Ladies at the cinema the other night and stood there grinning at them and nobody knew what to do so everybody pretended he wasn't there. Perhaps he was *not* there, either – supposing a man like that were to come up softly behind her, touch her shoulder, speak to her, she wouldn't be able to struggle, she would just lie down and die of fright, so much she hated that street. And she had to walk slowly because if she ran she would give whatever it was its opportunity and it would run after her. However, even walking slowly, it came to an end at last. Just round the corner in a placid ordinary street where all the damage had been tidied up was the third-floor flat which she shared with Monica, also a typist in a government office.

The radio was on full tilt. The smell of cabbage drifted down the stairs. Monica, for once, was getting the meal ready. They ate out on Mondays, Wednesdays and Fridays, in on Tuesdays, Thursdays, Saturdays and Sundays. Audrey usually did the housework and cooking and Monica took charge of the ration books, stood in long queues to shop and lugged the laundry back and forwards every week because the van didn't call any longer.

'Hullo,' said Monica.

Audrey answered her feebly, 'Hullo.'

Monica, a dark, pretty girl, put the food on the table and remarked at once, 'You're a bit green in the face. Have you been drinking mock gin?'

'Oh, don't be funny. I haven't had much to eat today – that's all.'

After a few minutes Monica said impatiently, 'Well why don't you eat then?'

'I think I've gone past it,' said Audrey, fidgeting with the sausage and cabbage on her plate.

Monica began to read from the morning paper. She spoke loudly above the music on the radio.

'Have you seen this article about being a woman in Germany? It says they can't get any scent or eau de Cologne or nail polish.'

'Fancy that!' Audrey said. 'Poor things!'

'It says the first thing Hitler stopped was nail polish. He began that way. I wonder why. He must have had a reason, mustn't he?'

'Why must he have had a reason?' said Audrey.

'Because,' said Monica, 'if they've got a girl thinking she isn't pretty, thinking she's shabby, they've got her where they want her, as a rule. And it might start with nail polish, see? And it says: "All the old women and the middle-aged women look most terribly unhappy. They simply *slink* about," it says.'

'You surprise me,' Audrey said. 'Different in the Isle of Dogs, isn't it?'

She was fed up now and she wanted to be rude to somebody. 'Oh *do* shut up,' she said. 'I'm not interested. Why should I have to cope with German women as well as all the women over here? What a nightmare!'

Monica opened her mouth to answer sharply; then shut it again. She was an even-tempered girl. She piled the plates on to a tray, took it into the kitchen and began to wash up.

As soon as she had gone Audrey turned off the radio and the light. Blissful sleep, lovely sleep, she never got enough of it . . . On Sunday mornings, long after Monica was up, she would lie unconscious. A heavy sleeper, you might call her, except that her breathing was noiseless and shallow and that she lay so still, without tossing or turning. And then *She (who?) sent the gentle sleep from Heaven that slid into my soul. That slid into my soul. Sleep, Nature's sweet, something-or-the-other. The sleep that knits up the ravelled* . . .

It seemed that she had hardly shut her eyes when she was awake again. Monica was shaking her.

'What's the matter? Is it morning?' Audrey said. 'What is it? What is it?'

'Oh, nothing at all,' Monica said sarcastically. 'You were only shrieking the place down.'

'Was I?' Audrey said, interested. 'What was I saying?'

'I don't know what you were saying and I don't care. But if you're trying to get us turned out, that's the way to do it. You know perfectly well that the woman downstairs is doing all she can to get us out because she says we are too noisy. You said something about jiggers. What *are* jiggers anyway?'

'It's slang for people in the Tube,' Audrey answered glibly, to her great surprise. 'Didn't you know that?'

'Oh is it? No, I never heard that.'

'The name comes from a tropical insect,' Audrey said, 'that gets in under your skin when you don't know it. It lays eggs and hatches them out and you don't know it. And there's another sort of tropical insect that lives in enormous cities. They have railways, Tubes, bridges, soldiers, wars, everything we have. And they have

109

big cities, and smaller cities with roads going from one to another. Most of them are what they call workers. They never fly because they've lost their wings and they never make love either. They're just workers. Nobody quite knows how this is done, but they think it's the food. Other people say it's segregation. Don't you believe me?' she said, her voice rising. 'Do you think I'm telling lies?'

'Of course I believe you,' said Monica soothingly, 'but I don't see why you should shout about it.'

Audrey drew a deep breath. The corners of her mouth quivered. Then she said, 'Look, I'm going to bed. I'm awfully tired. I'm going to take six aspirins and then go to bed. If the siren goes don't wake me up. Even if one of those things seems to be coming very close, don't wake me up. I don't want to be woken up whatever happens.'

'Very well,' Monica said. 'All right, old girl.'

Audrey rushed at her with clenched fists and began to shriek again. 'Damn you, don't call me that. Damn your soul to everlasting hell *don't call me that . . .*'

JESSIE KESSON

✍

from
The White Bird Passes

Day had ended in the Lane. But it was not yet night. Night didn't
come till the lamp in the causeway was lit. The hooter from the
tweed mill had sounded twenty minutes ago; like the belated echo
of its dying wail, the mill workers began to clatter up the Lane.
This was one of the regular periods in the Lane's existence when
Poll, and Battleaxe, and even the Duchess herself, were dispos-
sessed. They ruled their contemporaries, old and bound to the
Lane like themselves; they awed the children whose youngness
bound them to the precincts of the Lane; but the workers, coming
through the causeway in little groups, were impervious to the
Duchess's dictates. The Lane was their bed, their supper, their tea
and bread and dripping in the morning. Their lives began beyond
it. In the Rialto with Pearl White on Monday nights, with the
Charleston at the Lido on Tuesday nights, nearer home with a
threepenny poke of chips, and *It Ain't Gonna Rain No More*
scratched out for nothing at Joe's chip shop round the corner.
Thursdays were zero nights in their lives. The one night that the
Lane could hold them, and even then on unflattering terms: the
lack of the price to get beyond it.

The Duchess and her coterie diminished on Thursday night,
leaning against the causeway with silent disapproval while the
Lane's up-and-coming race held the cobbles and, even more
galling, held them in an idiom alien to her Grace; flaunting
overmuch of that tin jewellery from Woolworth's, that new store,
Nothing Over Sixpence, that had just opened in High Street;
drunk with the novelty and prodigality of jewellery so cheap;
hands on their hips; shimmying their bodies, like new-fangled

111

whores, for the old-fangled ones like Mysie Walsh and Liza MacVean still just kicked their legs and showed their garters; and the daft tunes they shimmied in rhythm with:

But yes,
We have no bananas,
We have no bananas today!

They had no feeling of protocol either. Didn't care tuppence which lavatory they used. When it had been the Duchess's rule for years that Right Laners used the lavatory by the causeway, and Left Laners used the one up beside the rag-store. They simply used the lavatory nearest their moment of need. And the Duchess strongly suspected, that, as in one other ancient time of need, they also went in two by two.

Fortunately the Duchess's peace of mind was disturbed only on Thursdays in particular, and for this short period of time which was neither night nor day but a transition between. Up the causeway they clattered, this little group of Laners, unknown to either Poll, or Battleaxe, or the Duchess.

'That's wee Lil's Betsy. She's shot up some in this past year.'

But they didn't know Betsy. Not now. She had outgrown them. She wasn't old enough to be behind with her rent. She wasn't young enough to have the School Board Man searching her out. And so she eluded them.

'You've got home again, young Betsy?'

'Aye.'

'They're saying you're all being put on half-time at the mill. Is that right?'

'*You* tell me!'

'Well!' The Duchess felt weary. 'Did you ever hear the like of that for cheek?'

'It's this picture-going!' Poll reflected. 'It's making them all like that. They'd bite the hand that feeds them.'

'I've never put foot in a picture palace in my life,' Battleaxe concluded. 'And I've no intention of starting now.'

Hugh, the lamp-lighter, set night on its course with one flick from his long pole, and Melodeon Mike set the final seal on it, the clop of his wooden leg distorting the sound of all other passing footsteps. The women round the causeway relaxed. They had come into their own again.

'It's *The Home Fire's Burning* and *The Long Long Trail Awinding* for them tonight, Cocks!' Mike shouted his greeting, knowing that the Duchess had no objection to the rest of the world being cheated as long as she was 'in the know'.

'I'll just squeeze them out of the old box, give my gammy leg a jerk behind me. And before you can spit, the coppers will be landing on my bonnet. "Poor Bugger" the folk will be thinking as they eye my leg. "Poor Sod that's what the war did." Not, mind you, that *I* ever blamed the war for the loss of my leg. I wouldn't have the lie of it on my soul. But if I were to tell them the truth now, Poll. If I were to turn right round and say I lost my leg in a brawl at Aikey Fair. What do you think they'd say? They'd say, "Drunken Brute. Serves him right." That's what they'd say. Folk's minds work queer. Dead queer. If they think I lost it in the war, they're glad because I lost it in a good cause. Or sorry because I lost it in a bad one. All according to how they feel about war. Either way they fling the coppers. What they don't see is that the loss of your leg is the loss of your leg. And it doesn't matter a damn how you lose it. It's still a loss to you.'

'And a gain too, though, Mike,' Poll pointed out, but without rancour. 'I bet you make more out of that gammy leg of yours and that squeeze box than Dodsie Jenner makes out of his lavender bags. And him went through the Dardanelles and all.'

'I'll grant you that,' Mike agreed, the love of an argument growing big within him. 'That's granted. But what has Dodsie Jenner got to show for being through the Dardanelles? Damn all, Poll. If he'd lost an arm now. Or even a coupla fingers itself, his lavender bags would go like nobody's business.'

'But Dodsie Jenner lost his mind,' Poll protested. 'Or at least what mind he did have. I knew him years before the war, he never did have much in his top storey. But what he had he lost after the Dardanelles.'

'But a mind's a different matter altogether, Poll,' Mike urged. 'Nobody knows if you got much of a mind in the first place. So how to hell can they tell when you've lost it? Outsiders I mean. Now I know a cove. He's brother to Bert Wylie's wife. He went through the lot. Got half his face blown off. He sells oranges down in the Green.'

'Oh, I know *him*!' Battleaxe broke in. 'He's called Pippins for a by-name.'

'The same. Pippins. That's him. Well . . .'

'God knows the poor soul can't help only having half a face, but I can never bring myself to buy his oranges,' Battleaxe went on. 'His face puts me off. I stick to Ned Wheeler when it comes to buying an orange, and of course that's just at the New Year.'

'Maybe that then.' Mike was impatient of interruptions. 'Now, where was I? Oh aye! This cove told me himself one night in The Hole In The Wall . . .'

'I thought Pippins was Pussyfoot,' Poll protested. 'He was a great one for the Salvation Army for a while.'

'He's not that now then,' Mike was patient. 'Though I did hear tell that it was the Army that helped to set him up in the Green. But when I saw him, he was in The Hole In The Wall. God, Poll, did you ever see a man with his nose shot away down a pint? You don't want to either. But, as I was saying, he told me himself that he makes more money now than he did when he had got all his face. It's proof folk want for their charity, Poll. Something they can see. No. I'll say till my dying day that Dodsie Jenner would have been better off if he'd lost a hand. My luck was just in, I lost my leg in 1916. If I'd lost it in a brawl at Aikey Fair in 1902, I'd have been a dead duck. That's what I mean by "luck", Poll.'

Luck. It was the invincible argument. Even the Duchess was wordless against it. Mike trailed himself away from the safety and comprehension of his own kind, out into the High Street. Only the sound of his melodeon echoed back to them:

. . . to the land of my dreams.

'Where the nightingales are singing.' Poll sang in solitary accompaniment.

'There was a lot that didn't come back,' Battleaxe ventured.

'And them that did come back, came back worse than they went off,' the Duchess added. Even the Duchess, who knew the truth, unconsciously accepted the lie of Mike Melodeon's wooden leg.

*

Up the Lane at 285 Janie, too, contemplated the results of her 'luck'.

'Mysie Walsh must be doing all right to give you two bob all in a once,' her mother said, through the hairpins in her teeth. 'Did you see my side combs anywhere, Janie? Was Mysie Walsh getting ready to go out, did you notice?'

'I don't know.' Janie was absorbed in clearing the table to find room for her book. 'She hadn't got her curlers in. She was just lying on top of her bed. She looked fed up. There's a new word for meadow, Mam. A Red Indian word. Muskoday. On the muskoday. The meadow. Muskoday. Musk-o-day. It's in this book. It sounds right fine, doesn't it?'

'Was that what you bought with your two bob?' Liza sounded amused.

'And your tobacco!' Janie protested against this forgetfulness. 'You are glad about the tobacco, aren't you, Mam?'

'Yes, of course I am. Get a lace out of one of my other shoes, Janie, this damned lace has snapped!'

'You'd hardly any tobacco left, had you, Mam?'

'No, hardly any. Not out of that shoe, Janie! Use your eyes, that's a brown one.'

'Your black shoe must be under the bed then. If you'd had one wish, it would have been for tobacco, wouldn't it?'

'Yes, Janie.' Liza's voice came slow and quiet and clear. 'I'm glad you bought tobacco. I had hardly any left. And if I'd had one wish, it would have been for tobacco. Now. Have you found my shoe?'

The surprise of Mysie Walsh's two bob was over. Dimly Janie realized that her mother's gladness at getting just didn't equal her own gladness in giving.

'Is this the right shoe, Mam?'

'That's it. That's the one.' Liza sat absorbed unlacing it. Janie, watching her down-bent head, thought, It's strange, I can hug Mysie Walsh. And smell her hair and I can't do that to my own Mam. Though she's much bonnier than Mysie Walsh. If Janie had been suddenly stricken with blindness she would have had a perpetual picture of her mother in her memory. Not a photograph. Her mother had so many faces. But a hundred little images. Each of which was some part of her mother. And her

115

mother some part of each. The way her red hair glistened and crept up into little curls when it rained. Her long legs sprawled across the fender. Her tall, swift stride. And her eyes that looked as if they were smiling when the rest of her face was in a rage.

'I'll maybe get diphtheria like Gertie did,' Janie thought, watching her, 'and have to go away in the ambulance. Maybe my Mam will hug me like Mysie Walsh does, then.'

'The Salacs are here, Janie,' Gertie shouted from the lobby below. 'There's going to be testimony and saving. Hurry up, or you'll miss it all.'

'Well.' Liza's eyes were smiling. 'That's something, Janie. Aren't you going?'

'I was going.' Janie was undecided. 'But there's a penny for the gas now. And I've got my book. The only thing is the Salacs only come on Saturdays. If I don't go tonight, I'll miss it all for a week.'

'And you want both things at once, Janie?' Liza was quizzical. 'Well. Nothing like it if you can get it. I'm away now. If you're in your bed before I get back, see and leave the sneck off the door.' Liza, remembering something, popped her head round the door again: 'Take my tip, Janie. If you go to the Salacs tonight, you'll still have your book left for tomorrow. That way of it, you'll get both things. But not at once, that's what makes it tough. Don't forget. Leave the sneck off the door for me.'

Five minutes later Janie and Gertie were pushing their way through the crowd gathered round the street lamp.

'You've made us late,' Gertie grumbled. 'And you've got an awful smell.'

'I know.' Janie was unoffended. 'It's cats. I'd to crawl under our bed. And Mysie Walsh's cat always comes in and does it under our bed. O look, Gertie, Annie Frigg's got a good shot in. I bet you anything she'll cry tonight, and give testimony, and kiss the Salacs. I love it when she does that. She's so funny.'

The crowd gathered round the Salvation Army was unchanging. The old Laners, who preferred the light of the lamp and the company to the darkness and loneliness of their rooms. The deformed Laners. White, fanatical, and selfish, not only laying claim to the best position round the lamp, but forcing a prior claim on God Himself, whining their Hallelujahs right up to the top of the lamp, where they thought the Mercy Seat must lie. And of course always the children of the Lane, who loved a noise anyhow. Later the drunks, reluctant to go home, would join the group. And if testimony wasn't over by the time they arrived, their testimony would be the most fervent of the lot. Beyond the group, leaning against the causeway, were the objective spectators, the Duchess, Poll, and Battleaxe. Without need of salvation in their own opinions, they nevertheless enjoyed the antics of their neighbours who were so very obviously in need of it.

> *He's the lily of the valley.*
> *He's the bright and morning star.*

Despite themselves, the objective spectators hummed the chorus. It was familiar. Like saying God bless you. Or God curse you. Something you had always said.

> *He's the fairest of ten thousand*
> *To my soul.*
> *To my soul.*

But Janie knew that she would always remember the sudden green and silver image the words had brought to the Lane at dusk. Gertie, unmoved by words and images, was becoming irritable.

'I thought they were going to be saving us tonight. It's a damned shame if they don't. So it is.'

'Wheesht,' admonished Chae Tastard, normally one of the best cursers in the Lane, but momentarily under the spell of the Salvationists. 'It's terrible the language that's on you two bairns. And the napkins hardly off your arses yet.'

And even more terrible the crowd's sudden and complete desertion of the Salvationists. It was Betsy's young Alan who started the whisper:

'Mysie Walsh's done herself in. Hanged herself. The bobbies are up at 284 now.'

'Making a right barney about her being cut down before they got the chance to do it themselves,' Betsy added to the information.

'Who cut her down, Son?' Battleaxe demanded like a furious general who had been overlooked, but still had a right to know. 'Who was it that cut her down?'

117

'Chae did. Chae Tastard, with his sharp cobbler's knife.'

'Liars!' Janie screamed in a small panic. 'She isn't dead. I took cheese to her.'

'Yeah?' Betsy's young Alan shot his tongue out at Janie and passed on, anxious to spread all the news to the more important grown-ups. 'And do you know what? A bit of cheese was stuck in her mouth when they took the rope off.'

Ted Howe, only drunkenly comprehending the news, forced his way through the crowd. 'Take my boots off when I die. When I die.' And beneath the lamp the Salvationists sang for their own edification:

> *Dare to do right.*
> *Dare to be true.*
> *God who created you*
> *Cares for you, too.*

For the crowd had deserted them and were following Ted towards the door of Mysie Walsh who was.

'Them,' Poll was saying, watching the police-guarded door morosely. 'Them that takes their own lives, don't get to rest in consecrated ground. It's yon bit of common ground behind the gaswork for them.'

'I saw this coming,' Battleaxe added, with the pride of a prophet whose vision has come true. '"Mark my words," I said to my man just the night before last, "Mysie Walsh will come to a bad end. She'll never die in her bed."'

'Not with the life she led,' the Duchess agreed. 'Running around with every Tom, Dick, and Harry. Enough to drive you mad, through time. And that time she was in hospital with the poomonia. I know what she had. And it wasn't poomonia either. I cut my wisdom teeth too early to be mistaken.'

The next of kin pushed her way through the crowd. Battleaxe, furious at her prerogative in getting past the Bobby unchallenged, spat out her commentary:

'See her? No show without Punch. Last time she saw Mysie Walsh she was pulling the hair out of her. Said she wouldn't spit in Mysie Walsh's direction because she owed her ten bob.'

A sense of fear took hold of Chae Tastard's small wife. Fear of what lay beyond the police-guarded door, fear of Battleaxe's anger, fear of everything. 'Death pays all debts,' she said in a quiet and already defeated attempt to escape.

The Duchess began to laugh harshly. 'That way of it, Lil, the sooner we're all in our wee, black boxes the better.'

The next of kin was coming out. 'Is she dead?' shouted Battleaxe, waiving aside personal differences out of a zeal for truth.

'Stone dead.' The next of kin was glad of a truce which lent her an attentive ear. 'As dead as a door nail. You wouldn't know her. You wouldn't know a bit of her. Her face black. Her tongue swollen twice the size of your fist. And a lump of cheese fit to choke her on its own stuck in her gullet.'

'I took the cheese to her,' Janie shouted from amongst the women's shawls. 'But I didn't know. Honest to God I didn't.'

The shawls wheeled round in attack.

'You shouldn't know either,' Battleaxe shouted, jealously eyeing the small girl who had last seen the corpse alive. 'You're too young to give evidence, anyhow.'

'You should have been in your bed long ago,' the Duchess added. 'If you were mine! But, thank God you're no' mine. Standing there all eyes and ears. Beat it now. Before I take the lights from you!'

The policeman saved Janie from sudden extinction. 'The show's over for tonight,' he said, with just the amount of humour needed for the crowd's mood. 'You lot got no homes to go to?'

'Only just,' cried Battleaxe, speaking for them all. 'The rent's behind.'

The crowd had gone, taking with them the cover which they had flung over the tenement. Mysie Walsh's window, covered with a blanket, lay exposed to Janie and Gertie. Gertie, who lived two doors away, flaunted her own safety: 'I'd just hate to be you, Janie, having to pass Mysie Walsh's door tonight. Maybe she'll jump out on you.'

'She can't. She's dead.' Janie used reason to fight fancy, but didn't succeed. 'Come on up with me, Gertie. Just till my Mam comes home.'

'I can't, I've got to go home or else I'll get a belting. But she

119

can't touch you, Janie,' and as if regretting her reassurances, Gertie shouted over her shoulder as she disappeared: 'I wouldn't be you for anything, Janie. She might just jump out on you.'

All black and her tongue purple, Janie thought, as the wooden stairs creaked beneath her feet. Ready to jump out on me when I reach second landing. For death, and this was Janie's first, near experience of it, could suddenly translate the loved and the living into the ghostly and the frightening. The scream poised itself in Janie's throat, ready for its flight through the tenement, the moment Mysie Walsh jumped out of death, through the door. And not really ready when the moment came. Only the figure who leapt from beside her door heard the cry that was a substitute for the scream.

'Shut your mouth, you little bastard. Do you want the whole house woken up?'

The dead don't speak so. The livingness of the words calmed Janie into surveying the speaker. It was a man. Her mother suddenly appeared from behind him, annoyance in her voice. 'Leave the bairn alone.'

'Yours?' the man asked.

'Aye. My first mistake. And my last one.'

The man jingled coppers in his pocket. 'Like to go and get yourself some chips, hen?'

'I can't. Chip shop's shut,' Janie said, contemplating him gratefully, since, whoever he was, he just wasn't Mysie Walsh back from the dead.

'Find out the time for us, then.'

'It's gone eleven. Gertie and me heard the clock not long since.'

'Scram, then.' The man was growing angry. 'Make yourself scarce, for God's sake.'

'She's my bairn,' Liza said resentfully, coming towards Janie. 'Look, luv, run into Mysie Walsh's for some coppers for the gas. Here's sixpence. Move over, you. Till the bairn gets past.'

'I can't.' Janie stood impassively. 'Mysie Walsh's dead.'

'Don't be daft. Don't act it,' Liza said harshly in the darkness. 'I spoke to Mysie Walsh when I went out.'

'She's dead since.' Janie stood small and impregnable in the safety of truth. 'She hanged herself. The bobbies were here and all. Chae Tastard cut her down with his big knife.'

Liza stared at Mysie Walsh's door, and backed away from it, no longer aware of the man: 'Come on, Janie. It's high time you and me were in our bed. Mind your feet on the first step. It won't be there much longer.'

'What about me?' The man's voice came plaintively behind them.

'You can keep,' Liza called down, as if she had forgotten him.

'What about my dough? I paid you, didn't I?'

'And I should have got you between the eyes with your lousy dough.' There was anger in Liza's voice. But Janie sensed that this anger wasn't directed at her. It was as if herself and her mother were in league, against the man. 'Mind your feet now, bairn,' her mother said. Warmly, intimately. The two of them taking care of each other on the stairs.

'You damned two-timer. You prick tormentor.' The man's voice came furiously from below. 'I paid you, didn't I?'

'And here's your money.' The sudden clatter of coppers in the darkness, the anger in Liza's voice, frightened the man. He mumbled himself down, and out of hearing.

'You stay here, Mam,' Janie cried, when he had gone. 'Just wait for me here, and I'll look for the money you threw. It's on the landing somewhere.'

Liza waited without protest. Throwing the money had been a sincere gesture, but a reckless one. 'There was two bob. A two-bob bit, and sixpence of coppers,' she shouted to Janie. 'Can you see, or will I light the lobby gas?'

'I've found the two-bob bit,' Janie answered. 'Maybe the pennies have rolled under Mysie Walsh's door!'

But Mysie Walsh was dead. At the other side of the door. Her face all black and her tongue all purple. Janie had forgotten. Now she remembered, and ran upstairs without the pennies, to where her mother waited.

ISABELLE EBERHARDT

∅

from
The Passionate Nomad

My discontent with people grows by leaps and bounds . . . dissatis-
faction with myself as well, for I have not managed to find a
suitable *modus vivendi*, and am beginning to fear that none is
possible with my temperament.

There is only one thing that can help me get through the years I
have on earth, and that is writing. It has the huge advantage of
giving the will a free hand, without making us have to cope with
the world out there. That in itself is vital, whatever else it may yield
in the way of career or gain, especially as I am more and more
convinced that life as such is hostile and a dead end.

As of now, I will probably go to Medeah and Bou-Saada once
the last five days of Ramadan are over.

Once again my soul is caught in a period of transition,
undergoing changes and, no doubt, growing darker still and more
oppressed. If this foray of mine into the world of darkness does not
stop, what will be its terrifying outcome?

Yet I do believe there is a remedy, but in all heartfelt humility ∪
it lies in the realm of the Islamic religion.

That is where I shall find peace at last, and solace for my heart.
The impure and, so to speak, hybrid atmosphere I now live in does
me no good. My soul is withering and turns inward for its
distressing observations.

As agreed, I set off for the Dahra on the evening of Thursday 11
December by the light of the Ramadan moon.

The night was clear and cool. There was total silence all over that desert town, as rider Muhammad and I slipped through like shadows. That man is so much a Bedouin and so close to nature that he is my favourite companion, for he is in total harmony with the landscape and the people . . . not to mention my own frame of mind. He is not aware of it, but he is as preoccupied as I am with the puzzle and enigma of the senses.

At Montenotte and Cavaignac we went to the Moorish cafés there. We crossed oueds, went up slopes and down ravines, past graveyards . . .

In a desert full of diss and doum, above a grim-looking shelf rather like those in the Sahara with shrubs perched high on the mounds, we dismounted to eat and to get some rest. The place felt so unsafe we started at the slightest noise. I spotted a vague white silhouette against one of the shrubs down below. The horses snorted restlessly . . . who was it? The shadow vanished, and when we went by that spot, the horses were uneasy.

Our path led through a narrow valley intersected by many oueds. Jackals howled nearby. Farther down we came to the mechta of Kaddour-bel-Korchi, the caïd of the Talassa.

The caïd was not there and we had to go farther still, until we found him in the mechta of a certain Abd-el-Kader ben Aïssa, a pleasant, hospitable man. We had our meal there and once the moon had set, we went off for Baach by paths that were riddled with holes and full of mud and rolling stones. At dawn the borj of Baach, the most beautiful in the area, came into sight high up on a pointed hill, looking very similar to a borj in the Sahara . . .

Algiers, 29 December 1902, 2.30 a.m.

How curious and dreamlike is my impression – is it a pleasant one? I can't tell – of life in Algiers, with all the weariness that goes with the end of Ramadan!

Ramadan! We spent its first few days in Ténès, in the soothing climate of family life the way it is at that time of year. What a curious family we are, made up of people who have drifted together by accident, Slimène and I, Bel-Hadj from Bou-Saada, and Muhammad, who has one foot in the unforgettable Souf and another on those poetic slopes overlooking the blue bay and road to Mostaganem . . .

31 December 1902, midnight

Another year has slipped by . . . One year less to live . . . I love life, out of curiosity and for the pleasure of discovering its mysteries.

Even when I was tiny, I used to think with terror of the time when our beloved elders would have to die. It seemed to me impossible they would! Five years have now gone by since Mama was laid to rest in a graveyard on Islamic soil . . . It will soon be four years ago that Vava was buried in Vernier over in the land of exile, next to Volodia whose death has never been explained . . .

And everything else is gone. That fateful, hapless house has passed into other hands . . . Augustin has vanished from my horizon where he used to loom so large. I have been roaming in anguish by myself, my only companion the man I found in the Souf, long may he stay at my side and bring me solace, ◡ *please Allah.*

What will next year bring us? What new hopes and disappointments? Despite so many changes, it is good to have a loving heart to call one's own, and friendly arms in which to rest.

ANNA MARIA ORTESE

Thunder in Naples

1. TOWARDS FORMIA

And once again I was in the train. The sky was grey (in Rome, as
I left, a storm seemed imminent). The countryside slipped past
the windows on both sides, far from monotonous, but rolling,
beautifully green, with groups of fruit trees with stubby trunks
and sticky leaves; often, under them, one glimpsed yellow hud-
dles of sheep, flocks of grey and white goats, a large quantity of
white cows lying in the uniformly bright green grass, often cut
through by short canals, little nameless streams. Grey or pink
farmhouses, with the peasant family gathered in the courtyard,
locked in a mysterious immobility which was later revealed to be
concentration on some slow-moving task. The women, in red or
yellow, their skirts held up with string, were barefoot, or had
their feet thrust into men's shoes thick with dust. Other women,
dressed in black, or deep violet, like huge olives, never turned
their heads as the train passed. Perhaps it was the effect of the
comparison with the speed of the train, but the countryside
seemed to have a sort of veil cast over it, a non-material shadow,
nothing to do with the clouds in the sky, but generated as it were
by time. Everything was so static that one was tempted to open
the window and let air in upon that tender countryside, as though
as yet there was none there, and it was all a dream.

There were a dozen or so people in the carriage. Stretched out
on the seats, as if at home, young men lay in their shirt-sleeves,
with hands on their sweaty foreheads, as though to induce sleep;
elderly men, middlemen perhaps, country people, with their belts

125

slackened to help digestion, talked and laughed mildly, almost effeminately, their voices and laughter coming from their whole person, with something soft and hoarse about it; while, out of the corner of their eye, they observed the surrounding objects and faces with cautious yet distant attention. There was a middle-aged woman, very beautiful, a sort of living cherry, with a red mouth and slanting eyes, lowered, but towards the temples. She never uttered a word throughout the journey. I imagined she was from Naples, one of those beautiful little women who never age, more fruits and flowers than women. Whereas on my right, on another seat, was a sort of yellow animal, with a low forehead and blue eyes, burnt brown by the country sun, with wide bare sun-coloured feet, stained with earth. Her attention was divided, not without a certain sullen calm, between her two children: a little girl, already ugly, with a pale face and open mouth, and a baby, a few months old, more than beautiful, stupendous. That baby, marvellously turned out, encased in a long white garment, with woolly jacket and shoes, all spotless, regarded us with an intelligence, a power and a goodness that was positively bewitching. Its forehead, high and barely domed beneath a little crown of golden curls, its perfect, minute features, its deep pink cheeks, its discriminating, glowing eyes, which brightened and then darkened in fleeting anxiety, then opened again joyfully, as though recognizing and acknowledging marvellous things, were in extraordinary contrast to its mother's brutishness. One felt the woman must have been looking after it for some city lady, that it was not her child, that she had been paid to rear it. But then, on careful inspection, it was clear that not only were the warm pink of the skin and the gold of the curls the same, but so were the small nose and the curve of the forehead. Except that the woman, who was barely out of her teens, had already walked upon this earth. And her child, as yet, had not.

A small child of about six came into the compartment, his handsome face already coarsened. He went around proffering sweets and oranges which nobody wanted. They did not even look at him. On his head, the sole vestige of childhood, he wore a chicken's feather stuck into a string. The feather, mangy as it was, undoubtedly picked up from the ground and slipped into the string for some game the boy had already forgotten, none the less gave him a curious authority. He went through the compartment with superb indifference, under the enchanted gaze of the youngest of the travellers and his sister, though without deigning to confer a single look upon them. He went out, immediately came back. He had seen something, and picked it up: a small wheel of greenish metal in a pool of spittle.

I would have given something to see the faces of my fellow-travellers liven at some point, express some trace of emotion, of any thought whatsoever. But the famed excitability and responsiveness of the Southerner seemed characteristically falsely bestowed, the stuff of legend. Take the Cherry-Woman: the sensuous, gratified sweetness of her perfect face, like pink ivory, never changes: whether she is looking out upon the vague, melancholy succession of fields and orchards; or turning her gaze upon her fellow-travellers – the shirt-sleeved men, the young men asleep, the animal-mother, the extraordinary and intense children – or noting the feather, the little tray of sweets, the wheel and the spittle, the Cherry-Woman expresses nothing. Her thoughts, if any, are locked into some unknown period, riveted upon some unknown houses in old Naples, full of mirrors, hangings, curvaceous little tables, consoles, bric-a-brac; heartened by a mild light coming in from the terrace and crossing the kitchen, and becoming laden with a sharp sweet smell of tomatoes. The Cherry-Woman has a husband and thriving children: her life, between bed and kitchen, and the very occasional visit to the milliner, remains frozen at some peaceful, unforgettable stage. Nothing can impair her peace. She will die that way.

The men saw nothing either, if one came to think about it. They looked without seeing, that much was clear. In their women's voices there quivered an immediate happiness, which was everything: a feeling of beatitude at the thought of recently ingested aubergines and wines; of creamy coffees shortly to be sipped. Such small things: a little matter to be wound up in Naples; another trip, tomorrow, to Nocera. Ritual greeting of relatives. The shade of the pergola which had eased the siesta yesterday and would do so again tomorrow, and tomorrow. Fifty-year-olds, in Naples, survive upon such minor but meaningful things.

For some reason I remembered a series of endless tunnels midway between Rome and Naples, but they never materialized – that is, they were short, and soon afterwards a faint sunlight lit up the drowsy countryside, glinted on little bridges and streams, and now the women raised their faces from their work in the fields – their hands on their hoes – with a touch of boldness, a smile that was a combination of the dumb and the strong, as eloquent as a long speech. (In the eyes of the women – but in the eyes of mule-women, of animal-women – I often see an intelligence, an avidity to understand, and a hopefulness, too, that are completely absent from the faces of their menfolk, and also almost completely absent from those of socially average men and women, although the faces are a positive inventory of threadbare life and humanity.) At Minturno the train stops: a tall young man, with baskets on his head, climbs on to the train like a Fury, sending the baskets flying forwards. Chaos ensues, because the animal-woman has got up to get out, with her icon-baby in her arms and the little girl holding her hand. The man almost flattens the three of them, swearing and flailing, as though he felt affronted by their very presence; but the woman offers no word of protest, as though for centuries such things had been part of the most moderate of civilizations. The little girl darts down like a little mouse, the mother follows her, accepting digs and shoves, with a covert smile. The eyes of the white-suited infant are unblinking: they continue to observe everything from the vantage point of the platform: the bully with the baskets, who has now found a seat, the Cherry-Woman and the traders, the trees, now flowerless, around Minturno station. I shall not easily forget those eyes, seeking out other eyes. Goodbye, little fellow. Goodbye, animal-mother.

2. STATION CAFÉ

Naples' new station seemed to me immense: I saw other things before this morning, but everything begins from there, from that square. The things I saw afterwards, and that square, are one inside the other, dissimilar and coherent, equally mysterious, like bones of an antediluvian animal stacked up in a shop of clouds.

Clouds and bones, that was my first impression. Nothing now where the old station used to be, an immense, bleached area, the

setting for a square virtually like a stretch of countryside, surrounded by small, featureless, regular buildings which opened in
slices on to old neglected streets. The station in question, from
whichever angle you look at it, is a sort of gigantic herring-bone,
with few components (pillars, glass, a long serrated platform
roof) suspended several metres above the ground, between the
tangle of the trains and the city.

The square still has everything it used to have, but diluted,
scattered, played down; smaller, older; more peaceable, more
resigned. Cabs and buses (the trams have disappeared), the
trolleys of long-suffering porters; men in livery unenthusiastically
following travellers, unhurriedly murmuring the name of some
hotel; well-mannered boys who accost you gracefully, beseeching
you to entrust them with your luggage, and immediately go away
again, still gracefully, resigned.

A wind was blowing, and a fine dust was settling on everything. Where the old Rettifilo starts, like an entrail, it was shady,
but on the upper part of the houses the sun, though remaining
hidden, laid a finger of light here and there, which soon disappeared. The air was still, despite the wind, and the city seemed
dressed, as people say, in half-mourning: white and grey with a
touch of black, and with the serenity of someone who has reached
the point where even memories are going.

Uncertain as to how to proceed, feeling that I would find that
mild confusion, that greying but still potent beauty everywhere, I
went into a *pasticceria* on the right, where the square seems more
than ever like a stretch of countryside and one can choose between
the little tables on the pavement and those inside. The room was
very long, as rooms are in dreams, and vaguely arcaded: yellow
walls with vast black-framed mirrors, all reflecting that square and
that dream. Certain tables were occupied by calm, ageing, fading,
withering men, with drooping jowls and hoarse voices, deep in
calm conversations, metal trays before them.

I haven't seen many works by El Greco, but I imagine to myself
that the couple of young men sitting a few metres from me, under
the mirrors, might have come down, a few days ago, from one of
his paintings. Each was sitting at a different table, under a
different mirror, with different old men, and they had a similarity

which could only be that of brothers, making them two works by the same hand.

I am describing the young man whom I could see full-face, because I could see the other only in profile, as if in a cloud. Here then is this pair of twins, born of the city or a foreign ship, of the Spaccanopoli or some storm which only apparently belongs to the Bay, Mediterranean perhaps. First the voices – the voice, rather, because there was a single voice: subdued, grave, light, with long pauses without resonance, almost without mood. Voices like jewels, pure and dry in the dust. Then their beauty. The twins are tall, black in all except skin, which has touches of grey or green. The faces are Latin, but lean, elongated, with eyes, noses and mouths purely delineated, but in a Byzantine immobility, within a frozen passion; tall, calm and sad. They are arguing, albeit in a whisper. They look like Picassos: faceted into two or three areas of attention, severity, silence.

The weather, in the mirrors, could be seen to be darkening, and the two handsome twins did not notice, still absorbed as they were in talking with the Old Men, though without leaning forward, or even taking umbrage at any of their smutty little comments, those lopsided, cunning smiles. Their hands too, lying on their knees, were long and beautiful, and must have sampled work: perhaps in the harbour, or at the counter of an American bar – perhaps, even, in dubious districts. It is of no importance. They were already hands touched by something akin to exorcism: midway between command and anguish.

A clock on the cash desk struck ten, and it was barely five. A black barrel organ appeared on the pavement, so that its side was visible from the café entrance; and that side, illustrated with traditional emblems of volcanoes and sails, women and guitars, proceeded to produce a music which no one listened to (as no one listens to an old woman dreaming) : the hoary 'Funiculí Funiculà'.

No one heard it, not even the old men. It did not so much as exist. Apocalyptic clouds, pierced by the rays of a dying sun, were growing in the mirrors, so that it soon began to seem as though a curtain had been drawn across them. The barrel organ gave out more raucous sounds, rhythmic noises like those made by a dying animal which still retains the power of memory, warding off the

final agony. No response from the twins. A human shape enters –
an old man, as it turns out – a jacket and a tuft of white hair
enters, with a news vendor selling *Napoli-Notte* underneath them.
Half-length photos of Kennedy, the Space Man. Not a sound from
the twins. As though for them future and present, let alone past,
summed up the harrowing voice of a barrel organ. And, unweary-
ing, laid down a truer future, a truer present.

Every so often, one of the pair would look at me. And it wasn't
such a simple look, either. It held neither animation, nor sympathy, nor goodness of heart, nor emotion: only a gleam of
consciousness. Yes, I found myself thinking, that is how Lazarus
would look, with that memory of the Judgement, that distaste and
expectation, if we were in Palestine, in the time of Christ, and not
in old Naples America twenty years after the last world eruption,
in this May of '61.

At one point – there, at that café table – I thought I had chosen
the wrong day for a visit to this city which, as travel agents
maintain, needs the magic of the clear blue sky. But it was too
late to alter that. And suddenly, as evening approached, any threat
or heaviness, in nature or the sky, melted away, turning them into
an azure penumbra, into a celebration of lights, a domestic welter
of streets, of balconies, vistas; became simply that mournfulness
of early summer, when winter vanishes mysteriously into May,
and a time of drama in any season. Anything haunting, tense,
conscious that I had glimpsed in the clouds, in the mirrors, in the
twins, in the colossal herring-bone which spanned the square . . .
had disappeared, and as though in the little white cloud at the feet
of the Madonna of Loreto, famous for transporting houses from
one region to another, the city of the Bourbons came before me
once again, with its lovely airy squares, old pink palazzi, rows of
lacy black balconies, a tender image of peace, streets full of
sheets, the Castello, the Royal Gardens, the Certosa, via Santa
Brigida, the Salita di Mezzo Cannone, the oblique Piazza del Gesù
with its grey entrance. Visions which seemed to have been
trawled, fresh and alive, as pink and silvery as nets full of fish,
from the night, from the secret depths of a sea, which is no longer
the idyllic sea of Mergellina but our own tragic impending
history.

There is a beauty about the pink houses, the pink palazzi of

Naples, with green shutters and grey or white frames, and their black and white balconies, which is no longer an architectural observation but the beginning of an age-old ballade. The cripple-women, the servant-women, the cherry-women, the exquisite gilded women of the smart neighbourhoods, pass by like ever-different waves in the ever-bright light of the shops, ambiguous in its artificiality; amidst the rolling, similar to that of lame sea birds, of the long seashore. There is no boisterousness, youthful explosion, joy; but an almost constant, almost painful happiness skin deep, snatched from death and offered up to life, emerging from the rubble, the alleys, the hovels; straining towards the villas, the Riviera, money, the sun, everything which is and is not, which is to all intents isolated, mute, exhausted, and to attain which, from now on, one has to reinvent or rob.

At nine o'clock, the wind having risen again, I went to find my room in a hotel on via Caracciolo. I soon forgot my weariness. I had forgotten that, emerging from Santa Lucia sulla Passeggiata, one came upon such wild and mournful piles of precious stones: diamonds and pearls, emeralds, opals, amethysts, topaz and rubies; and then, again, as though scattered across the black breast of an African queen, in long chains, more diamonds and pearls, which the sea wind – on the utterly dark, spent sea – sent rippling.

This was Posillipo; and in front of it lay the brief fan of Piazza della Vittoria and the great line of light of the hotels from which only soft American and French voices issued, and other incomprehensible languages, while – I do not think I am mistaken – apart from a doleful rustle, only the most absolute of silences came in from the sea.

3. AEROPLANES AND CROWDS

At six in the morning, drawing back the red and yellow flowered curtains over the room's two balconies, I saw the sea. Although the day looked fairly fine, an ashen touch of mist enveloped everything, from the parapets of the Passeggiata to one side of Vesuvius, equally anonymous and ashen. Between mountain and city, right in the middle of the water, one, two, three long, motionless metallic shapes: American warships.

Soon the sky opened up to a brighter light, which scattered a thin layer of gold, restless and wandering, over the broad expanse of water. Along with the monotonous rumble of the cars driving through the streets around the hotel, I began to hear the calls of fish-sellers, or possibly others – those sudden, singing calls which pierce the heart. Soon afterwards, and for the whole morning, the calls mingled with a violent roar of planes. I had forgotten that there was an airport in Naples; but it wasn't just the airport. That roar disturbed anything.

At midday the sun was hot, you could hardly hear the aeroplanes any longer, the whole city was opening itself up in light, Saturday and midday were sending torrents of people pouring from the narrow streets, the panoramic roads, the houses of the rich and the dark houses of the poor, and this would have made anyone forget whole fleets of planes, even had they flown lower.

Can one still talk of the people of Naples? Now that 'reconstruction fever, an overwhelming mood of eagerness and modernity' is sweeping the city, as the travel agents put it? I think one can.

Where so many people emerge from, only God knows. The city is not enormous, though the landscape is immense, there do not seem to be so many habitable houses; large areas – between one skyscraper and another – are literally falling apart, there is no precise flow of work, of production, to justify all these souls, yet the sight of the people reminds one of a stream of lava, the feeling of a flood of beings, like drops of rain. Where do they come from, and where are they going to? God must know.

A child, on the street below the Palazzo Reale (an enchanting, bright pink) and the gardens and steep blue view of the harbour, had selected the most beautiful, most light-filled spot for his physical needs: right opposite these wonders; and was aiming his jet at the wheels of the Cadillacs.

Nothing could be more serene, in its extravagant tranquillity; but the child looked like a coolie, so slight and old was he, and clothed in nothing, in dust: and so all this, at least for me, had a certain meaning.

The bells were ringing: from the first cafés on the Toledo (to call it via Roma is an absurdity) came a warm smell of vanilla –

the famous pastries known as *sfogliate*; in front of Vico Rotto there were little groups of people, everything was as it had always been: an extraordinary liveliness, the sense of festivity, an event, a tumult, and in reality – once you got close to it, nothing.

I recognized many faces – that is, I had difficulty recognizing them. The years had caused cheeks to broaden and sag, made eyes smaller, caused mouths to wither. The fine euphoria, too, the ready and lively gestures, had given way to a calmer gesturing, a more indolent step, the step of those who are no longer in a hurry and go around with only half their thoughts, minds, purposes and old hopes. Everything was more static, as though time had begun to run in such a way as to become confused with immobility, as if the wheel had begun to whirl forwards – or was this too just an impression, and was it actually spinning backwards?
Small young clerks, dogged traders, priests, sailors, girls, poor people: in unending torrents they came down from all the alleys around via Roma, up from all the streets around the post office, the port; they arrived from the Museum, from Foria, or were coming back from Chiaia or Rione Amedeo, where they had been to sunbathe; in two colourful streams, as an old river glitters with refuse, flowers and leaves, they sometimes poured, sometimes dribbled down that interminable street. I would have said they had grown, like a sea, although they did not make much noise. Even the shops, now, seemed to have grown, multiplied – it was as though there were more than need be, too many for the requirements or means of the population. Shops as ornaments, as floral or electric decorations on the village square on the patron saint's feast day: a blaze, a bounty of shop windows, of tiles, embellishments, of shop signs, and something in the faces of the people which did not match up to it. Something was missing. There was certainly less distress than previously, less desolation and suffering – fuller faces, people wore better clothes, there was more relaxed behaviour – but also a tonelessness, a greater indifference. So is there in fact less hope than before, or a hope to which these people are not party, which does not remotely concern them? – I found myself wondering.
There were faces among these people, at that almost holiday time of day, that I would have preferred not to see. That of the

man selling gold pins, for example. Who would need these pins, at this time of day, with this sun, this satiety, this festiveness? He is a man of no more than one metre twenty, with bones as slight as a child's, wearing a black hat, all nose and eyes and very pale beneath it. Nothing, simply nothing, could be paler. The place is permanently untouched by sun, spring, all the joyousness of light. He proffers his pins in a voice like a whisper – more than intimidated, terrified, as though he were talking from the depths of a chasm:

'Gold pins! Top-quality pins! Buy one now!'

The crowd surges on like a flower-covered wall, almost sweeping him away.

He was fainting, he was dying, or had already fainted or been dead for some time, but he continued to offer his wares, as slight as himself, in a pointless improbable cry of hunger – of despair.

But who listens to him?

On the other hand, an old woman – indeed, not just an old woman but a centenarian – was walking into the sun, eyes shut, wrapped in a red shawl, and she seemed sated, demented. Someone touched her on the shoulder and slipped something into her hand. Then the centenarian opened her eyes again, her lovely smile disappeared, and she began to shout (like a newborn baby catching sight of its mother's milk again) that God should bless that man's descendants down the centuries. It was as though the coin had burnt her. The man had moved off and the old woman was still calling God's name, with alarm rather than gratitude, and although I knew the poor people, the vagrants, the unfortunate of this city, and their calculated edginess, I sensed a genuineness and a weariness in that fear, the reflection of so deep-seated an ill, that I shuddered. How many, I wondered at that moment, how many in this crowd would cry out, if touched or gently greeted? Is kindness so rare – so terrible – nowadays?

Following the new via della Posta, you can still go from the old Toledo as far as Piazza del Gesù, and from there back to the Toledo through via Cisterna dell'Olio, or Port'Alba. Before going back to the Toledo you can go on as far as Benedetto Croce's house, plunge deeper into the oldest Naples.

This is what I did. And as chance would have it, at that very moment the sun's light, which until then had been brilliant and joyous, became veiled, while the fleet of clouds did not become thinner but opened out into curtains, pale windows, ranging from ashen to lilac; but the light too was still dulled by that haze and – suddenly – you could no longer hear a single noise, or voice. And this was the most extraordinary moment of that morning: when, as in a dream, creatures quite different from those who had just been thronging the Toledo now peopled what looked like a grey print. Now small nuns and priests were settling like doves on the oblique Piazza del Gesù. Schoolchildren and students came out of school and walked quietly, with chunks of bread in their hands. And little shops lit up with hidden lamps, patient glances, pained smiles. Minute figures of 'home nuns' slip from the street doors, girls old before their time, cripples, derelicts, 'welfare' people: while a scent of coffee, a smell of must, incense, washing, frying oil, tomatoes and bread, waft you away as if on a cloud. A smell of tomatoes and bread. Frying oil and caramelized sugar. Monkey nuts and roasted barley. You mean people *are eating*? I asked myself in amazement. Windows opened, revealing interiors: a black iron bedstead, a stony little olive branch, Our Lady of the Sorrows with her little lamps, the goldfinch's cage, the pensioner smoking his pipe with a frown; a mother bending over her coal stove, down there, which will not light.

Just as it used to be. Unchangeable.

And that light which was still, imperceptibly, fading!

I went back to via Constantinopoli. And here there was more air: here Foria began, red and green, like a red and green river flowing to some unknown sea. Here was the Naples of the first years of the century – a rampant paradise of colours, deserts, tumult, silence, never to be met with again; of vistas so airy that you no longer know if they belong to the world or the imagination; of noble *palazzi*, almost uninhabited; of gardens and orchards warmed by the sun and wreathed in clouds of blissful melancholy; Naples forgotten within an ocean of diaphanous curves, green and soft slopes, against the background of daring pinnacles like ever-quivering curtains, behind which wander a multitude of souls delivered from time, which extinguished Greece, the Gods, Rome;

souls which are still redolent of all this, and of gloomy Spanish courts as well.

Somewhere in the vast silence, a piano was repeating a simple, transparent aria by Scarlatti. Then even those notes died away. The sky was overcast. There was a rumble of thunder.

ELIZABETH TAYLOR

The Excursion to the Source

'England was like this when I was a child,' Gwenda said. She was fifteen years older than Polly, and had had a brief, baby's glimpse of the gay twenties – though, as an infant, could hardly have been really conscious of their charms.

It was France – the middle of France – which so much resembled that unspoilt England. In the hedgerows grew all the wild flowers that urbanization, ribbon development and sprayed insecticides had turned into rarities, delights of the past, in the South of England where Gwenda and Polly lived.

Polly had insisted on Gwenda's stopping the car so that she could get out and add to her bunch some new blue flower she was puzzling over. She climbed the bank to get a good specimen and stung her bare legs on nettles. Gwenda sat in the car with her eyes closed.

Polly, having spat into her palm and rubbed it on her smarting legs, began to search for the blue flower in *Fleurs de Prés et des Bois*, instead of looking at the map. Crossroads were on them suddenly and she had no directions to give. Gwenda pulled to the side of the road, having taken the wrong turning, and reached for the map, screwing in her monocle. As she was studying it, frowning, or looking up at the sun for her bearings, Polly said, 'I suppose it's a sort of campanula. What on earth does *"lancéolées"* mean? Oh, I *wish* I'd brought my proper flower book from home.'

'It's *this* road we want,' Gwenda said, following it on the map with her nicotined finger. 'If you could remember, we turn off *here*, and about eight kilometres further on bear right.' She handed back the map. Polly had scarcely glanced at it, but she took it obediently, although she could never read it unless they were travelling north, which at present they were not.

'And when we've surmounted *that* little problem, you'd better look in the Michelin for somewhere for tonight,' Gwenda added, and began to wrench the car round grimly, as if it were a five-ton lorry.

It was ten years since she had been in this part of France; with her husband then. They had travelled along the Dordogne Valley, from the mouth to the source, crossing from bank to bank. It was in the year that he died, and she remembered with a turn of her heart how, as she was driving, she would give secret glances at him, knowing him so well that he could never hide the signs of pain coming on – the difference in breathing, the slight shifting in his seat, the hand going involuntarily to his chest, and then at once returning to his lap to grip hold of the map. He could read maps in whichever direction they were heading.

Polly had put the flower book into the dashboard pocket and had her head in the Michelin guide. She was dreadfully short-sighted, but would not wear spectacles, however much Gwenda nagged her. She would not even use the subterfuge of lenses in sunglasses, which had been suggested.

'There's one with two pairs of those scissors at a place called – I think it's Sebonac.'

'Selonac,' Gwenda said. 'How much?'

'I can't see.'

'I'll have a look later. Can you find it on the map?'

'I already have,' Polly said with pride.

Gwenda was always fussing about money – heading Polly off the Menu Gastronomique on to the eleven-franc one. Although it was Polly's money, Polly sometimes thought.

Gwenda's husband had left her poorly provided for, and she had taken a job managing a hotel until Polly's mother, her own godmother, had begged her to look after Polly, *poor* Polly she always called her, and administer her affairs. This was before the operation from which she did not recover (as the doctor put it, but Gwenda did not), 'if anything should happen', as she put *that*. Polly was left very comfortable indeed. Long ago, people had thought Gwenda's parents clever to have chosen so rich a slight acquaintance to be Gwenda's godmother.

As soon as Mrs Hervey had died, Gwenda moved into her place; into the house in Surrey – red brick with a green dome, monkey-puzzle trees and dark banks of rhododendrons, everywhere smelling of pine trees. Polly was acquiescent. She could not have managed on her own. This was clear to everyone. And at twenty-seven it was thought unlikely that she would marry. In spite of the solid worth of her position, men seemed uncertain with her, found her scatterbrained and childish conversation maddening, wondered amongst themselves if she were really all there. She was like a lanky child with her pale, freckled face, soft, untidy hair, her awkwardness. She was forever tripping over carpets or walking into doors. She got on people's nerves.

The responsibility of having quite a little heiress on her hands was one Gwenda felt she could shoulder. She was ready to deal with impoverished widowers or ambitious younger men; but few came their way in Surrey. Fork luncheons for women was their manner of entertaining, or an evening's bridge which Polly did not join in. She would sit apart, sticking foreign stamps crookedly into an album. Besides stamps, she collected Victorian bun pennies, lustre jugs, fans, seashells, matchboxes and pressed wild flowers. There was a pile of albums full of pressed flowers, and what she seemed to love best about being in France was the chance of collecting different varieties. She hoped that Selonac, when they arrived there, would have more surprises. In a foreign country there was always the delight of not knowing what she might discover next – some rare strange orchid, perhaps, that she had never found before.

But Selonac was, at first sight, a disappointment – a few straggling houses on either side of the road. They were nearly through it when they saw a sign – '*Auberge*' – pointing down a lane to the right. 'There!' shouted Polly, trying to be efficient, but Gwenda was already turning the corner. They came to a little cobbled *Place*, with a church and a baker's shop and a garage and the *auberge* – with one or two umbrellaed tables and some box trees in tubs on the pavement before it.

'I'll go and ask,' Gwenda said. She always did all the fixing-up, while Polly sat mooning in the car over her wild flowers, or squinting short-sightedly at the Guide Michelin, looking up for the twentieth time the difference between a black bathtub and a white.

140

When Gwenda came back, she was followed by a young man, who dragged their suitcases out of the boot and lurched back into the darkness of the hotel with them.

It was a very dark and silent hotel. Polly felt depressed, as she went upstairs after Gwenda. She was never asked for her opinions about where they should stay. They never shared a room, and Gwenda always told her which was hers – and it was never the one nearest the bathroom or with the best view. She was glad that sharing a room was not one of Gwenda's economies. Gwenda snored like a man. She had heard her through many a thin wall.

This time they had the same view from their windows – across an orchard to a row of silvery trees which looked as if they bordered a stream. There was very little difference between the two rooms. Madame Peloux, the proprietress, showed Polly and Gwenda both, as if there were any chance of Polly making a choice; and then she began to chivvy her son, Jean, about the luggage. He was a clumsy, silent young man, and seemed to be sulking. His mother nagged him monotonously, as if from an old habit.

Like some wine, Polly did not travel well. She became more and more creased and greasy-faced. And the clothes in her suitcase, amongst the layers of tattered tissue-paper, all were creased, too, and all a little grubby, yet not *quite* grubby enough, she decided, to warrant all the fuss of getting them washed.

'Aren't you ready *yet*?' asked Gwenda at the door. 'After all that driving, what I need is some *violent* exercise.'

She usually said something like this, and once upon a time Polly had had amusing visions of her running across country or playing a few chukkas of polo. Now she knew that all that would happen would be that Gwenda would drape her cardigan over her shoulders and go for a stroll round the garden, or amble round the village, stopping to look in shop windows – longest at the *charcuteries* to marvel at terrines. She examined them with a professional eye; for her own pâté was quite the talk of their part of Surrey. When she was asked for the recipe, she became carefully vague and said she had none; that she just chucked in anything that came to hand.

This evening there was a pâté on the ten-franc menu, so she was happy. She had had her stroll through the orchard, and Polly, still unpacking, had watched her from the bedroom window. Gwenda pushed her way through the long grass, lifting her neat ankles over briars. She had a top-heavy look, especially when viewed from above. Her large bosom was out of character, Polly thought. It was altogether too motherly-looking. And to think of Gwenda with children was impossible.

In the end, the unpacking was done, and the little walk was over, and they went into the almost empty dining-room. There were red and pink tableclothes, and large damp napkins to match, and Jean, Madame Peloux's son, had combed his frizzy hair, and was waiting inexpertly at table.

'Mosquitoes,' Gwenda was saying. 'I'm afraid there might be. I went up and closed the shutters.'

There *was* a stream at the bottom of the orchard, across a narrow lane. She had come to it on her wanderings, and had been bitten a little by midges.

'The pâté's not bad,' she said, dipping into the jar of gherkins.

Polly thought it a bit 'off' – well, sour anyway; but she said nothing. She was too often told that the taste she objected to was the very one that had been aimed at, the absolute perfection of flavour.

Jean annoyed Gwenda by saying the name of everything he put on the table – as if she and Polly were children. '*Truites*', he announced, setting the dish down. They looked delicious – sprinkled with parsley and shredded almonds.

Gwenda, whose French – like everything else – was so much better than Polly's, asked if they were from the stream below the orchard, and Jean looked evasive, as if he could not understand her. '*Truites*', he said again, and turned away, knocking over a glass as he did so.

The only other guests sat across the room. They were obviously not newcomers. They were favoured by the best table at the garden window, whereas Gwenda and Polly looked out on to the square. They had a bottle of wine with their name scribbled on the label, and the man poured it out himself, looking very serious as he did so. The woman drank water, holding the glass in a shaking hand, tinkling it against her false teeth. She was ancient. He was in his sixties, and she was his mother.

As they were French, Gwenda had to listen with a little extra concentration to what they said – although they said little, and that in muted voices, as they stared before them, waiting for Jean to bring the next dish.

The old woman was thin and ashen and wore a sort of half-mourning of grey and mauve, and a hat – a floppy, linen garden hat. The only real colour about her was her crimson shiny lips, crookedly done, which she kept pressed together, and smudged, after every sip of water, with a purple handkerchief. Large diamond rings kept slipping on her old fingers.

'Mother and son,' Gwenda said in a low explanatory voice to Polly.

Jean had brought a tart to be cut from. Glazed slices of apple were slightly burnt. He made a great business of cutting their slices, frowning and pursing his lips as if it were a very tricky job.

Monsieur and Madame Devancourt, as he then addressed them, waved the tart away. Gwenda fastened on the name; repeated it once or twice in her mind, and had it secure.

'How *good* not to have anything frozen,' she said, as she said at nearly every mealtime.

'The tart is lovely,' Polly said. She loved sweet things, and longed for them through the other courses.

Madame Devancourt played with her rings and stared about her, while her tall, bald son was peeling an orange for her. They really were a very silent pair; but sometimes he made a little joke, and she gave a smothered snigger behind her handkerchief. It was surprising – sounded like a naughty little girl laughing in church.

Through the window, Polly watched one or two people sitting at the tables outside the inn, looking rather bored as they sipped their evening drink. A middle-aged woman, with a bitter, closed expression on her face, sat beside an older woman who was bowed over, so hunchbacked that she kept losing balance and slipping sideways. Then the younger woman – she was obviously her daughter – would put her right, and turn her head away again, without a word. After a while she suddenly stood up, got her mother to her feet and began a slow progress back across the *Place*.

Jean brought coffee to Gwenda and Polly and slopped it into the saucers pouring it out. Gwenda asked for another saucer and when he brought it, he looked so sulky that Polly smiled up at him, and thanked him in her atrocious accent. She knew so well herself what it was like to be clumsy and inadequate.

'Such a moron,' Gwenda said. 'Never mind, it's only for one night.'

Although it turned out to be for six.

Gwenda always got up for breakfast. She found French beds uncomfortable, and 'liked to be about', as she put it.

The Devancourts were also up. Madame was wearing her floppy hat, and a pair of grubby tennis shoes. Her son peeled another orange for her, and made a few more jokes. She seemed to be his life, and accepted his attentions placidly. But she was, in her own way, protective to *him*. When he half stood up, with his napkin in one hand and the orange in the other, and bowed to Gwenda and Polly as they came in, she stared hard at him, as if willing him back into his seat, and Polly could imagine her having guarded him from women since he was a young man, just as Gwenda had warded off young men from herself. When he had sat down again and resumed his careful orange-peeling, the old woman turned a cold and steady gaze on Gwenda, as if to say, 'Don't waste any time on *this* one. He is mine.' At Polly she did not so much as glance. Few people did. It was surprising that Jean darted forward and drew out her chair before he attended to Gwenda, although he shot it out so fast and so far that she almost fell on the floor.

'I really don't think he's all there,' Gwenda said.

She had brought the maps down to breakfast, and said that she thought they could get to the source of the river that day. It was so beautiful up there in the Auvergne, she said. The air so clear. The flowers so beautiful. At the thought of the flowers, Polly brightened; but there was also the thought of the day ahead, with all the difficulties of the map-reading and Gwenda's making a martyrdom of the driving – though it was she who forced the pace, who was determined to retrace every footstep of that last holiday with her husband. Why she wanted to do this, Polly found a puzzle – especially as that holiday must have been permeated with tragedy. Gwenda had always talked of it a great deal, and she talked of her husband more than Polly could endure. Such trivial repetitions – such as, every morning. '*How* Humphrey loved French bread!' and reminiscences all the way along the road. And there were implications that Polly knew none of the secret joys of matrimony, and would be unlikely ever to learn them. So Polly felt excluded, as well as bored.

Sometimes, alone in her bedroom, she lay for a little while face-down on the bed, upset by vague desires. If the desires were to be loved, she had no face to match her longing; simply nothing to define her daydreams. 'I want! I just *want!*' she sometimes moaned softly into the pillows.

'Oh, *lazy*-bones!' Gwenda would say, opening the door as she knocked on it. 'Even at *my* age, I wouldn't dream of lying down in the daytime.' As like as not, she would be on her way downstairs for some of her *violent* exercise. This morning, having mused once more on Humphrey's love of French bread, Gwenda put in her monocle and unfolded a map.

They were breakfasting in the bar, with a view through the open door across the *Place*. It was early in the morning, and children were gathered at the tables outside, waiting for the school bus. The boys smoked, and some of the older girls were playing a game of cards. They were very orderly, though gay, and made a sound like starlings. Gwenda kept glancing up in annoyance, and glaring through her monocle. Polly felt envious of the children.

Madame Devancourt padded past them in her tennis shoes, followed by her son. He bowed again, but she kept her eyes ahead. Presently, Jean appeared outside with a stiff broom and began to sweep beneath the tables; then he leaned on the broom and talked to some of the children; almost seeming to be one of them, without, for once, his shy or sullen look. Perhaps he too was envious of them, Polly thought.

'Jean, Jean!' Madame Peloux came in in her black overall and called her son's attention to his work, and he shrugged and glowered and began to sweep again.

The school bus came, was filled, and drove off, and there was silence except for the rasping of the broom on the pavement. When he had finished the sweeping, Jean watered the box-shrubs and a sharp, cold smell cut off the heat of the morning for a while.

'Have you packed?' Gwenda asked Polly, knowing that she had not.

As Polly got up, she bumped against the table, and Gwenda looked up sharply and clicked her tongue. Polly, catching Jean's eyes, blushed, ashamed to be rebuked in front of him. He was standing in the doorway, flicking the last drops from the watering-can about the pavement.

As she went upstairs, Polly thought, I'll bet old Humphrey never bumped into things, and she hoped for his sake that he hadn't.

Gwenda paid the bill, then she walked about the courtyard, smoking to soothe herself. The exasperation she felt at having to wait always for Polly was a trembling pain. She hated to wait, and now spent hours of her life doing so. She herself was quick and decisive, always thinking one step ahead. Routine things, like packing, for instance, were so boring that she would get them done with great speed, only to waste time she had saved pacing up and down while Polly dithered.

Jean brought down her case and put it in the boot of the car.

Monsieur Devancourt came out to the garage with his fishing-rods. He stopped to wish Gwenda a pleasant journey, then drove off in his old and dusty Citroën. As Gwenda looked back to the inn for any sign of Polly, she saw old Madame Devancourt, still wearing her hat, staring down at her from a window.

Already the sun was strong. Smells of baking came through the kitchen window, and Gwenda began to long for the cool air of the Auvergne.

At last Jean brought down Polly's suitcase, and Polly followed soon after. Madame Peloux came out from the kitchen, wiping her floury hands on her apron.

As they drove out of the courtyard, Polly thought, 'As soon as I get to like a place, we have to move on,' and she turned back and waved to Jean, who was staring after them in his vacant way.

But Gwenda was insistent on moving on, on retracing every mile of her holiday with Humphrey. They had to get up to the source and back through Northern France, and there were only ten days left. Then Gwenda had to go home to open a garden fête.

'I love this feeling of starting out fresh in the mornings,' she said, as they drove out of the square. 'Humphrey used to say . . .' She slowed down, reaching the main road; the engine stalled, and stopped, and would not start again.

'Oh, drat it,' said Gwenda.

Now the heat poured into the car. While Gwenda tugged at the starter and made her mild, but furious-sounding imprecations,

Polly placidly looked at her wild-flower book, as if the hitch did not involve her, and would soon be put right.

Jean, who had watched the car and seen it stop, came running towards them. He opened the bonnet and seemed to take a very grave view. After a while he fetched his friend from the garage. The car was towed away, and Gwenda and Polly decided to return temporarily to the *auberge* and drink a *citron pressé*.

'Now, we shall have a job to get to the mountains by this evening,' Gwenda said.

Polly was playing with a cat.

As the day went on, the idea of the mountains receded. Jean carried their suitcases back upstairs, and they unpacked.

'A week at *least*,' Gwenda moaned. 'And if they *say* that, goodness only knows what it might really mean. Stuck in this place.'

'It's quite a *nice* place,' said Polly.

'Yes, but it's not what we planned.'

The car was in the village garage, and a spare part had been telephoned for, and for once there seemed nothing that Gwenda could do. So she went to lie down, in the heat of the afternoon – the thing she said she never did. Polly, at a loose end, wandered in the orchard, looking for flowers. It was like the afternoons of her childhood, when her mother rested, and she was left to her own devices. In those days, she had felt under a spell. Through an open window she could hear the solid ticking of a grandfather clock and on the terrace, the peacocks squawked with a sound of rusty shears being forced open. Here there was only the busy noise of the cicadas in the grass.

At the bottom of the orchard, she saw Jean. He was beckoning to her eagerly, and she hurried forward, with a wading motion, through the long grass. He had few words to say – from habit, from *gaucherie*, from fear of her foreignness. To make up for his dumbness, his gestures were all exaggerated, like Harpo Marx's. They came out of the orchard and crossed the narrow, gritty lane, which was lanced by sunlight striking through birch trees.

With a complete disregard for Polly's bare legs, he took her hand and drew her through looped and tangled brambles, disturbing dozens of small blue butterflies. Polly could hear the stream, but not see it for all the undergrowth. She wondered where they were going, and what all the secrecy and haste and excitement were about. Jean parted some reeds and she could see the stream again. It looked less deep than it was, for it was very clear, and the fat brown stones on its bed seemed near the surface. Jean turned and lifted Polly with his hands round her waist. He swung her down over the bank on to a boulder. It had seemed a sudden, reckless thing to do and her breath was taken away; but she landed quite safely on the boulder, with his large rough hands steadying her.

He became more secretive than ever, carefully drawing aside branches to show to her a part of the stream, caged off by wire netting. The water flowed through the trap, which was full of trout, turning back and forth, and swimming as best they could. So this was his secret? Polly smiled, and he watched her face intently, and when she turned to him and nodded – she knew not why – he put a finger to his lips and narrowed his eyes. To an onlooker they would have seemed like people in a silent movie.

For a moment or two, they stood in contemplation, hypnotized by the slowly moving fish; then, suddenly, with more frantic gestures, Jean dashed off again. He took a spade from a hiding-place under a bush and began to try to thrust it into the earth. Polly turned to watch him with amazement. The earth was hard. He lifted a piece of rough turf and bent to examine the soil, clicking his tongue in disapproval. In spite of the dryness of the earth, he managed, as he dug deeper, to find a few worms. He brought them eagerly to Polly and put them into the palm of her hand, as if they were a handful of precious stones. She recoiled, but he did not notice and, to show her how, he took one of the worms from her and tore it into pieces and threw them to the fish. With a feeling of revulsion, Polly flung her handful suddenly into the trap. Some fell through, others lay on the wire netting, writhing. She bent down and dipped her hand into the cool water, while Jean poked at the worms with a stick, clicking his tongue in vexation.

'Jean! Jean!' They could hear his mother calling him across the orchard.

He frowned. He watched the trout a little longer, then he seemed to gather himself from a trance, braced himself, and gave his hands to Polly, dragging her clumsily up the bank. 'Jean! Jean!' the voice went on calling, getting shriller. He looped briars carefully over the trap and he and Polly set off.

Madame Peloux was standing in the orchard. She waved a basket at them, for there was some errand for Jean to run – he had to go to the farm to fetch a chicken for dinner. An old boiler, she explained rapidly, aside from Polly.

Polly stood, hesitating, unsure whether to walk on or not. Then, feeling very bold and having composed the sentence in French before she spoke it, she asked if she might go with him to the farm. His face at once lost its sulkiness, and the errand seemed to take on a bright aspect. Madame Peloux stood looking suspiciously after them as they set off.

'What *has* come over you?' Gwenda asked Polly, fearing that she knew. She had found the girl sitting by her bedroom window, studying a phrase-book. It was opened at *Le Marché*.

'You always said I should improve my French,' Polly replied defensively.

'But you never cared to try, did you? Before?'

It was a brilliant early evening, and Gwenda had looked in on her way downstairs. In the garden the acacias were full of sunlight against the pale blue sky. Martins and swallows darted about the terracotta, crenellated outhouse roof, catching, Gwenda hoped, the mosquitoes which otherwise might have plagued her later. There was a smell of lime blossom and honeysuckle and, down below, in the vegetable garden lilies grew like weeds.

'I could stay here for ever, I think,' Polly said, glancing across the orchard.

'This was hardly the object of our holiday,' Gwenda said. She was fretful to complete their journey. She talked continually of getting to the source, to the mountains, so infuriatingly near, where she and Humphrey had been so happy. As they were arrested on their travels, there were no fresh sights to discuss, so she talked about Humphrey, and Polly wished that she would not. Gwenda spoke of marriage as if it were something exclusive to herself and her late husband. She referred to past experiences, implying that Polly would never know similar ones.

'Humphrey and I climbed right to the summit,' she said. 'There was an enormous view, and gentians – great patches of gentians.'

'I should love to see gentians,' Polly said.

'Well, I doubt if we shall now,' Gwenda said briskly. 'It's so infuriating. You really ought not to read that small print. Your nose almost touches the page. So ridiculous. We shall have to see about getting you some spectacles when we get back.'

'I shan't wear them,' Polly said, in a mild but firm voice. Sometimes, quietly, she put her foot down, and then Gwenda let the matter go. It was such a rare occurrence that it did not constitute a threat. All the same, only that morning Polly had insisted on going to the market with Jean, and had left Gwenda at the garage and gone on with him alone. Gwenda was always at the garage, making the same complaints, asking the same questions.

'You'll find you'll come to them in the end,' she said, referring to the spectacles. 'Now do take your head out of that book, there's a dear girl. Let's go down and have a drink. I promised the Devancourts we'd join them.'

Madame Devancourt now seemed warmly disposed to them. She had decided that they were lesbians, and so of no danger to her son. Passing their table at breakfast, the day after the breakdown, the old lady had commiserated with them. She was formal and condescending. By dinner time, she had warmed a little more; and the following morning had come to them, with her son hovering behind her, to invite them to a drive out in the afternoon. 'Having no car you will see nothing of our country,' she said.

So they had driven out along rutted, dusty lanes to see a small château. It stood high on a slope over the river, bone-white, with black candle-snuffer turrets. Madame Devancourt had the name of a friend to mention, and the housekeeper admitted them. The family was away, and she went ahead from room to room, opening shutters, drawing dust-covers from furniture, lifting drugget from needlework carpets. There were some portraits, some pieces of tapestry, deers' heads and antlers growing from almost every wall, and a chilly smell from the stone floors. Madame Devancourt and Gwenda exclaimed over everything, drew one another to view this and that treasure or curiosity. Each was impressed by the other's knowledge. Monsieur Devancourt looked out of the windows, and Polly trailed behind, immeasurably bored.

She regretted this new friendship. Gwenda's fluency with French debarred Polly from any part in the conversation – not that she had anything to say. She was frightened of the old lady, and thought her son a pitiful creature. Now they must spend an hour with them sitting under the umbrellas outside the *auberge*. She took her wild-flower book with her, and looked for a picture of a gentian. '*Gentiane*', said Jean, pointing at the illustration, when he had set down her drink before her.

'*Oui,*' she said, smiling and blushing.

'*Oui, gentiane,*' he repeated, turning to take an order from another table.

'He will drive me *mad*,' said Gwenda.

Then there was the little commotion of having to get up as Madame Devancourt shuffled out to join them, her son following, carrying her handbag and her cardigan.

At another table came the other sorry pair, the *habituées*, the crippled mother and the bitter-faced daughter. Every evening, they sat for twenty minutes in the *Place*. The daughter sipped a drink, and kept propping up her mother. Not a word was spoken. When it was time to go, the daughter stood up in silence and helped her mother to her feet, and then to go slowly across the square. Homewards. Polly tried not to imagine any more – the dreadful ritual of getting mother to bed. All old, she thought, looking round her. Whenever Jean passed by, he nodded his head at her, as if he were saying, 'Ah, yes, you're still there.'

Gwenda, missing nothing, frowned.

He continued to madden her through dinner. When he brought the trout, he winked at Polly, collusively.

'One can grow tired even of trout,' Gwenda complained. 'Every evening. I do wish, Polly, you would try to ignore that terrible young man. He is quite oafish. I would have said he winked at you just now, if I could believe it possible.'

She had ordered a bottle of wine to be put on the Devancourts' table – a token of gratitude for their kindness – and now Monsieur Devancourt across the room raised his glass in a courtly gesture, and Madame her glass of water, with a shaking hand.

'Very affy,' said Polly in a low voice.

After dinner, the four of them sat in the stuffy little salon, and Gwenda told them stories about her husband.

'Excuse me,' Polly murmured, slipping away suddenly – the very thing Gwenda had been determined she snould not do.

In the courtyard, Jean was watering the tubs of geraniums. The air had a delicious smell.

At once, before Gwenda could find an excuse to come after them, he put down the watering-can and they set off across the orchard. Every evening he went to the stream to clean the trout-trap of drifting weeds and sticks and to dig up worms. They said very little – although Polly persevered with a few short sentences, and sometimes Jean pointed at plants and trees and said their name clearly in French, which she obediently repeated.

Although he was clumsy and unpredictable and could not speak a word of her language, Polly felt safe and at home with him. There was never anyone young in her life – neither here nor at home. She liked to go shopping with him in the market. It was the simplest, poorest of markets. Old women sat patiently beside whatever they had for sale – a few broad beans tied in a bundle, a live duck in a basket, lime flowers for tisane, a bucketful of arum lilies or Canterbury bells. She and Jean went from one to the other, comparing cheeses, and pressing the beanpods, and she felt a sense of intimacy, as if they were playing a game of being husband and wife. Nothing Gwenda could say would prevent her from going to the market.

This evening, she helped him to clean the trap, she fed worms to the fish, having lost her squeamishness. They were as busy and absorbed as children.

Throwing the last worm, she lost her balance on the boulder, and one foot went into the water; but he was there at once to steady her. She was annoyed with herself, wondering how to explain to Gwenda her soaking wet sandal, without revealing the secret of this place.

Jean lifted her up and sat her on the bank.

'I shall stay here for a while,' she said. Perhaps Gwenda would go up to bed early, although more likely not.

He understood her, and sat down beside her, feeling worried, because soon his mother would be calling 'Jean! Jean!' all round the garden – there would be some job to be done.

When they had been together before, there had always been something to be busy about – the marketing, the fish. Now each had only the other one in mind. He sat there staring in front of him, as if he were wondering what on earth to do next, for he had scarcely been allowed five minutes' idleness in his life. Then he suddenly had an inspiration. He turned and kissed her suddenly on the side of her face, then, less awkwardly, on her forehead. Polly had been kissed only by her mother and elderly relations; but she felt that she knew more about it than Jean. She put her hands behind his head and kissed him very strongly on the mouth. She felt quite faint with delight. But hardly had they had any time to enjoy their kissing, when that far-off, coming-and-going, mosquito-plaint began – 'Jean! Jean!' – across the orchard.

Until they were in sight of the house, they went hand in hand, saying nothing. Although the kissing was over, something remained – an excitement, a gladness. Something Gwenda, surely, could never have experienced.

That Gwenda guessed something of what had happened was shown by her coldness and huffiness. She had felt awkward, sitting in the salon with the Devancourts. Polly had excused herself so abruptly, and Madame Devancourt kept looking towards the door. Gwenda was glad when, at their usual time, Monsieur Devancourt fetched the draught-board and set out the counters. She watched for a little while, and realized that the son was making stupid mistakes so that his mother could win. Then, hearing Madame Peloux outside, calling for Jean, Gwenda got up uneasily, and said that she was going to have an early night. She went upstairs and threw open the window, regardless of mosquitoes.

Polly and Jean were coming back across the orchard. Gwenda began to shake violently, and moved back a few steps from the window. Jean answered his mother, but did not say a word to Polly, not even when she turned away from him to enter the house.

Gwenda was so unpleasantly disturbed that she felt unable to face Polly, and dreaded her coming to say goodnight. But she did not come. The footsteps stopped at the next room, and Gwenda heard the door open, and then shut. This was something that had never happened before. There were too many things happening for the first time. Gwenda lay in bed worrying about them, and she slept badly.

At breakfast, nothing was right. She snapped at Jean for slopping the coffee, she complained that the butter was rancid, and she found every word that Polly said in French excruciating. 'Your command of the language grows as fast as your accent deteriorates.' She preferred the days when Polly did not try, and had no reason for doing so. 'Whatever must the Devancourts think? They must wonder where on earth you picked up such an accent.'

'It's not *for* them to wonder,' Polly said calmly. 'They can't speak a *word* of English.'

She *was* calm. She was *too* calm, Gwenda decided. And Jean did not look at her this morning, nor she at him. It seemed to Gwenda that they no longer felt they needed to.

'Oh, *damn* the car,' she suddenly said.

Polly looked a little surprised, but said nothing.

'I think I'll have a look round the market this morning,' Gwenda said casually.

The three of them later set off, and there was only a brief chance to make an assignation, when Gwenda almost instinctively paused to look at a terrine on a stall.

The friendship with the Devancourts played into Polly's hands. Just at the right moment of the afternoon, Madame Devancourt came downstairs with a photograph album to show to Gwenda – her collection of photographs of great houses, all to be gone over and explained in detail, trapping Gwenda, who thought that she would scream. Monsieur Devancourt was attending to his fishing tackle, so the two women were left alone, sitting in the stuffy salon. It was too hot to go out of doors, Madame Devancourt said.

Polly, who had gone into the lavatory to try to plan her escape, saw the delightful sight of Gwenda with the album on her knees and Madame Devancourt leaning over, pointing at a photograph with a shaking finger. She slipped away without being seen. Jean, whose slack time it was, was waiting for her by the trout-trap. He pulled briars and bracken round them, like a nest and, without much being said, made love to her.

The old lady smelled of camphor and lavender. She leaned so close that Gwenda almost choked. Sometimes little flecks of spit fell on the pages of the album, and were quickly wiped away with the purple handkerchief. Gwenda tried to turn the pages quickly, but this would not do; for every coign and battlement and drawbridge had to be explained.

At last Monsieur Devancourt interrupted them. He had finished with his fishing tackle and had come to take them for a little drive. Where was Mademoiselle Polly, he wondered. Gwenda flushed, and said that she must be writing letters in her room; and she excused herself from the outing, having a headache, she explained.

When they had gone, Gwenda walked up and down the garden path. She strutted, with rather apart legs, like a starling. She listened and she looked about her. But there were no voices. It was a hot, humming afternoon. The Devancourts' car went off, and then there was nothing but the sound of insects, and hardly a leaf moved.

'Her mother!' Gwenda kept saying to herself. 'What would her mother think?'

It was a real headache she had, and the sun was making it much worse. It drove her inside – up to the vantage point of her bedroom window.

It was a long time before she saw Polly coming back across the orchard. She walked slowly, and was alone. But that was only a ruse, a piece of trickery, Gwenda was sure.

She leaned out of the window and called to her.

Polly seemed to come unwillingly, and stood hesitating at Gwenda's door.

'Where have you been?'

'For a walk.'

'With that dreadful loutish youth.'

Polly pressed her lips together.

'He's not even...' Gwenda shrugged and turned aside; and after a few moments in which nothing else was said, Polly went quietly to her own room. Although she foresaw all the agonizing awkwardness of the rest of the holiday – even, vaguely, of the rest of her life (Gwenda going on being huffy in Surrey) – she dismissed its importance. She stood before the looking-glass, combing her hair dreamily, staring at her freckled face with its band of sunburn across the forehead. It was she now, she decided, who had something exclusively her own, and it seemed to her that Gwenda had nothing – for even her memories were threadbare.

In the night, just before dawn, Gwenda woke up. Something had disturbed her, and she lay listening. There was silence, save for faraway cow-bells occasionally heard, then a floorboard creaked on the landing, and another. There was a gentle tapping on a bedroom door, and whispering.

She felt very cold, and sick, and deceived. She groped for her watch and peered at its luminous dial. It was nearly five o'clock. There was no real light in the sky, but perhaps a lessening of darkness.

Boards now creaked quite heavily along the passage, down the stairs. Gwenda got out of bed and went to the window, gently easing the shutters apart. As she did so, she heard an outside door open, and then a man's voice, speaking in low tones just below her. As her eyes grew used to the dark, she could make out two figures. After a moment, they moved off towards the courtyard, and she could see then that they were Jean and Monsieur Devancourt, both carrying fishing rods. After a while, she heard the car starting up. It drove away, and she listened to it fading into the distance. Then the church clock struck five.

She left the shutters opened, and got back into bed. The sky slowly lightened, and she turned about heavily on the rough, darned sheets, longing for day to come so that she could get on with it, hasten through it. She searched her mind for plans for escaping from this hated place and, faced with all the complications, found none.

At breakfast, Gwenda was tired and silent. She seemed to brood over her coffee, staring before her, the drooping lines of her face deeper than ever. Monsieur Devancourt and Jean returned, having caught a large pike. Jean quickly slipped on a white jacket and brought fresh coffee. Monsieur Devancourt joined his mother, and peeled her orange for her, was full of simple triumph at his successful expedition, and now wanted nothing but to devote the rest of the day to her. They discussed their plans with great pleasure.

As usual, Madame Devancourt stopped on her way past Gwenda's and Polly's table.

'How early a riser would it be possible for you to be?' she asked. She seemed playful, like a child with a secret. She hardly waited for Gwenda's reply. 'Then,' she went on, 'we have a little plan, Louis and I. We know your disappointment at not reaching the source of the river, and we think that if we can start early tomorrow we can make the journey and spend the following night *en route*. It would give us great pleasure. How does it strike you?'

It struck Gwenda very well, and she said so. She brightened at once. Polly, who never understood what Madame Devancourt said, had not tried to listen. When it was explained to her, she was appalled, and too artless to hide the fact. Gwenda touched her foot under the table to bring her to her senses; but she could only stammer her thanks, while looking quite dismayed.

'But it's dreadful for *me*,' she complained to Gwenda afterwards. 'I can't understand a single word they say. To have a long drive like that with them!'

She knew that she would have to go. She was not strong enough to resist Gwenda over this. After a while she forgot what was hanging over her. She was living in the present, and it was time to go to market with Jean. Gwenda, more relaxed now, let them go alone, while she visited the garage and made another fuss.

The next day, they left very early. Jean was up before them and brought them coffee and bread. It was a strange, cold dawn, and they moved about quietly, with lowered voices, putting things into the boot of the car. At the last moment, Polly found she had forgotten her wild-flower book and had to get out of the car and go and find it. It was her only solace – and such a small one to her in her altered life – that she might see gentians growing in the mountains. Jean stood ready to open the car door for her when she returned. His eyes rested mournfully upon her. As they drove off, she could see him standing there, staring after her, looking sulky.

Madame Devancourt was quite talkative this morning. She sat in front beside her son, and half turned her wedge-shaped face back towards Gwenda. Polly she completely ignored. She thought her an imbecile and wondered that Gwenda had not found a more intelligent and presentable partner. It seemed to her that they were not so very much in love, though in such cases, she found it difficult to tell.

They stopped for lunch at an inn full of memories for Gwenda. She was delighted. Her spirits had been rising all morning, as they climbed higher into the colder air. She became animated, and infected Madame Devancourt with her liveliness. Both had such recollections – and all along the route the two widows exchanged them. *La Bourboule! Le mont-Dore!* There were changes to be noted. Yet so much had remained the same. Monsieur Devancourt listened to them as he drove, smiling to see his mother so gay. It was unusual for her to have feminine companionship, and it seemed to do her good. Polly stared at the wild flowers along the way. She was obviously not allowed to stop to gather them. Monsieur Devancourt sometimes addressed a remark to her and then she started out of her dreams and became confused, and Gwenda had to rescue her.

After lunch, they went on to the source. The river they had driven beside became, at last, a thin fast trickle down the mountainside. The road ended. They got out of the car and felt the air cold on their faces, and Polly looked about for flowers. The gentians were higher up, Gwenda told her, and she said that she for one was determined to climb to the summit, as she and Humphrey had done. They could be taken nearly there in the funicular.

Madame Devancourt declined. She would sit in the car and wait for them, and be quite happy reading her novel, she explained.

'Your mother is charming,' Gwenda told Monsieur Devancourt as they waited for the lift to come down.

'It is altogether a charming day,' he said.

As they were hauled up by the cable car, Polly, although dizzy, peered down at the rocks for flowers. She saw miniature daffodils, drifts of white anemones, and then, in a crevice, a patch of gentians. The funicular swung high above them and came to a stop.

This much higher up, it was windy. Strands of hair kept lashing her cheeks. She hated the wind, and she hated being so high. Above them, at the top of a zigzagging path, she could see two tiny figures waving from the highest rock.

'I shouldn't like to go up there,' she said to Gwenda.

'But that's why we've come,' Gwenda said with a tone of scorn. 'Humphrey...' Then she changed her mind about what she was going to say. She would climb to the summit alone with Monsieur Devancourt and say not a word about her husband all the way.

Polly, on this lower slope, was quite content to scramble about and pick flowers. The tiny daffodils were exquisite, and there were varieties she could not classify until she got back to the car and found them in her book. But she could find no gentians. They seemed to grow in rockier parts. Here, there was only shabby, wind-bitten grass and patches of dirty snow. Barbed wire ran along the edge of the ridge. Beyond it rocks went sheer down to the valley.

From the summit, Gwenda and Monsieur Devancourt, rather out of breath, paused triumphantly and looked about them at the wide view. They could see Polly below, darting like a child or a bee, from one flower to another, and they called to her, but their voices were snatched out of their throats by the wind. Then Gwenda began to shout in earnest, for she could see that Polly was trying to crawl under the barbed wire. She was lying on her stomach, reaching for something. Gwenda and Monsieur Devancourt called out in warning and began to scramble down the slippery path as quickly as they could. Before they could come within Polly's hearing, there was a dreadful rushing noise of bouncing and cascading scree, of rocks dropping with an echo upon other rocks. The noise continued long after Polly had disappeared and Gwenda and Monsieur Devancourt had come to the newly opened fissure. Beside it was a handful of flowers, and a piece of gentian-blue chocolate-paper which Polly must have been reaching for.

Monsieur Devancourt had been a tower of strength. He had interviewed police officials and undertakers, intercepted newspapermen, booked the flight home, arranged about the coffin, sent telegrams, and brought Gwenda back to Selonac to pack the cases. And every now and then he bewailed the fact that the tragic excursion had been his idea.

Gwenda was stunned, rather than grief-stricken. She leaned on his kindness. She let him do everything for her.

Madame Devancourt now seemed to have withdrawn. Her son's solicitude was irksome and disturbing, and looks of suspicion were cast on him and Gwenda. The episode had been distasteful, encroaching – and she had had enough of her, this Englishwoman, with her demanding ways. Instead of taking command, as one of her kind should have done, she had clung to a man like any silly girl.

'I can never say "thank you" enough,' Gwenda said. She had come to them in the salon to bid them goodbye. 'When you visit England, I hope you will stay with me, in my house in Surrey.'

Madame Devancourt nodded forbiddingly; but Gwenda hardly noticed. In her mind, she was introducing Monsieur Devancourt – he had asked her to call him 'Louis' – to her friends. 'Do you play bridge?' she very nearly asked him; but she stopped herself in time. She shook hands. Once more Louis blamed himself for Polly's death, and his mother clicked her tongue impatiently.

Out in the courtyard, the car was waiting – ready at last; ready too late – and Jean was packing the cases into the boot. Gwenda had forgotten all about him. Madame Peloux stood by to wish her '*Bon voyage*'.

She looked into her bag for a tip, and advanced with it folded in her hand, ready to slip into Jean's. He slammed down the lid of the boot and, as Gwenda came up to him, he turned sulkily aside, and walked away.

His face was swollen; he made a blubbering noise, like a miserable child and, going faster and faster, made off across the orchard.

'Ah, Jean! Jean!' his mother said, with a sigh and a shake of her head, looking after him.

Gwenda got into the car. It started perfectly. She waved to Madame Peloux and to Louis Devancourt, who had come out of the inn to watch her go, and drove away, towards the airport.

DOROTHY PARKER

✑

Here We Are

The young man in the new blue suit finished arranging the glistening luggage in tight corners of the Pullman compartment. The train had leaped at curves and bounced along straightaways, rendering balance a praiseworthy achievement and a sporadic one; and the young man had pushed and hoisted and tucked and shifted the bags with concentrated care.

Nevertheless, eight minutes for the settling of two suitcases and a hatbox is a long time.

He sat down, leaning back against bristled green plush, in the seat opposite the girl in beige. She looked as new as a peeled egg. Her hat, her fur, her frock, her gloves were glossy and stiff with novelty. On the arc of the thin, slippery sole of one beige shoe was gummed a tiny oblong of white paper, printed with the price set and paid for that slipper and its fellow, and the name of the shop that had dispensed them.

She had been staring raptly out of the window, drinking in the big weathered signboards that extolled the phenomena of codfish without bones and screens no rust could corrupt. As the young man sat down, she turned politely from the pane, met his eyes, started a smile and got it about half done, and rested her gaze just above his right shoulder.

'Well!' the young man said.
'Well!' she said.
'Well, here we are,' he said.
'Here we are,' she said. 'Aren't we?'
'I should say we were,' he said. 'Eeyop. Here we are.'
'Well!' she said.

161

'Well!' he said. 'Well. How does it feel to be an old married lady?'

'Oh, it's too soon to ask me that,' she said. 'At least – I mean. Well, I mean, goodness, we've only been married about three hours, haven't we?'

The young man studied his wrist-watch as if he were just acquiring the knack of reading time.

'We have been married,' he said, 'exactly two hours and twenty-six minutes.'

'My,' she said. 'It seems like longer.'

'No,' he said. 'It isn't hardly half-past six yet.'

'It seems like later,' she said. 'I guess it's because it starts getting dark so early.'

'It does, at that,' he said. 'The nights are going to be pretty long from now on. I mean. I mean – well, it starts getting dark early.'

'I didn't have any idea what time it was,' she said. 'Everything was so mixed up, I sort of don't know where I am, or what it's all about. Getting back from the church, and then all those people, and then changing all my clothes, and then everybody throwing things, and all. Goodness, I don't see how people do it every day.'

'Do what?' he said.

'Get married,' she said. 'When you think of all the people, all over the world, getting married just as if it was nothing. Chinese people and everybody. Just as if it wasn't anything.'

'Well, let's not worry about people all over the world,' he said. 'Let's don't think about a lot of Chinese. We've got something better to think about. I mean. I mean – well, what do we care about them?'

'I know,' she said. 'But I just sort of got to thinking of them, all of them, all over everywhere, doing it all the time. At least, I mean – getting married, you know. And it's – well, it's sort of such a big thing to do, it makes you feel queer. You think of them, all of them, all doing it just like it wasn't anything. And how does anybody know what's going to happen next?'

'Let them worry,' he said. 'We don't have to. We know darn well what's going to happen next. I mean. I mean – well, we know it's going to be great. Well, we know we're going to be happy. Don't we?'

'Oh, of course,' she said. 'Only you think of all the people, and you have to sort of keep thinking. It makes you feel funny. An awful lot of people that get married, it doesn't turn out so well. And I guess they all must have thought it was going to be great.'

'Come on, now,' he said. 'This is no way to start a honeymoon, with all this thinking going on. Look at us – all married and everything done. I mean. The wedding all done and all.'

'Ah, it was nice, wasn't it?' she said. 'Did you really like my veil?'

'You looked great,' he said. 'Just great.'

'Oh, I'm terribly glad,' she said. 'Ellie and Louise looked lovely, didn't they? I'm terribly glad they did finally decide on pink. They looked perfectly lovely.'

'Listen,' he said. 'I want to tell you something. When I was standing up there in that old church waiting for you to come up, and I saw those two bridesmaids, I thought to myself, I thought, "Well, I never knew Louise could look like that!" Why, she'd have knocked anybody's eye out.'

'Oh, really?' she said. 'Funny. Of course, everybody thought her dress and hat were lovely, but a lot of people seemed to think she looked sort of tired. People have been saying that a lot, lately. I tell them I think it's awfully mean of them to go around saying that about her. I tell them they've got to remember that Louise isn't so terribly young any more, and they've got to expect her to look like that. Louise can say she's twenty-three all she wants to, but she's a good deal nearer twenty-seven.'

'Well, she was certainly a knock-out at the wedding,' he said. 'Boy!'

'I'm terribly glad you thought so,' she said. 'I'm glad someone did. How did you think Ellie looked?'

'Why, I honestly didn't get a look at her,' he said.

'Oh, really?' she said. 'Well, I certainly think that's too bad. I don't suppose I ought to say it about my own sister, but I never saw anybody look as beautiful as Ellie looked today. And always so sweet and unselfish, too. And you didn't even notice her. But you never pay attention to Ellie, anyway. Don't think I haven't noticed it. It makes me feel just terrible. It makes me feel just awful, that you don't like my own sister.'

'I do like her,' he said. 'I'm crazy for Ellie. I think she's a great kid.'

'Don't think it makes any difference to Ellie!' she said. 'Ellie's got enough people crazy about her. It isn't anything to her whether you like her or not. Don't flatter yourself she cares! Only, the only thing is, it makes it awfully hard for me you don't like her, that's the only thing. I keep thinking, when we come back and get in that apartment and everything, it's going to be awfully hard for me that you won't want my own sister to come and see me. It's going to make it awfully hard for me that you won't ever want my family around. I know how you feel about my family. Don't think I haven't seen it. Only, if you don't ever want to see them, that's your loss. Not theirs. Don't flatter yourself!'

'Oh, now, come on!' he said. 'What's all this talk about not wanting your family around? Why, you know how I feel about your family. I think your old lady – I think your mother's swell. And Ellie. And your father. What's all this talk?'

'Well, I've seen it,' she said. 'Don't think I haven't. Lots of people they get married, and they think it's going to be great and everything, and then it all goes to pieces because people don't like people's families, or something like that. Don't tell me! I've seen it happen.'

'Honey,' he said, 'what is all this? What are you getting all angry about? Hey, look, this is our honeymoon. What are you trying to start a fight for? Ah, I guess you're just feeling sort of nervous.'

'Me?' she said. 'What have I got to be nervous about? I mean. I mean, goodness, I'm not nervous.'

'You know, lots of times,' he said, 'they say that girls get kind of nervous and yippy on account of thinking about – I mean. I mean – well, it's like you said, things are all so sort of mixed up and everything, right now. But afterwards, it'll be all right. I mean. I mean – well, look, honey, you don't look any too comfortable. Don't you want to take your hat off? And let's don't ever fight, ever. Will we?'

'Ah, I'm sorry I was cross,' she said. 'I guess I did feel a little bit funny. All mixed up, and then thinking of all those people all over everywhere, and then being sort of 'way off here, all alone with you. It's so sort of different. It's sort of such a big thing. You can't blame a person for thinking, can you? Yes, don't let's ever, ever fight. We won't be like a whole lot of them. We won't fight or be nasty or anything. Will we?'

'You bet your life we won't,' he said.

'I guess I will take this darned old hat off,' she said. 'It kind of presses. Just put it up on the rack, will you, dear? Do you like it, sweetheart?'

'Looks good on you,' he said.

'No, but I mean,' she said, 'do you really like it?'

'Well, I'll tell you,' he said. 'I know this is the new style and everything like that, and it's probably great. I don't know anything about things like that. Only I like the kind of a hat like that blue hat you had. Gee, I liked that hat.'

'Oh, really?' she said. 'Well, that's nice. That's lovely. The first thing you say to me, as soon as you get me off on a train away from my family and everything, is that you don't like my hat. The first thing you say to your wife is you think she has terrible taste in hats. That's nice, isn't it?'

'Now, honey,' he said, 'I never said anything like that. I only said –'

'What you don't seem to realize,' she said, 'is this hat cost twenty-two dollars. Twenty-two dollars. And that horrible old blue thing you think you're so crazy about, that cost three ninety-five.'

'I don't give a darn what they cost,' he said. 'I only said – I said I liked that blue hat. I don't know anything about hats. I'll be crazy about this one as soon as I get used to it. Only it's kind of not like your other hats. I don't know about the new styles. What do I know about women's hats?'

'It's too bad,' she said, 'you didn't marry somebody that would get the kind of hats you'd like. Hats that cost three ninety-five. Why didn't you marry Louise? You always think she looks so beautiful. You'd love her taste in hats. Why didn't you marry her?'

'Ah, now, honey,' he said. 'For heaven's sakes!'

'Why didn't you marry her?' she said. 'All you've done, ever since we got on this train, is talk about her. Here I've sat and sat, and just listened to you saying how wonderful Louise is. I suppose that's nice, getting me all off here alone with you, and then raving about Louise right in front of my face. Why didn't you ask her to marry you? I'm sure she would have jumped at the chance. There aren't so many people asking her to marry them. It's too bad you didn't marry her. I'm sure you'd have been much happier.'

'Listen, baby,' he said, 'while you're talking about things like

that, why didn't you marry Joe Brooks? I suppose he could have
given you all the twenty-two dollar hats you wanted, I suppose!'

'Well, I'm not so sure I'm not sorry I didn't,' she said. 'There!
Joe Brooks wouldn't have waited until he got me all off alone and
then sneered at my taste in clothes. Joe Brooks wouldn't ever hurt
my feelings. Joe Brooks has always been fond of me. There!'

'Yeah,' he said. 'He's fond of you. He was so fond of you he
didn't even send a wedding present. That's how fond of you he
was.'

'I happen to know for a fact,' she said, 'that he was away on
business, and as soon as he comes back he's going to give me
anything I want, for the apartment.'

'Listen,' he said. 'I don't want anything he gives you in our
apartment. Anything he gives you, I'll throw right out the window.
That's what I think of your friend Joe Brooks. And how do you
know where he is and what he's going to do, anyway? Has he been
writing to you?'

'I suppose my friends can correspond with me,' she said. 'I
didn't hear there was any law against that.'

'Well, I suppose they can't!' he said. 'And what do you think of
that? I'm not going to have my wife getting a lot of letters from
cheap traveling salesmen!'

'Joe Brooks is not a cheap traveling salesman!' she said. 'He is
not! He gets a wonderful salary.'

'Oh yeah?' he said. 'Where did you hear that?'

'He told me so himself,' she said.

'Oh, he told you so himself,' he said. 'I see. He told you so
himself.'

'You've got a lot of right to talk about Joe Brooks,' she said.
'You and your friend Louise. All you ever talk about is Louise.'

'Oh, for heaven's sakes!' he said. 'What do I care about Louise?
I just thought she was a friend of yours, that's all. That's why I
ever even noticed her.'

'Well, you certainly took an awful lot of notice of her today,' she
said. 'On our wedding day! You said yourself when you were
standing there in the church you just kept thinking of her. Right up
at the altar. Oh, right in the presence of God! And all you thought
about was Louise.'

'Listen, honey,' he said, 'I never should have said that. How does anybody know what kind of crazy things come into their heads when they're standing there waiting to get married? I was just telling you that because it was so kind of crazy. I thought it would make you laugh.'

'I know,' she said. 'I've been all sort of mixed up today, too. I told you that. Everything so strange and everything. And me all the time thinking about all those people all over the world, and now us here all alone, and everything. I know you get all mixed up. Only I did think, when you kept talking about how beautiful Louise looked, you did it with malice and forethought.'

'I never did anything with malice and forethought!' he said. 'I just told you that about Louise because I thought it would make you laugh.'

'Well, it didn't,' she said.

'No, I know it didn't,' he said. 'It certainly did not. Ah, baby, and we ought to be laughing, too. Hell, honey lamb, this is our honeymoon. What's the matter?'

'I don't know,' she said. 'We used to squabble a lot when we were going together and then engaged and everything, but I thought everything would be so different as soon as you were married. And now I feel so sort of strange and everything. I feel so sort of alone.'

'Well, you see, sweetheart,' he said, 'we're not really married yet. I mean. I mean – well, things will be different afterwards. Oh, hell. I mean, we haven't been married very long.'

'No,' she said.

'Well, we haven't got much longer to wait now,' he said. 'I mean – well, we'll be in New York in about twenty minutes. Then we can have dinner, and sort of see what we feel like doing. Or I mean. Is there anything special you want to do tonight?'

'What?' she said.

'What I mean to say,' he said, 'would you like to go to a show or something?'

'Why, whatever you like,' she said. 'I sort of didn't think people went to theaters and things on their – I mean, I've got a couple of letters I simply must write. Don't let me forget.'

'Oh,' he said. 'You're going to write letters tonight?'

'Well, you see,' she said. 'I've been perfectly terrible. What with all the excitement and everything. I never did thank poor old Mrs

Sprague for her berry spoon, and I never did a thing about those book ends the McMasters sent. It's just too awful of me. I've got to write them this very night.'

'And when you've finished writing your letters,' he said, 'maybe I could get you a magazine or a bag of peanuts.'

'What?' she said.

'I mean,' he said, 'I wouldn't want you to be bored.'

'As if I could be bored with you!' she said. 'Silly! Aren't we married? Bored!'

'What I thought,' he said, 'I thought when we got in, we could go right up to the Biltmore and anyway leave our bags, and maybe have a little dinner in the room, kind of quiet, and then do whatever we wanted. I mean. I mean – well, let's go right up there from the station.'

'Oh, yes, let's,' she said. 'I'm so glad we're going to the Biltmore. I just love it. The twice I've stayed in New York we've always stayed there. Papa and Mamma and Ellie and I, and I was crazy about it. I always sleep so well there. I go right off to sleep the minute I put my head on the pillow.'

'Oh, you do?' he said.

'At least, I mean,' she said. 'Way up high it's so quiet.'

'We might go to some show or other tomorrow night instead of tonight,' he said. 'Don't you think that would be better?'

'Yes, I think it might,' she said.

He rose, balanced a moment, crossed over and sat down beside her.

'Do you really have to write those letters tonight?' he said.

'Well,' she said, 'I don't suppose they'd get there any quicker than if I wrote them tomorrow.'

There was a silence with things going on in it.

'And we won't ever fight any more, will we?' he said.

'Oh, no,' she said. 'Not ever! I don't know what made me do like that. It all got so sort of funny, sort of like a nightmare, the way I got thinking of all those people getting married all the time; and so many of them, everything spoils on account of fighting and everything. I got all mixed up thinking about them. Oh, I don't want to be like them. But we won't be, will we?'

'Sure we won't,' he said.

'We won't go all to pieces,' she said. 'We won't fight. It'll all be

168

different, now we're married. It'll all be lovely. Reach me down my hat, will you, sweetheart? It's time I was putting it on. Thanks. Ah, I'm so sorry you don't like it.'

'I do so like it!' he said.

'You said you didn't,' she said. 'You said you thought it was perfectly terrible.'

'I never said any such thing,' he said. 'You're crazy.'

'All right, I may be crazy,' she said. 'Thank you very much. But that's what you said. Not that it matters – it's just a little thing. But it makes you feel pretty funny to think you've gone and married somebody that says you have perfectly terrible taste in hats. And then goes and says you're crazy, beside.'

'Now, listen here,' he said. 'Nobody said any such thing. Why, I love that hat. The more I look at it the better I like it. I think it's great.'

'That isn't what you said before,' she said.

'Honey,' he said. 'Stop it, will you? What do you want to start all this for? I love the damned hat. I mean, I love your hat. I love anything you wear. What more do you want me to say?'

'Well, I don't want you to say it like that,' she said.

'I said I think it's great,' he said. 'That's all I said.'

'Do you really?' she said. 'Do you honestly? Ah, I'm so glad. I'd hate you not to like my hat. It would be – I don't know, it would be sort of such a bad start.'

'Well, I'm crazy for it,' he said. 'Now we've got that settled, for heaven's sakes. Ah, baby. Baby lamb. We're not going to have any bad starts. Look at us – we're on our honeymoon. Pretty soon we'll be regular old married people. I mean. I mean, in a few minutes we'll be getting in to New York, and then we'll be going to the hotel, and then everything will be all right. I mean – well, look at us! Here we are married! Here we are!'

'Yes, here we are,' she said. 'Aren't we?'

COLETTE

Journey's End

'Well I never! Who'd'ave thought our paths would ever cross again! How long is it now since I last set eyes on you! Why, Marseilles of course, remember? You were on tour with the Pitard Company, and I with the Dubois. We both played the same night. It was up to our group not to be outdone by yours, and vice versa. That didn't stop us going out to have a bite together that night, shellfish, eh! on the terrace, at Basso's.

'. . . No, you've not changed much, I must say. You've looked after number one, all right; you're lucky! Your digestion's been your saving, but if you'd got thirteen years of touring in your system, like me, you wouldn't be looking so nifty!

'Yes, go ahead, you can tell me I've changed! At forty-six, it's a bit hard having to play duenna parts, when there are so many skittish youngsters of fifty and sixty to be seen footling about in juvenile leads on the Grands Boulevards, who'll throw up their parts, as likely as not, if there's a brat of over twelve in the cast! It was Saigon knocked me out, and long before my time too. I sang in operetta at Saigon, I did, in a theatre lit by eight hundred oil lamps!

'. . . And what else? Well, apart from that, there's not much to tell. I go on "touring", like so many others. I keep saying I've had enough of it, and this'll be the last time I'll do it; I go on saying to all who'll listen that I'd rather be a theatre attendant or travel in perfumery. So what? Here I am back again with Pitard, and you're back with Pitard too. We came back to find work, and it's noses to the grindstone once again.

'. . . I don't need you to tell me that prices have dropped all around. If it got about what I'm working for this time, my

170

reputation would be gone. It really seems as if they think we don't need to eat when on tour.

'Not to mention that I've got my sister with me, you know. It may make two on the payroll but it means two mouths to feed. Oh, she's taken to the life right enough, the poor kid; she's got guts! More guts than health, if you ask me! She'll tackle any part. Take the time when we had a fifty-day contract with the Miral Touring Company, in a mixed bill of three plays nightly: the child took the part of the maid who lays the table in the first – ten lines; then an old peasant woman who tells everyone a few home truths – two hundred lines; and to end up, a girl of seventeen married off against her will who never stops crying throughout. Just think of the poor thing having to cope with all those changes of make-up!

'And for starvation fees, too, I'll have you know! On top of that we had the doctor's and chemist's bills to pay – it was the winter, my bronchitis was so bad – not to mention the nurse's charge for cupping, thirty-seven francs' worth! I went on rehearsing with forty cups on my back and so hid the fact I was suffering. When I was seized by a fit of coughing, I rushed off to the lav, otherwise they'd have replaced me within the hour, you bet!

'I was able to get away, but doctors and their drugs had ruined me in advance. It was then the child began to knit woollen garments, you know, those loose coatees that are fashionable just now, with a little woollen jumper to match. She works when we're travelling, on the train; she's got the knack of it. When we're in for a journey, eight or nine hours by rail, she'll reel off a coatee in four days and post it off at once to a firm in Paris.

' ... Yes, yes, I know, you've got the music hall to keep you going. There's still a living to be made in the halls; but what d'you suppose there's left for me? They'll bury my bones on one of these tours, and believe me, I'm not the only one ... Oh, I'm not trying to plead constant illness, you know. I still have my good moments; I was happy-go-lucky enough when young! If only my liver let me alone for three weeks, or if my cough left off for a fortnight, or the blessed varicose veins didn't make my left leg weigh so heavy, then I'd be my old self again!

'If, granted that, I chanced on a few good companions, not too mangy a lot, but sporty, who don't spend their lives harping on their woes and retailing their maladies and confinements, then I promise you I'd soon get my fair share of fun again.

'Provided, of course, I'm not laid out like Marizot . . . didn't you know? It wasn't in the papers, but the story might have come your way. We were . . . now, where were we? . . . in Belgium, in pouring rain. We'd just finished a passable dinner, that is, my sister and I, Marizot and Jacquard. Marizot goes out first, while we stay behind to settle the bill. You know how short-sighted he is. He misses his way, and off he goes down a dark narrow street, and there at the end was a stream, a river, I don't know, the Scheldt, or something: to be brief, he falls into the water and gets carried away. They only found him two days later. It all happened so quick that the first night after, we hadn't even begun to feel sad, believe me! It wasn't till the next night, when the under-manager played Marizot's part, that we all began to get weepy and cried on the stage . . .

'Anyhow, people don't drown every day, thank God! We did find some consolation at the time of the railway strike. Yes, and it played us a most unusual trick. Listen to this: we ended up the tour with *Fiasco* – the devil of a title – and the night before we'd played it in Rouen. When we reach Mantes, the train stops. "All change! Everyone to leave the train! We go no farther!" The strike was on! Off I went to have a good moan. I had acute liver trouble, rheumatism in my left leg, a high temperature, the whole boiling. I sat down on a bench in the waiting room, saying to myself, "After a knock like this nothing will get me to budge again, my luck's right out, I'd rather die on the spot!" Jacquard was there, same as ever, with his big overcoat and his pipe, and he comes up to me and says, "Why don't you just go home. You'd better take the Pigalle-Halle-aux-vins bus, which drops you on your doorstep."

'"Oh, leave me in peace!" I give him for answer. "Have you no heart at all? Here we are, stuck for Lord knows how long by this filthy strike? D'you think I get much fun out of spending my miserable salary on drugs and digs, eh! I'd like you to be standing in my shoes and then see what you'd do in my place!"

'"In your place?" he says. "In your place I'd take the Pigalle-Halle-aux-vins bus."

'I could have cried with rage, dearie. I could have struck him, that Jacquard, with his pipe and his wooden mug! I flayed him alive with my tongue! When I'm finished, he takes me by the arm and forcibly leads me to the glass door. And what d'you suppose I see in the station-yard? *Pigalle-Halle-aux-vins*, dearie! *Pigalle*, in so many words! Three Pigalle buses, which had been used to bring along another troupe that very morning! And there they were, having a soft drink, right in front of that station at Mantes!

'I started to giggle, not but what my liver was killing me, and on I giggled till I thought I would never stop. And the best of it was that we went back to Paris in *Pigalle-Halle-aux-vins*, dearie, by the special authority of the sub-prefect. It cost us a bit more than two and a half francs, but what a time we all had! Jacquard and Marval sat on the top deck and threw down sausage skins to us inside, and you should have seen the faces of the "bystanders"! That alone was worth the whole trip!

'And what a shaking we had, I felt as if my liver were being torn from my body at every jolt! It might well have been worse, for I laughed the whole length of the way, and that's always something to the good!

'And when all's said and done, as Jacquard put it, "What are speed and altitude records to the likes of us? Give me a nice little bus ride *Mantes–Paris* on a *Pigalle-Halle-aux-vins* every time! There's an endurance test quite out of the ordinary!"'

JEANETTE WINTERSON

✍

The Lives of Saints

That day we saw three Jews in full-length black coats and black hats standing on identical stools looking into the funnel of a pasta machine. One stepped down from his little stool and went to the front where the pasta was stretching out in orange strands. He took two strands and held them up high so that they dropped against his coat. He looked as if he'd been decorated with medal ribbon.

They bought the machine. The Italian boys in T-shirts carried it to the truck. They bought the machine because they wanted to make pasta like ringlets to sell in their shop. Their shop sold sacred food and the blinds were always half-drawn. The floor was just boards, not polished, and the glass counter stood chest high. They served together in their hats and coats. They wrapped things in greaseproof paper. They did this every day except Saturday and after the machine came they made pasta too. They lined the top of the glass counter with wooden trays and they lined the wooden trays with greaseproof paper. Then they laid out the ringlets of fusilli in colours they liked, liking orange best in memory of the first day. The shop was dark but for the pasta that glowed and sang from the machine.

It is true that on bright days we are happy. This is true because the sun on the eyelids effects a chemical change in the body. The sun also diminishes the pupils to pinpricks, letting the light in less. When we can hardly see we are most likely to fall in love. Nothing is commoner in summer than love and I hesitate to tell you of the commonplace, but I have only one story and this is it.

In the shop where the Jews stood in stone relief like Shadrach, Meshach and Abednego in the fiery furnace, there was a woman

174

who liked to do her shopping in 4ozs. Even the pasta that fell from the scales in flaming waterfalls trickled into her bag. I was always behind her, coming in from the hot streets to the cool dark that hit like a church. What did she do with her tiny parcels laid in lines on the glass top? Before she paid for them, she always counted them; if there were not sixteen she asked for something else and if there were more than sixteen she had a thing taken away.

I began following her. To begin with I followed just a little way, then, as my obsession grew, I followed in ever-increasing circles from the shop to her home, through the park past the hospital. I lost all sense of time and space and sometimes it seemed to me that I was in the desert or the jungle and still following. Sometimes we were aboriginal in our arcane pathways and other times we walked one street.

I say we. She was oblivious of me. To begin with I kept a respectful distance. I walked on the other side of the road. Then because she never noticed, I got closer and closer, close enough to see that she coloured her hair. The shade was not constant. One day her skirt had a hanging thread and I cut it off without disturbing her. At last I started to walk beside her. We fell in step without the least difficulty. And still she gave no sign of my presence. I began to wonder about myself and took to carrying a mirror to see if I was still there. So far we had walked side by side in silence. Eventually I said, 'Did you know that parrots are left-handed? This is very rare in the animal kingdom. Most creatures are right-handed like us.'

She said nothing and I dredged my mind for things that might please her.

From that day I told her everything I knew. The origin of The Magic Carpet, the nature of cities that last only one day and disappear at nightfall, the register of notes available to a frog during courtship and every story I could remember, including the shortest story in the world. It is by a Guatemalan writer called Augusto Monterroso, *'Cuando desperto, el dinosauro todavía estaba alli.'* (When I woke up, the dinosaur was still there.) Just as Scheherazade prevented her death, so I prolonged our life together with my stories. I bound us head to foot in words.

Nothing I said had any effect. I felt like Marco Polo who criss-crossed the world searching for a single treasure to please Kublai

Khan. The Great Khan was not interested in the Silk Road or the cedar forests he owned. Rich beyond measure, he desired something he could not possess. Only one thing could please him and he did not know what that thing was. Polo brought home intricate and fabulous toys and shamans who could teach the emperor how to fly. But when the emperor died, old and exhausted, he knew the world had eluded him.

I rummaged through the out-of-print sections in second-hand bookshops and spent all my spare time in the library. I learned astronomy and mathematics and studied the drawings of Leonardo da Vinci in order to explain how a watermill worked. I was so impatient to tell her all I had discovered that I started waiting for her outside her house. Eventually I knocked on the door and knocked on the door at 7 a.m. sharp every morning after that. She was always ready. In winter she carried a torch.

After a few months we were spending the whole of each day together. I made sandwiches for our lunch. She never questioned my choice of filling, though I noticed she usually threw away the ones with sardine.

St Teresa of Avila: 'I have no defence against affection. I could be bribed with a sardine.'

So it is with me, for whom kindness has always been a surprise. In the lives of saints I look for confirmation of excess. To them it is not strange to spend the nights on a mountain or to forgo food. For them the visionary and the everyday coincide. Above all they have no domestic virtues, preferring intensity to comfort. Despite their inhospitable ways they ferment with unexpected life like those bleak railway cuttings that host horizontal dandelions. They know there is no passion without pain.

As I told her this, as I had told her so many things, she turned to me and said, 'Sixteen years ago I lived in a hot country with my husband, who was important. We had servants and three children. There was a young man who worked for us. I used to watch his body through the window.

'In the house we lived such clean lives, always washed and talcumed against the sweat. Not the heat of the day nor the heavy night could unsettle us. We knew how to dress. One evening when the boards were creaking with the weather he came to us where we sat eating small biscuits and dropped two baskets of limes on the floor. He was so tired that he spilt the baskets and went on his knees under my husband's feet. I looked down and saw my husband's black socks within his black shoes. His toe kicked at a lime. I ducked under the table collecting what I could and I could smell the young man smelling of the day and the sun. My husband crossed his legs and I heard him say, "No need for that, Jane."

'Later, when we put out the lamps and I went to my room and Stephen went to his, my armpits were wet and my face looked as though I'd been drinking. I knew he'd come. I took my nightgown on and off four or five times wondering how to greet him. It didn't matter. Not then or afterwards. Not any of the two months that followed. My heart swelled. I had a whale's heart. The arteries of a whale's heart are so wide that a child could crawl through. I found I was pregnant.

'On the night I told him he told me he had to go away. He asked me to go with him and I looked at the verandah and the lamps and Stephen's door that was closed and the children's door that was slightly ajar. I looked at his body. I said I had to stay and he put his head on my stomach and cried. On the day he left I lay in my room and when I heard his flight coming over the house I wrapped my head in a towel. Stephen opened the door and said, "Are you staying?" I said I was. He said, "Never mention this again." I never did. Not that or anything else.'

We walked on in silence. We walked through the hours of the day until we arrived at nightfall and came to a castle protected by a moat. Lions guarded the gateway. 'I'm going in now,' she said.

I looked up from my thoughts and saw an ordinary house fronted by a pretty garden and a pair of tabbies washing their paws. Which was the story and which was real? Could it be true that a woman who had not spoken for sixteen years except to order her food was now walking into this small house full of everyday things? Was it not more likely that she would disappear into her magic kingdom and leave me on the other side of the water, my throat clogged with feelings that resist words?

I followed her across the moat and saw our reflections in the water. I wanted to reach down and scoop her in my arms, let her run over my body until both of us were wet through. I wanted to swim inside her. We crossed the moat and she fed me on boiled cabbage. I have heard it is a cure for gout. She never spoke as we

ate and afterwards she took a candle and took me upstairs. I was
surprised to see a mosquito net in England.

Time is not constant and time in stories least of all. Anyone can
fall asleep and lose generations in their dreams. The night I spent
with her has taken up my whole life and now I live attached to
myself like a codicil. It is not because I lack interests; indeed, I have
recently reworked Leonardo's drawings and built for myself a very
fine watermill. It is simply that being with her allowed me to be
myself. There was no need to live normally. Now, I know so many
stories and such a collection of strange things and I wonder who
would like them since I cannot do them justice on my own. The
heart of a whale is the height of a man . . .

I left her at dawn. The street was quiet, only a cat and the electric
whirr of a milk van. I kept looking back at the candle in the
window until it was as far away as the faint point of a fading star.
In the early sky all the stars had faded by the time I got home.
There was the retreating shape of the moon and nothing more.

Every day I went to the shop where the Jews stood in stone relief
and I bought things that pleased me. I took my time, time being
measured in 4ozs. She never came in. I waited outside her house for
some years until a 'FOR SALE' sign appeared and a neighbour told
me the woman next door had vanished. I felt such pleasure then, to
know that she was wandering the world and that one day, one day,
I might find her again. When I do, all the stories that are folded into
this one can be shaken out and let loose. But until then, like the
lives of saints, more is contained than can be revealed. The world
itself will roll up like a scroll taking time and space away. All
stories end here.

BERYL MARKHAM

🖋

Something I Remember

When I think about it, it seems to me that in twenty-odd years of breeding and training racehorses, I ought to have encountered at least one with human qualities. I have read about such horses but I have never known one and I can't help feeling a little cheated. Whenever I have heard someone say, 'Now there's a horse so intelligent he's almost human,' I have had to admit to myself a little sadly that no horse I can bring to memory ever deserved that laudatory phrase. Of course, it may be that such a comparison is, to a horse, of doubtful virtue. That was certainly the case with Wee MacGregor.

Wee MacGregor maintained throughout his life a gentle contempt for both men and the works of men, and I am convinced that his willing response to their demands was born wholly of tolerance. He rarely ignored a word or resisted a hand; and it was not until he began his blood feud with Chaldean that anyone realized the intensity of the fire that burned in his heart.

Wee MacGregor was an Arab. His coat was chestnut, and his mane and tail were black, and he wore a white star on his forehead – jauntily and a little to one side, more or less as an impudent street urchin might wear his cap. He was an urchin, too, by the standards prevailing in our stables. He was perfectly built but very small, and though he was a stallion, he was not bought to breed, certainly not to race, but only to work at carrying myself or my father – and even, if need be, to draw a pony cart. I still remember the day he came.

Horses were always coming and going on our farm in Kenya. Some arrived for training, and others left for the races at Nairobi,

179

Eldoret, Nakuru, or even Durban, more than two thousand miles away. Until the advent of Wee MacGregor, they were all thoroughbreds of course and, to the uninitiated, they must have looked alike, except for colour. They were tall, tense horses of supreme arrogance and insolent beauty. They were pampered, they were groomed, they were cherished like the heirs to so many thrones.

They were, I am afraid, a snobbish clique, for when Wee MacGregor was led for the first time to his stall (in the lesser stable) he was greeted with silence. Not even a stallion raised his voice, and the brood mares in their spacious boxes scarcely stirred. There may have been other reasons for it, but the controlled dismay with which our thoroughbreds looked upon Wee MacGregor was, in effect, similar to the way a gathering of the socially illustrious might view the arrival in their midst of a labourer with calloused hands.

Nevertheless, in the days that followed, the little Arab worked hard and kept his peace; he toiled with patience and gave everyone to understand that he bore no grudge and that his was a placid soul. He was intelligent, he handled beautifully, he refused no effort asked of him, and it may have been that if Chaldean had not come to the farm, we would never have been disillusioned about Wee MacGregor's pacific nature. But Chaldean did come – and on a bad day, too.

We were clearing the trees from our farm – or rather we were fighting the great Mau forest, which, in its centuries of unhampered growth, had raised a rampart of trees so tall I used to think their branches brushed the sky. The trees were cedar, olive, yew, and bamboo, and often the cedars rose to heights of two hundred feet, blocking the sun.

Men said the forest could not be beaten, and this was true, but at least my father made it retreat. Under his command, a corps of Dutchmen with hundreds of oxen and an axe to every man assaulted the bulwark, day after day, and in time its outer walls began to fall.

On one such day, my father said to me, 'Get Wee MacGregor and take this note to Mostert. The rains are due, and I don't want the teams bogged in the forest.'

Christiaan Mostert was our foreman and when, an hour later, he took my father's message from my hand and read it, he looked upward involuntarily, but he could not see the sky.

'Ja,' he said, 'I see nothing, but I think the baas is right. I smell rain, and the monkeys have lost their tongues.'

He spat on his hands and shouted an order, but it was too late. Thunder swallowed his voice, and rain swallowed the forest. It was a typical equatorial storm – instantaneous, violent, and all-encompassing. It made the world black, then split the blackness with knives of light. It made the great trees creak and the bamboos moan. Forest hogs ran for cover, terrified parrots darted in green and scarlet arcs through the lightning, and the oxen plunged and strained in their traces.

It was not a new thing for Christiaan Mostert, or for any of his men, or for me. It was new for Wee MacGregor, and yet the little Arab took the whole monstrous nightmare in his stride. He neither reared nor even trembled, and as I rode him from ox team to ox team through the roaring forest aisles, his manner was one of dutiful resignation.

Even when a massive cedar, ripped by lightning, fell across a span of oxen and broke the backs of two, he did not wince; and when Christiaan Mostert put rifle bullets into the suffering beasts, Wee MacGregor only tilted his ears in mild curiosity, as if the insanity of his masters had begun to bore him.

For an hour he worked, disdainful even of the storm, lending his strength to a bogged wagon more than once, carrying me back and forth with Mostert's orders to his men; and when the storm ended as abruptly as it had begun, Wee MacGregor met Chaldean for the first time.

Chaldean had arrived that day from England. He stood, bristling arrogance, blanketed and angry-eyed in the broad space between our stables. My father was there, standing proudly beside him, and a dozen syces and farm boys, marvelling at his beauty.

It was more than beauty. It was pride in heritage and conscious-ness of ability, for Chaldean's breeding and his record were clean as fire. He was a descendant of St Simon, and a champion, and his colts were champions and he knew it.

He was black and smooth as a rifle barrel, and as hard. The cast of his head was classic. He was deep-chested and clean-legged and the promise of a magnificent stride lay in his height and in the power of his quarters. He was to Wee MacGregor as a Doric column to a beam of wood, and he clothed his beauty in insolence.

Wee MacGregor felt it. Straight from his labours in the forest, still wet with the rain that mingled with his sweat, he raised his head and looked upon this pampered paragon – and trembled. He let a low sound escape his throat, and Chaldean heard it.

For a moment, the two horses – one a drudge and one a prince – regarded each other, and then Chaldean whirled on his tether and reared from the ground and screamed the shrill scream of an angered stallion. He rose higher, against my father's strength, and beat the air with his forelegs and screamed again. My father swore and jerked him down, and the syces ran forward to hold him.

Wee MacGregor plunged, but I held him back. He fought the bridle, but I turned him. It did not last long, but it was not finished. I knew then, as I rode to the stable, that the giant thoroughbred and the little Arab had made their quarrel and what remained was only the settling of it.

Still, under the pressure of regular work, you forget such things. If you have a stable of fifty horses, you have not time to concern yourself with the grudges and foibles of one or two. You remember certain rules and you follow them. The rule that two warring stallions must never meet is axiomatic – so self-evident that you take it for granted that they never will.

My days passed, and when on occasion I had to use Wee MacGregor again on some routine duty or other, it did not seem to me that anything about him had changed. He brooded a lot, the way some horses do, or appear to do, and often I would find him in his stall standing in the farthest corner, out of the light, staring at the wall and seeing nothing.

It is true that once or twice I noticed that the wooden latch on his door had been partly slipped back, but there again I thought nothing of it because many horses will, out of boredom, fondle a latch with their teeth or toy with a halter rope. I always shot the latch home and forgot about it.

When Rêve d'Or came to the farm, Chaldean's ego began to assert itself to such an extent that at times he was almost beyond control. Rêve d'Or was a whaler filly (that is to say, an Australian thoroughbred filly), a dark bay and beautiful in the eyes of horsemen, but I never knew why her daily passage down the area-way between Chaldean's stable and Wee MacGregor's should have brought their vendetta to the white heat that it did; there were dozens of other mares and fillies on the place.

It may have been that, in fact, she was wholly forgotten by both of them once they had established a new reason for their enmity, but however that was, her groom never led her past the stables without drawing from the little Arab and the haughty thoroughbred screams of mutual rage and hatred. It ought to have been obvious to everybody that one day this burning bitterness must bring a climax, but no one thought about it.

It was not so long a time that Rêve d'Or had a lovely foal, and Chaldean (since he was of St Simon strain) was, of course, its sire. Horse breeders are not given to romanticism in their work but rather to considerations of profit and loss, and a colt by Chaldean out of Rêve d'Or gave great expectations to my father and to those horse-wise friends who frequented our house.

It is a strange but a true thing that the appearance of a new foal in a stable will always excite the stallions and even the geldings to the most exorbitant antics. They will neigh and scream and beat against their boxes in a kind of wild gaiety. If they are in pasture, they will gallop its length time and again, kicking their heels, drumming out the good word with swift and sparkling hooves like tireless performers at a week-long jubilee. No birthdays go unheralded. And yet, in the case of Rêve d'Or's foal, Wee MacGregor was a silent bystander.

This, I suppose, was due to his breeding. Arabs are not so excitable as thoroughbreds, and Wee MacGregor was valued all the more for his steady (if increasingly dour) character. He had even got to the point where he no longer returned Chaldean's insults, but only stood and glared at his enemy from the darkest depths of his stall. He worked hard while Chaldean basked in the sun; he arrived home clotted with sweat while Chaldean fretted under the ministrations of some diligent syce; his feet were left unshod for labour while Chaldean's were deftly plated for glory on the track. We forgot, but Wee MacGregor remembered these things. He hoarded the memories until his heart was full of them and would hold no more.

It is a hideous thing to watch two stallions fight. If you are on the back of one, it is terrifying.

For many months, not a morning had passed on which Wee MacGregor had not seen me mount Chaldean and ride him away to his exercise. For many months, I had forgotten the half-open latch on Wee MacGregor's door, I had forgotten that patience and practice make for perfection. Nowadays I can only believe that Wee MacGregor knew it from the first.

He caught us not far from the house. The path we always took wandered through a wattle grove that had a clearing in it. It was a big clearing surrounded by trees and shaded by their lacelike leaves and yellow blossoms. The earth underneath was red clay and hard. It was so hard that it gave a kind of ring to Wee MacGregor's hooves – a bold and forthright ring, for he used no cunning in his attack; he did not come from behind.

He came straight for his enemy, not cantering or rushing headlong, but lifting his firm little legs high and proudly, making taut the bow of his neck, flaunting his black tail like a battle plume. Nor were his ears laid back in anger. They were alert, anticipant, and eager – as if this, at last, were the joyful moment he had dreamt of all his quiet life.

I remember that the little scraps of sunlight fallen through the leaves lay on his chestnut coat and burnished it like armour; I remember that his eyes were bright. I remember, too, that Chaldean swung round with graceful majesty to face this puny David and his shining courage. I could feel Chaldean's muscles harden; I could feel his veins swell to rigid ropes beneath his skin. I could hear the first notes of his battle cry, deep and low in his throat, and I looked around me.

Through the trees I could see our house, but it was far. No one was near – not my father, not a syce, not a farm-hand. I might have dismounted, but you do not abandon a valuable horse to his fury; you do not throw away the rules. You hang on – and tremble. I hung on. I trembled. The two stallions were alone in their anger and I was alone in my fear.

When Wee MacGregor charged, when Chaldean screamed his challenge, when blood spurted on my clothes and on my bare arms, and the cyclones of dust hid all but trenchant teeth and hooves like iron cudgels, my fear was frozen still – and I was a forgotten watcher.

I watched the little Arab's first lunge. He came in, head outstretched, swift as a sword, using only his teeth – flashing his teeth – hoping to cripple Chaldean's foreleg. He was fearless. He was quick, and in this quickness he was deadly.

Chaldean went to his knees, parrying the thrust and screaming his war cry with what seemed the volume of a thousand trembling trumpets. The vibrations of that cry ran through my body.

Chaldean went down. He struck his shoulder on a root, gashing the flesh, adding crimson to our vortex of whirling colour, but he rose again with inspired fury. He reared high, while I clung to him, and he caught the Arab on the flank, striking both blood and pain as a smith strikes fire from steel.

I suppose I cried out. I suppose I flailed my whip and let the reins cut my tugging hands. I was alone and not yet fifteen, and it may even have been that I wept, but these are things I don't remember. I only remember the sudden realization of the terrible power, the destruc've strength that can pour from the sinews of this most docile of animals, this nodding slave of men.

Wee MacGregor fought with so cold a determination that he made almost no sound. It was clear at once that he wanted not just to win but to kill. It was clear, too, that he felt that his anger compensated for his lack of size.

Chaldean towered above him. He had advantages and he used them. He reared until the Arab was beneath him, then plunged and sank his teeth into Wee MacGregor's neck and held fast and reared again and hurled his enemy from him into the dust and blood; and there was a moment of silence.

There was a moment of silence as the little Arab found his legs and stood sucking breath into his lungs. The wound on his neck was deep and it was scarlet, but it might have been no wound at all. He gave no sign of pain.

For a frantic instant, I tried to turn Chaldean, to drive him home, but he would not budge. He knew what was coming, and it came.

If Wee MacGregor had fought viciously before, he fought insanely now. He came in with eyes like burning coals, and I tried to beat him off, but for him, I was not there. For him, nothing existed save his anger and his enemy. Abandoning caution, he closed, and the impact almost threw me from the saddle.

Again Chaldean caught him by the neck and hurled him bleeding to the ground, and again he rose, staggering a little now, but not hesitating. His courage was like a shield that beat away the thought of fear. Three times he came on and three times he fell before Chaldean's strength and fury. But on the fourth try, he found his moment.

I do not know how it happened, but somehow in the maelstrom of screams and dust and thudding hooves, the little Arab caught in his teeth a strip of the pressure bandage bound around Chaldean's foreleg. The bandage had come undone. It was like a net, and the Arab meant to make it one. He held it firmly in his teeth and pulled, and Chaldean was helpless. He pawed and plunged and tottered and swayed, fighting to free himself. There was panic in him – and I prepared to leap from his back at last. It seemed madness to hang on for, if he fell, I should fall with him – perhaps under him.

I beat Wee MacGregor with my whip, sparing no strength, lashing his head and his neck and his withers, but he was aware of nothing save the promise of triumph. His teeth clamped tight on the bandage, he threw the whole power of his body into the effort of downing his enemy.

Chaldean faltered. He was trapped, and the Arab knew it. I knew it. I put my hands on the pommel and made ready to throw myself clear, I could hear voices coming up the road, but now there was not time. It was too late.

I was raising myself from the saddle when the bandage broke in Wee MacGregor's teeth. The ripping of the cloth and Chaldean's lunge were simultaneous. So, almost, was my own cry and Wee MacGregor's single shriek of pain when Chaldean's teeth closed on the little Arab's foreleg, twisting it, breaking the bone as if it were a stalk of corn. Chaldean reared high and, for the last time, threw his challenger to earth.

The Arab lay almost still, but he was not dead, and Chaldean would not have it so. Not I, but his rage was master. Wee MacGregor tried once more to rise, but the bone of his leg was broken through. David was down, and Goliath moved forward to kill him, but he did not.

My father had come, and with him, his men. They had bound grass to sticks and made torches of them and now they beat Chaldean back with fire. They thrust the fire in his face and beat him back, step by step, and shouted at him, and I gathered the reins tight in my hands, which were bleeding now, and urged him home at last, down the dusty road, not bothering to hold my tears.

Most times you destroy a crippled horse, but Wee MacGregor was made to live, though he never worked again. He was brought home on a rope stretcher and for weeks he stood in his stall supported by a sling until, in time, he walked once more, with halting steps.

Of course, he was never any trouble after that; he could not have been. He was pensioned, as faithful horses often are, and he never again slipped the latch of his stall – or at least not more than once.

One day, or rather at the end of one day, when the sun was almost gone and I rode Rêve d'Or through the clearing in the wattle grove, we came upon the little Arab standing still as marble in what had been the arena of his great defeat. He was older then, and the fire had gone from his eye, and his chestnut coat was dull in the horizontal light. But there he stood, looking not at Rêve d'Or and not at me, but at the earth, and we passed him by. He did not whinny or make any sound or lift his head. He only stood there like a man with a dream.

But of course that was only the way it seemed to me. Horses are not like humans – at least no horse that I have ever known – and I suspect that he had come there only to catch the last warmth of the sun. I don't know, and so I can't be sure. It is all just something I remember.

ELIZABETH BOWEN

❦

Love

It was a funny experience, it was really – not like a thing that happened, more like a dream. Sometimes I think I did dream it – for all I can get out of Edna, I might have done. It's like Edna to put the whole thing on me – she does that by keeping on saying nothing. So of course I can never refer to it. And I don't know that I want to – not to Edna. Anyhow, Edna's shut up, just like a clam.

The minute we came round the rocks into that bay I felt there was something ... The day, with that sea glare and at the same time no sun, made everything look unnatural, and we were dead beat. We'd kept slogging along in that loose sand: our shoes were full of it. For miles we hadn't seen anything you could call anything – only rocks, and slopes coming down, and the same sea. So when we came round that rock and saw the hotel, it gave us quite a shock. The bay was ever so narrow, it looked private; the hotel stood back but sand came right up to it. There was a sort of jetty, but that had rotted. The hotel must have been pink, with a name painted across it, but the name and the colour had faded right out. All the shutters were up, but for one window: it looked like a dead person winking at you. I never did like being stared at. I said, 'Why, Edna, it's shut up.'

She said, 'Well, it *is* a poor-looking place!'

The hotel (I can see it now) had only two storeys, but it was quite long. And at one side they'd tacked on a sort of a wooden annexe, maybe for a dance-hall or restaurant. That was all shuttered up, too, inside the coloured glass. Along the front of it, though, went a great iron verandah, that looked as though it had come from some other place. Quite massive, it was, all pillars and scrolls and lace-work: it looked heavy enough to pull the whole annexe down. There were great steps, with the bottom buried in sand. What drew my eye to it was the bright blue dress of the lady sitting up there. She was not the sort of person you'd see anywhere. She sat up there, simply looking at us.

So Edna, to show she was within her rights, bumped down there on the sand and took her shoes off and shook all the sand out of them, one after the other. 'That's better,' she said. 'Why don't you? Go on,' but somehow I didn't like to. 'You are a silly,' she said. 'It's only just a hotel!'

I looked sideways and saw a board with 'Luncheons, Teas, Suppers', stuck there in the sand – but the writing ever so faint. 'I daresay it's all right,' I said. 'We might have come for our teas.'

'You and your tea,' she said. 'You're always on about tea.'

But I saw she wanted her tea as much as I did, from the way she whacked the sand out of her skirt. You can't help getting to notice a person's character when you work in the same office and go on holidays with them. If you asked me how I liked Edna I wouldn't know how to answer, but a girl on her own like I am has to put up with some things, and it's slow to go on your holiday all alone. I wouldn't mind keeping on noticing Edna's character if she wouldn't keep on saying she keeps on noticing mine. Still, we'd booked our room, so we had to get along somehow – and it was only the fortnight, after all. You get better value for money in quiet places, so she and I had picked on a quiet place. Edna and I aren't like some other girls in business, always off where you can pick up a boy. For one thing, Edna hasn't got much appeal – and I always was one to keep myself to myself. It was quite a nice place Edna and I had picked on, it was refined – but I must say it was a bit slow. No other place up or down the coast for ever so many miles; we really did ought to have brought bikes. We sunbathed a bit, but we somehow only burned red. It was nice, safe bathing, but when it was cold for that, or too windy for deck-chairs, there was nothing to do but go for a trudge on the sands. That suited Edna all right – she always was quite a hiker – and I didn't like to be left. We never walked much inland, as you'll understand, because of the awful cows. I often said I did wish the sand wasn't so soft, and Edna'd say, 'Whatever do you expect?'

This day I'm talking about was the last day but one of our

holiday – that may have been the reason that, once we'd started off walking, we'd come further along than we ever had. I'd been wanting my tea some time, though I wasn't going to say so, to make Edna start picking at me.

'I doubt they serve teas,' I said. 'The place looks shut up, to me.' 'Then what they want to leave that board for?' said Edna. 'If they say teas, they've got to serve teas.' She got quite red. 'Besides, look,' she said, sort of spying at the verandah, 'besides, look; they've got a visitor there.' So she started marching towards the place. I went too – though it somehow didn't seem right.

The person on the verandah sat as still as an image. Only her eyes kept moving, following us. She let us come on till we were near up, then said, 'Oh, no, you mustn't go in!'

I must say Edna did jump, too, but she said, 'Well, this is a hotel all right, isn't it?'

The person looked sort of puzzled: she just said, 'You mustn't; they wouldn't like you to.'

'What are you up to, then?' said Edna, ever so sharp.

That gave the lady even more of a puzzle. Then she said, 'But I always sit outside.'

Being interfered with settled the thing for Edna; she just gave my elbow a sort of pull, and we walked away from the lady, past all those shut shutters, round the end of the hotel. We made a guess that the front door must be on the inland side. The last we saw of the lady, she'd shot up and was banging ever so frightenedly on the window behind her, calling, 'Oh, mind, oh, mind!' 'If you ask me,' said Edna, 'this is a loony-bin. But if so, why do they put up "Teas"?'

On the land side of the hotel, the grass went sloping quite steep up. Awful cows had trodden and messed up all over the place. We looked round but we didn't see any cows. There was the hall door, all right, under a glass porch with one pane gone. The door was ever so shut and the bell out of its socket so nothing would do Edna but to start hammering, I'd have ten times sooner gone missing my tea; I could have slapped Edna, being stubborn like that.

'Oh give over, do, Edna,' I was starting to say – when quite of a sudden the door opened and a young fellow looked out – in his shirt-sleeves, he was. He'd come ever so quiet, in those rubber-soled shoes. He didn't smile or frown, he just looked at us – the way he had no expression was quite rude. He held the door half-shut, keeping his hand on it.

'We want tea for two,' said Edna – right out flat.

'Sorry,' he said, 'we don't serve teas.' He stepped back and started shutting the door. But Edna pushed in her shoulder as quick as quick. She started to say, 'Well, what I want to know is –' and I started to ask her to come off it. Then, though, something made me look round at the hill, and – oh, my goodness, I could have dropped! There were those awful cows, the pack of them, awful black cows, with their horns and everything, coming downhill behind us ever so stealthy ready to spring on us. I grabbed Edna, and she saw – before we half knew what had happened, we'd fought past the young man in at the door. Edna snatched the door from him and gave it a slam shut. I felt her shake all over, just like a piece of paper. She said, 'My girl friend doesn't like cows.'

The first minute, it was so dark we couldn't see anything, it was so dark in there. The place smelled ever so musty. There must have been an archway through to the front; there were chinks of light round the shutters on the sea side. When I started to see, I saw what looked like a row of corpses, all hanging along on the one wall. Later, I noticed these were gentlemen's mackintoshes. I should have told that first go off, by the smell. There they all hung, not moving – why should they move?

Edna said, 'Those cows of yours are not safe.'

He said, 'Those aren't my cows. Are you two from town?'

I daresay Edna gave him one of her looks. She shrilled up and said, 'Then what about that board?' 'Which board? – Oh, that,' he said, as easy as anything. He walked off like a cat, in his rubber shoes, and began unbolting the shutter we'd seen the light come through. So we saw the sea out through the window, and felt better – a bit. And we saw through there, through the arch, now he'd got the shutter open, a lounge – but no palms, and dust over the mirrors, and wicker chairs and tables all coming untwined. 'We did serve teas, all right,' he said, 'but it isn't convenient now.' He went on, 'Then you two came round by the sea?'

I don't think he meant to cheek us, it was just his manner, I don't think he more than half knew we were there. After a bit he said, 'It seems a shame, doesn't it? Did you come from far?' I told him where we'd come from. Then he said, 'Ha⁻e you two got friends, where you are?'

'What's that to you?' said Edna.

He simply went on, 'If you've got friends, or anyone that you talk to, where you're staying – well, just *don't* talk this time – see? I don't serve teas any more, and I don't serve anything, and I don't want locals or visitors coming nosing round here after teas or anything else that I don't serve.' He stood with his arms crossed and his thumbs tucked under his elbows, looking at Edna and me in the calmest way. 'You've no right in here,' he said. 'This place isn't even open. You wouldn't come pushing in if you were a nice pair of girls. All the same, though' (he said to us like an emperor), 'I'll give you your teas, all right, *if you won't go off and talk.*'

So then I piped up (I could see no harm in it, really) and said, how Edna and I always kept ourselves to ourselves. And I told him we'd be back in London the day after tomorrow. Edna said she wasn't sure that she did fancy her tea now, after one thing and another and what had been said. 'Oh yes, you do,' he said. 'Women always fancy their teas.' He rubbed one hand on a table and rubbed some dust off, then stood and watched the dust on his hand. Then he did something queerer – he went and opened the window and stuck his head right out and looked up and down. Whatever he thought he'd see, it didn't seem to be there. So then he pulled his head in and shut the window and said, 'OK; I'll go and see what I've got.'

'You mean, tea?' we said.

'Tea,' he said. 'If you'll sit in those two chairs.' He pulled two chairs out – they were ever so dusty – and stuck the two of us down in a chair each. 'If you move out of those,' he said, 'you won't get any tea. See? And if a lady should pass, you don't have to talk to her – see? The lady's like you, she keeps herself to herself.'

That was the way he went on – as if we'd been a pair of kids. I and Edna dared hardly look at each other – but she put her finger up and gave her forehead a tap. Still, whatever were we to do, just two girls like her and me – and with those cows waiting just outside the door? He got as far as the archway, to give a last look at us. Then he frowned – and we all three looked at the window. There *she* was, the one in blue, with her eyes starting out of her head. She saw him, and began to bang on the glass. I and Edna were sitting back, and so she couldn't see us. We could see her talking away, but we couldn't hear what she said. In the glare out there her blue dress looked ever so queer. She kept banging harder and harder, with the flat of her hands. 'If you don't watch out,' said Edna, 'she'll smash your window. Not that it's my affair.'

For the minute, he seemed to me to quite lose his head. Then he gave us each such a look – like an awful warning, it was – then made a dart at the window and threw it up. Then we *did* hear her – her voice came out in a wail. 'Oh, Oswald, oh, my darling Oswald!' she said.

Before he could step away from the window she reached in, as quick as quick, and got her arms round his neck. 'Oh, I did watch,' she said. 'I *did*! But they got in. Oh, Oswald, forgive me. Forgive me, Oswald,' she said. 'What's going to happen? They'll take you away. I've failed you!' He wriggled his head, but she held on ever so tight. Her wrists were as thin as wire, with gold bracelets slipping into her cuff.

'That's all right, Miss Tope,' he said. 'Nothing's happened; I'm safe, really I am.'

'But they got in. Where are they?'

'They didn't,' he said. 'They've gone.'

She glared past him in at the window – and I tell you, I and Edna stiffened back in our chairs. 'But what did they see?' she said. 'What did they guess? Suppose they're somewhere? Let me come in and look.'

'Ah,' he said, 'but if you come in, who's going to keep lookout? Go back and keep lookout. You know I depend on you.' That made her let him go and come over puzzled for a minute. She stood there puzzling it out, with her eyes fixed on his face. 'I'm *depending* on you,' he said – he was like a father to her. And she could have been his mother – as years go. She looked ready to cry. 'Are you really safe?' she said.

'I'm always safe,' he said, 'while you keep watch.' He gave her a sort of nod, and she crinkled her whole face up and gave him the same sort of nod – then she went away. He waited another minute, then shut the window and walked off, as calm as anything, through the arch.

Well, Edna and I just sat; we stayed in those two chairs and didn't utter or even look at each other. I don't know how that time ever went by. We heard Oswald off somewhere, putting out china, and we could smell the oil stove – he must have left the door open; *he* was listening, all right. Then when he came back and put the tray down he said, 'Well, here you are.' Edna reached for the pot, but he'd got to it first; he pulled up a chair and sat down, ever so at his ease. That was his way of showing we weren't to pay: it was not our tea, it was his. Edna hates being put under compliment – how she did flush up. And I'm sure I was glad to keep my face in my cup. He cut me and Edna each a slice off the loaf. I saw Edna ready to fire up.

'It's all very fine to say not to talk,' she said. 'But how are my friend and me to know what not to talk about? That Miss Tope, I daresay? Whatever is eating her?'

He said, 'She thinks I did a murder.'

'Does she?' said Edna. 'Did you?'

'No,' says he, as offhand as anything. 'But she thinks every minute they'll be coming for me. The fact is, I don't want them coming round after *her*. Her people are all on to get her shut up. They wouldn't care what she suffered. She gave them the slip once, though, and now they don't know she's here. If they did, they'd be round here for her in a jiffy – they don't care *what* she might suffer, wouldn't care if it killed her. But I'd see them all to blazes before I'd let them touch her. I'm the one friend she's got.'

'I must say,' said Edna, 'you take a lot on yourself. Why, she's bats, she is really. She might do anyone harm. Look at those hands of hers – they're as strong as strong.'

'She won't do me harm,' said Oswald.

'She might do herself harm, too.'

'Not while she's with me.'

'Where did she get that, then, about that murder you did?'

Oswald went all quite different when he talked of Miss Tope; he wasn't cool and please-yourself any longer. You might think he was a mother just had her first. 'I kidded her that,' he said. 'If they weren't to come and take her she and I were bound to keep lying low. And when she first came back here she was out all over the place – along the main road, round the village – just like a child, so trustful, talking away to everyone. Of course she got remarked on – how could she not be? Her people would have been here for her in a week. So I had to think up some way to keep her quiet without letting on it was *her*: she'd have died of that. So I told her I'd done something awful, and that they'd be coming for me, and that she'd have to hide me, and keep watch. Since then, she's never budged from this place.'

'Poor soul,' I said.

He said, 'You don't know her. She's as sweet and lovely as she was when a girl.'

'No doubt,' said Edna, 'she is the perfect lady. All the same, she's willing to stay where she thinks there's been a murder done. Do you mean to say *that* didn't give her a turn against you?'

'Why, no,' Oswald said. 'She'd never judge what *I* did. She just sometimes cries and calls me her poor thing. She and I have been like that – friends with each other – since I was a little kid and she was the loveliest girl. You see her and my fathers, they were so thick – though her father was a rich gentleman; at one time he could have bought England; he had a yacht and all. It was her father set my father up in this business, this hotel. Then they were always coming here, Miss Meena and him. And where Major Tope came, in those days, his crowd used to follow him. Ever so many gentlemen, and Miss Meena – they used to call this their headquarters – my father's place. I remember all these windows blazing down on the sand, and Miss Meena in her lace dress on that verandah, singing to her guitar. She was like a queen to them all – and she was my queen all right. They used to laugh at me, always round after her. But in those days I was only a little kid. When Major Tope's crash came, all that crowd that used to come here melted away like snow. I guess they lost money, too. Major Tope had invested for *my* father all my father had made out of this place. So when the crash came, my father went down too. Major Tope couldn't stand it all; he put himself out. My father wasn't left long after that lot went: I was left with this place, and I did carry on for a bit, just with teas and that, but when Miss Tope came back I shut down. It wouldn't do – not with her.'

'Then you didn't ought to have left that board up, with "Teas"!'

'That's for her,' he said. 'I did try taking it down, once, but how she did take on – she won't see a thing changed. The day she came back she said, "Here I am, back, Oswald. Now we'll be happy. We've always been happy here." She hates to see anything go – I couldn't hurt like that.'

'That's all very well,' said Edna, 'but how ever do you make out? With no custom or anything? You've got your own life to think of – a young fellow like you.'

He said, as stand-offish as anything, 'Oh, I make out all right. This premises is still mine, and I get a bit for the grass.'

'Still, you can't keep on,' Edna said. He said: 'Leave that to her and me.'

He got up and piled back the things on the tray. 'Well, if you must go . . .' he said. 'Thanks for your company.' So she and I got up. When he saw Edna eyeing out of the window he said, 'No, not that way; you're going back inland.' He got us out through the hall – oh, it echoed, it did sound empty – past the mackintoshes all those people had left. 'Well, I'm sure you've been very kind,' I said, 'giving us tea and everything. Thank you, I'm sure.'

'The way to thank me,' he said, 'is by keeping your mouths shut.'

While he was opening the door I said, 'Oh, Edna, the cows!' He gave a sort of grin and said he'd make that all right. As a matter of fact, the cows were off up another hill. Oswald started us off up a path that he said would bring us down again on the sands in the next bay. (And it did.) He stayed, with a stick, as he'd promised, between us and that other hill where the cows were. We walked fast and were ever so out of breath. I looked back once and saw Oswald, looking quite little, and his hotel down there looking just like a little box. I thought when we got our breaths we were bound to start saying something. Then I saw Edna'd put on one of her funny manners, so I didn't say anything – I didn't want to, either. Because what can you say when you don't know what you think? And what can you think when a thing doesn't make sense?

MALACHI WHITAKER

✍

Landlord of the Crystal Fountain

A tall, good-looking, red-haired school teacher of about thirty stood in King's Cross Station one Friday afternoon trying to find enough change for her ticket. She had a violent headache, and frowned as she fumbled in her brown leather bag.

Her name was Brenda Millgate, and she was going north for the weekend to see her sister. It was purely a visit of duty; she had nothing whatever in common with Doris, and she looked upon the weekend as wasted already.

Nothing would go right for her. A few coppers rolled from her fingers, and she felt embarrassed as obsequious strangers handed pennies back to her. But at length the ticket was bought, and she picked up her weekend case and walked resolutely on to Platform Ten. The bookstall was further down on her left, but she felt too tired to go down and buy any of the alluring-looking magazines offered for sale. There was not much time. She had had to hurry as it was. And now she found the train was crowded.

She was dressed very neatly in brown, and had on a cream-coloured blouse with buttons that very nearly matched the colour of her hair. She had also a brown silk umbrella with a shining orange knob on it, and there was an orange leather band across her brown handbag.

In spite of her knowledge that she looked both well and intelligent, there seemed to be no room for her. There was a place or two in the non-smoking carriages, but she did not like the stink that came out of them. 'You can get the smell of smoke out of your clothes,' she thought, 'but not that – that other.' She did not know what to call it. But though she walked quickly up and down the platform in her brown shoes, she could find nowhere suitable, and had to jump up and stand in the corridor at last. Just behind her, she heard a loud, hearty voice saying something that was followed by a burst of laughter. She put down her case, and watched the bookstall glide smoothly past the window. Then she turned her head to see how many people were in the carriage behind her.

Why, there was a seat! In fact, only five men were sitting down, but five such big men she had never before seen together. They seemed to fill the place to overflowing. Probably there were lots more seats on the train, but her head was so bad that she could hardly see them. The door of the carriage opened, and a friendly voice said, 'Do come in here, miss. There's plenty of room.'

'Thank you,' she said gratefully. She felt tired enough to faint or to fall asleep.

The five big men rearranged themselves and let her sit in a corner seat near the window. For a few minutes they gave her all their attention until they had her settled and comfortable. One put her case on the rack, another even helped her off with her hat, the one opposite moved so that she could put her feet up on the seat, the fourth asked her if she would like a paper to read, and the fifth one stood up laughing and said, 'Now we're all comfortable, aren't we?'

She sank back with a sigh of relief. 'I've got such an awful headache. This is lovely, lovely.'

One of them made a joke about her red hair, and she laughed softly. 'You're all together, aren't you?' she asked. 'Friends?'

'Yes, friends,' they answered, and one of them said, 'All together.'

She sank almost immediately into a kind of stupor, in which she could hear the dulled rattle of the train wheels and the quiet hum of voices. 'Why are these men so pleasant?' she wondered. 'So steeped in comfortableness?' It felt nice to be with them.

After a short while she woke, feeling much better, and began to study her fellow-travellers. 'What great hulking men,' she thought, 'and yet how considerate they are.' Not one of them had started to smoke.

'Smoke if you like,' she said. 'I like the smell. But first of all, do tell me what you are. What do you do? I've been wondering ever since I saw you.'

The man in the far corner leaned forward. He had thinning black hair brushed as far as it would go round a dome-like forehead.

'We're landlords, my girl,' he said. 'Landlords, all of us. We've every one got licensed houses.'

'Pubs,' her mind flashed.

'You're all very big landlords,' she said.

He wagged his finger at her, 'Ah, it's the life.' He took out a pipe and filled it, and began to smoke.

'Tell me the names of your – your houses,' she said.

'The Golden Lion at Firley Green; The White Horse at Itterington; The Case is Altered (that's a puzzler, isn't it, miss?) just at the entrance to Hay Park; The Crown, Bridge Road.'

They were all busy but one, pulling card-cases out of their pockets. 'We've been up to a convention; a spree, by God. Hush, we've had the time of our lives!'

Then she looked across at the man who sat opposite, the one who had moved so that she might put her feet up. He was, she thought, the tallest of them all. He had a red face and tight, straw-coloured curls thick over his head. His eyes were blue-grey. He wore a dark suit and a black tie. He had not yet spoken. 'What's the name of yours?'

'I'm proud of the name of mine,' he said, 'but I haven't any cards on me.'

The others all handed their cards to her, and she took them impatiently, leaning forward, looking at the straw-haired giant, whose deep voice had at the same time pleased and startled her. 'What is it? What's the name of yours?'

'All in good time,' he said, smiling slowly. 'It's called the Crystal Fountain.'

Then the others began to talk about their homes and their lives. They discussed their wives, and announced themselves as hen-pecked men, all but the landlord of the Crystal Fountain, who kept silent. He and Brenda sat looking at each other in perfect contentment, listening to the talk around them.

Casually they brought out stacks of sandwiches, and made her share them. At first, she was full of dismay. Sandwiches – dry sandwiches in a train! Yet presently she was eating one of salmon and cucumber.

'But this is real salmon,' she cried in astonishment, 'and the cucumber's as fresh as a drink of water.'

'Of course it is,' one shouted. 'We know what to buy and where to buy it.'

'You didn't get them near here, I'll bet.'

'But we did. And within a stone's throw of King's Cross, too.'

The sandwiches melted away like snow in a thaw. There was enough for everybody. Brenda got plenty of compliments – on her height, on her appetite, on her red hair. She blushed with pleasure.

After the meal, they all relaxed, leaning back and unfastening buttons that had become too tight. One or two smoked. The dome-headed one offered her cigarettes, and when she refused one, he was glad.

'Not speaking in a business way, of course,' he said. 'I've nothing against it. We see it, practically speaking, every evening of our lives. It wouldn't do for us to be prejudiced. But I'm glad.'

Brenda slipped her feet down from the opposite seat, sighing with joy. She had not the least idea why she now felt so happy.

'I've never met any landlords socially,' she thought. 'No, I've never met a landlord before in my life. Publicans. Publicans and sinners. Perhaps they were like this when Jesus was alive. No wonder He . . .' She dozed again.

She thought of her life, of her mother's ambition that she should be a teacher. She thought with astonishment of the examinations she had passed, the years of pleasant training. She was not in the least clever. She had no retentive memory. But somehow everything had come to her. Flukes, flukes. And she *was* good with children – just plain good at getting on with people, with the heads, with her fellow-teachers.

And because she had liked the children who flowed under, rather than passed through her hands, and had spent her time hoping that here and there a silk purse dwelt among the pigs' ears, she had not thought a great deal about men.

There was one who thought of her, and she knew it. But she was not in any way satisfied with him. He was shorter than she was – small, dark, dry and meticulous. He liked her to be a kind of imitation of himself. He had the power of making her feel that she would eventually marry him; that one day, when she was

200

tired and sick of school and all that it meant, she would turn to him. So he simply waited.

She did not dislike him physically. She was tolerant, and adaptable, ready to make the best of anything. His name was Claud Foden.

She opened her eyes and looked across at the landlord of the Crystal Fountain. He was studying her gravely. He leaned forward and spoke quietly. 'My God,' he said, 'but you're a nice woman. I suppose you're more a lady, though.'

'No,' she answered him just as quietly, 'woman's the word,' and soon she was telling him about herself.

'My father kept a shop. Well, my stepfather, and Doris – that's my sister – and I went to school on his money. He was a butcher, a big fine man with curly hair like yours, only white. I don't remember my own father. My mother always used to tell us that she had married again so that we could have a good education. She didn't know much, but she was ambitious. I'm supposed to know a lot, but I'm not ambitious that way, at all. I'm a teacher, but I've just begun to wonder why I'm a teacher, for my heart isn't in it. It's with the children, all right, but not with what I'm supposed to be teaching them.'

She felt astonished to hear these words coming from her mouth. She did not usually talk like that. No, she used a sort of jargon, a 'we're all girls together' kind of language. Anything to crush down her height and healthiness, her over-exuberance. She really envied the dim creatures who tripped about like neat mice, knowing she could never grow like them. Her red hair was thick and curly, and it shone; when she saw it in a mirror, she knew that it was beautiful, but always thought disparagingly of people who liked that kind of thing.

The two sat looking at each other, admiring each other. The other four men were talking among themselves. They leaned back, stretching out their legs. Their firm calves touched each other, so that their blood seemed to flow through one body rather than two. They kept on looking at each other with absorbed pleasure as the train rushed through the gathering darkness.

Brenda began to think dreamily that she would like to have a dressing-gown of orange and green, and a link of great amber beads like lumps of sucked toffee. And imitation pearls – only they must be great big ones, too. She would like to have rings on her fingers, 'and bells on my toes' she murmured, and dangling gold earrings.

'And now listen to me,' the man opposite said, in his voice that could be deep and quiet at the same time, 'for I've got a lot to say to you. I don't know much about you – you're not married, by any chance, are you?'

'No.'

'Well, I have been, to a fine girl, none better. For five years. But she's dead now. She's gone and can't be brought back. I'm wanting another wife. I'm wanting her quick, and I think you'll do. What do you say?'

'You'll have to let me think.'

'Well, don't take long, then, for we haven't far to go. I want you to come with me to see the place, but you'll like it. I've no fear of that. I like it. It's out at Ella Syke, on the moor edge. You might find it a bit quiet, but I don't. What do you say, lass?'

She was thinking. 'This can't often happen to people. It's never happened to anyone I know. But I'm going to do it.'

A silence had fallen over the carriage. She said, 'All right, then, as soon as you like.'

'That's good.'

'I'll have to send a telegram to Doris. She's expecting me. But do you think I'd make you a good wife – in a business way, I mean?' She had no other qualms.

'I'll soon teach you. But you might have been born to it.' He stood up and presented her gravely to his four friends. 'Any one of them'll vouch for me,' he said. 'There's no underhand business here. And I expect to call and see your sister in a day or so. We'll make a special day of the wedding.'

The five big men took everything for granted, and fell to talking again, while the girl leaned back and thought. There would certainly be a lot of fuss about her job. Doris would be astounded. It would mean a fresh start in life. She would never see Claud Foden again as long as she lived.

On the other hand, this new bliss that had grown up in her would never leave her. She was ready to go on. 'It'll be hard work, and different work, but I'll do it.' There must be some of her mother's ambition in her, she thought. Here it was. Her eyes blazed with a new light.

She carried her own case, because he had one of his own. They walked across the grey northern station to find a telegraph office behind the closed post office. But he took hold of her arm with his free hand, and she liked the firm way it held her. Yet she could think of nothing to put in the telegram except: 'Don't worry about me. I am going to the Crystal Fountain.'

KATHERINE MANSFIELD

🙟

An Indiscreet Journey

I

She is like St Anne. Yes, the concierge is the image of St Anne, with that black cloth over her head, the wisps of grey hair hanging, and the tiny smoking lamp in her hand. Really very beautiful, I thought, smiling at St Anne, who said severely: 'Six o'clock. You have only just got time. There is a bowl of milk on the writing-table.' I jumped out of my pyjamas and into a basin of cold water like any English lady in any French novel. The concierge, persuaded that I was on my way to prison cells and death by bayonets, opened the shutters and the cold clear light came through. A little steamer hooted on the river; a cart with two horses at a gallop flung past. The rapid swirling water; the tall black trees on the far side, grouped together like Negroes conversing. Sinister, very, I thought, as I buttoned on my age-old Burberry. (That Burberry was very significant. It did not belong to me. I had borrowed it from a friend. My eye lighted upon it hanging in her little dark hall. The very thing! The perfect and adequate disguise – an old Burberry. Lions have been faced in a Burberry. Ladies have been rescued from open boats in mountainous seas wrapped in nothing else. An old Burberry seems to me the sign and the token of the undisputed venerable traveller, I decided, leaving my purple peg-top with the real seal collar and cuffs in exchange.)

'You will never get there,' said the concierge, watching me turn up the collar. 'Never! Never!' I ran down the echoing stairs – strange they sounded, like a piano flicked by a sleepy housemaid – and on to the Quai. 'Why so fast, *ma mignonne?*' said a lovely little boy in coloured socks, dancing in front of the electric lotus buds that curve over the

entrance to the Metro. Alas! there was not even time to blow him a
kiss. When I arrived at the big station I had only four minutes to spare,
and the platform entrance was crowded and packed with soldiers,
their yellow papers in one hand and big untidy bundles. The Commissaire of Police stood on one side, a Nameless Official on the other.
Will he let me pass? Will he? He was an old man with a fat swollen face
covered with big warts. Horn-rimmed spectacles squatted on his
nose. Trembling, I made an effort. I conjured up my sweetest early-
morning smile and handed it with the papers. But the delicate thing
fluttered against the horn spectacles and fell. Nevertheless, he let me
pass, and I ran, ran in and out among the soldiers and up the high steps
into the yellow-painted carriage.

'Does one go direct to X?' I asked the collector who dug at my
ticket with a pair of forceps and handed it back again. 'No,
Mademoiselle, you must change at XYZ.'

'At – ?'

'XYZ.'

Again I had not heard. 'At what time do we arrive there, if you
please?'

'One o'clock.' But that was no good to me. I hadn't a watch.
Oh, well – later.

Ah! the train had begun to move. The train was on my side. It swung
out of the station, and soon we were passing the vegetable gardens,
passing the tall blind houses to let, passing the servants beating carpets. Up already and walking in the fields, rosy from the rivers and the
red-fringed pools, the sun lighted upon the swinging train and stroked
my muff and told me to take off that Burberry. I was not alone in the
carriage. An old woman sat opposite, her skirt turned back over her
knees, a bonnet of black lace on her head. In her fat hands, adorned
with a wedding and two mourning rings, she held a letter. Slowly,
slowly, she sipped a sentence, and then looked up and out of the
window, her lips trembling a little, and then another sentence, and
again the old face turned to the light, tasting it . . . Two soldiers leaned
out of the window, their heads nearly touching – one of them was
whistling, the other had his coat fastened with some rusty safety-
pins. And now there were soldiers everywhere working on the railway line, leaning against trucks or standing hands on hips, eyes fixed
on the train as though they expected at least one camera at every
window. And now we were passing big wooden sheds like rigged-up

dancing-halls or seaside pavilions, each flying a flag. In and out of them walked the Red Cross men; the wounded sat against the walls sunning themselves. At all the bridges, the crossings, the stations, a *petit soldat*, all boots and bayonet. Forlorn and desolate he looked – like a little comic picture waiting for the joke to be written underneath. Is there really such a thing as war? Are all these laughing voices really going to the war? These dark woods lighted so mysteriously by the white stems of the birch and the ash – these watery fields with the big birds flying over – these rivers green and blue in the light – have battles been fought in places like these?

What beautiful cemeteries we are passing! They flash gay in the sun. They seem to be full of cornflowers and poppies and daisies. How can there be so many flowers at this time of the year? But they are not flowers at all. They are bunches of ribbons tied on to the soldiers' graves.

I glanced up and caught the old woman's eye. She smiled and folded the letter. 'It is from my son – the first we have had since October. I am taking it to my daughter-in-law.'

'. . . ?'

'Yes, very good,' said the old woman, shaking down her skirt and putting her arm through the handle of her basket. 'He wants me to send him some handkerchiefs and a piece of stout string.'

What is the name of the station where I have to change? Perhaps I shall never know. I got up and leaned my arms across the window rail, my feet crossed. One cheek burned as in infancy on the way to the seaside. When the war is over I shall have a barge and drift along these rivers with a white cat and a pot of mignonette to bear me company.

Down the side of the hill filed the troops, winking red and blue in the light. Far away, but plainly to be seen, some more flew by on bicycles. But really, *ma France adorée*, this uniform is ridiculous. Your soldiers are stamped upon your bosom like bright irreverent transfers.

The train slowed down, stopped . . . Everybody was getting out except me. A big boy, his *sabots* tied to his back with a piece of string, the inside of his tin wine cup stained a lovely impossible pink, looked very friendly. Does one change here perhaps for X? Another whose képi had come out of a wet paper cracker swung my suitcase to earth. What darlings soldiers are! '*Merci bien, Monsieur, vous êtes tout à fait aimable* . . .' 'Not this way,' said a bayonet. 'Nor this,' said another. So I followed the crowd. 'Your passport, Mademoiselle . . .' *'We, Sir Edward Grey* . . .' I ran through the muddy square and into the buffet.

A green room with a stove jutting out and tables on each side. On the counter, beautiful with coloured bottles, a woman leans, her breasts in her folded arms. Through an open door I can see a kitchen, and the cook in a white coat breaking eggs into a bowl and tossing the shells into a corner. The blue and red coats of the men who are eating hang upon the walls. Their short swords and belts are piled upon chairs. Heavens! what a noise. The sunny air seemed all broken up and trembling with it. A little boy, very pale, swung from table to table, taking the orders, and poured me out a glass of purple coffee. *Ssssh,* came from the eggs. They were in a pan. The woman rushed from behind the counter and began to help the boy. *Toute de suite, tout'suite!* she chirruped to the loud impatient voices. There came a clatter of plates and the pop-pop of corks being drawn.

Suddenly in the doorway I saw someone with a pail of fish – brown speckled fish, like the fish one sees in a glass case, swimming through forests of beautiful pressed seaweed. He was an old man in a tattered jacket, standing humbly, waiting for someone to attend to him. A thin beard fell over his chest, his eyes under the tufted eyebrows were bent on the pail he carried. He looked as though he had escaped from some holy picture, and was entreating the soldiers' pardon for being there at all . . .

But what could I have done? I could not arrive at X with two fishes hanging on a straw; and I am sure it is a penal offence in France to throw fish out of railway-carriage windows, I thought, miserably climbing into a smaller, shabbier train. Perhaps I might have taken them to – *ah, mon Dieu* – I had forgotten the name of my uncle and aunt again! Buffard, Buffon – what was it? Again I read the unfamiliar letter in the familiar handwriting.

My dear niece,

Now that the weather is more settled, your uncle and I would be charmed if you would pay us a little visit. Telegraph me when you are coming. I shall meet you outside the station if I am free. Otherwise our good friend, Madame Grinçon, who lives in the little toll-house by the bridge, *juste en face de la gare*, will conduct you to our home. *Je vous embrasse bien tendrement.*

JULIE BOIFFARD.

A visiting card was enclosed: *M. Paul Boiffard.*

Boiffard – of course that was the name. *Ma tante Julie et mon oncle Paul* – suddenly they were there with me, more real, more solid than any relations I had ever known. I saw *tante Julie* bridling, with the soup-tureen in her hands, and *oncle Paul* sitting at the table with a red and white napkin tied round his neck. Boiffard – Boiffard – I must remember the name. Supposing the Commissaire Militaire should ask me who the relations were I was going to and I muddled the name – Oh, how fatal! Buffard – no, Boiffard. And then for the first time, folding Aunt Julie's letter, I saw scrawled in a corner of the empty back page: *Venez vite, vite.* Strange impulsive woman! My heart began to beat . . .

'Ah, we are not far off now,' said the lady opposite. 'You are going to X, Mademoiselle?'

'Oui, Madame.'

'I also . . . You have been there before?'

'No, Madame. This is the first time.'

'Really, it is a strange time for a visit.'

I smiled faintly, and tried to keep my eyes off her hat. She was quite an ordinary little woman, but she wore a black velvet toque, with an incredibly surprised looking seagull camped on the very top of it. Its round eyes, fixed on me so inquiringly, were almost too much to bear. I had a dreadful impulse to shoo it away, or to lean forward and inform her of its presence . . .

'Excusez-moi, Madame, but perhaps you have not remarked there is an *espèce de* seagull *couché sur votre chapeau.'*

Could the bird be there on purpose? I must not laugh . . . I must not laugh. Had she ever looked at herself in a glass with that bird on her head?

'It is very difficult to get into X at present, to pass the station,' she said, and she shook her head with the seagull at me. 'Ah, such an affair. One must sign one's name and state one's business.'

'Really, is it as bad as all that?'

'But naturally. You see the whole place is in the hands of the military, and' – she shrugged – 'they have to be strict. Many people do not get beyond the station at all. They arrive. They are put in the waiting-room, and there they remain.'

Did I or did I not detect in her voice a strange, insulting relish?

208

'I suppose such strictness is absolutely necessary,' I said coldly, stroking my muff.

'Necessary!' she cried. 'I should think so. Why, Mademoiselle, you cannot imagine what it would be like otherwise! You know what women are like about soldiers' – she raised a final hand – 'mad, completely mad. But' – and she gave a little laugh of triumph – 'they could not get into X. *Mon Dieu*, no! There is no question about that.'

'I don't suppose they even try,' said I.

'Don't you?' said the seagull.

Madame said nothing for a moment. 'Of course the authorities are very hard on the men. It means instant imprisonment, and then – off to the firing-line without a word.'

'What are *you* going to X for?' said the seagull. 'What on earth are *you* doing here?'

'Are you making a long stay in X, Mademoiselle?'

She had won, she had won. I was terrified. A lamp-post swam past the train with the fatal name upon it. I could hardly breathe – the train had stopped. I smiled gaily at Madame and danced down the steps to the platform . . .

It was a hot little room completely furnished with two colonels seated at two tables. They were large grey-whiskered men with a touch of burnt red on their cheeks. Sumptuous and omnipotent they looked. One smoked what ladies love to call a heavy Egyptian cigarette, with a long creamy ash, the other toyed with a gilded pen. Their heads rolled on their tight collars, like big overripe fruits. I had a terrible feeling, as I handed my passport and ticket, that a soldier would step forward and tell me to kneel. I would have knelt without question.

'What's this?' said God I, querulously. He did not like my passport at all. The very sight of it seemed to annoy him. He waved a dissenting hand at it, with a *'Non, je ne peux pas manger ça'* air.

'But it won't do. It won't do at all, you know. Look – read for yourself,' and he glanced with extreme distaste at my photograph, and then with even greater distaste his pebble eyes looked at me.

'Of course the photograph is deplorable,' I said, scarcely breathing with terror, 'but it has been viséd and viséd.'

He raised his big hulk and went over to God II.

209

'Courage!' I said to my muff and held it firmly, 'Courage!'

God II held up a finger to me, and I produced Aunt Julie's letter and her card. But he did not seem to feel the slightest interest in her. He stamped my passport idly, scribbled a word on my ticket, and I was on the platform again.

'That way – you pass out that way.'

Terribly pale, with a faint smile on his lips, his hand at salute, stood the little corporal. I gave no sign, I am sure I gave no sign. He stepped behind me.

'And then follow me as though you do not see me,' I heard him half-whisper, half-sing.

How fast he went, through the slippery mud towards a bridge. He had a postman's bag on his back, a paper parcel and the *Matin* in his hand. We seemed to dodge through a maze of policemen, and I could not keep up at all with the little corporal, who began to whistle. From the toll-house 'our good friend, Madame Grinçon', her hands wrapped in a shawl, watched our coming, and against the toll-house there leaned a tiny faded cab. *Montez vite, vite!* said the little corporal, hurling my suitcase, the postman's bag, the paper parcel and the *Matin* on to the floor.

'A-ie! A-ie! Do not be so mad. Do not ride yourself. You will be seen,' wailed 'our good friend, Madame Grinçon'.

'Ah, je m'en f . . .' said the little corporal.

The driver jerked into activity. He lashed the bony horse and away we flew, both doors, which were the complete sides of the cab, flapping and banging.

'Bonjour, mon amie.'

'Bonjour, mon ami.'

And then we swooped down and clutched at the banging doors. They would not keep shut. They were fools of doors.

'Lean back, let me do it!' I cried. 'Policemen are as thick as violets everywhere.'

At the barracks the horses reared up and stopped. A crowd of laughing faces blotted the window.

'Prends ça, mon vieux,' said the little corporal, handing the paper parcel.

'It's all right,' called someone.

We waved, we were off again. By a river, down a strange

white street, with little houses on either side, gay in the late sunlight.

'Jump out as soon as he stops again. The door will be open. Run straight inside. I will follow. The man is already paid. I know you will like the house. It is quite white. And the room is white too, and the people are –'

'White as snow.'

We looked at each other. We began to laugh. 'Now,' said the little corporal.

Out I flew and in at the door. There stood, presumably, my Aunt Julie. There in the background hovered, I supposed, my Uncle Paul.

'*Bonjour, Madame!*' '*Bonjour, Monsieur!*'

'It is all right, you are safe,' said my Aunt Julie. Heavens, how I loved her! And she opened the door of the white room and shut it upon us. Down went the suitcase, the postman's bag, the *Matin*. I threw my passport up into the air, and the little corporal caught it.

II

What an extraordinary thing. We had been there to lunch and to dinner each day; but now in the dusk and alone I could not find it. I clop-clopped in my borrowed *sabots* through the greasy mud, right to the end of the village, and there was not a sign of it. I could not even remember what it looked like, or if there was a name painted on the outside, or any bottles or tables showing at the window. Already the village houses were sealed for the night behind big wooden shutters. Strange and mysterious they looked in the ragged drifting light and thin rain, like a company of beggars perched on the hillside, their bosoms full of rich unlawful gold. There was nobody about but the soldiers. A group of wounded stood under a lamp-post, petting a mangy, shivering dog. Up the street came four big boys singing:

'*Dodo, mon homme, fais vit' dodo . . .*'

and swung off down the hill to their sheds behind the railway station. They seemed to take the last breath of the day with them. I began to walk slowly back.

211

'It must have been one of these houses. I remember it stood far back from the road – and there were no steps, not even a porch – one seemed to walk right through the window.' And then quite suddenly the waiting-boy came out of just such a place. He saw me and grinned cheerfully, and began to whistle through his teeth.

'*Bonsoir, mon petit.*'

'*Bonsoir, Madame.*' And he followed me up the café to our special table, right at the far end by the window, and marked by a bunch of violets that I had left in a glass there yesterday.

'You are two?' asked the waiting-boy, flicking the table with a red and white cloth. His long swinging steps echoed over the bare floor. He disappeared into the kitchen and came back to light the lamp that hung from the ceiling under a spreading shade, like a haymaker's hat. Warm light shone on the empty place that was really a barn, set out with dilapidated tables and chairs. Into the middle of the room a black stove jutted. At one side of it there was a table with a row of bottles on it, behind which Madame sat and took the money and made entries in a red book. Opposite her desk a door led into the kitchen. The walls were covered with a creamy paper patterned all over with green and swollen trees – hundreds and hundreds of trees reared their mushroom heads to the ceiling. I began to wonder who had chosen the paper and why. Did Madame think it was beautiful, or that it was a gay and lovely thing to eat one's dinner at all seasons in the middle of a forest ... On either side of the clock there hung a picture: one, a young gentleman in black tights wooing a pear-shaped lady in yellow over the back of a garden seat, *Premier Rencontre*; two, the black and yellow in amorous confusion, *Triomphe d'Amour*.

The clock ticked to a soothing lilt, *C'est ça, c'est ça.* In the kitchen the waiting-boy was washing up. I heard the ghostly chatter of the dishes.

And years passed. Perhaps the war is long since over – there is no village outside at all – the streets are quiet under the grass. I have an idea this is the sort of thing one will do on the very last day of all – sit in an empty café and listen to a clock ticking until –

Madame came through the kitchen door, nodded to me and took her seat behind the table, her plump hands folded on the red book. *Ping* went the door. A handful of soldiers came in, took off their coats and began to play cards, chaffing and poking fun at the pretty

212

waiting-boy, who threw up his little round head, rubbed his thick fringe out of his eyes and cheeked them back in his broken voice. Sometimes his voice boomed up from his throat, deep and harsh, and then in the middle of a sentence it broke and scattered in a funny squeaking. He seemed to enjoy it himself. You would not have been surprised if he had walked into the kitchen on his hands and brought back your dinner turning a catherine wheel.

Ping went the door again. Two more men came in. They sat at the table nearest Madame, and she leaned to them with a birdlike movement, her head on one side. Oh, they had a grievance! The Lieutenant was a fool – nosing about – springing out at them – and they'd only been sewing on buttons. Yes, that was all – sewing on buttons, and up comes this young spark. 'Now then, what are you up to?' They mimicked the idiotic voice. Madame drew down her mouth, nodding sympathy. The waiting-boy served them with glasses. He took a bottle of some orange-coloured stuff and put it on the table edge. A shout from the card-players made him turn sharply, and crash! over went the bottle, spilling on the table, the floor – smash! to tinkling atoms. An amazed silence. Through it the drip-drip of the wine from the table on to the floor. It looked very strange dropping so slowly, as though the table were crying. Then there came a roar from the card-players. 'You'll catch it, my lad! That's the style! Now you've done it ... *Sept, huit, neuf.*' They started playing again. The waiting-boy never said a word. He stood, his head bent, his hands spread out, and then he knelt and gathered up the glass, piece by piece, and soaked the wine up with a cloth. Only when Madame cried cheerfully, 'You wait until *he* finds out,' did he raise his head.

'He can't say anything, if I pay for it,' he muttered, his face jerking, and he marched off into the kitchen with the soaking cloth.

'*Il pleure de colère,*' said Madame delightedly, patting her hair with her plump hands.

The café slowly filled. It grew very warm. Blue smoke mounted from the tables and hung about the haymaker's hat in misty wreaths. There was a suffocating smell of onion soup and boots and damp cloth. In the din the door sounded again. It opened to let

213

in a weed of a fellow, who stood with his back against it, one hand shading his eyes.

'Hullo! you've got the bandage off?'

'How does it feel, *mon vieux?*'

'Let's have a look at them.'

But he made no reply. He shrugged and walked unsteadily to a table, sat down and leaned against the wall. Slowly his hand fell. In his white face his eyes showed, pink as a rabbit's. They brimmed and spilled, brimmed and spilled. He dragged a white cloth out of his pocket and wiped them.

'It's the smoke,' said someone. 'It's the smoke tickles them up for you.'

His comrades watched him a bit, watched his eyes fill again, again brim over. The water ran down his face, off his chin on to the table. He rubbed the place with his coat-sleeve, and then, as though forgetful, went on rubbing, rubbing with his hand across the table, staring in front of him. And then he started shaking his head to the movement of his hand. He gave a loud strange groan and dragged out the cloth again.

'*Huit, neuf, dix,*' said the card-players.

'*P'tit,* some more bread.'

'Two coffees.'

'*Un Picon!*'

The waiting-boy, quite recovered, but with scarlet cheeks, ran to and fro. A tremendous quarrel flared up among the card-players, raged for two minutes, and died in flickering laughter. 'Ooof!' groaned the man with the eyes, rocking and mopping. But nobody paid any attention to him except Madame. She made a little grimace at her two soldiers.

'*Mais vous savez, c'est un peu dégoûtant, ça,*' she said severely.

'*Ah, oui, Madame,*' answered the soldiers, watching her bent head and pretty hands, as she arranged for the hundredth time a frill of lace on her lifted bosom.

'*V'là Monsieur!*' cawed the waiting-boy over his shoulder to me. For some silly reason I pretended not to hear, and I leaned over the table smelling the violets, until the little corporal's hand closed over mine.

'Shall we have *un peu de charcuterie* to begin with?' he asked tenderly.

III

'In England,' said the blue-eyed soldier, 'you drink whisky with your meals. *N'est-ce pas, Mademoiselle?* A little glass of whisky neat before eating. Whisky and soda with your *bifteks*, and after, more whisky with hot water and lemon.'

'Is it true, that?' asked his great friend who sat opposite, a big red-faced chap with a black beard and large moist eyes and hair that looked as though it had been cut with a sewing-machine.

'Well, not quite true,' said I.

'*Si, si,*' cried the blue-eyed soldier. 'I ought to know. I'm in business. English travellers come to my place, and it's always the same thing.'

'Bah, I can't stand whisky,' said the little corporal. 'It's too disgusting the morning after. Do you remember, *ma fille*, the whisky in that little bar at Montmartre?'

'*Souvenir tendre,*' sighed Blackbeard, putting two fingers in the breast of his coat and letting his head fall. He was very drunk.

'But I know something that you've never tasted,' said the blue-eyed soldier, pointing a finger at me: 'something really good.' *Cluck*, he went with his tongue. '*É-pat-ant!* And the curious thing is that you'd hardly know it from whisky except that it's' – he felt with his hand for the word – 'finer, sweeter perhaps, not so sharp, and it leaves you feeling gay as a rabbit next morning.'

'What is it called?'

'Mirabelle!' He rolled the word round his mouth, under his tongue. 'Ah-ha, that's the stuff.'

'I could eat another mushroom,' said Blackbeard. 'I would like another mushroom very much. I am sure I could eat another mushroom if Mademoiselle gave it to me out of her hand.'

'You ought to try it,' said the blue-eyed soldier, leaning both hands on the table and speaking so seriously that I began to wonder how much more sober he was than Blackbeard. 'You ought to try it, and tonight. I would like you to tell me if you don't think it's like whisky.'

'Perhaps they've got it here,' said the little corporal, and he called the waiting-boy. '*P'tit!*'

'*Non, Monsieur,*' said the boy, who never stopped smiling. He served us with dessert plates painted with blue parrots and horned beetles.

'What is the name for this in English?' said Blackbeard, pointing. I told him 'Parrot.'

'Ah, *mon Dieu!* . . . Pair-rot . . .' He put his arms round his plate. 'I love you, *ma petite* pair-rot. You are sweet, you are blonde, you are English. You do not know the difference between whisky and mirabelle.'

The little corporal and I looked at each other, laughing. He squeezed up his eyes when he laughed, so that you saw nothing but the long curly lashes.

'Well, I know a place where they do keep it,' said the blue-eyed soldier. '*Café des Amis*. We'll go there – I'll pay – I'll pay for the whole lot of us.' His gesture embraced thousands of pounds.

But with a loud whirring noise the clock on the wall struck half-past eight; and no soldier is allowed in a café after eight o'clock at night.

'It is fast,' said the blue-eyed soldier. The little corporal's watch said the same. So did the immense turnip that Blackbeard produced, and carefully deposited on the head of one of the horned beetles.

'Ah, well, we'll take the risk,' said the blue-eyed soldier, and he thrust his arms into his immense cardboard coat. 'It's worth it,' he said. 'It's worth it. You just wait.'

Outside, stars shone between wispy clouds, and the moon fluttered like a candle flame over a pointed spire. The shadows of the dark plume-like trees waved on the white houses. Not a soul to be seen. No sound to be heard but the *Hsh! Hsh!* of a faraway train, like a big beast shuffling in its sleep.

'You are cold,' whispered the little corporal. 'You are cold, *ma fille.*'

'No, really not.'

'But you are trembling.'

'Yes, but I'm not cold.'

'What are the women like in England?' asked Blackbeard. 'After the war is over I shall go to England. I shall find a little English woman and marry her – and her pair-rot.' He gave a loud choking laugh.

'Fool!' said the blue-eyed soldier, shaking him; and he leaned over to me. 'It is only after the second glass that you really taste it,' he whispered. 'The second little glass and then – ah! – then you know.'

Café des Amis gleamed in the moonlight. We glanced quickly up and down the road. We ran up the four wooden steps, and opened the ringing glass door into a low room lighted with a hanging lamp, where about ten people were dining. They were seated on two benches at a narrow table.

'Soldiers!' screamed a woman, leaping up from behind a white soup-tureen – a scrag of a woman in a black shawl. 'Soldiers! At this hour! Look at that clock, look at it.' And she pointed to the clock with the dripping ladle.

'It's fast,' said the blue-eyed soldier. 'It's fast, Madame. And don't make so much noise, I beg of you. We will drink and we will go.'

'Will you?' she cried, running round the table and planting herself in front of us. 'That's just what you won't do. Coming into an honest woman's house this hour of the night – making a scene – getting the police after you. Ah, no! Ah, no! It's a disgrace, that's what it is.'

'Sh!' said the little corporal, holding up his hand. Dead silence. In the silence we heard steps passing.

'The police,' whispered Blackbeard, winking at a pretty girl with rings in her ears, who smiled back at him, saucy. 'Sh!'

The faces lifted, listening. 'How beautiful they are!' I thought. 'They are like a family party having supper in the New Testament . . .' The steps died away.

'Serve you very well right if you had been caught,' scolded the angry woman. 'I'm sorry on your account that the police didn't come. You deserve it – you deserve it.'

'A little glass of mirabelle and we will go,' persisted the blue-eyed soldier.

Still scolding and muttering, she took four glasses from the cupboard and a big bottle. 'But you're not going to drink in here. Don't you believe it.' The little corporal ran into the kitchen. 'Not there! Not there! Idiot!' she cried. 'Can't you see there's a window there, and a wall opposite where the police come every evening to . . .'

'Sh!' Another scare.

'You are mad and you will end in prison – all four of you,' said the woman. She flounced out of the room. We tiptoed after her into a dark-smelling scullery, full of pans of greasy water, of salad leaves and meat-bones.

'There now,' she said, putting down the glasses. 'Drink and go!'

'Ah, at last!' The blue-eyed soldier's happy voice trickled through the dark. 'What do you think? Isn't it just as I said? Hasn't it got a taste of excellent – *ex-cellent* whisky?'

MILES FRANKLIN

✐

from
My Brilliant Career

An Introduction to Possum Gully

I was nearly nine summers old when my father conceived the idea
that he was wasting his talents by keeping them rolled up in the
small napkin of an out-of-the-way place like Bruggabrong and the
Bin Bin stations. Therefore he determined to take up his residence
in a locality where he would have more scope for his ability.

When giving his reason for moving to my mother, he put the
matter before her thus: The price of cattle and horses had fallen so
of late years that it was impossible to make much of a living by
breeding them. Sheep were the only profitable article to have
nowadays, and it would be impossible to run them on Bruggabrong
or either of the Bin Bins. The dingoes would work havoc among
them in no time, and what they left the duffers would soon dispose
of. As for bringing police into the matter, it would be worse than
useless. They could not run the offenders to earth, and their efforts
to do so would bring down upon their employer the wrath of the
duffers. Result, all the fences on the station would be fired for a
dead certainty, and the destruction of more than a hundred miles of
heavy log fencing on rough country like Bruggabrong was no
picnic to contemplate.

This was the feasible light in which father shaded his desire to
leave. The fact of the matter was that the heartless harridan,
discontent, had laid her claw-like hand upon him. His guests were
ever assuring him he was buried and wasted in Timlinbilly's
gullies. A man of his intelligence, coupled with his wonderful
experience among stock, would, they averred, make a name and
fortune for himself dealing or auctioneering if he only liked to try.

Richard Melvyn began to think so too, and desired to try. He did try.

He gave up Bruggabrong, Bin Bin East and Bin Bin West, bought Possum Gully, a small farm of one thousand acres, and brought us all to live near Goulburn. Here we arrived one autumn afternoon. Father, mother, and children packed in the buggy, myself, and the one servant-girl, who had accompanied us, on horseback. The one man Father had retained in his service was awaiting our arrival. He had preceded us with a bullock-drayload of furniture and belongings, which was all Father had retained of his household property. Just sufficient for us to get along with, until he had time to settle and purchase more, he said. That was ten years ago, and that is the only furniture we possess yet – just enough to get along with.

My first impression of Possum Gully was bitter disappointment – an impression which time has failed to soften or wipe away.

How flat, common, and monotonous the scenery appeared after the rugged peaks of the Timlinbilly Ranges!

Our new house was a ten-roomed wooden structure, built on a barren hillside. Crooked stunted gums and stringybarks, with a thick underscrub of wild cherry, hop, and hybrid wattle, clothed the spurs which ran up from the back of the detached kitchen. Away from the front of the house were flats, bearing evidence of cultivation, but a drop of water was nowhere to be seen. Later, we discovered a few round, deep, weedy waterholes down on the flat, which in rainy weather swelled to a stream which swept all before it. Possum Gully is one of the best-watered spots in the district, and in that respect has stood to its guns in the bitterest drought. Use and knowledge have taught us the full value of its fairly clear and beautifully soft water. Just then, however, coming from the mountains where every gully had its limpid creek, we turned in disgust from the idea of having to drink this water.

I felt cramped on our new run. It was only three miles wide at its broadest point. Was I always, always, always to live here, and never, never, never to go back to Bruggabrong? That was the burden of the grief with which I sobbed myself to sleep on the first night after our arrival.

Mother felt dubious of her husband's ability to make a living off a thousand acres, half of which were fit to run nothing but wallabies, but Father was full of plans, and very sanguine concerning his future. He was not going to squat henlike on his place as the cockies around him did. He meant to deal in stock, making of Possum Gully merely a depot on which to run some of his bargains until reselling.

Dear, oh dear! It was terrible to think he had wasted the greater part of his life among the hills where the mail came but once a week, and where the nearest town, of 650 inhabitants, was forty-six miles distant. And the road had been impassable for vehicles. Here, only seventeen miles from a city like Goulburn, with splendid roads, mail thrice weekly, and a railway platform only eight miles away, why, man, my fortune is made! Such were the sentiments to which he gave birth out of the fullness of his hopeful heart.

Ere the diggings had broken out on Bruggabrong, our nearest neighbour, excepting, of course, boundary-riders, was seventeen miles distant. Possum Gully was a thickly populated district, and here we were surrounded by homes ranging from half a mile to two and three miles away. This was a new experience for us, and it took us some time to become accustomed to the advantage and disadvantage of the situation. Did we require an article, we found it handy, but decidedly the reverse when our neighbours borrowed from us, and, in the greater percentage of cases, failed to return the loan.

To Life

It is indelibly imprinted on my memory in a manner which royal joy, fame, pleasure, and excitement beyond the dream of poets could never efface, not though I should be cursed with a life of five-score years. I will paint it truthfully – letter for letter as it was.

It was twenty-six miles from Yarnung to Barney's Gap, as M'Swat's place was named. He had brought a light wagonette and pair to convey me thither.

As we drove along, I quite liked my master. Of course, we were of calibre too totally unlike ever to be congenial companions, but I appreciated his sound common sense in the little matters within his range, and his bluntly straightforward, fairly good-natured, manner. He was an utterly ignorant man, with small ideas according to the sphere which he fitted, and which fitted him; but he was 'a man for a' that, an' a' that'.

221

He and my father had been boys together. Years and years ago M'Swat's father had been blacksmith on my father's station, and the little boys had played together, and, in spite of their then difference in station, had formed a friendship which lived and bore fruit at this hour. I wished that their youthful relations had been inimical, not friendly.

We left the pub in Yarnung at nine, and arrived at our destination somewhere about two o'clock in the afternoon.

I had waxed quite cheerful, and began to look upon the situation in a sensible light. It was necessary that I should stand up to the guns of life at one time or another, and why not now? M'Swat's might not be so bad after all. Even if they were dirty, they would surely be willing to improve if I exercised tact in introducing a few measures. I was not afraid of work, and would do many things. But all these ideas were knocked on the head, like a dairyman's surplus calves, when on entering Barney's Gap we descended a rough road to the house, which was built in a narrow gully between two steep stony hills, which, destitute of grass, rose like grim walls of rock, imparting a desolate and prison-like aspect.

Six dogs, two pet lambs, two or three pigs, about twenty fowls, eight children which seemed a dozen, and Mrs M'Swat bundled out through the back door at our approach. Those children, not through poverty – M'Swat made a boast of his substantial banking account – but on account of ignorance and slatternliness, were the dirtiest urchins I have ever seen, and were so ragged that those parts of them which should have been covered were exposed to view. The majority of them had red hair and wide hanging-open mouths. Mrs M'Swat was a great, fat, ignorant, pleasant-looking woman, shockingly dirty and untidy. Her tremendous, flabby, stockingless ankles bulged over her unlaced hobnailed boots; her dress was torn and unbuttoned at the throat, displaying one of the dirtiest necks I have seen. It did not seem to worry her that the infant she held under her arm like a roll of cloth howled killingly, while the other little ones clung to her skirts, attempting to hide their heads in its folds like so many emus. She greeted me with a smacking kiss, consigned the baby to the charge of the eldest child, a big girl of fourteen, and seizing upon my trunks as though they were feather-weight, with heavy clodhopping step disappeared into the house with them. Returning, she invited me to enter, and following in her wake, I was followed by the children through the dirtiest passage into the dirtiest room, to sit upon the dirtiest chair, to gaze upon the other dirtiest furniture of which I have ever heard. One wild horrified glance at the dirt, squalor, and total benightedness that met me on every side, and I trembled in every limb with suppressed emotion and the frantic longing to get back to Caddagat which possessed me. One instant showed me that I could never, never live here.

'Have ye had yer dinner?' my future mistress inquired in a rough uncultivated voice. I replied in the negative.

'Sure, ye'll be dyin' of hunger; but I'll have it in a twinklin'.'

She threw a crumpled and disgustingly filthy cloth three-cornered ways on to the dusty table and clapped thereon a couple of dirty knives and forks, a pair of cracked plates, two poley cups and chipped saucers. Next came a plate of salt meat, red with saltpetre, and another of dark, dry, sodden bread. She then disappeared to the kitchen to make the tea, and during her absence two of the little boys commenced to fight. One clutched the tablecloth, and over went the whole display with a bang – meat-dish broken, and meat on the dusty floor; while the cats and fowls, ever on the alert for such occurrences, made the most of their opportunities. Mrs M'Swat returned carrying the tea, which was spilling by the way. She gave those boys each a clout on the head which dispersed them roaring like the proverbial town bull, and alarmed me for the safety of their ear-drums. I wondered if their mother was aware of their having ear-drums. She grabbed the meat, and wiping it on her greasy apron, carried it around in her hand until she found a plate for it, and by that time the children had collected the other things. A cup was broken, and another, also a poley, was put in its stead.

Mr M'Swat now appeared, and after taking a nip out of a rum bottle which he produced from a cupboard in the corner, he invited me to sit up to dinner.

There was no milk. M'Swat went in entirely for sheep, keeping only a few cows for domestic purposes: these, on account of the drought, had been dry for some months. Mrs M'Swat apologized for the lack of sugar, stating she was quite out of it and had forgotten to send for a fresh supply.

'You damned fool, to miss such a chance wen I was goin' to town with the wagonette! I mightn't be goin' in again for munce [months]. But sugar don't count much. Them as can't do without a useless luxury like that for a spell will never make much of a show at gettin' on in the wu-r-r-r-ld,' concluded Mr M'Swat, sententiously.

The children sat in a row and, with mouths open and interest in their big wondering eyes, gazed at me unwinkingly till I felt I must rush away somewhere and shriek to relieve the feeling of over-strained hysteria which was overcoming me. I contained myself sufficiently, however, to ask if this was all the family.

'All but Peter. Where's Peter, Mary Ann?'

'He went to the Red Hill to look after some sheep, and won't be back till dark.'

'Peter's growed up,' remarked one little boy, with evident pride in this member of the family.

'Yes; Peter's twenty-one, and hes a mustatche and shaves,' said the eldest girl, in a manner indicating that she expected me to be struck dumb with surprise.

'She'll be surprised wen she sees Peter,' said a little girl in an audible whisper.

Mrs M'Swat vouchsafed the information that three had died between Peter and Lizer, and this was how the absent son came to be so much older than his brothers and sisters.

'So you have had twelve children?' I said.

'Yes,' she replied, laughing fatly, as though it were a joke.

'The boys found a bees' nest in a tree an' have been robbin' it the smornin',' continued Mrs M'Swat.

'Yes; we have ample exemplification of that,' I responded. It was honey here and honey there and honey everywhere. It was one of the many varieties of dirt on the horrible foul-smelling tablecloth. It was on the floor, the door, the chairs, the children's heads, and the cups. Mrs M'Swat remarked contentedly that it always took a couple of days to wear 'off of' things.

After 'dinner' I asked for a bottle of ink and some paper, and scrawled a few lines to Grannie and my mother, merely reporting my safe arrival at my destination. I determined to take time to collect my thoughts before petitioning for release from Barney's Gap.

I requested my mistress to show me where I was to sleep, and she conducted me to a fairly respectable little bedroom, of which I

224

was to be sole occupant, unless I felt lonely and would like Rose Jane to sleep with me. I looked at pretty, soft-eyed, dirty little Rose Jane, and assured her kind-hearted mother I would not be the least lonely, as the sickening despairing loneliness which filled my heart was not of a nature to be cured by having as a bedmate a frowzy wild child.

Upon being left alone I barred my door and threw myself on the bed to cry – weep wild hot tears that scalded my cheeks, and sobs that shook my whole frame and gave me a violent pain in the head.

Oh, how coarse and grating were the sounds to be heard around me! Lack, nay, not lack, but utter freedom from the first instincts of cultivation, was to be heard even in the great heavy footfalls and the rasping sharp voices which fell on my ears. So different had I been listening in a room at Caddagat to my grannie's brisk pleasant voice, or to my Aunt Helen's low refined accents; and I am such a one to see and feel these differences.

However, I pulled together in a little while, and called myself a fool for crying. I would write to Grannie and Mother explaining matters, and I felt sure they would heed me, as they had no idea what the place was like. I would have only a little while to wait patiently, then I would be among all the pleasures of Caddagat again; and how I would revel in them, more than ever, after a taste of a place like this, for it was worse than I had imagined it could be, even in the nightmares which had haunted me concerning it before leaving Caddagat.

The house was of slabs, unlimed, and with very low iron roof, and having no sign of a tree near it, the heat was unendurable. It was reflected from the rocks on either side, and concentrated in this spot like an oven, being 122 degrees in the verandah now. I wondered why M'Swat had built in such a hole, but it appears it was the nearness of the point to water which recommended it to his judgement.

With the comforting idea that I would not have long to bear this, I bathed my eyes, and walked away from the house to try and find a cooler spot. The children saw me depart but not return, to judge from a discussion of myself which I heard in the dining-room, which adjoined my bed-chamber.

Peter came home, and the children clustered around to tell the news.

'Did she come?'

'Yes.'

'Wot's she like?'

'Oh, a rale little bit of a thing, not as big as Lizer!'

'And, Peter, she hes teeny little hands, as wite as snow, like that woman in the picter Ma got off of the tea.'

'Yes, Peter,' chimed in another voice; 'and her feet are that little that she don't make no nise wen she walks.'

'It ain't only becos her feet are little, but cos she's got them beautiful shoes like wot's in picters,' said another.

'Her hair is tied with two great junks of ribbing, one up on her head an' another near the bottom; better than that bit er red ribbing wot Lizer keeps in the box agin the time she might go to town some day.'

'Yes,' said the voice of Mrs M'Swat, 'her hair is near to her knees, and a plait as thick as yer arm; and wen she writ a couple of letters in a minute, you could scarce see her hand move it was that wonderful quick; and she uses them big words wot you couldn't understand without bein' eddicated.'

'She has tree brooches, and a necktie better than your best one wots you keeps to go seeing Susie Duffy in,' and Lizer giggled slyly.

'You shut up about Susie Duffy, or I'll whack yuz up aside of the ear,' said Peter angrily.

'She ain't like Ma. She's fat up here, and goes in like she'd break in the middle, Peter.'

'Great scissors! she must be a flyer,' said Peter. 'I'll bet she'll make you sit up, Jimmy.'

'I'll make *her* sit up,' retorted Jimmy, who came next to Lizer. 'She thinks she's a toff, but she's only old Melvyn's darter, that Pa has to give money to.'

'Peter,' said another, 'her face ain't got them freckles on like yours, and it ain't dark like Lizer's. It's reel wite, and pinky round here.'

'I bet she won't make me knuckle down to her, no matter wot colour she is,' returned Peter, in a surly tone.

No doubt it was this idea which later in the afternoon induced him to swagger forward to shake hands with me with a flash insolent leer on his face. I took pains to be especially nice to him, treating him with deference, and making remarks upon the extreme heat of the weather with such pleasantness that he was nonplussed, and looked relieved when able to escape. I smiled to myself, and apprehended no further trouble from Peter.

The table for tea was set exactly as it had been before, and was lighted by a couple of tallow candles made from bad fat, and their odour was such as my jockey travelling companion of the day before would have described as a tough smell.

'Give us a toon on the peeany,' said Mrs M'Swat after the meal, when the dishes had been cleared away by Lizer and Rose Jane. The tea and scraps, of which there was any amount, remained on the floor, to be picked up by the fowls in the morning.

The children lay on the old sofa and on the chairs, where they always slept at night until their parents retired, when there was an all-round bawl as they were wakened and bundled into bed, dirty as they were, and very often with their clothes on.

I acceded to Mrs M'Swat's request with alacrity, thinking that while forced to remain there I would have one comfort, and would spend all my spare time at the piano. I opened the instrument, brushed a little of the dust from the keys with my pocket-handkerchief, and struck the opening chords of Kowalski's 'Marche Hongroise'.

I have heard of pianos sounding like a tin dish, but this was not as pleasant as a tin dish by long chalks. Every note that I struck stayed down not to rise, and when I got them up the jarring, clanging, discordant clatter they produced beggars description. There was not the slightest possibility of distinguishing any tune on the thing. Worthless to begin with, it had stood in the dust, heat, and wind so long that every sign that it had once made music had deserted it.

I closed it with a feeling of such keen disappointment that I had difficulty in suppressing tears.

'Won't it play?' inquired Mr M'Swat.

'No; the keys stay down.'

'Then, Rose Jane, go ye an' pick 'em up while she tries again.'

I tried again, Rose Jane fishing up the keys as I went along. I perceived instantly that not one had the least ear for music or idea what it was; so I beat on the demented piano with both hands, and often with all fingers at once, and the bigger row I made the better they liked it.

LISA ST AUBIN DE TERÁN

☞

Zapa, the Fire Child Who Looked Like a Toad

On the east side of the hacienda, on the slope that stretched across from the rift of hidden orange trees to the low crest, La Ciega's house spread down the hill in a series of low-roofed mud walls that lengthened and expanded with his family. La Ciega was both rich and blind. He had been so for many years. He was an optimist, so he never accepted his lack of sight. The fortune that he was amassing from his illicit still and his continual sales of rot-gut rum would, he believed, one day pay for the miracle that would return his sight to him. Because La Ciega was also a realist, he knew that even miracles had to be paid for; only calamity was free. So he kept his money in a pit under the hearth like a hoard of future visions. Since he didn't care for his money as such, what he wanted was to see, he never felt that just his savings made him rich. His true riches lay in the cropped heads of his many sons and in the thick hair of his daughters. La Ciega had fifteen children: fourteen of his own and his orphaned niece, the fire child Zapa.

When the rains turned all the tracks to mud and hindered the working of the old copper distillery and leaked through the tin roofs, blackened the corncakes and mildewed the pots, all the workers used to find their way to La Ciega's to drink there and describe his children to him. Elsa, his favourite, was the prettiest with her hair like a fair horse's mane and eyes the colour of smothered grass. While the plainest – not only of his, but of all the estate children – was Zapa, who never had a proper name. Somehow, though he did favour Elsa, the blind man loved these two girls nearly the same. Had not Zapa been given to him, and she was his kin, saved as a baby from a burning hut; people called her

228

survival a miracle. La Ciega loved miracles, even if they happened to other people. They inspired him rather in the way his own gold teeth inspired the workers. Few men were envious of his gold-studded mouth; there was a collective pride in his metal dentistry. It was enough just to live near such a mouth: to sit and speak and hear the answers tumbling from the shining barricades.

Zapa was so plain that it had given her her name. It meant 'a toad'. When she was first dragged from the fire, saved by her screams (and the natural curiosity that always lured the workers and their families to the site of a disaster), she was only a few weeks old. At first they thought that Zapa's mother was in the hut as well and that they'd watched her burn. But when the ashes cooled and the debris was checked, there was no sign of any bones except for the charred splinters of the guinea pigs trapped in their inner pen. For weeks and months they thought her mother would return to claim her baby, but she never came. Waiting for her, they felt reluctant to choose a name, so they called her Zapa to match her strange face, and the nickname stuck to her, as she to them.

No one knew what made her perform her odd rituals; only Elsa seemed to understand the importance of crouching on stones and staring silently into water. Every day Elsa and Zapa shared their chores, sweeping the dirt floors and making brooms, gathering twigs for kindling and grinding corn; then all their spare time would be spent inventing games, making shrines and saying chants into the dark rift of trees. Zapa was always the high priestess, while Elsa, who was four years older, was the acolyte.

Every year, when the rains stopped and the layer of mould that had gathered on everything – from the hammock strings to the used milk tins that sat clustered around their house, with their muddy geraniums – had powdered and dried, people began to gossip again. It was not that they stopped during the rainy season, it was just that the floods, and the inevitable sickness and fever that followed, held back the tide of conjecture. There was less time for speculation. The workers still monitored each other's affairs, but they laid down their stores of information like salt fish for such time as they might need them. Life took longer to live in the wet weather. The best place to gossip was on the low wall outside La Ciega's and the track was too slippery then, and the wall itself too chilly.

La Ciega was a moneylender – not by any special inclination, more because he was the only person other than the *Patrón* who had any money. Everyone, in their time, would wind up the steep slope to his house and borrow from him, watching him notch the tally on to his lending stick. Then, within minutes, everyone else for miles around would know about the transaction. There were no secrets on the hacienda. Nothing was or could be hidden except for the tops of the tall orange trees that grew in the dank rift of the valley. In lieu of interest, La Ciega charged information. Blind as he was, he made himself the centre of that world. Nothing moved without his knowledge. No wedding or funeral was possible without his loans. No bribe or debt could be paid without his assistance. Because instead of drudging in the cane fields he had had the wit to distil the cane juice, he was treated somewhat as an oracle. Any man who could prosper despite his disability and have fifteen children all clothed and fed, a gold mouth, and an unlimited stash of inside information must be wiser than most, without a doubt. So when the wives and the widows sent their children across the pink tasselled grass to fill up their empty bottles with new rum or to borrow the coins for a new sack of seed, they often asked Ciega for his advice on this or that dispute.

To his own household, he said: 'I am like the old man of Mototán. My voice is the voice of all this valley. They live their lives by mine, just as we all live ours by the sun's clock. Their sons and daughters fear me because I have my fingers caught in all their parents' veins. In the beginning all I wanted was to see, but now, though I am blind, I can see that the example I lease to others must come from me.'

La Ciega's wife had heard this speech before and she would sidle back into her kitchen before he got halfway through, smiling with a mixture of pride and mockery. Perhaps because she never had to borrow money from him, she didn't find him as imposing as the others. Or perhaps it was because he was helpless without her and she had borne him fourteen children. When the elections came round, filling the towns and villages with their bribes, La Ciega and his wife, Juana, had been to hear some of the speeches. Maybe Juana smiled at her husband because she recognized the rhetoric as coming from the Christian Democrat campaigner who had given them the new copper pipes for their stills. Whatever the reason,

Juana never showed the others her ambiguous smile. It was something she kept for herself as she patted out the corncakes for their evening meal.

It was only the words that came between them, because Juana, too, wanted her sons home by nightfall. It kept her from worrying, and it kept them safe. She knew herself how easily led astray a girl could be – even by a blind man. Her family had once teased her for her marriage. She supposed they must have despised La Ciega. In principle she did too, but in practice he was too fine a man to harbour any prejudice against. And who else had a husband with a headful of gold? And who else had as many live children, or even half as much food? So Juana was happy with her lot, and as watchful as her husband for her children's safety. There was no shame in her family, no blot, and it was a fine thing to be envied by so many other women. Not even their gossiping scratches reached their mark. What did it matter that La Ciega had never been able to see her fine looks? He had felt her and loved her, and now that childbirth had harrowed her flesh, she was glad that he would never see her face fade. She saw her beauty repeated in Elsa with pride, and she saw the poor thin hair and the pale wide mouth of her niece with pity. Poor Zapa; La Ciega loved her because she was his sister's child, his blood. But Juana loved her for her motherlessness. Her own daughters were so pretty that Zapa's lack of grace never bothered her; she was a good girl, and that was all that mattered.

Zapa rarely paused to think about her place in the family; she was neither the eldest nor the youngest. Her chores were simple and her rewards were greater than the dusty mugs of syrupy water for the poorer children on the estate. On Sundays she ate eggs and chicken and sardines with her rice. She had a comb of her own, and a new cotton frock every Christmas time, and sandals for her feet. Sometimes she thought of her real mother, the one who had left her to burn, but she could never put a face to the idea. When the sun was at its hottest, and the yard and rooms were swept and the brooms had been dismantled and fresh twigs had been collected for the afternoon's sweep, Zapa would lie in the grass and squint at the sun, searching for a hint of her lost mother. The lights in front of her eyelids were as near as she ever came to seeing her, red and orange lights that hovered on the edge of sleep.

Most days, though, she was content with her passport to love, and her cult of the swept yard and her games and Elsa. She knew that everyone needed to belong somewhere, and she did, right there on her uncle's porch every night at six when the silent curfew filled the hills and all the weary workers staggered back home across the terraces. The drag-bellied pigs were shut away for the night, as were the hens and goats. La Ciega's lumpy cow was tethered and his dogs unleashed. All the stray children divided and scattered to their own places to eat and rest. Everyone was counted. Not even the boys missed the beginning of the curfew. It was true that they crept out again sometimes, but the world as they knew it began and ended at six and six. An enormous amount of scandal could be squeezed in between those times, but the times themselves were sacred. Work began and ended then. It seemed, almost, as though life itself began and ended there too.

For eight years Zapa had learned to ply her broom, then for two years she was mistress of the sweeping. She mastered her craft so well that she knew all the places where the escoba bush grew, and she picked the twigs faster and tied them quicker than any other child. Sometimes people would come and ask to borrow her so that she might make up their brooms. Zapa could make brooms that would last a whole week. She had a knack of stuffing the bundle of twigs through the cut cylinder of an empty sardine tin in such a way that the twigs would stay put. People used to poke at her straggly hair and say, 'Juana did a good job the day she dragged you screaming from that fire. And to think all we saw was a bundle of rags and burns, when really you were an infant prodigy. What do you say to that, Zapa?'

But Zapa was a shy child who had, some said, lost her tongue in the fire. Often, instead of answering, she would hold up the backs of her hands and flash her fingernails. It was her way of communicating. Only Elsa knew how much she loved to chatter. When there were just the two of them playing in the rift, Zapa never stopped talking. She'd squat on her favourite flat stone and blink her wide eyes and make up reasons for everything around them. Zapa could explain the existence of every seed and fruit; she'd pretend to know how the sand and the boulders came to be there. She would watch the blue birds settling in the tree tops and then tell Elsa where they came from and where they were going to.

Zapa could trace the tracks of the red ants and list the nests of the beetles and lizards who clung to the rocks. Whatever Elsa asked her, Zapa knew. She seemed to rake the cobwebs that looped from one wide leaf of the red-studded onoto to the next and weave them into gossamer lies. She told Elsa that God had given her the face of a toad so that everyone would notice only her beautiful hands.

'Look,' she'd say, showing her manicured fingers yet again. 'Look, not even the *doña* has hands like mine. I could sweep the porch down to its bare bone and my skin would still be as soft and my nails as fine.'

Elsa loved Zapa's hands. She worshipped them and begged her to tell the secrets of the potion and leaves that she rubbed into them. Sometimes Zapa shared her spells, mixing up creams for Elsa, but she never told her how they were made. When the first signs of the workers' return drifted up to them, they would make their way home. Zapa often lingered for a while in the wood, but she never missed the curfew – no one did. No one dared.

The day had begun like any day. It was not special, there was no saint hovering over it. There was no market out of range or visitor on the estate. Elsa had seen Antonio José, her admirer, but then she saw him every day. He wanted to marry her but she was only fourteen and he didn't seem like half as much fun as staying at home, where there was plenty of everything, and sleeping near Zapa, whom she loved. Zapa was only ten and would have years to go until she married, so Antonio José would have to wait or choose again. After the sweeping, she and Zapa had gone to the rift. Their frangipani tree had opened its first flower, and Zapa had caught a frog and a water snake in her net. Elsa had wanted to tie the frog in a plantain bag and then watch it struggle, but Zapa had told her that this frog was the keeper of all the flowers, and a special friend of hers who came in through the hole in the kitchen door; if they let it be, it would sing 'Las Mañanitas' to them next year.

It had been a day of little things with nothing but a trickle of trivia to show for itself. Nothing had happened to announce its importance. There were no portents, no kneeling boughs or tapping winds, no formation of birds in flight. Nothing. In years to come, Elsa felt retrospectively cheated by this. She looked back and sifted the events, the whispers and comments, searching for some significance or some pattern to explain why their lives were shattered then. But there was nothing.

Elsa sat on the porch and waited impatiently. It never occurred to her that Zapa would be really late. No one was ever late. She waited uneasily only because the quality of her own life improved when Zapa was beside her. The others began to grumble long before she began to feel alarm. Zapa had a reason and an excuse for everything; she would find a way to darn her absence to the law. If only she came back she could make La Ciega forgive her, but she didn't come. Juana began to move in slow motion, the paste of wet corn started to stick to her fingers. In retrospect, she would call this the first omen. As the moments passed, the thin house filled with dread. The boys tried to laugh off the tension; but one by one they found themselves swallowing teazles as La Ciega ran through and repeated his head count.

At dawn and dusk, the double six of every day, each child knelt before La Ciega and his tally stick. The blind man would reach out and touch each proffered crown.

'Bless me, father.'

'May God bless you and your life be good.'

Fourteen varying heads passed under his palm. He knew them all so well.

'Where is Zapa?' he asked each time, running and rerunning the head count through his hands.

'Where is Zapa?'

La Ciega had a gold fob watch which he kept on a chain round his neck for safekeeping. Between each demand he called out, 'Pedro, time?'

It was six fifteen, eighteen, twenty-three, thirty, then seven o'clock and eight. Elsa watched, taking her ritual part in the charade, passing and repassing in her place in the count. She watched Zapa's prospective scolding turned into a beating and then a thrashing, and then take off into the realms of the unknown. She was tempted to run and find her, but she knew that such action would be a clumsy admission of a guilt that Elsa felt sure Zapa would be able to explain away.

The night was thick with shadows when Zapa walked up to the line of stunned silence. Her family all looked to her to ease their confusion and the chill that was coming from the evening air into the base of their spines. Elsa watched her adoptive sister's wispy hair caught in the small light of their lamp. She remembered there were fireflies in the bracken and trees around her. As though by Zapa's orchestration, the cicadas began to sing with their usual tunelessness as she arrived. All she had to do was to speak up over their low background of noise, and Zapa was always good with insects.

The minutes of waiting became worse than the preceding two hours. Zapa said nothing except, kneeling, she asked for her '*Bendición*'.

Their world fragmented in La Ciega's silence. The blessing was refused: the house was shamed, and Zapa herself condemned, with never so much as a word spoken.

The others pushed and poked her and made eyes such as could roll excuses from behind their own sockets. Zapa said nothing except for the three times she knelt in front of her uncle and asked for his blessing. By the third denial, Juana had Zapa's bundle ready for her: the frock and comb, her emery boards and a stack of corncakes for the night. She handed it to the child to make her see how final her silence would be. Zapa took it sadly, looking around her with her wide, slightly protruding eyes.

'*Bendición*' she asked, this time of Juana. In reply there were only that tired woman's tears, which seemed to speak more clearly than any words might have done: 'May He forgive you, Zapa, for you know we can't. You have brought shame into this house, you must take it away again.' Zapa took the bundle and shuffled backwards across the porch, avoiding Elsa's eyes. She held out her hand to Juana, who had been a mother: '*Bendición*, Mamma?'

No one ever knew why Zapa wouldn't explain where she had been, not even Elsa. It couldn't have changed everything, whatever the excuse, but the leaving would have been more gentle had words been allowed to bear witness. As it was, Zapa found herself making her way through the dark, past the barking dogs of every hut that lay between home and the road that she would have to reach to leave the hacienda. There was nowhere else to go but away. No one would dare to go against La Ciega. Zapa knew that no one would want to. Men and women who had turned their own

235

daughters away for just such misdemeanours would scarcely harbour her, after what she had done. She had broken the form, and the form was everything. She had splintered their life. The lust that she was tacitly accused of had no reason to escape at such a time. Dozens of bastards were conceived in the night between the blessings. By defying La Ciega she had made herself a rebel woman in the eyes of the world and shunned his protection.

As she picked her way over the loose stones of the track, the implications of her loss began to possess her. She walked past the low-slung avocado trees and the leaves rustled against her face. There were noises all around her, the night noises that she had been brought up to fear. Anyone who went out at night was prey to El Coco, the wild man who ate children like herself. Only a lover and a great deal of lust could conquer such fears. Zapa had neither. Juana would assume that Zapa had been led astray by a man – were it not so, she would have talked in her defence and mitigated her sentence to being banished into service. Zapa didn't know why she hadn't talked. Even without her usual weave of fantasy she could have told the truth: she had fallen asleep on a huge cold stone. The fire took her tongue.

It didn't take long to flush Zapa out from the dusty roadside to the town. A few days spent hanging around the market scrounging food soon brought her down to the place where she would be cared for. It even seemed vaguely like a mythical home. She was taken to the Calle Vargas, a street of brothels on the far side of the little market town. She had never seen or heard of the red-light zone before, but she liked the sound of it. It was all she had left of her mother, that flicker of red lights on her eyelids when the sun beat down. The women on the Vargas were mostly kind, but the turnover was fast, so no one really had time to help a ten-year-old child prostitute with an ugly face and a broad grin, wide eyes and a lack of grace.

Some of the old regulars who had proved themselves immune to the fevers and the infections remembered her. They remembered her plainness and her impossibly thin hair and her gift for sweeping and her perfect nails. She had won several hearts by doing the manicures in between customers. 'Poor Zapa,' they would say, 'she had some very nasty customers.'

When Elsa married Antonio José, she did so to gain her freedom to seek Zapa out. As a married woman, she had the right to go to market. She hadn't wanted to wed so young, but somewhere she knew that Zapa needed her, and life itself was empty without Zapa. She didn't love Antonio José, but she preferred him to her life at Ciega's house as it had come to be since Zapa left. Everyone missed her. A whole year passed before she tracked her sister down. It was a year of buying herbs and asking questions. It was possible to get to market only occasionally. She didn't know what would happen when she found her; just that she had to look.

Elsa followed Zapa as she shifted from one brothel to the next, never quite managing to catch up with her in the minutes she stole from her shopping trips. Elsa left notes and messages and presents of soft cheese and eggs. At one point she seemed so close, but when she returned, they said Zapa had fled.

One by one her own babies were born, weighing her down as they filled her womb and tying her down at home. She had less time to search for her sister. Whenever she did, the news was confusing. Zapa had gone, disappeared, died of a fever, died of a fight, run away with a cowboy, run away with a gambler, found her family, gone home. Eventually Elsa despaired, and made a shrine to Zapa in the rift, loading it with flowers and leaves and piles of flat grey stones. Every time she felt her breasts harden and a new life stir within her, she prayed tearfully for the sign of a toad in her womb.

GRACE PALEY

The Long-Distance Runner

One day, before or after forty-two, I became a long-distance runner. Though I was stout and in many ways inadequate to this desire, I wanted to go far and fast, not as fast as bicycles and trains, not as far as Taipei, Hingwen, places like that, islands of the slant-eyed cunt, as sailors in bus stations say when speaking of travel, but round and round the county from the sea side to the bridges, along the old neighborhood streets a couple of times, before old age and urban renewal ended them and me.

I tried the country first, Connecticut, which being wooded is always full of buds in spring. All creation is secret, isn't that true? So I trained in the wide-zoned suburban hills where I wasn't known. I ran all spring in and out of dogwood bloom, then laurel.

People sometimes stopped and asked me why I ran, a lady in silk shorts halfway down over her fat thighs. In training, I replied and rested only to answer if closely questioned. I wore a white sleeveless undershirt as well, with excellent support, not to attract the attention of old men and prudish children.

Then summer came, my legs seemed strong. I kissed the kids goodbye. They were quite old by then. It was near the time for parting anyway. I told Mrs Raftery to look in now and then and give them some of that rotten Celtic supper she makes.

I told them they could take off any time they wanted to. Go lead your private life, I said. Only leave me out of it.

A word to the wise . . . said Richard.

You're depressed, Faith, Mrs Raftery said. Your boyfriend Jack, the one you think's so hotsy-totsy, hasn't called and you're as gloomy as a tick on Sunday.

Cut the folkshit with me, Raftery, I muttered. Her eyes filled with tears because that's who she is: folkshit from bunion to topknot. That's how she got liked by me, loved, invented and endured.

When I walked out the door they were all reclining before the television set, Richard, Tonto and Mrs Raftery, gazing at the news. Which proved with moving pictures that there *had* been a voyage to the moon and Africa and South America hid in a furious whorl of clouds.

I said, Goodbye. They said, Yeah, OK, sure.

If that's how it is, forget it, I hollered and took the Independent subway to Brighton Beach.

At Brighton Beach I stopped at the Salty Breezes Locker Room to change my clothes. Twenty-five years ago my father invested $500 in its future. In fact he still clears about $3.50 a year, which goes directly (by law) to the Children of Judea to cover their deficit.

No one paid too much attention when I started to run, easy and light on my feet. I ran on the boardwalk first, past my mother's leafleting station – between a soft-ice-cream stand and a degenerated dune. There she had been assigned by her comrades to halt the tides of cruel American enterprise with simple socialist sense.

I wanted to stop and admire the long beach. I wanted to stop in order to think admiringly about New York. There aren't many rotting cities so tan and sandy and speckled with citizens at their salty edges. But I had already spent a lot of life lying down or standing and staring. I had decided to run.

After about a mile and a half I left the boardwalk and began to trot into the old neighborhood. I was running well. My breath was long and deep. I was thinking pridefully about my form.

Suddenly I was surrounded by about three hundred blacks.

Who you?

Who that?

Look at her! Just look! When you seen a fatter ass?

Poor thing. She ain't right. Leave her, you boys, you bad boys.

I used to live here, I said.

Oh yes, they said, in the white old days. That time too bad to last.

But we loved it here. We never went to Flatbush Avenue or Times Square. We loved our block.

Tough black titty.

I like your speech, I said. Metaphor and all.

Right on. We get that from talking.

Yes, my people also had a way of speech. And don't forget the Irish. The gift of gab.

Who they? said a small boy.

Cops.

Nowadays, I suggested, there's more than Irish on the police force.

You right, said two ladies. More more, much much more. They's French Chinamen Russkies Congoleans. Oh missee, you too right.

I lived in that house, I said. That apartment house. All my life. Till I got married.

Now that *is* nice. Live in one place. My mother live that way in South Carolina. One place. Her daddy farmed. She said. They ate. No matter winter war bad times. Roosevelt. Something! Ain't that wonderful! And it weren't cold! Big trees!

That apartment. I looked up and pointed. There. The third floor.

They all looked up. So what! You blubrous devil! said a dark young man. He wore horn-rimmed glasses and had that intelligent look that City College boys used to have when I was eighteen and first looked at them.

He seemed to lead them in contempt and anger, even the littlest ones who moved toward me with dramatic stealth singing, Devil, Oh Devil. I don't think the little kids had bad feeling because they poked a finger into me, then laughed.

Still I thought it might be wise to keep my head. So I jumped right in with some facts. I said, How many flowers' names do you know? Wild flowers, I mean. My people only knew two. That's what they say now anyway. Rich or poor, they only had two flowers' names. Rose and violet.

Daisy, said one boy immediately.

Weed, said another. That *is* a flower, I thought. But everyone else got the joke.

Saxifrage, lupine, said a lady. Viper's bugloss, said a small Girl Scout in medium green with a dark green sash. She held up a *Handbook of Wild Flowers*.

How many you know, fat mama? a boy asked warmly. He wasn't against my being a mother or fat. I turned all my attention to him.

Oh sonny, I said, I'm way ahead of my people. I know in yellows alone: common cinquefoil, trout lily, yellow adder's-tongue, swamp buttercup and common buttercup, golden sorrel, yellow or hop clover, devil's-paintbrush, evening primrose, black-eyed Susan, golden aster, also the yellow pickerelweed growing down by the water if not in the water, and dandelions of course. I've seen all these myself. Seen them.

You could see China from the boardwalk, a boy said. When it's nice.

I know more flowers than countries. Mostly young people these days have traveled in many countries.

Not me. I ain't been nowhere.

Not me either, said about seventeen boys.

I'm not allowed, said a little girl. There's drunken junkies.

But *I! I!* cried out a tall black youth, very handsome and well dressed. I am an African. My father came from the high stolen plains. *I* have been everywhere. I was in Moscow six months, learning machinery. I was in France, learning French. I was in Italy, observing the peculiar Renaissance and the people's sweetness. I was in England, where I studied the common law and the urban blight. I was at the Conference of Dark Youth in Cuba to understand our passion. I am now here. Here am I to become an engineer and return to my people, around the Cape of Good Hope in a Norwegian sailing vessel. In this way I will learn the fine old art of sailing in case the engines of the new society of my old inland country should fail.

We had an extraordinary amount of silence after that. Then one old lady in a black dress and high white lace collar said to another old lady dressed exactly the same way, Glad tidings when someone got brains in the head not fish juice. Amen, said a few.

Whyn't you go up to Mrs Luddy living in your house, you lady, huh? The Girl Scout asked this.

Why she just groove to see you, said some sarcastic snickerer.

She got palpitations. Her man, he give it to her.

That ain't all, he a natural gift-giver.

I'll take you, said the Girl Scout. My name is Cynthia. I'm in Troop 355, Brooklyn.

I'm not dressed, I said, looking at my lumpy knees.

You shouldn't wear no undershirt like that without no runnin number or no team writ on it. It look like a undershirt.

Cynthia! Don't take her up there, said an important boy. Her head strange. Don't you take her. Hear?

Lawrence, she said softly, you tell me once more what to do I'll wrap you round that lamp-post.

Git! she said, powerfully addressing *me*.

In this way I was led into the hallway of the whole house of my childhood.

The first door I saw was still marked in flaky gold, 1A. That's where the janitor lived, I said. He was a Negro.

How come like that? Cynthia made an astonished face. How come the janitor was a black man?

Oh Cynthia, I said. Then I turned to the opposite door, first floor front, 1B. I remembered. Now, here, this was Mrs Goreditsky, very very fat lady. All her children died at birth. Born, then one, two, three. Dead. Five children, then Mr Goreditsky said, I'm bad luck on you Tessie and he went away. He sent $15 a week for seven years. Then no one heard.

I know her, poor thing, said Cynthia. The city come for her summer before last. The way they knew, it smelled. They wrapped her up in a canvas. They couldn't get through the front door. It scraped off a piece of her. My Uncle Ronald had to help them, but he got disgusted.

Only two years ago. She was still here! Wasn't she scared?

So we all, said Cynthia. White ain't everything.

Who lived up here, she asked, 2B? Right now, my best friend Nancy Rosalind lives here. She got two brothers, and her sister married and got a baby. She very light-skinned. Not her mother. We got all colors amongst us.

Your best friend? That's funny. Because it was *my* best friend. Right in that apartment. Joanna Rosen.

What become of her? Cynthia asked. She got a running shirt too?

Come on Cynthia, if you really want to know, I'll tell you. She married this man, Marvin Steirs.

Who's he?

I recollected his achievements. Well, he's the president of a big corporation, JoMar Plastics. This corporation owns a steel company, a radio station, a new Xerox-type machine that lets you do twenty-five different pages at once. This corporation has a foundation, The JoMar Fund for Research in Conservation. Capitalism is like that, I added, in order to be politically useful.

How come you know? You go over their house a lot?

No. I happened to read all about them on the financial page, just last week. It made me think: a different life. That's all.

Different spokes for different folks, said Cynthia.

I sat down on the cool marble steps and remembered Joanna's cousin Ziggie. He was older than we were. He wrote a poem which told us we were lovely flowers and our legs were petals, which nature would force open no matter how many times we said no.

Then I had several other interior thoughts that I couldn't share with a child, the kind that give your face a blank or melancholy look.

Now you're not interested, said Cynthia. Now you're not gonna say a thing. Who lived here, 2A? Who? Two men lives here now. Women coming and women going. My mother says, Danger sign: Stay away, my darling, stay away.

I don't remember, Cynthia. I really don't.

You got to. What'd you come for, anyways?

Then I tried. 2A. 2A. Was it the twins? I felt a strong obligation as though remembering was in charge of the *existence* of the past. This is not so.

Cynthia, I said, I don't want to go any further. I don't even want to remember.

Come on, she said, tugging at my shorts, don't you want to see Mrs Luddy, the one lives in your old house? That be fun, no?

No. No, I don't want to see Mrs Luddy.

Now you shouldn't pay no attention to those boys downstairs. She will like you. I mean, she is kind. She don't like most white people, but she might like you.

No Cynthia, it's not that, but I don't want to see my father and mother's house now.

I didn't know what to say. I said, Because my mother's dead. This was a lie, because my mother lives in her own room with my father in the Children of Judea. With her hand over her socialist

243

heart, she reads the paper every morning after breakfast. Then she says sadly to my father, Every day the same. Dying . . . dying, dying from killing.

My mother's dead, Cynthia. I can't go in there.

Oh . . . oh, the poor thing, she said, looking into my eyes. Oh, if my mother died, I don't know what I'd do. Even if I was old as you. I could kill myself. Tears filled her eyes and started down her cheeks. If my mother died, what would I do? She is my protector, she won't let the pushers get me. She hold me tight. She gonna hide me in the cedar box if my Uncle Rudford comes try to get me back. She *can't* die, my mother.

Cynthia – honey – she won't die. She's young. I put my arm out to comfort her. You could come live with me, I said. I got two boys, they're nearly grown up. I missed it, not having a girl.

What? What you mean now, live with you and boys. She pulled away and ran for the stairs. Stay away from me, honky lady. I know them white boys. They just gonna try and jostle my black womanhood. My mother told me about that, keep you white honky devil boys to your devil self, you just leave me be you old bitch you. Somebody help me, she started to scream, you hear. Somebody help. She gonna take me away.

She flattened herself to the wall, trembling. I was too frightened by her fear of me to say, honey, I wouldn't hurt you, it's me. I heard her helpers, the voices of large boys crying, We coming, we coming, hold your head up, we coming. I ran past her fear to the stairs and up them two at a time. I came to my old own door. I knocked like the landlord, loud and terrible.

Mama not home, a child's voice said. No, no, I said. It's me! a lady! Someone's chasing me, let me in. Mama not home, I ain't allowed to open up for nobody.

It's me! I cried out in terror. Mama! Mama! let me in!

The door opened. A slim woman whose age I couldn't invent looked at me. She said, Get in and shut that door tight. She took a hard pinching hold on my upper arm. Then she bolted the door herself. Them hustlers after you. They make me pink. Hide this white lady now, Donald. Stick her under your bed, you got a high bed.

Oh that's OK. I'm fine now, I said. I felt safe and at home.

You in my house, she said. You do as I say. For two cents, I throw you out.

I squatted under a small kid's pissy mattress. Then I heard the knock. It was tentative and respectful. My mama don't allow me to open. Donald! someone called. Donald!

Oh no, he said. Can't do it. She gonna wear me out. You know her. She already tore up my ass this morning once. Ain't *gonna* open up.

I lived there for about three weeks with Mrs Luddy and Donald and three little baby girls nearly the same age. I told her a joke about Irish twins. Ain't Irish, she said.

Nearly every morning the babies woke us at about 6.45. We gave them all a bottle and went back to sleep till 8.00. I made coffee and she changed diapers. Then it really stank for a while. At this time I usually said, Well listen, thanks really, but I've got to go I guess. I guess I'm going. She'd usually say, Well, guess again. *I* guess you ain't. Or if she was feeling disgusted she'd say, Go on now! Get! You wanna go, I guess by now I have snorted enough white lady stink to choke a horse. Go on!

I'd get to the door and then I'd hear voices. I'm ashamed to say I'd become fearful. Despite my wide geographical love of mankind, I would be attacked by local fears.

There was a sentimental truth that lay beside all that going and not going. It *was* my house where I'd lived long ago my family life. There was a tile on the bathroom floor that I myself had broken, dropping a hammer on the toe of my brother Charles as he stood dreamily shaving, his prick halfway up his undershorts. Astonishment and knowledge first seized me right there. The kitchen was the same. The table was the enameled table common to our class, easy to clean, with wooden undercorners for indigent and old cockroaches that couldn't make it to the kitchen sink. (However, it was not the same table, because I have inherited that one, chips and all.)

The living-room was something like ours, only we had less plastic. There may have been less plastic in the world at that time. Also, my mother had set beautiful cushions everywhere, on beds and chairs. It was the way she expressed herself, artistically, to embroider at night or take strips of flowered cotton and sew them across ordinary white or blue muslin in the most delicate designs, the way women have always used materials that live and die in hunks and tatters to say: This is my place.

Mrs Luddy said, Uh huh!

245

Of course, I said, men don't have that outlet. That's how come they run around so much.

Till they drunk enough to lay down, she said.

Yes, I said, on a large scale you can see it in the world. First they make something, then they murder it. Then they write a book about how interesting it is.

You got something there, she said. Sometimes she said, Girl, you don't know *nothing*.

We often sat at the window looking out and down. Little tufts of breeze grew on that windowsill. The blazing afternoon was around the corner and up the block.

You say men, she said. Is that men? she asked. What you call – a Man?

Four flights below us, leaning on the stoop, were about a dozen people and around them devastation. Just a minute, I said. I had seen devastation on my way, running, gotten some of the pebbles of it in my running shoe and the dust of it in my eyes. I had thought with the indignant courtesy of a citizen, This is a disgrace to the City of New York which I love and am running through.

But now, from the commanding heights of home, I saw it clearly. The tenement in which Jack my old and present friend had come to gloomy manhood had been destroyed, first by fire, then by demolition (which is a swinging ball of steel that cracks bedrooms and kitchens). Because of this work, we could see several blocks wide and a block and a half long. Crazy Eddy's house still stood, famous 1510 gutted, with black window frames, no glass, open laths. The stubbornness of the supporting beams! Some persons or families still lived on the lowest floors. In the lots between, a couple of old sofas lay on their fat faces, their springs sticking up into the air. Just as in wartime a half-dozen ailanthus trees had already found their first quarter inch of earth and begun a living attack on the dead yards. At night, I knew animals roamed the place, squalling and howling, furious New York dogs and street cats and mighty rats. You would think you were in Bear Mountain Park, the terror of venturing forth.

Someone ought to clean that up, I said.

Mrs Luddy said, Who you got in mind? Mrs Kennedy? –

Donald made a stern face. He said, That just what I gonna do when I get big. Gonna get the Sanitary Man in and show it to him.

You see that, you big guinea you, you clean it up right now! Then he stamped his feet and fierced his eyes.

Mrs Luddy said, Come here, you little nigger. She kissed the top of his head and gave him a whack on the backside all at one time.

Well, said Donald, encouraged, look out there now you all! Go on I say, look! Though we had already seen, to please him we looked. On the stoop men and boys lounged, leaned, hopped about, stood on one leg, then another, took their socks off, and scratched their toes, talked, sat on their haunches, heads down, dozing.

Donald said, Look at them. They ain't got self-respect. They got Afros *on* their heads, but they don't know they black *in* their heads.

I thought he ought to learn to be more sympathetic. I said, There are reasons that people are that way.

Yes, ma'am, said Donald.

Anyway, how come you never go down and play with the other kids, how come you're up here so much?

My mama don't like me do that. Some of them is bad. Bad. I might become a dope addict. I got to stay clear.

You just a dope, that's a fact, said Mrs Luddy.

He ought to be with kids his age more, I think.

He see them in school, miss. Don't trouble your head about it if you don't mind.

Actually, Mrs Luddy didn't go down into the street either. Donald did all the shopping. She let the welfare investigator in, the meterman came into the kitchen to read the meter. I saw him from the back room, where I hid. She did pick up her check. She cashed it. She returned to wash the babies, change their diapers, wash clothes, iron, feed people, and then in free half hours she sat by that window. She was waiting.

I believed she was watching and waiting for a particular man. I wanted to discuss this with her, talk lovingly like sisters. But before I could freely say, Forget about that son of a bitch, he's a pig, I did have to offer a few solid facts about myself, my kids, about fathers, husbands, passers-by, evening companions, and the life of my father and mother in this room by this exact afternoon window.

I told her, for instance, that in my worst times I had given myself one extremely simple physical pleasure. This was cream cheese for breakfast. In fact, I insisted on it, sometimes depriving the children of very important articles and foods.

Girl, you don't know nothing, she said.

Then for a little while she talked gently as one does to a person who is innocent and insane and incorruptible because of stupidity. She had had two such special pleasures for hard times she said. The first, men, but they turned rotten, white women had ruined the best, give them the idea their dicks made of solid gold. The second pleasure she had tried was wine. She said, I do like wine. You *has* to have something just for yourself by yourself. Then she said, But you can't raise a decent boy when you liquor-dazed every night.

White or black, I said, returning to men, they did think they were bringing a rare gift, whereas it was just sex, which is common like bread, though essential.

Oh, you can do without, she said. There's folks does without.

I told her Donald deserved the best. I loved him. If he had flaws, I hardly noticed them. It's one of my beliefs that children do not have flaws, even the worst do not.

Donald was brilliant – like my boys except that he had an easier disposition. For this reason I decided, almost the second moment of my residence in that household, to bring him up to reading level at once. I told him we would work with books and newspapers. He went immediately to his neighborhood library and brought some hard books to amuse me. *Black Folktales* by Julius Lester and *The Pushcart War*, which is about another neighborhood but relevant.

Donald always agreed with me when we talked about reading and writing. In fact, when I mentioned poetry, he told me he knew all about it, that David Henderson, a known black poet, had visited his second-grade class. So Donald was, as it turned out, well ahead of my nosy tongue. He was usually very busy shopping. He also had to spend a lot of time making faces to force the little serious baby girls into laughter. But if the subject came up, he could take *the* poem right out of the air into which language and event had just gone.

An example: That morning, his mother had said, Whew, I just got too much piss and diapers and wash. I wanna just sit down by that window and rest myself. He wrote a poem:

> *Just got too much pissy diapers*
> *and wash and wash*
> *just wanna sit down by that window*
> *and look out*
> *   ain't nothing there.*

248

Donald, I said, you are plain brilliant. I'm never going to forget you. For God's sakes don't you forget me.

You fool with him too much, said Mrs Luddy. He already don't even remember his grandma, you never gonna meet someone like her, a curse never come past her lips.

I do remember, Mama, I remember. She lying in bed, right there. A man standing in the door. She say, Esdras, I put a curse on you head. You worsen tomorrow. How come she said like that?

Gomorrah, I believe Gomorrah, she said. She know the Bible inside out.

Did she live with you?

No. No, she visiting. She come up to see us all, her children, how we doing. She come up to see sights. Then she lay down and died. She was old.

I remained quiet because of the death of mothers. Mrs Luddy looked at me thoughtfully, then she said:

My mama had stories to tell, she raised me on. *Her* mama was a little thing, no sense. Stand in the door of the cabin all day, sucking her thumb. It was slave times. One day a young field boy come storming along. He knock on the door of the first cabin hollering, Sister, come out, it's freedom. She come out. She say, Yeah? When? He say, Now! It's freedom now! Then he knock at the next door and say, Sister! It's freedom! Now! From one cabin he run to the next cabin, crying out, Sister, it's freedom now!

Oh I remember that story, said Donald. Freedom now! Freedom now! He jumped up and down.

You don't remember nothing boy. Go on, get Eloise, she want to get into the good times.

Eloise was two but undersized. We got her like that, said Donald. Mrs Luddy let me buy her ice cream and green vegetables. She was waiting for kale and chard, but it was too early. The kale liked cold. You not about to be here November, she said. No, no. I turned away, lonesomeness touching me, and sang our Eloise song:

> *Eloise loves the bees*
> *the bees they buzz*
> *like Eloise does.*

Then Eloise crawled all over the splintery floor, buzzing wildly.

Oh you crazy baby, said Donald, buzz buzz buzz.

Mrs Luddy sat down by the window.

You all make a lot of noise, she said sadly. You just right on noisy.

The next morning Mrs Luddy woke me up.

Time to go, she said.

What?

Home.

What? I said.

Well, don't you think your little spoiled boys crying for you? Where's Mama? They standing in the window. Time to go lady. This ain't Free Vacation Farm. Time we was by ourself a little.

Oh Ma, said Donald, she ain't a lot of trouble. Go on, get Eloise, she hollering. And button up your lip.

She didn't offer me coffee. She looked at me strictly all the time. I tried to look strictly back, but I failed because I loved the sight of her.

Donald was teary, but I didn't dare turn my face to him, until the parting minute at the door. Even then, I kissed the top of his head a little too forcefully and said, Well, I'll see you.

On the front stoop there were about half a dozen mid-morning family people and kids arguing about who had dumped garbage out of which window. They were very disgusted with one another.

Two young men in handsome dashikis stood in counsel and agreement at the street corner. They divided a comment. How come white womens got rotten teeth? And look so old? A young woman waiting at the light said, Hush . . .

I walked past them and didn't begin my run till the road opened up somewhere along Ocean Parkway. I was a little stiff because my way of life had used only small movements, an occasional stretch to put a knife or teapot out of reach of the babies. I ran about ten, fifteen blocks. Then my second wind came, which is classical, famous among runners, it's the beginning of flying.

In the three weeks I'd been off the street, jogging had become popular. It seemed that I was only one person doing her thing, which happened like most American eccentric acts to be the most 'in' thing I could have done. In fact, two young men ran alongside of me for nearly a mile. They ran silently beside me and turned off at Avenue H. A gentleman with a mustache, running poorly in the opposite direction, waved. He called out, Hi, señora.

Near home I ran through our park, where I had aired my children on weekends and late-summer afternoons. I stopped at the northeast playground, where I met a dozen young mothers intelligently handling their little ones. In order to prepare them, meaning no harm, I said, In fifteen years, you girls will be like me, wrong in everything.

At home it was Saturday morning. Jack had returned looking as grim as ever, but he'd brought cash and a vacuum cleaner. While the coffee perked, he showed Richard how to use it. They were playing tick tack toe on the dusty wall.

Richard said, Well! Look who's here! Hi!

Any news? I asked.

Letter from Daddy, he said. From the lake and water country in Chile. He says it's like Minnesota.

He's never been to Minnesota, I said. Where's Anthony?

Here I am, said Tonto, appearing. But I'm leaving.

Oh yes, I said. Of course. Every Saturday he hurries through breakfast or misses it. He goes to visit his friends in institutions. These are well-known places like Bellevue, Hillside, Rockland State, Central Islip, Manhattan. These visits take him all day and sometimes half the night.

I found some chocolate-chip cookies in the pantry. Take them, Tonto, I said. I remember nearly all his friends as little boys and girls always hopping, skipping, jumping and cookie-eating. He was annoyed. He said, No! Chocolate cookies is what the commissaries are full of. How about money?

Jack dropped the vacuum cleaner. He said, No! They have parents for that.

I said, Here, five dollars for cigarettes, one dollar each.

Cigarettes! said Jack. Goddamnit! Black lungs and death! Cancer! Emphysema! He stomped out of the kitchen, breathing. He took the bike from the back room and started for Central Park, which has been closed to cars but opened to bicycle riders. When he'd been gone about ten minutes, Anthony said, It's really open only on Sundays.

Why didn't you say so? Why can't you be decent to him? I asked. It's important to me.

Oh Faith, he said, patting me on the head because he'd grown so tall, all that air. It's good for his lungs. And his muscles! He'll be back soon.

You should ride too, I said. You don't want to get mushy in your legs. You should go swimming once a week.

I'm too busy, he said. I have to see my friends.

Then Richard, who had been vacuuming under his bed, came into the kitchen. You still here, Tonto?

Going going gone, said Anthony, don't bat your eye.

Now listen, Richard said, here's a note. It's for Judy, if you get as far as Rockland. Don't forget it. Don't open it. Don't read it. I know he'll read it.

Anthony smiled and slammed the door.

Did I lose weight? I asked. Yes, said Richard. You look OK. You never look too bad. But where were you? I got sick of Raftery's boiled potatoes. Where were you, Faith?

Well! I said. Well! I stayed a few weeks in my old apartment, where Grandpa and Grandma and me and Hope and Charlie lived, when we were little. I took you there long ago. Not so far from the ocean where Grandma made us very healthy with sun and air.

What are you talking about? said Richard. Cut the baby talk.

Anthony came home earlier than expected that evening because some people were in shock therapy and someone else had run away. He listened to me for a while. Then he said, I don't know what she's talking about either.

Neither did Jack, despite the understanding often produced by love after absence. He said, Tell me again. He was in a good mood. He said, You can even tell it to me twice.

I repeated the story. They all said, What?

Because it isn't usually so simple. Have you known it to happen much nowadays? A woman inside the steamy energy of middle age runs and runs. She finds the houses and streets where her childhood happened. She lives in them. She learns as though she was still a child what in the world is coming next.

Medley

I could tell the minute I got in the door and dropped my bag, I wasn't staying. Dishes piled sky-high in the sink looking like some circus act. Glasses all ghosty on the counter. Busted tea bags, curling cantaloupe rinds, white cartons from the Chinamen, green sacks from the deli, and that damn dog creeping up on me for me to wrassle his head or kick him in the ribs one. No, I definitely wasn't staying. Couldn't even figure why I'd come. But picked my way to the hallway anyway till the laundry-stuffed pillowcases stopped me. Larry's bass blocking the view to the bedroom.

'That you, Sweet Pea?'

'No, man, ain't me at all,' I say, working my way back to the suitcase and shoving that damn dog out the way. 'See ya round,' I holler, the door slamming behind me, cutting off the words abrupt.

Quite naturally sitting cross-legged at the club, I embroider a little on the homecoming tale, what with an audience of two crazy women and a fresh bottle of Jack Daniels. Got so I could actually see shonuff toadstools growing in the sink. Cantaloupe seeds sprouting in the muck. A goddamn compost heap breeding near the stove, garbage gardens on the grill.

'Sweet Pea, you oughta hush, cause you can't possibly keep on lying so,' Pot Limit's screaming, tears popping from her eyes. 'Lawd hold my legs, cause this liar bout to kill me off.'

'Never mind about Larry's housekeeping girl,' Sylvia's soothing me, sloshing perfectly good bourbon all over the table. 'You can come and stay with me till your house comes through. It'll be like old times at Aunt Merriam's.'

I ease back into the booth to wait for the next set. The drummer's fooling with the equipment, tapping the mikes, hoping he's watched, so I watch him. But feeling worried in my mind about Larry, cause I've been through days like that myself. Cold cream caked on my face from the day before, hair matted, bathrobe funky, not a clean pair of drawers to my name. Even the emergency ones, the draggy cotton numbers stuffed way in the back of the drawer under the scented paper gone. And no clean silverware in the box and the last of the paper cups gone too. Icebox empty cept for a rock of cheese and the lone water jug that ain't even half full that's how anyhow the thing's gone on. And not a clue as to the next step. But then Pot Limit'll come bamming on the door to say So-and-so's in town and can she have the card table for a game. Or Sylvia'll send a funny card inviting herself to dinner and even giving me the menu. Then I zoom through that house like a manic work brigade till me and the place ready for white-glove inspection. But what if somebody or other don't intervene for Larry, I'm thinking.

The drummer's messin round on the cymbals, head cocked to the side, rings sparkling. The other dudes are stepping out from behind the curtain. The piano man playing with the wah-wah doing splashy, breathy science fiction stuff. Sylvia checking me out to make sure I ain't too blue. Blue got hold to me, but I lean forward out of the shadows and babble something about how off the bourbon tastes these days. Hate worryin Sylvia, who is the kind of friend who bleeds at the eyes with your pain. I drain my glass and hum along with the opening riff of the guitar and I keep my eyes strictly off the bass player, whoever he is.

Larry Landers looked more like a bass player than ole Mingus himself. Got these long arms that drape down over the bass like they were grown special for that purpose. Fine, strong hands with long fingers and muscular knuckles, the dimples deep black at the joints. His calluses so other-colored and hard, looked like Larry had swiped his grandmother's tarnished thimbles to play with. He'd move in on that bass like he was going to hump it or something, slide up behind it as he lifted it from the rug, all slinky. He'd become one with the wood. Head dipped down sideways bobbing out the rhythm, feet tapping, legs jiggling, he'd look good. Thing about it, though, ole Larry couldn't play for shit. Couldn't never find the right placement for the notes. Never plucking with enough strength, despite the perfectly capable hands. Either you didn't hear him at all or what you heard was off. The man couldn't play for nuthin is what I'm saying. But Larry Landers was baad in the shower, though.

He'd soap me up and down with them great, fine hands, doing a deep bass walking in the back of his mouth. And I'd just have to sing, though I can't sing to save my life. But we'd have one hellafyin musical time in the shower, lemme tell you. 'Green Dolphin Street' never sounded like nuthin till Larry bopped out them changes and actually made me sound good. On 'My Funny Valentine' he'd do a whizzing sounding bow thing that made his throat vibrate real sexy and I'd cutesy up the introduction, which is, come to think of it, my favorite part. But the main number when the hot water started running out was 'I Feel Like Making Love'. That was usually the wind-up of our repertoire cause you can imagine what that song can do to you in the shower and all.

Got so we spent a helluva lotta time in the shower. Just as well, cause didn't nobody call Larry for gigs. He a nice man, considerate, generous, baad in the shower, and good taste in music. But he just wasn't anybody's bass player. Knew all the stances, though, the postures, the facial expressions, had the choreography down. And right in the middle of supper he'd get some Ron Carter thing going in his head and hop up from the table to go get the bass. Haul that sucker right in the kitchen and do a number in dumb show, all the playing in his throat, the acting with his hands. But that ain't nuthin. I mean that can't get it. I can impersonate Betty Carter if it comes to that. The arms crooked just so, the fingers popping, the body working, the cap and all, the teeth, authentic. But I got sense enough to know I ain't nobody's singer. Actually, I am a mother, though I'm only just now getting it together. And too, I'm an A-1 manicurist.

Me and my cousin Sinbad come North working our show in cathouses at first. Set up a salon right smack in the middle of Miz Maybry's Saturday traffic. But that wasn't no kind of life to be bringing my daughter into. So I parked her at a boarding school till

I could make some other kind of life. Wasn't no kind of life for Sinbad either, so we quit.

Our first shop was a three-chair affair on Austin. Had a student barber who could do anything – blow-outs, do's, corn rows, weird cuts, Afros, press and curl, whatever you wanted. Plus he din't gab you to death. And he always brought his sides and didn't blast em neither. He went on to New York and opened his own shop. Was a bootblack too then, an old dude named James Noughton, had a crooked back and worked at the post office at night, and knew everything about everything, read all the time.

'Whatcha want to know about Marcus Garvey, Sweet Pea?'

If it wasn't Garvey, it was the rackets or the trucking industry or the flora and fauna of Greenland or the planets or how the special effects in the disaster movies were done. One Saturday I asked him to tell me about the war, cause my nephew'd been drafted and it all seemed so wrong to me, our men over there in Nam fighting folks who fighting for the same things we are, to get that bloodsucker off our backs.

Well, what I say that for. Old dude gave us a deep knee bend, straight up eight-credit dissertation on World Wars I and II – the archduke getting offed, Africa cut up like so much cake, Churchill and his cigars, Gabriel Heatter on the radio, Hitler at the Olympics igging Owens, Red Cross doing Bloods dirty refusing donuts and bandages, A. Philip Randolph scaring the white folks to death, Mary McLeod Bethune at the White House, Liberty Bond drives, the Russian front, frostbite of the feet, the Jew stiffs, the gypsies no one mourned . . . the whole johnson. Talked straight through the day, Miz Mary's fish dinner growing cold on the radiator, his one and only customer walking off with one dull shoe. Fell out exhausted, his shoe rag limp in his lap, one arm draped over the left foot platform, the other clutching his heart. Took Sinbad and our cousin Pepper to get the old man home. I stayed with him all night with the ice pack and a fifth of Old Crow. He liked to die.

After while trade picked up and with a better class of folk too. Then me and Sinbad moved to North and Gaylord and called the shop Chez Sinbad. No more winos stumbling in or deadbeats wasting my time talking raunchy shit. The paperboy, the numbers man, the dudes with classier hot stuff coming in on Tuesday mornings only. We did up the place nice. Light globes from a New

Orleans whorehouse, Sinbad likes to lie. Brown-and-black-and-silver-striped wallpaper. Lots of mirrors and hanging plants. Them old barber chairs spruced up and called antiques and damn if someone didn't buy one off us for eight hundred, cracked me up.

I cut my schedule down to ten hours in the shop so I could do private sessions with the gamblers and other business men and women who don't like sitting around the shop even though it's comfy, specially my part. Got me a cigar showcase with a marble top for serving coffee in clear glass mugs with heatproof handles too. My ten hours in the shop are spent leisurely. And my twenty hours out are making me a mint. Takes dust to be a mother, don't you know.

It was a perfect schedule once Larry Landers came into my life. He part-timed at a record shop and bartended at Topp's on the days and nights I worked at the shops. That gave us most of Monday and Wednesdays to listen to sides and hit the clubs. Gave me Fridays all to myself to study in the library and wade through them college bulletins and get to the museum and generally chart out a routine for when Debbie and me are a team. Sundays I always drive to Delaware to see her, and Larry detours to DC to see his sons. My bankbook started telling me I was soon going to be a full-time mama again and a college girl to boot, if I can ever talk myself into doing a school thing again, old as I am.

Life with Larry was cool. Not just cause he wouldn't hear about me going halves on the bills. But cause he was an easy man to be easy with. He liked talking softly and listening to music. And he liked having folks over for dinner and cards. Larry a real nice man and I liked him a lot. And I liked his friend Hector, who lived in the back of the apartment. Ole moon-face Hector went to school with Larry years ago and is some kind of kin. And they once failed in the funeral business together and I guess those stories of them times kinda keep them friends.

The time they had to put Larry's brother away is their best story, Hector's story really, since Larry got to play a little grief music round the edges. They decided to pass up a church service, since Bam was such a treacherous desperado wouldn't nobody want to preach over his body and wouldn't nobody want to come to hear no lies about the dearly departed untimely ripped or cut down or whatever. So Hector and Larry set up some kind of pop stand awning right at the gravesite, expecting close blood only. But seems the whole town turned out to make sure ole evil, hell-raising Bam was truly dead. Dudes straight from the barber chair, the striped ponchos blowing like wings, fuzz and foam on they face and all, lumbering up the hill to the hole taking bets and talking shit, relating how Ole Crazy Bam had shot up the town, shot up the jail, shot up the hospital pursuing some bootlegger who'd come up one keg short of the order. Women from all around come to demand the lid be lifted so they could check for themselves and be sure that Bam was stone cold. No matter how I tried I couldn't think of nobody bad enough to think on when they told the story of the man I'd never met.

Larry and Hector so bent over laughing bout the funeral, I couldn't hardly put the events in proper sequence. But I could surely picture some neighbor lady calling on Larry and Bam's mama reporting how the whole town had turned out for the burying. And the mama snatching up the first black thing she could find to wrap around herself and make an appearance. No use passing up a scene like that. And Larry prancing round the kitchen being his mama. And I'm too stunned to laugh, not at somebody's mama, and somebody's brother dead. But him and Hector laughing to beat the band and I can't help myself.

Thing about it, though, the funeral business stories are Hector's stories and he's not what you'd call a good storyteller. He never gives you the names, so you got all these he's and she's floating around. And he don't believe in giving details, so you got to scramble to paint your own pictures. Toward the end of that particular tale of Bam, all I could picture was the townspeople driving a stake through the dead man's heart, then hurling that coffin into the hole right quick. There was also something in that story about the civil rights workers wanting to make a case cause a white cop had cut Bam down. But looked like Hector didn't have a hold to that part of the story, so I just don't know.

Stories are not Hector's long suit. But he is an absolute artist on windows. Ole Moon-Face can wash some windows and make you cry about it too. Makes these smooth little turns out there on that little bitty sill just like he wasn't four stories up without a belt. I'd park myself at the breakfast counter and thread the new curtains on the rods while Hector mixed up the vinegar solution real chef-like. Wring out the rags just so, scrunch up the newspapers into soft wads that make you think of cat's paws. Hector was a cat himself out there on the sill, making these marvelous circles in the glass, rubbing the hardhead spots with a strip of steel wool he had pinned to his overalls.

Hector offered to do my car once. But I put a stop to that after that first time. My windshield so clear and sparkling felt like I was in an accident and heading over the hood, no glass there. But it was a pleasure to have coffee and watch Hector. After while, though, Larry started hinting that the apartment wasn't big enough for four. I agreed, thinking he meant Earl had to go. Come to find Larry meant Hector, which was a real drag. I love to be around people who do whatever it is they do with style and care.

Larry's dog's named Earl P. Jessup Bowers, if you can get ready for that. And I should mention straightaway that I do not like dogs one bit, which is why I was glad when Larry said somebody had to go. Cats are bad enough. Horses are a total drag. By the age of nine I was fed up with all that noble horse this and noble horse that. They got good PR, horses. But I really can't use em. Was a fire once when I was little and some dumb horse almost burnt my daddy up messin around, twisting, snorting, broncing, rearing up, doing everything but comin on out the barn like even the chickens had sense enough to do. I told my daddy to let that horse's ass burn. Horses be as dumb as cows. Cows just don't have good press agents is all.

I used to like cows when I was real little and needed to hug me something bigger than a goldfish. But don't let it rain, the dumbbells'll fall right in a ditch and you break a plow and shout yourself hoarse trying to get them fools to come up out the ditch. Chipmunks I don't mind when I'm at the breakfast counter with my tea and they're on their side of the glass doing Disney things in the yard. Blue jays are law-and-order birds, thoroughly despicable. And there's one prize fool in my Aunt Merriam's yard I will one day surely kill. He tries to 'whip whip whippoorwill' like the Indians do in the Fort This or That movies when they're signaling to each other closing in on George Montgomery but don't never get around to wiping that sucker out. But dogs are one of my favorite hatreds. All the time woofing, bolting down their food,

259

slopping water on the newly waxed linoleum, messin with you when you trying to read, chewin on the slippers.

Earl P. Jessup Bowers was an especial drag. But I could put up with Earl when Hector was around. Once Hector was gone and them windows got cloudy and gritty, I was through. Kicked that dog every chance I got. And after thinking what it meant, how the deal went down, place too small for four and it was Hector not Earl – I started moving up my calendar so I could get out of there. I ain't the kind of lady to press no ultimatum on no man. Like 'Choose, me or the dog.' That's unattractive. Kicking Hector out was too. An insult to me, once I got to thinking on it. Especially since I had carefully explained from jump street to Larry that I got one item on my agenda, making a home for me and my kid. So if anybody should've been given walking papers, should've been me.

Anyway. One day Moody comes waltzing into Chez Sinbad's and tips his hat. He glances at his nails and glances at me. And I figure here is my house in a green corduroy suit. Pot Limit had just read my cards and the jack of diamonds kept coming up on my resource side. Sylvia and me put our heads together and figure it got to be some gambler or hustler who wants his nails done. What other jacks do I know to make my fortune? I'm so positive about Moody, I whip out a postcard from the drawer where I keep the emeries and write my daughter to start packing.

'How much you make a day, Miss Lady?'

'Thursdays are always good for fifty,' I lie.

He hands me fifty and glances over at Sinbad, who nods that it's cool. 'I'd like my nails done at four-thirty. My place.'

'Got a customer at that time, Mr Moody, and I like to stay reliable. How bout five-twenty?'

He smiles a slow smile and glances at Sinbad, who nods again, everything's cool. 'Fine,' he says. 'And do you think you can manage a shave without cutting a person's throat?'

'Mr Moody, I don't know you well enough to have just cause. And none of your friends have gotten to me yet with that particular proposition. Can't say what I'm prepared to do in the future, but for now I can surely shave you real careful-like.'

Moody smiles again, then turns to Sinbad, who says it's cool and he'll give me the address. This look-nod dialogue burns my ass.

That's like when you take a dude to lunch and pay the check and the waiter's standing there with *your* money in his paws asking *the dude* was everything all right and later for *you*. Shit. But I take down Moody's address and let the rest roll off me like so much steaming lava. I start packing up my little alligator case – buffer, batteries, clippers, emeries, massager, sifter, arrowroot and cornstarch, clear sealer, magnifying glass, and my own mixture of green and purple pigments.

'Five-twenty ain't five-twenty-one, is it, Miss Lady?'

'Not in my book,' I say, swinging my appointment book around so he can see how full it is and how neatly the times are printed in. Course I always fill in phony names case some creep starts pressing me for a session.

For six Thursdays running and two Monday nights, I'm at Moody's bending over them nails with a miner's light strapped to my forehead, the magnifying glass in its stand, nicking just enough of the nails at the sides, tinting just enough with the color so he can mark them cards as he shuffles. Takes an hour to do it proper. Then I sift my talc concoction and brush his hands till they're smooth. Them cards move around so fast in his hands, he can actually tell me he's about to deal from the bottom in the next three moves and I miss it and I'm not new to this. I been a gambler's manicurist for more years than I care to mention. Ten times he'll cut and each time the same fifteen cards in the top cut and each time in exactly the same order. Incredible.

Now, I've known hands. My first husband, for instance. To see them hands work their show in the grandstands, at a circus, in a parade, the pari-mutuels – artistry in action. We met on the train. As a matter of fact, he was trying to burgle my bag. Some story to tell the grandchildren, hunh? I had to get him straight about robbing from folks. I don't play that. Ya gonna steal, hell, steal back some of them millions we got in escrow is my opinion. We spent three good years on the circuit. Then credit cards moved in. Then choke-and-grab muggers killed the whole tradition. He was reduced to a mere shell of his former self, as they say, and took to putting them hands on me. I try not to think on when things went sour. Try not to think about them big slapping hands, only of them working hands. Moody's working hands were something like that, but even better. So I'm impressed and he's impressed. And he pays me fifty and tips me fifty and shuts up when I shave him and keeps his hands off my lovely person.

I'm so excited counting up my bread, moving up the calendar, making impulsive calls to Delaware and the two of us squealing over the wire like a coupla fools, that what Larry got to say about all these goings-on just rolls off my back like so much molten lead.

'Well, who be up there while he got his head in your lap and you squeezing his goddamn blackheads?'

'I don't squeeze his goddamn blackheads, Larry, on account of he don't have no goddamn blackheads. I give him a shave, a steam, and an egg-white face mask. And when I'm through, his face is as smooth as his hands.'

'I'll bet,' Larry says. That makes me mad cause I expect some kind of respect for my work, which is better than just good.

'And he doesn't have his head in my lap. He's got a whole barbershop set up on his solarium.'

'His what?' Larry squinting at me, raising the wooden spoon he stirring the spaghetti with, and I raise the knife I'm chopping the onions with. Thing about it, though, he don't laugh. It's funny as hell to me, but Larry got no sense of humor sometimes, which is too bad cause he's a lotta fun when he's laughing and joking.

'It's not a bedroom. He's got this screened-in sun porch where he raises African violets and —'

'Please, Sweet Pea. Why don't you quit? You think I'm dumb?'

'I'm serious. I'm serious and I'm mad cause I ain't got no reason to lie to you whatever was going on, Larry.' He turns back to the pot and I continue working on the sauce and I'm pissed off cause this is silly. 'He sits in the barber chair and I shave him and give him a manicure.'

'What else you be giving him? A man don't be paying a good-looking woman to come to his house and all and don't —'

'Larry, if you had the dough and felt like it, wouldn't you pay Pot Limit to come read your cards? And couldn't you keep your hands to yourself and she a good-looking woman? And couldn't you see yourself paying Sylvia to come and cook for you and no funny stuff, and she's one of the best-looking women in town?'

Larry cooled out fast. My next shot was to bring up the fact that he was insulting my work. Do I go around saying the women who pass up Bill the bartender and come to him are after his joint? No, cause I respect the fact that Larry Landers mixes the best piña coladas this side of Barbados. And he's flashy with the blender and the glasses and the whole show. He's good and I respect that. But he cooled out so fast I didn't have to bring it up. I don't believe in overkill, besides I like to keep some things in reserve. He cooled out so fast I realized he wasn't really jealous. He was just going through one of them obligatory male numbers, all symbolic, no depth.

Like the time this dude came into the shop to talk some trash and Sinbad got his ass on his shoulders, talking about the dude showed no respect for him cause for all he knew I could be Sinbad's woman. And me arguing that since that ain't the case, what's the deal? I mean why get hot over what if if what if ain't. Men are crazy. Now there is Sinbad, my blood cousin who grew up right in the same house like a brother damn near, putting me through simple-ass changes like that. Who's got time for grand opera and comic strips, I'm trying to make a life for me and my kid. But men are like that. Gorillas, if you know what I mean.

Like at Topp's sometimes. I'll drop in to have a drink with Larry when he's on the bar and then I leave. And maybe some dude'll take it in his head to walk me to the car. That's cool. I lay it out right quick that me and Larry are a we and then we take it from there, just two people gassing in the summer breeze and that's just fine. But don't let some other dude holler over something like 'Hey, man, can you handle all that? Why don't you step aside, junior, and let a man . . .' and blah-de-da-de-dah. They can be the best of friends or total strangers just kidding around, but right away they two gorillas pounding on their chest, pounding on their chest and talking over my head, yelling over the tops of cars just like I'm not a person with some say-so in the matter. It's a man-to-man ritual that ain't got nothing to do with me. So I just get in my car and take off and leave them to get it on if they've a mind to. They got it.

But if one of the gorillas is a relative, or a friend of mine, or a nice kinda man I got in mind for one of my friends, I will stick around long enough to shout em down and point out that they are some ugly gorillas and are showing no respect for me and therefore owe me an apology. But if they don't fit into one of them categories, I figure it ain't my place to try to develop them so they can make the leap from gorilla to human. If their own mamas and daddies didn't care whether they turned out to be amoebas or catfish or whatever, it ain't my weight. I got my own weight. I'm a mother. So they got it.

Like I use to tell my daughter's daddy, the key to getting along and living with other folks is to keep clear whose weight is whose. His drinking, for instance, was not my weight. And him waking me up in the night for them long, rambling, ninety-proof monologues bout how the whole world's made up of victims, rescuers, and executioners and I'm the dirty bitch cause I ain't rescuing him fast enough to suit him. Then got so I was the executioner, to hear him tell it. I don't say nuthin cause my philosophy of life and death is this – I'll go when the wagon comes, but I ain't going out behind somebody else's shit. I arranged my priorities long ago when I jumped into my woman stride. Some things I'll go off on. Some things I'll hold my silence and wait it out. Some things I just bump off, cause the best solution to some problems is to just abandon them.

But I struggled with Mac, Debbie's daddy. Talked to his family, his church, AA, hid the bottles, threatened the liquor man, left a good job to play nurse, mistress, kitten, buddy. But then he stopped calling me Dahlin and started calling me Mama. I don't play that. I'm my daughter's mama. So I split. Did my best to sweeten them last few months, but I'd been leaving for a long time.

The silliest thing about all of Larry's grumblings back then was Moody had no eyes for me and vice versa. I just like the money. And I like watching him mess around with the cards. He's exquisite, dazzling, stunning shuffling, cutting, marking, dealing from the bottom, the middle, the near top. I ain't never seen nothing like it, and I seen the whole lot. The thing that made me mad, though, and made me know Larry Landers wasn't ready to deal with no woman full grown, was the way he kept bringing it up, always talking about what he figured was on Moody's mind, like what's on my mind don't count. So I finally did have to use up my reserves and point out to Larry that he was insulting my work and that I would never dream of accusing him of not being a good bartender, of just being another pretty face, like they say.

'You can't tell me he don't have eyes,' he kept saying.

'What about my eyes? Don't my eyes count?' I gave it up after a coupla tries. All I know is, Moody wasn't even thinking about me. I was impressed with his work and needed the trade and vice versa.

One time, for instance, I was doing his hands on the solarium and thought I saw a glint of metal up under his jacket. I rearranged myself in the chair so I could work my elbow in there to see if he was carrying heat. I thought I was being cool about it.

'How bout keeping your tits on your side of the table, Miss Lady.'

I would rather he think anything but that. I would rather he think I was clumsy in my work even. 'Wasn't about tits, Moody. I was just trying to see if you had a holster on and was too lazy to ask.'

'Would have expected you to. You a straight-up, direct kind of person.' He opened his jacket away with the heel of his hand, being careful with his nails. I liked that.

'It's not about you,' he said quietly, jerking his chin in the direction of the revolver. 'Had to transport some money today and forgot to take it off. Sorry.'

I gave myself two demerits. One for the tits, the other for setting up a situation where he wound up telling me something about his comings and goings. I'm too old to be making mistakes like that. So I apologized. Then gave myself two stars. He had a good opinion of me and my work. I did an extra-fine job on his hands that day.

Then the house happened. I had been reading the rental ads and For Sale columns for months and looking at some awful, tacky places. Then one Monday me and Sylvia lucked up on this cute little white-brick job up on a hill away from the street. Lots of light and enough room and not too much yard to kill me off. I paid my money down and rushed them papers through. Got back to Larry's place all excited and found him with his mouth all poked out.

Half grumbling, half proposing, he hinted around that we all should live at his place like a family. Only he didn't quite lay it out plain in case of rejection. And I'll tell you something, I wouldn't want to be no man. Must be hard on the heart always having to get out there, setting yourself up to be possibly shot down, approaching the lady, calling, the invitation, the rap. I don't think I could handle it myself unless everybody was just straight up at all times from day one till the end. I didn't answer Larry's nonproposed proposal cause it didn't come clear to me till after dinner. So I just let my silence carry whatever meaning it will. Ain't nuthin too much changed from the first day he came to get me from my Aunt Merriam's place. My agenda is still to make a home for my girl. Marriage just ain't one of the things on my mind no more, not after two. Got no regrets or bad feelings about them husbands neither. Like the poem says, when you're handed a lemon, make lemonade, honey, make lemonade. That's Gwen Brook's motto, that's mine too. You get a lemon, well, just make lemonade.

'Going on the road next week,' Moody announces one day through the steam towel. 'Like you to travel with me, keep my hands in shape. Keep the women off my neck. Check the dudes at my back. Ain't asking you to carry heat or money or put yourself in no danger. But I could use your help.' He pauses and I ease my buns into the chair, staring at the steam curling from the towel.

'Wicked schedule though – Mobile, Birmingham, Sarasota Springs, Jacksonville, then Puerto Rico and back. Can pay you two thousand and expenses. You're good, Miss Lady. You're good and you got good sense. And while I don't believe in nothing but my skill and chance, I gotta say you've brought me luck. You a lucky lady, Miss Lady.'

He raises his hands and cracks his knuckles and it's like the talking towel has eyes as well cause damn if he ain't checking his cuticles.

'I'll call you later, Moody,' I manage to say, mind reeling. With two thousand I can get my stuff out of storage, and buy Debbie a real nice bedroom set, pay tuition at the college too and start my three-credit-at-a-time grind.

Course I never dreamed the week would be so unnerving, exhausting, constantly on my feet, serving drinks, woofing sisters, trying to distract dudes, keeping track of fifty-leven umpteen goings-on. Did have to carry the heat on three occasions and had to do a helluva lotta driving. Plus was most of the time holed up in the hotel room close to the phone. I had pictured myself lazying on the beach in Florida dreaming up cruises around the world with two matching steamer trunks with the drawers and hangers and stuff. I'd pictured traipsing through the casinos in Puerto Rico ordering chicken salad and coffee liqueur and tipping the croupiers with blue chips. Shit no. Was work. And I sure as hell learned how Moody got his name. Got so we didn't even speak, but I kept those hands in shape and his face smooth and placid. And whether he won, lost, broke even, or got wiped out, I don't even know. He gave me my money and took off for New Orleans. That trip liked to kill me.

'You never did say nothing interesting about Moody,' Pot Limit says insinuatingly, swinging her legs in from the aisle cause ain't nobody there to snatch so she might as well sit comfortable.

'Yeah, she thought she'd put us off the trail with a riproaring tale about Larry's housekeeping.'

They slapping five and hunching each other and making a whole lotta noise, spilling Jack Daniels on my turquoise T-straps from Puerto Rico.

'Come on, fess up, Sweet Pea,' they crooning. 'Did you give him some?'

'Ahhh, yawl bitches are tiresome, you know that?'

'Naaw, naaw,' says Sylvia, grabbing my arm. 'You can tell us. We wantta know all about the trip, specially the nights.' She winks at Pot Limit.

'Tell us about this Moody man and his wonderful hands one more time, cept we want to hear how the hands feel on the flesh, honey.' Pot Limit doing a bump and grind in the chair that almost makes me join in the fun, except I'm worried in my mind about Larry Landers.

Just then the piano player comes by and leans over Sylvia, blowing in her ear. And me and Pot Limit mimic the confectionary goings-on. And just as well, cause there's nothin to tell about Moody. It wasn't a movie after all. And in real life the good-looking gambler's got cards on his mind. Just like I got my child on my mind. Onliest thing to say about the trip is I'm five pounds lighter, not a shade darker, but two thousand closer toward my goal.

'Ease up,' Sylvia says, interrupting the piano player to fuss over me. Then the drummer comes by and eases in on Pot Limit. And I ease back into the shadows of the booth to think Larry over.

I'm staring at the entrance half expecting Larry to come into Topp's, but it's not his night. Then too, the thing is ended if I'd only know it. Larry the kind of man you're either living with him or you're out. I for one would've liked us to continue, me and Debbie in our place, him and Earl at his. But he got so grumpy the time I said that, I sure wasn't gonna bring it up again. Got grumpy in the shower too, got so he didn't want to wash my back.

But that last night fore I left for Birmingham, we had us one crazy musical time in the shower. I kept trying to lure him into 'Maiden Voyage', which I really can't do without back-up, cause I can't sing all them changes. After while he comes out from behind his sulk and did a Jon Lucien combination on vocal and bass, alternating the sections, eight bars of singing words, eight bars of singing bass. It was baad. Then he insisted on doing 'I Love You More Today Than Yesterday'. And we like to break our arches, stomping out the beat against the shower mat.

The bathroom was all steamy and we had the curtains open so we could see the plants and watch the candles burning. I had bought us a big fat cake of sandalwood soap and it was matching them candles scent for scent. Must've been two o'clock in the morning and looked like the hot water would last for ever and ever and ever. Larry finally let go of the love songs, which were making me feel kinda funny cause I thought it was understood that I was splitting, just like he'd always made it clear either I was there or nowhere.

Then we hit on a tune I don't even know the name of cept I like to scat and do my thing Larry calls Swahili wailing. He laid down the most intricate weaving, walking, bopping, strutting bottom to my singing I ever heard. It inspired me. Took that melody and went right on out that shower, them candles bout used up, the fatty soap long since abandoned in the dish, our bodies barely visible in the steamed-up mirrors walling his bathroom. Took that melody right on out the room and out of doors and somewhere out this world. Larry changing instruments as fast as I'm changing moods, colors. Took an alto solo and gave me a rest, worked an intro up on the piano playing the chords across my back, drove me all up into the high register while he weaved in and out around my head on a flute sounding like them chilly pipes of the Andes. And I was Yma Sumac for one minute there, up there breathing some rare air and losing my mind, I was so high on just sheer music. Music and water, the healthiest things in the world. And that hot water pounding like it was part of the group with a union card and all. And I could tell that if that bass could've fit in the tub, Larry would've dragged that bad boy in there and played the hell out of them soggy strings once and for all.

Toni Cade Bambara *Medley*

I dipped way down and reached way back for snatches of Jelly Roll Morton's 'Deep Creek Blues' and Larry so painful, so stinging on the bass, could make you cry. Then I'm racing fast through Bessie and all the other Smith singers, Mildred Bailey, Billie and imitators, Betty Roche, Nat King Cole vintage 46, a little Joe Carroll, King Pleasure, some Babs. Found myself pulling lines out of songs I don't even like, but ransacked songs just for the meaningful lines or two cause I realized we were doing more than just making music together, and it had to be said just how things stood.

Then I was off again and lost Larry somewhere down there doing scales, sound like. And he went back to that first supporting line that had drove me up into the Andes. And he stayed there waiting for me to return and do some more Swahili wailing. But I was elsewhere and liked it out there and ignored the fact that he was aiming for a wind-up of 'I Love You More Today Than Yesterday'. I sang myself out till all I could ever have left in life was 'Brown Baby' to sing to my little girl. Larry stayed on the ground with the same supporting line, and the hot water started getting funny and I knew my time was up. So I came crashing down, jarring the song out of shape, diving back into the melody line and somehow, not even knowing what song each other was doing, we finished up together just as the water turned cold.

EDITH WHARTON

Souls Belated

I

Their railway carriage had been full when the train left Bologna; but at the first station beyond Milan their only remaining companion – a courtly person who ate garlic out of a carpet-bag – had left his crumb-strewn seat with a bow.

Lydia's eye regretfully followed the shiny broadcloth of his retreating back till it lost itself in the cloud of touts and cab-drivers hanging about the station; then she glanced across at Gannett and caught the same regret in his look. They were both sorry to be alone.

'*Par-ten-ʒa!*' shouted the guard. The train vibrated to a sudden slamming of doors; a waiter ran along the platform with a tray of fossilized sandwiches; a belated porter flung a bundle of shawls and bandboxes into a third-class carriage; the guard snapped out a brief *Partenʒa!* which indicated the purely ornamental nature of his first shout; and the train swung out of the station.

The direction of the road had changed, and a shaft of sunlight struck across the dusty red velvet seats into Lydia's corner. Gannett did not notice it. He had returned to his *Revue de Paris*, and she had to rise and lower the shade of the farther window. Against the vast horizon of their leisure such incidents stood out sharply.

Having lowered the shade, Lydia sat down, leaving the length of the carriage between herself and Gannett. At length he missed her and looked up.

'I moved out of the sun,' she hastily explained.

He looked at her curiously: the sun was beating on her through the shade.

270

'Very well,' he said pleasantly; adding, 'You don't mind?' as he drew a cigarette-case from his pocket.

It was a refreshing touch, relieving the tension of her spirit with the suggestion that, after all, if he could *smoke* – ! The relief was only momentary. Her experience of smokers was limited (her husband had disapproved of the use of tobacco) but she knew from hearsay that men sometimes smoked to get away from things; that a cigar might be the masculine equivalent of darkened windows and a headache. Gannett, after a puff or two, returned to his review.

It was just as she had foreseen; he feared to speak as much as she did. It was one of the misfortunes of their situation that they were never busy enough to necessitate, or even to justify, the postponement of unpleasant discussions. If they avoided a question it was obviously, unconcealably because the question was disagreeable. They had unlimited leisure and an accumulation of mental energy to devote to any subject that presented itself; new topics were in fact at a premium. Lydia sometimes had premonitions of a famine-stricken period when there would be nothing left to talk about, and she had already caught herself doling out piecemeal what, in the first prodigality of their confidences, she would have flung to him in a breath. Their silence therefore might simply mean that they had nothing to say; but it was another disadvantage of their position that it allowed infinite opportunity for the classification of minute differences. Lydia had learned to distinguish between real and factitious silences; and under Gannett's she now detected a hum of speech to which her own thoughts made breathless answer.

How could it be otherwise, with that thing between them? She glanced up at the rack overhead. The *thing* was there, in her dressing-bag, symbolically suspended over her head and his. He was thinking of it now, just as she was; they had been thinking of it in unison ever since they had entered the train. While the carriage had held other travellers they had screened her from his thoughts; but now that he and she were alone she knew exactly what was passing through his mind; she could almost hear him asking himself what he should say to her . . .

The thing had come that morning, brought up to her in an innocent-looking envelope with the rest of their letters, as they were leaving the hotel at Bologna. As she tore it open, she and Gannett were laughing over some ineptitude of the local guidebook – they had been driven, of late, to make the most of such incidental humors of travel. Even when she had unfolded the document she took it for some unimportant business paper sent abroad for her signature, and her eye travelled inattentively over the curly *Whereases* of the preamble until a word arrested her: – Divorce. There it stood, an impassable barrier, between her husband's name and hers.

She had been prepared for it, of course, as healthy people are said to be prepared for death, in the sense of knowing it must come without in the least expecting that it will. She had known from the first that Tillotson meant to divorce her – but what did it matter? Nothing mattered, in those first days of supreme deliverance, but the fact that she was free; and not so much (she had begun to be aware) that freedom had released her from Tillotson as that it had given her to Gannett. This discovery had not been agreeable to her self-esteem. She had preferred to think that Tillotson had himself embodied all her reasons for leaving him; and those he represented had seemed cogent enough to stand in no need of reinforcement. Yet she had not left him till she met Gannett. It was her love for Gannett that had made life with Tillotson so poor and incomplete a business. If she had never, from the first, regarded her marriage as a full cancelling of her claims upon life, she had at least, for a number of years, accepted it as a provisional compensation, – she had made it 'do'. Existence in the commodious Tillotson mansion in Fifth Avenue – with Mrs Tillotson senior commanding the approaches from the second-story front windows – had been reduced to a series of purely automatic acts. The moral atmosphere of the Tillotson interior was as carefully screened and curtained as the house itself: Mrs Tillotson senior dreaded ideas as much as a draught on her back. Prudent people liked an even temperature; and to do anything unexpected was as foolish as going out in the rain. One of the chief advantages of being rich was that one need not be exposed to unforeseen contingencies: by the use of ordinary firmness and common sense one could make sure of doing exactly the same thing every day at the same hour. These doctrines, reverentially imbibed with his mother's milk, Tillotson (a model son who had never given his parents an hour's anxiety) complacently expounded to his wife, testifying to his sense of their importance by the regularity with which he wore goloshes on damp days, his punctuality at meals, and his elaborate precautions against burglars and contagious diseases. Lydia, coming from a smaller town, and entering New York life through the portals of the Tillotson mansion, had mechanically accepted this point of view as inseparable from having a front pew in church and a parterre box at the opera. All the people who came to the house revolved in the same small circle of prejudices. It was the kind of society in which, after dinner, the ladies compared the exorbitant charges of their children's teachers, and agreed that, even with the new duties on French clothes, it was cheaper in the end to get everything from Worth; while the husbands, over their cigars, lamented municipal corruption, and decided that the men to start a reform were those who had no private interests at stake.

To Lydia this view of life had become a matter of course, just as lumbering about in her mother-in-law's landau had come to seem the only possible means of locomotion, and listening every Sunday to a fashionable Presbyterian divine the inevitable atonement for having thought oneself bored on the other six days of the week. Before she met Gannett her life had seemed merely dull: his coming made it appear like one of those dismal Cruikshank prints in which the people are all ugly and all engaged in occupations that are either vulgar or stupid.

It was natural that Tillotson should be the chief sufferer from this readjustment of focus. Gannett's nearness had made her husband ridiculous, and a part of the ridicule had been reflected on herself. Her tolerance laid her open to a suspicion of obtuseness from which she must, at all costs, clear herself in Gannett's eyes.

She did not understand this until afterwards. At the time she fancied that she had merely reached the limits of endurance. In so large a charter of liberties as the mere act of leaving Tillotson seemed to confer, the small question of divorce or no divorce did not count. It was when she saw that she had left her husband only to be with Gannett that she perceived the significance of anything affecting their relations. Her husband, in casting her off, had virtually flung her at Gannett: it was thus that the world viewed it. The measure of alacrity with which Gannett would receive her would be the subject of curious speculation over afternoon-tea tables and in club corners. She knew what would be said – she had heard it so often of others! The recollection bathed her in misery.

The men would probably back Gannett to 'do the decent thing'; but the ladies' eyebrows would emphasize the worthlessness of such enforced fidelity; and after all, they would be right. She had put herself in a position where Gannett 'owed' her something; where, as a gentleman, he was bound to 'stand the damage'. The idea of accepting such compensation had never crossed her mind; the so-called rehabilitation of such a marriage had always seemed to her the only real disgrace. What she dreaded was the necessity of having to explain herself; of having to combat his arguments; of calculating, in spite of herself, the exact measure of insistence with which he pressed them. She knew not whether she most shrank from his insisting too much or too little. In such a case the nicest sense of proportion might be at fault; and how easy to fall into the error of taking her resistance for a test of his sincerity! Whichever way she turned, an ironical implication confronted her: she had the exasperated sense of having walked into the trap of some stupid practical joke.

Beneath all these preoccupations lurked the dread of what he was thinking. Sooner or later, of course, he would have to speak; but that, in the meantime, he should think, even for a moment, that there was any use in speaking, seemed to her simply unendurable. Her sensitiveness on this point was aggravated by another fear, as yet barely on the level of consciousness; the fear of unwillingly involving Gannett in the trammels of her dependence. To look upon him as the instrument of her liberation; to resist in herself the least tendency to a wifely taking possession of his future; had seemed to Lydia the one way of maintaining the dignity of their relation. Her view had not changed, but she was aware of a growing inability to keep her thoughts fixed on the essential point – the point of parting with Gannett. It was easy to face as long as she kept it sufficiently far off: but what was this act of mental postponement but a gradual encroachment on his future? What was needful was the courage to recognize the moment when, by some word or look, their voluntary fellowship should be transformed into a bondage the more wearing that it was based on none of those common obligations which make the most imperfect marriage in some sort a centre of gravity.

When the porter, at the next station, threw the door open, Lydia drew back, making way for the hoped-for intruder, but none came,

274

and the train took up its leisurely progress through the spring wheatfields and budding copses. She now began to hope that Gannett would speak before the next station. She watched him furtively, half-disposed to return to the seat opposite his, but there was an artificiality about his absorption that restrained her. She had never before seen him read with so conspicuous an air of warding off interruption. What could he be thinking of? Why should he be afraid to speak? Or was it her answer that he dreaded?

The train paused for the passing of an express, and he put down his book and leaned out of the window. Presently he turned to her with a smile.

'There's a jolly old villa out here,' he said.

His easy tone relieved her, and she smiled back at him as she crossed over to his corner.

Beyond the embankment, through the opening in a mossy wall, she caught sight of the villa, with its broken balustrades, its stagnant fountains, and the stone satyr closing the perspective of a dusky grass-walk.

'How should you like to live there?' he asked as the train moved on.

'There?'

'In some such place, I mean. One might do worse, don't you think so? There must be at least two centuries of solitude under those yew trees. Shouldn't you like it?'

'I – I don't know,' she faltered. She knew now that he meant to speak.

He lit another cigarette. 'We shall have to live somewhere, you know,' he said as he bent above the match.

Lydia tried to speak carelessly. '*Je n'en vois pas le nécessité!* Why not live everywhere, as we have been doing?'

'But we can't travel forever, can we?'

'Oh, forever's a long word,' she objected, picking up the review he had thrown aside.

'For the rest of our lives then,' he said, moving nearer.

She made a slight gesture which caused his hand to slip from hers.

'Why should we make plans? I thought you agreed with me that it's pleasanter to drift.'

He looked at her hesitatingly. 'It's been pleasant, certainly; but I suppose I shall have to get at my work again some day. You know I haven't written a line since – all this time,' he hastily emended.

She flamed with sympathy and self-reproach. 'Oh, if you mean *that* – if you want to write – of course we must settle down. How stupid of me not to have thought of it sooner! Where shall we go? Where do you think you could work best? We oughtn't to lose any more time.'

He hesitated again. 'I had thought of a villa in these parts. It's quiet; we shouldn't be bothered. Should you like it?'

'Of course I should like it.' She paused and looked away. 'But I thought – I remember your telling me once that your best work had been done in a crowd – in big cities. Why should you shut yourself up in a desert?'

Gannett, for a moment, made no reply. At length he said, avoiding her eye as carefully as she avoided his: 'It might be different now; I can't tell, of course, till I try. A writer ought not to be dependent on his *milieu*; it's a mistake to humor oneself in that way; and I thought that just at first you might prefer to be –'

She faced him. 'To be what?'

'Well – quiet. I mean –'

'What do you mean by "at first"?' she interrupted.

He paused again. 'I mean after we are married.'

She thrust up her chin and turned toward the window. 'Thank you!' she tossed back at him.

'Lydia!' he exclaimed blankly; and she felt in every fibre of her averted person that he had made the inconceivable, the unpardonable mistake of anticipating her acquiescence.

The train rattled on and he groped for a third cigarette. Lydia remained silent.

'I haven't offended you?' he ventured at length, in the tone of a man who feels his way.

She shook her head with a sigh. 'I thought you understood,' she moaned. Their eyes met and she moved back to his side.

'Do you want to know how not to offend me? By taking it for granted, once for all, that you've said your say on this odious question and that I've said mine, and that we stand just where we did this morning before that – that hateful paper came to spoil everything between us!'

'To spoil everything between us? What on earth do you mean? Aren't you glad to be free?'

'I was free before.'

'Not to marry me,' he suggested.

'But I don't *want* to marry you!' she cried.

She saw that he turned pale. 'I'm obtuse, I suppose,' he said slowly. 'I confess I don't see what you're driving at. Are you tired of the whole business? Or was I simply a – an excuse for getting away? Perhaps you didn't care to travel alone? Was that it? And now you want to chuck me?' His voice had grown harsh. 'You owe me a straight answer, you know; don't be tenderhearted!'

Her eyes swam as she leaned to him. 'Don't you see it's because I care – because I care so much? Oh, Ralph! Can't you see how it would humiliate me? Try to feel it as a woman would! Don't you see the misery of being made your wife in this way? If I'd known you as a girl – that would have been a real marriage! But now – this vulgar fraud upon society – and upon a society we despised and laughed at – this sneaking back into a position that we've voluntarily forfeited: don't you see what a cheap compromise it is? We neither of us believe in the abstract "sacredness" of marriage; we both know that no ceremony is needed to consecrate our love for each other; what object can we have in marrying, except the secret fear of each that the other may escape, or the secret longing to work our way back gradually – oh, very gradually – into the esteem of the people whose conventional morality we have always ridiculed and hated? And the very fact that, after a decent interval, these same people would come and dine with us – the women who talk about the indissolubility of marriage, and who would let me die in a gutter today because I am "leading a life of sin" – doesn't that disgust you more than their turning their backs on us now? I can stand being cut by them, but I couldn't stand their coming to call and asking what I meant to do about visiting that unfortunate Mrs So-and-so!'

She paused, and Gannett maintained a perplexed silence.

'You judge things too theoretically,' he said at length, slowly. 'Life is made up of compromises.'

'The life we ran away from – yes! If we had been willing to accept them' – she flushed – 'we might have gone on meeting each other at Mrs Tillotson's dinners.'

He smiled slightly. 'I didn't know that we ran away to found a new system of ethics. I supposed it was because we loved each other.'

'Life is complex, of course; isn't it the very recognition of that fact that separates us from the people who see it *tout d'une pièce?* If *they* are right – if marriage is sacred in itself and the individual must always be sacrificed to the family – then there can be no real marriage between us, since our – our being together is a protest against the sacrifice of the individual to the family.' She interrupted herself with a laugh. 'You'll say now that I'm giving you a lecture on sociology! Of course one acts as one can – as one must, perhaps – pulled by all sorts of invisible threads; but at least one needn't pretend, for social advantages, to subscribe to a creed that ignores the complexity of human motives – that classifies people by arbitrary signs, and puts it in everybody's reach to be on Mrs Tillotson's visiting-list. It may be necessary that the world should be ruled by conventions – but if we believe in them, why did we break through them? And if we don't believe in them, is it honest to take advantage of the protection they afford?'

Gannett hesitated. 'One may believe in them or not; but as long as they do rule the world it is only by taking advantage of their protection that one can find a *modus vivendi.*'

'Do outlaws need a *modus vivendi?*'

He looked at her hopelessly. Nothing is more perplexing to man than the mental process of a woman who reasons her emotions.

She thought she had scored a point and followed it up passionately. 'You do understand, don't you? You see how the very thought of the thing humiliates me! We are together today because we choose to be – don't let us look any farther than that!' She caught his hands. '*Promise* me you'll never speak of it again; promise me you'll never *think* of it even,' she implored, with a tearful prodigality of italics.

Through what followed – his protests, his arguments, his final unconvinced submission to her wishes – she had a sense of his but half-discerning all that, for her, had made the moment so tumultuous. They had reached that memorable point in every heart-history when, for the first time, the man seems obtuse and the woman irrational. It was the abundance of his intentions that consoled her, on reflection, for what they lacked in quality. After all, it would have been worse, incalculably worse, to have detected any overreadiness to understand her.

II

When the train at nightfall brought them to their journey's end at the edge of one of the lakes, Lydia was glad that they were not, as usual, to pass from one solitude to another. Their wanderings, during the year, had indeed been like the flight of outlaws: through Sicily, Dalmatia, Transylvania and Southern Italy they had persisted in their tacit avoidance of their kind. Isolation, at first, had deepened the flavor of their happiness, as night intensifies the scent of certain flowers; but in the new phase on which they were entering, Lydia's chief wish was that they should be less abnormally exposed to the action of each other's thoughts.

She shrank, nevertheless, as the brightly looming bulk of the fashionable Anglo-American hotel on the water's brink began to radiate toward their advancing boat its vivid suggestion of social order, visitors' lists, Church services, and the bland inquisition of the *table-d'hôte*. The mere fact that in a moment or two she must take her place on the hotel register as Mrs Gannett seemed to weaken the springs of her resistance.

They had meant to stay for a night only, on their way to a lofty village among the glaciers of Monte Rosa; but after the first plunge into publicity, when they entered the dining-room, Lydia felt the relief of being lost in a crowd, of ceasing for a moment to be the centre of Gannett's scrutiny; and in his face she caught the reflection of her feeling. After dinner, when she went upstairs, he strolled into the smoking-room, and an hour or two later, sitting in the darkness of her window, she heard his voice below and saw him walking up and down the terrace with a companion cigar at his side. When he came up he told her he had been talking to the hotel chaplain – a very good sort of fellow.

'Queer little microcosms, these hotels! Most of these people live here all summer and then migrate to Italy or the Riviera. The English are the only people who can lead that kind of life with dignity – those soft-voiced old ladies in Shetland shawls somehow carry the British Empire under their caps. *Civis Romanus sum*. It's a curious study – there might be some good things to work up here.'

He stood before her with the vivid preoccupied stare of the novelist on the trail of a 'subject'. With a relief that was half painful she noticed that, for the first time since they had been together, he was hardly aware of her presence.

'Do you think you could write here?'

'Here? I don't know.' His stare dropped. 'After being out of things so long one's first impressions are bound to be tremendously vivid, you know. I see a dozen threads already that one might follow –'

He broke off with a touch of embarrassment.

'Then follow them. We'll stay,' she said with sudden decision.

'Stay here?' He glanced at her in surprise, and then, walking to the window, looked out upon the dusky slumber of the garden.

'Why not?' she said at length, in a tone of veiled irritation.

'The place is full of old cats in caps who gossip with the chaplain. Shall you like – I mean, it would be different if –'

She flamed up.

'Do you suppose I care? It's none of their business.'

'Of course not; but you won't get them to think so.'

'They may think what they please.'

He looked at her doubtfully.

'It's for you to decide.'

'We'll stay,' she repeated.

Gannett, before they met, had made himself known as a successful writer of short stories and of a novel which had achieved the distinction of being widely discussed. The reviewers called him 'promising', and Lydia now accused herself of having too long interfered with the fulfilment of his promise. There was a special irony in the fact, since his passionate assurances that only the stimulus of her companionship could bring out his latent faculty had almost given the dignity of a 'vocation' to her course: there had been moments when she had felt unable to assume, before posterity, the responsibility of thwarting his career. And, after all, he had not written a line since they had been together: his first desire to write had come from renewed contact with the world! Was it all a mistake then? Must the most intelligent choice work more disastrously than the blundering combinations of chance? Or was there a still more humiliating answer to her perplexities? His sudden impulse of activity so exactly coincided with her own wish to withdraw, for a time, from the range of his observation, that she wondered if he too were not seeking sanctuary from intolerable problems.

'You must begin tomorrow!' she cried, hiding a tremor under the laugh with which she added, 'I wonder if there's any ink in the inkstand?'

Whatever else they had at the Hotel Bellosguardo, they had, as Miss Pinsent said, 'a certain tone'. It was to Lady Susan Condit that they owed this inestimable benefit; an advantage ranking in Miss Pinsent's opinion above even the lawn tennis courts and the resident chaplain. It was the fact of Lady Susan's annual visit that made the hotel what it was. Miss Pinsent was certainly the last to underrate such a privilege: – 'It's so important, my dear, forming as we do a little family, that there should be some one to give *the tone*; and no one could do it better than Lady Susan – an earl's daughter and a person of such determination. Dear Mrs Ainger now – who really *ought*, you know, when Lady Susan's away – absolutely refuses to assert herself.' Miss Pinsent sniffed derisively. 'A bishop's niece! – my dear, I saw her once actually give in to some South Americans – and before us all. She gave up her seat at table to oblige them – such a lack of dignity! Lady Susan spoke to her very plainly about it afterwards.'

Miss Pinsent glanced across the lake and adjusted her auburn front.

'But of course I don't deny that the stand Lady Susan takes is not always easy to live up to – for the rest of us, I mean. Monsieur Grossart, our good proprietor, finds it trying at times, I know – he has said as much, privately, to Mrs Ainger and me. After all, the poor man is not to blame for wanting to fill his hotel, is he? And Lady Susan is so difficult – so very difficult – about new people. One might almost say that she disapproves of them beforehand, on principle. And yet she's had warnings – she very nearly made a dreadful mistake once with the Duchess of Levens, who dyed her hair and – well, swore and smoked. One would have thought that might have been a lesson to Lady Susan.' Miss Pinsent resumed her knitting with a sigh. 'There are exceptions, of course. She took at once to you and Mr Gannett – it was quite remarkable, really. Oh, I don't mean that either – of course not! It was perfectly natural – we *all* thought you so charming and interesting from the first day – we knew at once that Mr Gannett was intellectual, by the magazines you took in; but you know what I mean. Lady Susan is so very – well, I won't say prejudiced, as Mrs Ainger does – but so prepared *not* to like new people, that her taking to you in that way was a surprise to us all, I confess.'

Miss Pinsent sent a significant glance down the long laurustinus alley from the other end of which two people – a lady and gentleman – were strolling toward them through the smiling neglect of the garden.

'In this case, of course, it's very different; that I'm willing to admit. Their looks are against them; but, as Mrs Ainger says, one can't exactly tell them so.'

'She's very handsome,' Lydia ventured, with her eyes on the lady, who showed, under the dome of a vivid sunshade, the hour-glass figure and superlative coloring of a Christmas chromo.

'That's the worst of it. She's too handsome.'

'Well, after all, she can't help that.'

'Other people manage to,' said Miss Pinsent skeptically.

'But isn't it rather unfair of Lady Susan – considering that nothing is known about them?'

'But, my dear, that's the very thing that's against them. It's infinitely worse than any actual knowledge.'

Lydia mentally agreed that, in the case of Mrs Linton, it possibly might be.

'I wonder why they came here?' she mused.

'That's against them too. It's always a bad sign when loud people come to a quiet place. And they've brought van-loads of boxes – her maid told Mrs Ainger's that they meant to stop indefinitely.'

'And Lady Susan actually turned her back on her in the *salon*?'

'My dear, she said it was for our sakes; that makes it so unanswerable! But poor Grossart *is* in a way! The Lintons have taken his most expensive *suite*, you know – the yellow damask drawing-room above the portico – and they have champagne with every meal!'

They were silent as Mr and Mrs Linton sauntered by; the lady with tempestuous brows and challenging chin; the gentleman, a blond stripling, trailing after her, head downward, like a reluctant child dragged by his nurse.

'What does your husband think of them, my dear?' Miss Pinsent whispered as they passed out of earshot.

Lydia stooped to pick a violet in the border.

'He hasn't told me.'

'Of your speaking to them, I mean. Would he approve of that? I know how very particular nice Americans are. I think your action might make a difference; it would certainly carry weight with Lady Susan.'

'Dear Miss Pinsent, you flatter me!'

Lydia rose and gathered up her book and sunshade.

'Well, if you're asked for an opinion – if Lady Susan asks you for one – I think you ought to be prepared,' Miss Pinsent admonished her as she moved away.

III

Lady Susan held her own. She ignored the Lintons, and her little family, as Miss Pinsent phrased it, followed suit. Even Mrs Ainger agreed that it was obligatory. If Lady Susan owed it to the others not to speak to the Lintons, the others clearly owed it to Lady Susan to back her up. It was generally found expedient, at the Hotel Bellosguardo, to adopt this form of reasoning.

Whatever effect this combined action may have had upon the Lintons, it did not at least have that of driving them away. Monsieur Grossart, after a few days of suspense, had the satisfaction of seeing them settle down in his yellow damask *premier* with what looked like a permanent installation of palm trees and silk sofa-cushions, and a gratifying continuance in the consumption of champagne. Mrs Linton trailed her Doucet draperies up and down the garden with the same challenging air, while her husband, smoking innumerable cigarettes, dragged himself dejectedly in her wake; but neither of them, after the first encounter with Lady Susan, made any attempt to extend their acquaintance. They simply ignored their ignorers. As Miss Pinsent resentfully observed, they behaved exactly as though the hotel were empty.

It was therefore a matter of surprise, as well as of displeasure, to Lydia, to find, on glancing up one day from her seat in the garden that the shadow which had fallen across her book was that of the enigmatic Mrs Linton.

'I want to speak to you,' that lady said, in a rich hard voice that seemed the audible expression of her gown and her complexion.

Lydia started. She certainly did not want to speak to Mrs Linton.

'Shall I sit down here?' the latter continued, fixing her intensely shaded eyes on Lydia's face, 'or are you afraid of being seen with me?'

'Afraid?' Lydia colored. 'Sit down, please. What is it that you wish to say?'

Mrs Linton, with a smile, drew up a garden chair and crossed one open-work ankle above the other.

'I want you to tell me what my husband said to your husband last night.'

Lydia turned pale.

'My husband – to yours?' she faltered, staring at the other.

'Didn't you know they were closeted together for hours in the smoking-room after you went upstairs? My man didn't get to bed until nearly two o'clock and when he did I couldn't get a word out of him. When he wants to be aggravating I'll back him against anybody living!' Her teeth and eyes flashed persuasively upon Lydia. 'But you'll tell me what they were talking about, won't you? I know I can trust you – you look so awfully kind. And it's for his own good. He's such a precious donkey and I'm so afraid he's got into some beastly scrape or other. If he'd only trust his own old woman! But they're always writing to him and setting him against me. And I've got nobody to turn to.' She laid her hand on Lydia's with a rattle of bracelets. 'You'll help me, won't you?'

Lydia drew back from the smiling fierceness of her brows.

'I'm sorry – but I don't think I understand. My husband has said nothing to me of – of yours.'

The great black crescents above Mrs Linton's eyes met angrily.

'I say – is that true?' she demanded.

Lydia rose from her seat.

'Oh, look here, I didn't mean that, you know – you mustn't take one up so! Can't you see how rattled I am?'

Lydia saw that, in fact, her beautiful mouth was quivering beneath softened eyes.

'I'm beside myself!' the splendid creature wailed, dropping into her seat.

'I'm so sorry,' Lydia repeated, forcing herself to speak kindly; 'but how can I help you?'

Mrs Linton raised her head sharply.

'By finding out – there's a darling!'

'Finding what out?'

'What Trevenna told him.'

'Trevenna –?' Lydia echoed in bewilderment.

Mrs Linton clapped her hand to her mouth.

'Oh, Lord – there, it's out! What a fool I am! But I supposed of course you knew; I supposed everybody knew.' She dried her eyes and bridled. 'Didn't you know that he's Lord Trevenna? I'm Mrs Cope.'

Lydia recognized the names. They had figured in a flamboyant elopement which had thrilled fashionable London some six months earlier.

'Now you see how it is – you understand, don't you?' Mrs Cope continued on a note of appeal. 'I knew you would – that's the reason I came to you. I suppose *he* felt the same thing about your husband; he's not spoken to another soul in the place.' Her face grew anxious again. 'He's awfully sensitive, generally – he feels our position, he says – as if it wasn't *my* place to feel that! But when he does get talking there's no knowing what he'll say. I know he's been brooding over something lately, and I *must* find out what it is – it's to his interest that I should. I always tell him that I think only of his interest; if he'd only trust me! But he's been so odd lately – I can't think what he's plotting. You will help me, dear?'

Lydia, who had remained standing, looked away uncomfortably.

'If you mean by finding out what Lord Trevenna has told my husband, I'm afraid it's impossible.'

'Why impossible?'

'Because I infer that it was told in confidence.'

Mrs Cope stared incredulously.

'Well, what of that? Your husband looks such a dear – anyone can see he's awfully gone on you. What's to prevent your getting it out of him?'

Lydia flushed.

'I'm not a spy!' she exclaimed.

'A spy – a spy? How dare you?' Mrs Cope flamed out. 'Oh, I don't mean that either! Don't be angry with me – I'm so miserable.' She essayed a softer note. 'Do you call that spying – for

one woman to help out another? I do need help so dreadfully! I'm
at my wits' end with Trevenna, I am indeed. He's such a boy – a
mere baby, you know; he's only two-and-twenty.' She dropped
her orbed lids. 'He's younger than me – only fancy! a few months
younger. I tell him he ought to listen to me as if I was his mother;
oughtn't he now? But he won't, he won't! All his people are at
him, you see – oh, I know *their* little game! Trying to get him away
from me before I can get my divorce – that's what they're up to. At
first he wouldn't listen to them; he used to toss their letters over to
me to read; but now he reads them himself, and answers 'em too, I
fancy; he's always shut up in his room, writing. If I only knew
what his plan is I could stop him fast enough – he's such a
simpleton. But he's dreadfully deep too – at times I can't make him
out. But I know he's told your husband everything – I knew that
last night the minute I laid eyes on him. And I *must* find out – you
must help me – I've got no one else to turn to!'

She caught Lydia's fingers in a stormy pressure.

'Say you'll help me – you and your husband.'

Lydia tried to free herself.

'What you ask is impossible; you must see that it is. No one
could interfere in – in the way you ask.'

Mrs Cope's clutch tightened.

'You won't, then? You won't?'

'Certainly not. Let me go, please.'

Mrs Cope released her with a laugh.

'Oh, go by all means – pray don't let me detain you! Shall you
go and tell Lady Susan Condit that there's a pair of us – or shall I
save you the trouble of enlightening her?'

Lydia stood still in the middle of the path, seeing her antagonist
through a mist of terror. Mrs Cope was still laughing.

'Oh, I'm not spiteful by nature, my dear; but you're a little more
than flesh and blood can stand! It's impossible, is it? Let you go,
indeed! You're too good to be mixed up in my affairs, are you?
Why, you little fool, the first day I laid eyes on you I saw that you
and I were both in the same box – that's the reason I spoke to you.'

She stepped nearer, her smile dilating on Lydia like a lamp
through a fog.

'You can take your choice, you know; I always play fair. If
you'll tell I'll promise not to. Now then, which is it to be?'

286

Lydia, involuntarily, had begun to move away from the pelting storm of words; but at this she turned and sat down.

'You may go,' she said simply. 'I shall stay here.'

IV

She stayed there for a long time, in the hypnotized contemplation, not of Mrs Cope's present, but of her own past. Gannett, early that morning, had gone off on a long walk – he had fallen into the habit of taking these mountain-tramps with various fellow-lodgers; but even had he been within reach she could not have gone to him just then. She had to deal with herself first. She was surprised to find how, in the last months, she had lost the habit of introspection. Since their coming to the Hotel Bellosguardo she and Gannett had tacitly avoided themselves and each other.

She was aroused by the whistle of the three o'clock steamboat as it neared the landing just beyond the hotel gates. Three o'clock! Then Gannett would soon be back – he had told her to expect him before four. She rose hurriedly, her face averted from the inquisitorial façade of the hotel. She could not see him just yet; she could not go indoors. She slipped through one of the overgrown garden-alleys and climbed a steep path to the hills.

It was dark when she opened their sitting-room door. Gannett was sitting on the window-ledge smoking a cigarette. Cigarettes were now his chief resource: he had not written a line during the two months they had spent at the Hotel Bellosguardo. In that respect, it had turned out not to be the right *milieu* after all.

He started up at Lydia's entrance.

'Where have you been? I was getting anxious.'

She sat down in a chair near the door.

'Up the mountain,' she said wearily.

'Alone?'

'Yes.'

Gannett threw away his cigarette: the sound of her voice made him want to see her face.

'Shall we have a little light?' he suggested.

She made no answer and he lifted the globe from the lamp and put a match to the wick. Then he looked at her.

'Anything wrong? You look done up.'

She sat glancing vaguely about the little sitting-room, dimly lit by the pallid-globed lamp, which left in twilight the outlines of the furniture, of his writing-table heaped with books and papers, of the tea-roses and jasmine drooping on the mantelpiece. How like home it had all grown – how like home!

'Lydia, what is wrong?' he repeated.

She moved away from him, feeling for her hatpins and turning to lay her hat and sunshade on the table.

Suddenly she said: 'That woman has been talking to me.'

Gannett stared.

'That woman? What woman?'

'Mrs Linton – Mrs Cope.'

He gave a start of annoyance, still, as she perceived, not grasping the full import of her words.

'The deuce! She told you –?'

'She told me everything.'

Gannett looked at her anxiously.

'What impudence! I'm so sorry that you should have been exposed to this, dear.'

'Exposed!' Lydia laughed.

Gannett's brow clouded and they looked away from each other.

'Do you know *why* she told me? She had the best of reasons. The first time she laid eyes on me she saw that we were both in the same box.'

'Lydia!'

'So it was natural, of course, that she should turn to me in a difficulty.'

'What difficulty?'

'It seems she has reason to think that Lord Trevenna's people are trying to get him away from her before she gets her divorce –'

'Well?'

'And she fancied he had been consulting with you last night as to – as to the best way of escaping from her.'

Gannett stood up with an angry forehead.

'Well – what concern of yours was all this dirty business? Why should she go to you?'

'Don't you see? It's so simple. I was to wheedle his secret out of you.'

'To oblige that woman?'

288

'Yes; or, if I was unwilling to oblige her, then to protect myself.'

'To protect yourself? Against whom?'

'Against her telling everyone in the hotel that she and I are in the same box.'

'She threatened that?'

'She left me the choice of telling it myself or of doing it for me.'

'The beast!'

There was a long silence. Lydia had seated herself on the sofa, beyond the radius of the lamp, and he leaned against the window. His next question surprised her.

'When did this happen? At what time, I mean?'

She looked at him vaguely.

'I don't know – after luncheon, I think. Yes, I remember; it must have been at about three o'clock.'

He stepped into the middle of the room and as he approached the light she saw that his brow had cleared.

'Why do you ask?' she said.

'Because when I came in, at about half-past three, the mail was just being distributed, and Mrs Cope was waiting as usual to pounce on her letters; you know she was always watching for the postman. She was standing so close to me that I couldn't help seeing a big official-looking envelope that was handed to her. She tore it open, gave one look at the inside, and rushed off upstairs like a whirlwind, with the director shouting after her that she had left all her other letters behind. I don't believe she ever thought of you again after that paper was put into her hand.'

'Why?'

'Because she was too busy. I was sitting in the window, watching for you, when the five o'clock boat left, and who should go on board, bag and baggage, valet and maid, dressing-bags and poodle, but Mrs Cope and Trevenna. Just an hour and a half to pack up in! And you should have seen her when they started. She was radiant – shaking hands with everybody – waving her handkerchief from the deck – distributing bows and smiles like an empress. If ever a woman got what she wanted just in the nick of time, that woman did. She'll be Lady Trevenna within a week, I'll wager.'

'You think she has her divorce?'

'I'm sure of it. And she must have got it just after her talk with you.'

Lydia was silent.

At length she said, with a kind of reluctance, 'She was horribly angry when she left me. It wouldn't have taken long to tell Lady Susan Condit.'

'Lady Susan Condit has not been told.'

'How do you know?'

'Because when I went downstairs half an hour ago I met Lady Susan on the way –'

He stopped, half smiling.

'Well?'

'And she stopped to ask if I thought you would act as patroness to a charity concert she is getting up.'

In spite of themselves they both broke into a laugh. Lydia's ended in sobs and she sank down with her face hidden. Gannett bent over her, seeking her hands.

'That vile woman – I ought to have warned you to keep away from her; I can't forgive myself! But he spoke to me in confidence; and I never dreamed – well, it's all over now.'

Lydia lifted her head.

'Not for me. It's only just beginning.'

'What do you mean?'

She put him gently aside and moved in her turn to the window. Then she went on, with her face turned toward the shimmering blackness of the lake, 'You see of course that it might happen again at any moment.'

'What?'

'This – this risk of being found out. And we could hardly count again on such a lucky combination of chances, could we?'

He sat down with a groan.

Still keeping her face toward the darkness, she said, 'I want you to go and tell Lady Susan – and the others.'

Gannett, who had moved toward her, paused a few feet off.

'Why do you wish me to do this?' he said at length, with less surprise in his voice than she had been prepared for.

'Because I've behaved basely, abominably, since we came here: letting these people believe we were married – lying with every breath I drew –'

'Yes, I've felt that too,' Gannett exclaimed with sudden energy.

The words shook her like a tempest: all her thoughts seemed to fall about her in ruins.

'You – you've felt so?'

'Of course I have.' He spoke with low-voiced vehemence. 'Do you suppose I like playing the sneak any better than you do? It's damnable.'

He had dropped on the arm of a chair, and they stared at each other like blind people who suddenly see.

'But you have liked it here,' she faltered.

'Oh, I've liked it – I've liked it.' He moved impatiently. 'Haven't you?'

'Yes,' she burst out; 'that's the worst of it – that's what I can't bear. I fancied it was for your sake that I insisted on staying – because you thought you could write here; and perhaps just at first that really was the reason. But afterwards I wanted to stay myself – I loved it.' She broke into a laugh. 'Oh, do you see the full derision of it? These people – the very prototypes of the bores you took me away from, with the same fenced-in view of life, the same keep-off-the-grass morality, the same little cautious virtues and the same little frightened vices – well, I've clung to them. I've delighted in them, I've done my best to please them. I've toadied Lady Susan, I've gossiped with Miss Pinsent, I've pretended to be shocked with Mrs Ainger. Respectability! It was the one thing in life that I was sure I didn't care about, and it's grown so precious to me that I've stolen it because I couldn't get it in any other way.'

She moved across the room and returned to his side with another laugh.

'I who used to fancy myself unconventional! I must have been born with a card-case in my hand. You should have seen me with that poor woman in the garden. She came to me for help, poor creature, because she fancied that, having "sinned", as they call it, I might feel some pity for others who have been tempted in the same way. Not I! She didn't know me. Lady Susan would have been kinder, because Lady Susan wouldn't have been afraid. I hated the woman – my one thought was not to be seen with her – I could have killed her for guessing my secret. The one thing that mattered to me at that moment was my standing with Lady Susan!'

Gannett did not speak.

'And you – you've felt it too!' she broke out accusingly. 'You've enjoyed being with these people as much as I have; you've let the chaplain talk to you by the hour about "The Reign of Law" and

Professor Drummond. When they asked you to hand the plate in church I was watching you – *you wanted to accept.*'

She stepped close, laying her hand on his arm.

'Do you know, I begin to see what marriage is for. It's to keep people away from each other. Sometimes I think that two people who love each other can be saved from madness only by the things that come between them – children, duties, visits, bores, relations – the things that protect married people from each other. We've been too close together – that has been our sin. We've seen the nakedness of each other's souls.'

She sank again on the sofa, hiding her face in her hands.

Gannett stood above her perplexedly: he felt as though she were being swept away by some implacable current while he stood helpless on its bank.

At length he said, 'Lydia, don't think me a brute – but don't you see yourself that it won't do?'

'Yes, I see it won't do,' she said without raising her head.

His face cleared.

'Then we'll go tomorrow.'

'Go – where?'

'To Paris; to be married.'

For a long time she made no answer; then she asked slowly, 'Would they have us here if we were married?'

'Have us here?'

'I mean Lady Susan – and the others.'

'Have us here? Of course they would.'

'Not if they knew – at least, not unless they could pretend not to know.'

He made an impatient gesture.

'We shouldn't come back here, of course; and other people needn't know – no one need know.'

She sighed. 'Then it's only another form of deception, and a meaner one. Don't you see that?'

'I see that we're not accountable to any Lady Susans on earth!'

'Then why are you ashamed of what we are doing here?'

'Because I'm sick of pretending that you're my wife when you're not – when you won't be.'

She looked at him sadly.

'If I were your wife you'd have to go on pretending. You'd have to pretend that I'd never been – anything else. And our friends would have to pretend that they believed what you pretended.'

Gannett pulled off the sofa-tassel and flung it away.

'You're impossible,' he groaned.

'It's not I – it's our being together that's impossible. I only want you to see that marriage won't help it.'

'What will help it then?'

She raised her head.

'My leaving you.'

'Your leaving me?' He sat motionless, staring at the tassel, which lay at the other end of the room. At length some impulse of retaliation for the pain she was inflicting made him say deliberately:

'And where would you go if you left me?'

'Oh!' she cried, wincing.

He was at her side in an instant.

'Lydia – Lydia – you know I didn't mean it; I couldn't mean it! But you've driven me out of my senses; I don't know what I'm saying. Can't you get out of this labyrinth of self-torture? It's destroying us both.'

'That's why I must leave you.'

'How easily you say it!' He drew her hands down and made her face him. 'You're very scrupulous about yourself – and others. But have you thought of me? You have no right to leave me unless you've ceased to care –'

'It's because I care –'

'Then I have a right to be heard. If you love me you can't leave me.'

Her eyes defied him.

'Why not?'

He dropped her hands and rose from her side.

'Can you?' he said sadly.

The hour was late and the lamp flickered and sank. She stood up with a shiver and turned toward the door of her room.

V

At daylight a sound in Lydia's room woke Gannett from a troubled sleep. He sat up and listened. She was moving about softly, as though fearful of disturbing him. He heard her push back one of the creaking shutters; then there was a moment's silence, which seemed to indicate that she was waiting to see if the noise had roused him.

Presently she began to move again. She had spent a sleepless night, probably, and was dressing to go down to the garden for a breath of air. Gannett rose also; but some undefinable instinct made his movements as cautious as hers. He stole to his window and looked out through the slats of the shutter.

It had rained in the night and the dawn was gray and lifeless. The cloud-muffled hills across the lake were reflected in its surface as in a tarnished mirror. In the garden, the birds were beginning to shake the drops from the motionless laurustinus-boughs.

An immense pity for Lydia filled Gannett's soul. Her seeming intellectual independence had blinded him for a time to the feminine cast of her mind. He had never thought of her as a woman who wept and clung: there was a lucidity in her intuitions that made them appear to be the result of reasoning. Now he saw the cruelty he had committed in detaching her from the normal conditions of life; he felt, too, the insight with which she had hit upon the real cause of their suffering. Their life was 'impossible', as she had said – and its worst penalty was that it had made any other life impossible for them. Even had his love lessened, he was bound to her now by a hundred ties of pity and self-reproach; and she, poor child! must turn back to him as Latude returned to his cell . . .

A new sound startled him: it was the stealthy closing of Lydia's door. He crept to his own and heard her footsteps passing down the corridor. Then he went back to the window and looked out.

A minute or two later he saw her go down the steps of the porch and enter the garden. From his post of observation her face was invisible, but something about her appearance struck him. She wore a long travelling cloak and under its folds he detected the outline of a bag or bundle. He drew a deep breath and stood watching her.

She walked quickly down the laurustinus alley toward the gate; there she paused a moment, glancing about the little shady square. The stone benches under the trees were empty, and she seemed to gather resolution from the solitude about her, for she crossed the square to the steamboat landing, and he saw her pause before the ticket office at the head of the wharf. Now she was buying her ticket. Gannett turned his head a moment to look at the clock: the boat was due in five minutes. He had time to jump into his clothes and overtake her –

He made no attempt to move; an obscure reluctance restrained him. If any thought emerged from the tumult of his sensations, it was that he must let her go if she wished it. He had spoken last night of his rights: what were they? At the last issue, he and she were two separate beings, not made one by the miracle of common forbearances, duties, abnegations, but bound together in a *noyade* of passion that left them resisting yet clinging as they went down.

After buying her ticket, Lydia had stood for a moment looking out across the lake; then he saw her seat herself on one of the benches near the landing. He and she, at that moment, were both listening for the same sound: the whistle of the boat as it rounded the nearest promontory. Gannett turned again to glance at the clock: the boat was due now.

Where would she go? What would her life be when she had left him? She had no near relations and few friends. There was money enough ... but she asked so much of life, in ways so complex and immaterial. He thought of her as walking barefooted through a stony waste. No one would understand her – no one would pity her – and he, who did both, was powerless to come to her aid ...

He saw that she had risen from the bench and walked toward the edge of the lake. She stood looking in the direction from which the steamboat was to come; then she turned to the ticket office, doubtless to ask the cause of the delay. After that she went back to the bench and sat down with bent head. What was she thinking of?

The whistle sounded; she started up, and Gannett involuntarily made a movement toward the door. But he turned back and continued to watch her. She stood motionless, her eyes on the trail of smoke that preceded the appearance of the boat. Then the little craft rounded the point, a dead-white object on the leaden water: a minute later it was puffing and backing at the wharf.

The few passengers who were waiting – two or three peasants and a snuffy priest – were clustered near the ticket office. Lydia stood apart under the trees.

The boat lay alongside now; the gangplank was run out and the peasants went on board with their baskets of vegetables, followed by the priest. Still Lydia did not move. A bell began to ring querulously; there was a shriek of steam, and someone must have called to her that she would be late, for she started forward, as though in answer to a summons. She moved waveringly, and at the edge of the wharf she paused. Gannett saw a sailor beckon to her; the bell rang again and she stepped upon the gangplank.

Halfway down the short incline to the deck she stopped again; then she turned and ran back to the land. The gangplank was drawn in, the bell ceased to ring, and the boat backed out into the lake. Lydia, with slow steps, was walking toward the garden . . .

As she approached the hotel she looked up furtively and Gannett drew back into the room. He sat down beside a table; a Bradshaw lay at his elbow, and mechanically, without knowing what he did, he began looking out the trains to Paris . . .

EUDORA WELTY

Clytie

It was late afternoon, with heavy silver clouds which looked bigger and wider than cotton fields, and presently it began to rain. Big round drops fell, still in the sunlight, on the hot tin sheds, and stained the white false fronts of the row of stores in the little town of Farr's Gin. A hen and her string of yellow chickens ran in great alarm across the road, the dust turned river-brown, and the birds flew down into it immediately, sitting out little pockets in which to take baths. The bird dogs got up from the doorways of the stores, shook themselves down to the tail, and went to lie inside. The few people standing with long shadows on the level road moved over into the post office. A little boy kicked his bare heels into the sides of his mule, which proceeded slowly through the town toward the country.

After everyone else had gone under cover, Miss Clytie Farr stood still in the road, peering ahead in her near-sighted way, and as wet as the little birds.

She usually came out of the old big house about this time in the afternoon, and hurried through the town. It used to be that she ran about on some pretext or other, and for a while she made soft-voiced explanations that nobody could hear, and after that she began to charge up bills, which the postmistress declared would never be paid any more than anyone else's, even if the Farrs were too good to associate with other people. But now Clytie came for nothing. She came every day, and no one spoke to her any more: she would be in such a hurry, and couldn't see who it was. And every Saturday they expected her to be run over, the way she darted out into the road with all the horses and trucks.

It might be simply that Miss Clytie's wits were all leaving her, said the ladies standing in the door to feel the cool, the way her sister's had left her; and she would just wait there to be told to go home. She would have to wring out everything she had on – the waist and the jumper skirt, and the long black stockings. On her head was one of the straw hats from the furnishing store, with an old black satin ribbon pinned to it to make it a better hat, and tied under the chin. Now, under the force of the rain, while the ladies watched, the hat slowly began to sag down on each side until it looked even more absurd and done for, like an old bonnet on a horse. And indeed it was with the patience almost of a beast that Miss Clytie stood there in the rain and stuck her long empty arms out a little from her sides, as if she were waiting for something to come along the road and drive her to shelter.

In a little while there was a clap of thunder.

'Miss Clytie! Go in out of the rain, Miss Clytie!' someone called.

The old maid did not look around, but clenched her hands and drew them up under her armpits, and sticking out her elbows like hen wings, she ran out of the street, her poor hat creaking and beating about her ears.

'Well, there goes Miss Clytie,' the ladies said, and one of them had a premonition about her.

Through the rushing water in the sunken path under the four wet black cedars, which smelled bitter as smoke, she ran to the house.

'Where the devil have you been?' called the older sister, Octavia, from an upper window.

Clytie looked up in time to see the curtain fall back.

She went inside, into the hall, and waited, shivering. It was very dark and bare. The only light was falling on the white sheet which covered the solitary piece of furniture, an organ. The red curtains over the parlor door, held back by ivory hands, were still as tree trunks in the airless house. Every window was closed, and every shade was down, though behind them the rain could still be heard.

Clytie took a match and advanced to the stair post, where the bronze cast of Hermes was holding up a gas fixture; and at once above this, lighted up, but quite still, like one of the unmovable relics of the house, Octavia stood waiting on the stairs.

She stood solidly before the violet-and-lemon-colored glass of the window on the landing, and her wrinkled, unresting fingers took hold of the diamond cornucopia she always wore in the bosom of her long black dress. It was an unwithered grand gesture of hers, fondling the cornucopia.

'It is not enough that we are waiting here – hungry,' Octavia was saying, while Clytie waited below. 'But you must sneak away and not answer when I call you. Go off and wander about the streets. Common – common –!'

'Never mind, Sister,' Clytie managed to say.

'But you always return.'

'Of course . . .'

'Gerald is awake now, and so is Papa,' said Octavia, in the same vindictive voice – a loud voice, for she was usually calling.

Clytie went to the kitchen and lighted the kindling in the wood stove. As if she were freezing cold in June, she stood before its open door, and soon a look of interest and pleasure lighted her face, which had in the last years grown weather-beaten in spite of the straw hat. Now some dream was resumed. In the street she had been thinking about the face of a child she had just seen. The child, playing with another of the same age, chasing it with a toy pistol, had looked at her with such an open, serene, trusting expression as she passed by! With this small, peaceful face still in her mind, rosy like these flames, like an inspiration which drives all other thoughts away, Clytie had forgotten herself and had been obliged to stand where she was in the middle of the road. But the rain had come down, and someone had shouted at her, and she had not been able to reach the end of her meditations.

It had been a long time now, since Clytie had first begun to watch faces, and to think about them.

Anyone could have told you that there were not more than 150 people in Farr's Gin, 'counting Negroes'. Yet the number of faces seemed to Clytie almost infinite. She knew now to look slowly and carefully at a face; she was convinced that it was impossible to see it all at once. The first thing she discovered about a face was always that she had never seen it before. When she began to look at people's actual countenances there was no more familiarity in the world for her. The most profound, the most moving sight in the whole world must be a face. Was it possible to comprehend the eyes and the mouths of other people, which concealed she knew not what, and secretly asked for still another unknown thing? The mysterious smile of the old man who sold peanuts by the church gate returned to her; his face seemed for a moment to rest upon the iron door of the stove, set into the lion's mane. Other people said Mr Tom Bate's Boy, as he called himself, stared away with a face as clean-blank as a watermelon seed, but to Clytie, who observed grains of sand in his eyes and in his old yellow lashes, he might have come out of a desert, like an Egyptian.

But while she was thinking of Mr Tom Bate's Boy, there was a terrible gust of wind which struck her back, and she turned around. The long green window shade billowed and plunged. The kitchen window was wide open – she had done it herself. She closed it gently. Octavia, who never came all the way downstairs for any reason, would never have forgiven her for an open window, if she knew. Rain and sun signified ruin, in Octavia's mind. Going over the whole house, Clytie made sure that everything was safe. It was not that ruin in itself could distress Octavia. Ruin or encroachment, even upon priceless treasures and even in poverty, held no terror for her; it was simply some form of prying from without, and this she would not forgive. All of that was to be seen in her face.

Clytie cooked the three meals on the stove, for they all ate different things, and set the three trays. She had to carry them in proper order up the stairs. She frowned in concentration, for it was hard to keep all the dishes straight, to make them come out right in the end, as Old Lethy could have done. They had had to give up the cook long ago when their father suffered the first stroke. Their father had been fond of Old Lethy, she had been his nurse in childhood, and she had come back out of the country to see him when she heard he was dying. Old Lethy had come and knocked at the back door. And as usual, at the first disturbance, front or back. Octavia had peered down from behind the curtain and cried, 'Go away! Go away! What the devil have you come *here* for?' And although Old Lethy and their father had both pleaded that they might be allowed to see each other, Octavia had shouted as she always did, and sent the intruder away. Clytie had stood as usual, speechless in the kitchen, until finally she had repeated after her sister, 'Lethy, go away'. But their father had not died. He was, instead, paralyzed, blind, and able only to call out in unintelligible sounds and to swallow liquids. Lethy still would come to the back door now and then, but they never let her in, and the old man no longer heard or knew enough to beg to see her. There was only one caller admitted to his room. Once a week the barber came by appointment to shave him. On this occasion not a word was spoken by anyone.

Clytie went up to her father's room first and set the tray down on a little marble table they kept by his bed.

'I want to feed Papa,' said Octavia, taking the bowl from her hands.

'You fed him last time,' said Clytie.

Relinquishing the bowl, she looked down at the pointed face on the pillow. Tomorrow was the barber's day, and the sharp black points, at their longest, stuck out like needles all over the wasted cheeks. The old man's eyes were half closed. It was impossible to know what he felt. He looked as though he were really far away, neglected, free . . . Octavia began to feed him.

Without taking her eyes from her father's face, Clytie suddenly began to speak in rapid, bitter words to her sister, the wildest words that came to her head. But soon she began to cry and gasp, like a small child who has been pushed by the big boys into the water.

'That is enough,' said Octavia.

But Clytie could not take her eyes from her father's unshaven face and his still-open mouth.

'And I'll feed him tomorrow if I want to,' said Octavia. She stood up. The thick hair, growing back after an illness and dyed almost purple, fell over her forehead. Beginning at her throat, the long accordion pleats which fell the length of her gown opened and closed over her breasts as she breathed. 'Have you forgotten Gerald?' she said. 'And I am hungry too.'

Clytie went back to the kitchen and brought her sister's supper.

Then she brought her brother's.

Gerald's room was dark, and she had to push through the usual barricade. The smell of whisky was everywhere; it even flew up in the striking of the match when she lighted the jet.

'It's night,' said Clytie presently.

Gerald lay on his bed looking at her. In the bad light he resembled his father.

'There's some more coffee down in the kitchen,' said Clytie.

'Would you bring it to me?' Gerald asked. He stared at her in an exhausted, serious way.

She stooped and held him up. He drank the coffee while she bent over him with her eyes closed, resting.

Presently he pushed her away and fell back on the bed, and began to describe how nice it was when he had a little house of his own down the street, all new, with all conveniences, gas stove, electric lights, when he was married to Rosemary. Rosemary – she had given up a job in the next town, just to marry him. How had it happened that she had left him so soon? It meant nothing that he had threatened time and again to shoot her, it was nothing at all that he had pointed the gun against her breast. She had not understood. It was only that he had relished his contentment. He had only wanted to play with her. In a way he had wanted to show her that he loved her above life and death.

'Above life and death,' he repeated, closing his eyes.

Clytie did not make an answer, as Octavia always did during these scenes, which were bound to end in Gerald's tears.

Outside the closed window a mockingbird began to sing. Clytie held back the curtain and pressed her ear against the glass. The rain had stopped. The bird's song sounded in liquid drops down through the pitch-black trees and the night.

'Go to hell,' Gerald said. His head was under the pillow.

She took up the tray, and left Gerald with his face hidden. It was not necessary for her to look at any of their faces. It was their faces which came between.

Hurrying, she went down to the kitchen and began to eat her own supper.

Their faces came between her face and another. It was their faces which had come pushing in between, long ago, to hide some face that had looked back at her. And now it was hard to remember the way it looked, or the time when she had seen it first. It must have been when she was young. Yes, in a sort of arbor, hadn't she laughed, leaned forward . . . and that vision of a face – which was a little like all the other faces, the trusting child's, the innocent old traveler's, even the greedy barber's and Lethy's and the wandering peddlers' who one by one knocked and went unanswered at the door – and yet different, yet far more – this face had been very close to hers, almost familiar, almost accessible. And then the face of Octavia was thrust between, and at other times the apoplectic face of her father, the face of her brother Gerald and the face of her brother Henry with the bullet hole through the forehead . . . It was purely for a resemblance to a vision that she examined the secret, mysterious, unrepeated faces she met in the street of Farr's Gin.

But there was always an interruption. If anyone spoke to her, she fled. If she saw she was going to meet someone on the street, she had been known to dart behind a bush and hold a small branch in front of her face until the person had gone by. When anyone called her by name, she turned first red, then white, and looked somehow, as one of the ladies in the store remarked, *disappointed*.

She was becoming more frightened all the time, too. People could tell because she never dressed up any more. For years, every once in a while, she would come out in what was called an 'outfit', all in hunter's green, a hat that came down around her face like a bucket, a green silk dress, even green shoes with pointed toes. She would wear the outfit all one day, if it was a pretty day, and then next morning she would be back in the faded jumper with her old hat tied under the chin, as if the outfit had been a dream. It had been a long time now since Clytie had dressed up so that you could see her coming.

Once in a while when a neighbor, trying to be kind or only being curious, would ask her opinion about anything – such as a pattern of crochet – she would not run away; but, giving a thin trapped smile, she would say in a childish voice, 'It's nice'. But, the ladies always added, nothing that came anywhere close to the Farrs' house was nice for long.

'It's nice', said Clytie when the old lady next door showed her the new rosebush she had planted, all in bloom.

But before an hour was gone, she came running out of her house screaming, 'My sister Octavia says you take that rosebush up! My sister Octavia says you take the rosebush up and move it away from our fence! If you don't I'll kill you! You take it away.'

And on the other side of the Farrs lived a family with a little boy who was always playing in his yard. Octavia's cat would go under the fence, and he would take it and hold it in his arms. He had a song he sang to the Farrs' cat. Clytie would come running straight out of the house, flaming with her message from Octavia. 'Don't you do that! Don't you do that!' she would cry in anguish. 'If you do that again, I'll have to kill you!'

And she would run back to the vegetable patch and begin to curse.

The cursing was new, and she cursed softly, like a singer going over a song for the first time. But it was something she could not stop. Words which at first horrified Clytie poured in a full, light stream from her throat, which soon, nevertheless, felt strangely relaxed and rested. She cursed all alone in the peace of the vegetable garden. Everybody said, in something like deprecation, that she was only imitating her older sister, who used to go out to that same garden and curse in that same way, years ago, but in a remarkably loud, commanding voice that could be heard in the post office.

Sometimes in the middle of her words Clytie glanced up to where Octavia, at her window, looked down at her. When she let the curtain drop at last, Clytie would be left there speechless.

Finally, in a gentleness compounded of fright and exhaustion and love, an overwhelming love, she would wander through the gate and out through the town, gradually beginning to move faster, until her long legs gathered a ridiculous, rushing speed. No one in town could have kept up with Miss Clytie, they said, giving them an even start.

She always ate rapidly, too, all alone in the kitchen, as she was eating now. She bit the meat savagely from the heavy silver fork and gnawed the little chicken bone until it was naked and clean.

Halfway upstairs, she remembered Gerald's second pot of coffee, and went back for it. After she had carried the other trays down again and washed the dishes, she did not forget to try all the doors and windows to make sure that everything was locked up absolutely tight.

The next morning, Clytie bit into smiling lips as she cooked breakfast. Far out past the secretly opened window a freight train was crossing the bridge in the sunlight. Some Negroes filed down the road going fishing, and Mr Tom Bate's Boy, who was going along, turned and looked at her through the window.

Gerald had appeared dressed and wearing his spectacles, and announced that he was going to the store today. The old Farr furnishing store did little business now, and people hardly missed Gerald when he did not come; in fact, they could hardly tell when he did because of the big boots strung on a wire, which almost hid the cagelike office. A little high-school girl could wait on anybody who came in.

Now Gerald entered the dining-room.

'How are you this morning, Clytie?' he asked.

'Just fine, Gerald, how are you?'

'I'm going to the store,' he said.

He sat down stiffly, and she laid a place on the table before him.

From above, Octavia screamed, 'Where in the devil is my thimble, you stole my thimble, Clytie Farr, you carried it away, my little silver thimble!'

'It's started,' said Gerald intensely. Clytie saw his fine, thin, almost black lips spread in a crooked line. 'How can a man live in the house with women? How can he?'

He jumped up, and tore his napkin exactly in two. He walked out of the dining-room without eating the first bite of his breakfast. She heard him going back upstairs into his room.

'My thimble!' screamed Octavia.

She waited one moment. Crouching eagerly, rather like a little squirrel, Clytie ate part of her breakfast over the stove before going up the stairs.

At nine Mr Bobo, the barber, knocked at the front door.

Without waiting, for they never answered the knock, he let himself in and advanced like a small general down the hall. There was the old organ that was never uncovered or played except for funerals, and then nobody was invited. He went ahead, under the arm of the tiptoed male statue and up the dark stairway. There they were, lined up at the head of the stairs, and they all looked at him with repulsion. Mr Bobo was convinced that they were every one mad. Gerald, even, had already been drinking, at nine o'clock in the morning.

Mr Bobo was short and had never been anything but proud of it, until he had started coming to this house once a week. But he did not enjoy looking up from below at the soft, long throats, the cold, repelled, high-reliefed faces of those Farrs. He could only imagine what one of those sisters would do to him if he made one move.

305

(As if he would!) As soon as he arrived upstairs, they all went off and left him. He pushed out his chin and stood with his round legs wide apart, just looking around. The upstairs hall was absolutely bare. There was not even a chair to sit down in.

'Either they sell away their furniture in the dead of night,' said Mr Bobo to the people of Farr's Gin, 'or else they're just too plumb mean to use it.'

Mr Bobo stood and waited to be summoned, and wished he had never started coming to this house to shave old Mr Farr. But he had been so surprised to get a letter in the mail. The letter was on such old, yellowed paper that at first he thought it must have been written a thousand years ago and never delivered. It was signed 'Octavia Farr', and began without even calling him 'Dear Mr Bobo'. What it said was: 'Come to this residence at nine o'clock each Friday morning until further notice, where you will shave Mr James Farr.'

He thought he would go one time. And each time after that, he thought he would never go back – especially when he never knew when they would pay him anything. Of course, it was something to be the only person in Farr's Gin allowed inside the house (except for the undertaker, who had gone there when young Henry shot himself, but had never to that day spoken of it). It was not easy to shave a man as bad off as Mr Farr, either – not anything like as easy as to shave a corpse or even a fighting-drunk field hand. Suppose you were like this, Mr Bobo would say: you couldn't move your face; you couldn't hold up your chin, or tighten your jaw, or even bat your eyes when the razor came close. The trouble with Mr Farr was his face made made no resistance to the razor. His face didn't hold.

'I'll never go back,' Mr Bobo always ended to his customers. 'Not even if they paid me. I've seen enough.'

Yet here he was again, waiting before the sickroom door.

'This is the last time,' he said. 'By God!'

And he wondered why the old man did not die.

Just then Miss Clytie came out of the room. There she came in her funny, sideways walk, and the closer she got to him the more slowly she moved.

'Now?' asked Mr Bobo nervously.

Clytie looked at his small, doubtful face. What fear raced

through his little green eyes! His pitiful, greedy, small face – how very mournful it was, like a stray kitten's. What was it that this greedy little thing was so desperately needing?

Clytie came up to the barber and stopped. Instead of telling him that he might go in and shave her father, she put out her hand and with breathtaking gentleness touched the side of his face.

For an instant afterward, she stood looking at him inquiringly, and he stood like a statue, like the statue of Hermes.

Then both of them uttered a despairing cry. Mr Bobo turned and fled, waving his razor around in a circle, down the stairs and out the front door; and Clytie, pale as a ghost, stumbled against the railing. The terrible scent of bay rum, of hair tonic, the horrible moist scratch of an invisible beard, the dense, popping green eyes – what had she got hold of with her hand! She could hardly bear it – the thought of that face.

From the closed door to the sickroom came Octavia's shouting voice.

'Clytie! Clytie! You haven't brought Papa the rain water! Where in the devil is the rain water to shave Papa?'

Clytie moved obediently down the stairs.

Her brother Gerald threw open the door of his room and called after her, 'What now? This is a madhouse! Somebody was running past my room, I heard it. Where do you keep your men? Do you have to bring them home?' He slammed the door again, and she heard the barricade going up.

Clytie went through the lower hall and out the back door. She stood beside the old rain barrel and suddenly felt that this object, now, was her friend, just in time, and her arms almost circled it with impatient gratitude. The rain barrel was full. It bore a dark, heavy, penetrating fragrance, like ice and flowers and the dew of night.

Clytie swayed a little and looked into the slightly moving water. She thought she saw a face there.

Of course. It was the face she had been looking for, and from which she had been separated. As if to give a sign, the index finger of a hand lifted to touch the dark cheek.

Clytie leaned closer, as she had leaned down to touch the face of the barber.

It was a wavering, inscrutable face. The brows were drawn

together as if in pain. The eyes were large, intent, almost avid, the nose ugly and discolored as if from weeping, the mouth old and closed from any speech. On either side of the head dark hair hung down in a disreputable and wild fashion. Everything about the face frightened and shocked her with its signs of waiting, of suffering.

For the second time that morning, Clytie recoiled, and as she did so, the other recoiled in the same way.

Too late, she recognized the face. She stood there completely sick at heart, as though the poor, half-remembered vision had finally betrayed her.

'Clytie! Clytie! The water! The water!' came Octavia's monumental voice.

Clytie did the only thing she could think of to do. She bent her angular body further, and thrust her head into the barrel, under the water, through its glittering surface into the kind, featureless depth, and held it there.

When Old Lethy found her, she had fallen forward into the barrel, with her poor ladylike black-stockinged legs up-ended and hung apart like a pair of tongs.

PATRICE CHAPLIN

✐

from
Albany Park

ONE

I first saw José Tarres on the stairs of the Hotel Residencia
Internacional in Gerona, Spain. I looked at him, he looked at me. I
carried on walking down to the main door, he went up the stairs to
the bar. It didn't seem like too much to me but then I wasn't aware,
in those days, just how important a look could be. I went on south
with my friend Beryl and he did whatever he did, which I never
really found out. I still don't know thirty years later. But he had a
lot of front over a lot of subterfuge.

Gerona is a pre-Roman town, forty miles inland from the Costa
Brava. It has a vast old quarter with a much-visited cathedral, Arab
baths, monumental churches. Bells ring across the town each
fifteen minutes day and night. The cobbled alleys and sharp
stairways, deep arches and courtyards, are all stone, most of it
medieval, some from earlier times. The buildings, huge buttresses
of stone, lean together across the strip of street leaving only a shine
of brilliant sky. Parts of the original city wall still remain – clumps
of stones almost covered with weed, supposedly 4,000 years old.
The stone makes the town echo and enhances every sound. Only
the bells are free as they toll high above the buildings. The stone
makes the town very cold in winter. It holds on to atmosphere. It
makes sure the past is there always, solid, unconquered by decay.
It's said the stones have a magnetism that draws certain people
back time and time again to the city. I believe it. Carcassonne has
the same legend. I've heard it's to do with ley lines. At certain
points across the earth the energy builds up and creates a pull, a
pulse, and in these places unusual and mystical things can happen.

309

It was mid-morning when I saw José Tarres for the first time. Beryl saw him too. She was always quick to follow up what she fancied but I thought we should get going and hitch a lift to Barcelona before it got too hot. It was May in the mid 1950s and she and I were fifteen. We didn't eat much because we didn't have money but we were full of shivery excitement. We had all our life ahead of us. Spain in those days was sensual and hospitable. The infestation of tourists hadn't begun. And we had the big one on our side – youth, but we didn't even consider that. Ageing, like death, was a process that didn't happen to us.

We wore arty rope Roman sandals that you could buy in the Charing Cross Road for three and sixpence, and very tight drainpipe trousers. Our black sleeveless tops were lopsided and handmade and falling apart. Our very long nails were painted black and we wore white lipstick. We dressed the same as we did when dancing to trad jazz at Cy Laurie's club in Soho. The Spanish had never seen anything like it. The women threw round prickly things that stuck to us, the kids threw stones and men threw glances, long and curious. They were more concerned with what was underneath our weird black clothes. Beryl wore enormous gold hoop earrings, mine were dangling silvered chandeliers. We put on a lot of make-up – the longest task of the day was getting that on. We had huge Brigitte Bardot kisscurls over our ears and our hair was streaked with a gold dust that in certain climates turned green.

Beryl was very beautiful, which made being her friend difficult. I didn't compete – even at fifteen I knew that was a mistake but I certainly tried to always be at my best. She in turn had an incredible older sister who'd been out with every attractive boy in Albany Park. That caused a great deal of misery. Her sister's body for example – well, she should have been a film starlet but life, having one of its ironical turns, fitted her out with a desire, not for fame, but ironing. The body was kept indoors in the living-room toiling over a businesslike ironing-board. Whenever I saw her she was pressing delicate knickers or brassières with large cups and starched blouses. Johnny Ray would sing 'Glad Rag Doll', then she'd change the 78 record to 'All of Me' or 'Cry'. She was neat and fastidious, her waist was so tiny – everyone remarked on her waist. She was what they call in Albany Park, 'developed'. She had a pronounced interest in clothes and an enviable style, but she was straight. I think she was one of the main reasons Beryl left home when she did, so early. I left because I wanted adventure. Also my mother was unbalanced again, definitely dodgy, and Albany Park was too small for all that sort of thing. Anyway, I'd always had wanderlust. I used to lie on the lawn on a summer's day and the very sky seemed to call to me. I'd jump up, and beyond the rose bushes I could see the woods and I'd hunger to plunge through their darkness and run across the meadow and go beyond the other woods, out of the known into the unknown, and so reach the coast. And then it would really begin. I wanted to be a gypsy and go to Bohemia. My father didn't consider that a career. But I knew I'd travel because I longed to. Also, I had a real love of life in those days. My father, anyway, never really interfered with something I wanted to do. It was not so much a gift of freedom to an already wayward child. It was just that he had his hands full with my mother, like carrying her unconscious body out of the river where she'd tried to drown herself. He tried very hard to stop her killing herself. In the end it depressed him but he still carried on, even when he had little reason for living himself.

Beryl's sister was the only girl with a natural beauty spot just under her eye. In retaliation Beryl used to pencil in two, and her mascara was so thick, her lashes looked like spiders' legs. Beryl's sister would saunter down the high street in the nearby town, Sidcup, wearing a pink coat that emphasized her remarkable waist and everything else, and the boys would gather on the other side of the road and just stare. Boys respected her and would not approach. Whereas Beryl and I would prowl around the park, also in Sidcup, looking for boys. We got the sister's rejects. We did not get respect. That sister really had got glamour. And not only that, she was nice. It was as though she knew how lucky she was and was grateful. I realize the only thing Beryl could do was go completely arty and extraordinary or commit suicide.

I don't know how we got permission to have passports so young, under sixteen, or what lies we'd told to get them. The lies would have come from me. I was the one with ideas. Beryl just went along with it and shared the consequences.

When Beryl and I got to the bottom of the stairs in the Hotel Residencia Internacional, she had to get her mirror out and apply more make-up. This was a ritual that could happen anywhere, at

311

any time. I totally approved of it. The door of the hotel swung shut with a distinctive sound and, because of the narrowness of the street, it echoed up to the very top rooms. Even if you were on the roof you could tell if someone was leaving or entering. It turned out to be very useful for José.

Beryl wanted another large *café con leche*. She had very bad nerves that hit her stomach. It was caused by being slapped with a ruler in primary school. I remember the incident – it was too everyday for comment, but as Mr Jones hit the back of her legs her cheeks turned crimson which made her large eyes even browner. I can't remember anything sensational about the punishment but she used it at the local doctor's and got a generous sicknote that got her out of all educational activities she considered tiresome. She was easily bored. Mr Jones was always swinging the ruler about. He liked today's choice up on a chair and the class counted aloud as the ruler hit the back of the knees. It was the only time the class counted accurately. There was no sympathy, just curiosity as to whether the child would cry before six strokes or get to twelve. It was also interesting to see how pain changed someone's face. These attacks with the ruler had nothing to do with discipline, naturally. The teacher just happened to like it. Otherwise he was getting his rocks off with Miss Ashwood, a raucous type on the other side of the blackboard. As a result of his sexual lapses my friend was not well educated but she still got into grammar school. I wondered what having nerves was like. As far as I knew I'd never in my life encountered a nerve, but Beryl was defensive, even secretive. Although our friendship had begun at the age of four and was very close there were things she did not talk about. I never knew what went on in her house. Whenever I visited, Johnny Ray or Frankie Laine would be singing loudly and her sister would be at the ironing-board or standing in front of the living-room mirror (won at a fairground) putting on make-up. There was always a boyfriend waiting for her on the step. Because my family were a quarter of an inch higher up the social scale, our parents didn't speak. Beryl's mother's choice, not mine. They came from the East End and kept to their own kind.

The high atmosphere in Gerona had overstimulated Beryl. Because her stomach nerves were on she had to go to the first café we passed and spend half our remaining money on another breakfast. I told her we'd miss lunch but she didn't care. She was quite defiant when she wanted something. She smiled at the waiter, he loved her dimples. Breakfast was on the house.

She admitted then that the nerves story was a lot of shit. She'd just hated the teacher. The way Mr Jones dressed made her sick. Anyway, she preferred being at home listening to records, reading magazines and pinning up pictures of Bardot and Elsa Martinelli in her room.

We put our rucksacks over one shoulder, which was more attractive than the usual way. The jukebox was playing 'Johnny Guitar' as we left. I'd never seen streets so narrow, with the buildings leaning across nearly hiding the sky. It was like walking through a forest. I was already entranced by the light, it completely changed colours. I loved the smell of the woodsmoke, the loud eau de Cologne. The alleys were symphonies of smells – hot olive oil, vanilla, leather, drains. All of it made me shiver with expectation. What we were doing seemed a very good way to be alive. We crossed the river by the tall bridge, an iron one with a canopy – the traffic began in the modern part away from the river. Hitch-hiking was a difficult activity to pin down in Spain because cars stopped before we even signalled. Men wanted to give us a ride, both varieties. We got a lift immediately to Calella, just outside Barcelona. In those days it was an attractive, almost deserted resort with one bar. We sunbathed and drank chocolate milk and ate bread covered with oil and tomato. Because it was May there weren't many people about; visitors, if they came, arrived in June.

Beryl said we should get into Barcelona and work in a club. We'd say we were eighteen so where was the problem? There was no language difficulty – not pouring drinks. We waded at the edge of the sea to the next resort, a fishing village, and it was so lovely we promised to go back and stay. When I next did go there, ten years later, it was unrecognizable. Only the name remained of what was once so exquisite.

I remember it took us ages to get into Barcelona and even longer to get out. The women looked so sensuous and glamorous and the men belonged to them. I felt so left out, sad. Nobody noticed us in the big towns. I longed to grow up so I could be very beautiful and sought after. I wanted to buy Toledo gold jewellery and Spanish perfume. The town excited me but made me desperate to become something else. It stoked ambition. I think for the first time I needed to be somebody. In Barcelona we found out hitching was illegal in Spain. The Guardia Civil would pick up not only us, but the driver. A gypsy youth took us up to Barcelonetta, an encampment so dangerous no outsider ventured there. Even the police went in groups. Yet nothing happened to us, perhaps because we didn't see it as dangerous. I think we even asked them for money which was a reversal in that place. The dwellings were constructed inside caves. Outside there were dozens of abandoned cars and vans, covered in bits of cloth. It was messy and complicated but the music was marvellous and the kids, although some of their noses dripped with snot, had marvellous seeing eyes. It was like visiting a colony of dangerous birds. I'd only go up there today if I wanted to kill myself and couldn't think of another way.

We didn't decide to go to Sitges. We just felt we should keep going, and south sounded better than north. Our Spanish was limited. *Guapa* – beautiful, *dinero* – money, *rubia* – blonde, *morena* – dark. That way we missed a lot of indelicate talk. But the men didn't know what to make of us. They just hadn't seen two very young girls hitching alone before, not in Spain. The Soho clothes belonged to another race. And our obvious youth. They just couldn't get it at all. But we were out to see the world. We took the roads as they came and we had time. As long as it was new and different from Albany Park. That was all we asked.

Cars wouldn't stop on the main road out of Barcelona because there were too many police about, so we had to keep walking through intense heat which danced hypnotically on and off the freshly tarred road. Plants moved in the wind made by the passing cars; tough plants, grey and dusty like old spiders. Run-down cafés and brightly painted shacks lined the road and a multitude of radios played the haunting Spanish song that we thought was a flamenco chart buster. It was in fact an advertising jingle for national chocolate. It was full of the melancholy and desire that the south conjured up. I thought it announced the beginning of a huge and deathly passion. How right I was.

I told Beryl I knew how I'd look when I grew up. I'd be brown and curvaceous with lustrous hair like the Barcelona women. I'd adorn myself with Toledo gold jewellery, wear filmstar shoes and exude sexual magnetism. There were some things too ridiculous

314

even to reply to, so she stayed silent. I could see it was like turning a kangaroo into a tiger, but desire was on my side and with desire you could do anything.

After two kilometres we started signalling to the cars. It was always wise to be settled with a place to sleep before nightfall. We'd have got a train at that point but had no money. Then a long-distance lorry pulled alongside and we asked the driver where he was going. He didn't understand but opened the door. The step up into his cab was too high so he had to get out and push us up from behind, his hands cupping our buttocks. He was going directly to Valencia which was great, but all the giggling and physical intimacy getting into the cab had given him ideas and it didn't feel safe. Especially when he said, 'Hitch-hiking dangerous. Men sexy. Maybe you like sex?' He swished open a curtain behind him and pointed to a makeshift bed amongst the lorry's produce. We tried to get his mind off all that by asking him about his travels. He did a circuitous route from Bilbao that wound up in Murcia twice a week. Sometimes he drove thirty hours without sleep. I asked him the Spanish word for 'to drive'. He told me one which I learnt effortlessly. Later it turned out it was the verb 'to fuck'.

He turned on the radio and we all sang along to 'Johnny Guitar' and the atmosphere was great, but I still thought we should get out. Our way of survival was to say we were thirsty, after a certain time in each vehicle. Usually the driver pulled up at a café and sometimes offered us food. This one had everything in the back, unfortunately, and pulled out a litre of dark wine.

'No, no, *café con leche,*' said Beryl.

She didn't want that either. She wanted a paella and salad, a seafood platter. Then an icecream cake, some fruit, a slab of *torrone,* a black coffee. But she hadn't got the words for any of her deepest needs, even in English.

'Spanish wine good. You make love with me.'

I couldn't tell whether it was a question or a promise. He pulled into a petrol station and got out. In the next line a youth with very pale hair and a beautiful face like James Dean, as Beryl was quick to point out, was getting into his car. We jumped down from the lorry and asked him for a ride. The youth tossed our rucksacks into the back and we drove away before the lorry driver had even asked for petrol.

The boy said we should stay at Sitges. It was a resort, '*muy guapo*', but he reckoned there were cheaper hotels in nearby Casteldefels. It wasn't a question of cheap. We needed free. We had eight pesetas left. Communication was difficult but he got the drift of Beryl's interest and asked her name. I think he explained who he was and what he did, where he lived, all of it impossible to understand. So he made a gesture and it looked as though he was sewing.

'I think he does needlework,' said Beryl, and her eyes rolled. It didn't occur to us he could be gay because 'gay' wasn't a word in use then. We'd only come across 'queers' once and that was when a lord of the realm made love with a boy and went to prison. We heard about that during a domestic science lesson at Dartford Grammar School. We thought it was a rare occurrence like being albino. Albany Park was dreadful in every way but it was a hive of heterosexual activity. It occurred to me later that the blond youth was not suggesting he did needlework but that our homemade tops needed sewing up.

Casteldefels was next to Sitges, about twenty miles from Barcelona, and we arrived as the sun was setting. It was completely deserted. There were two, maybe three, freshly built hotels and they all appeared empty. To one side was an army camp. What about nightlife? That was more important than food or sleep. The boy said the nearest club for dancing was on the outskirts of Sitges. We needed to ask him for money but he was too much like us. He shook our hands politely and drove away.

There was a double room at the first hotel but the owner wanted money in advance. Also he didn't like the look of us. At the second we ran into luck. The owner and his wife, childless, had a lot of pent-up caring instinct. Also they spoke English.

'But you are little girls,' he said, when I asked if we could work for him. 'Twelve. No more than twelve.' We showed him our passports but he stayed with twelve. He liked that. His wife wanted to think we were waifs who had run away from unsatisfactory homes. She took us into the kitchen and gave us home-made soup, olives and fresh sardines. She was fascinated by our make-up, how long did it take to put on? Trying to seem normal, I said fifteen minutes. Actually it took twice that. She was appalled. Five minutes was all she spent on her face. I thought her proud boast might be a mistake. Her husband was giving us too much attention. She sincerely hoped we'd run away from our parents. She looked as though she could handle a drama. May in Casteldefels was boring for her. We explained our career was travelling and we were making our way to Bohemia in Czechoslovakia. She said her husband couldn't advance our travelling plans by giving us work because the season hadn't started but we could have a small plain room at the back at a reduced rate. We accepted that. She did not ask for anything in advance. 'Who needs a St Christopher's medal?' said Beryl. 'This place has all the luck we need.'

I felt so free and light as we walked along the seashore towards the danceclub on the outskirts of Sitges. The chirp of insects, the delicious breeze, the distant music and the Mediterranean night sky made me thrilled to be alive. It was all there – all the joyous things. Life promised me, that night, I'd be happy.

TWO

The sand was dazzling white and quite empty. The owner's wife had brought us breakfast without even being asked. She wanted to mend our home-made clothes but Beryl thought she'd do something frightful to them, like add sleeves and a neckline. We had a dozen boys' names on cigarette packets. Our début at the nightclub had been all we'd hoped for, but then we excelled in clubs because we were good at rock and roll and jive and in South London won prizes. A day never passed that we didn't dance. If there were no clubs we'd dance in the streets.

Although sunbathing was more important than something as mundane as survival, the money thing had to be talked about. We'd begged in France and it wasn't difficult, not if you asked for money for the Métro or a bus. The problem with Casteldefels was that there was no one to beg from. I wanted to move on to a town and get something together but Beryl chose to hang around. She'd liked the look of the blond youth who'd given us a lift and reckoned he'd show up at the club. If we were going to move it would have to be that morning because of paying, or rather not paying, for the room. I'd offer the woman our earrings and promise to pay something on the way back through.

'But we won't be coming back through,' said Beryl. 'We won't pass this way again.'

Then we'd have to spend a day in Barcelona begging. A growing hotel bill was a nasty thing. We put on bikinis and lay in the sun and Beryl said something would turn up. It did. One minute the beach was deserted, the next, we were surrounded by soldiers. I opened my eyes because I thought the sun had gone in. They were standing around us, a dozen of them. They'd made no noise approaching. Because we had no reason to be frightened of men we were pleased to see them. We asked their names, they offered cigarettes. They were polite and wanted a date. Only two would get that, so there was a lot of banter and showing off. They liked dancing so that was a good start. They didn't speak a word of English but managed to convey that the nearby nightclub was a joke and the real places were in Barcelona. The atmosphere changed, they jumped to attention, saluting. Captain Pascual ordered them back to barracks. He spoke English and asked where we were staying. He had Paul Newman blue twinkling eyes and cropped fair hair bleached by the sun. He was lean, brown and his eyelashes were long. He looked like the cover of a *Woman's Realm* romance and I thought he was good-looking. Beryl said he was far too old. He was twenty-four. He said we were foolish. To sit alone on a beach with soldiers was very dangerous. 'Don't go near soldiers. They will sexually molest you. If I hadn't rescued you you would now be molested.' He escorted us back to the hotel and Beryl let him look after her. He sexually molested her immediately.

We had a sexual code: 26 was the real thing, going all the way, having intercourse, losing it; 25 was a slither, which meant there was no penetration; 24 was putting up a finger; 23 was caressing inside your clothes, 22 outside, and so on. We hadn't got to 26 which meant we were still virgins – so Beryl said. I believe she reached 26 in as many minutes with Captain Pascual but her virginity, like her nerves, was something she didn't talk about. I had to wait outside in the garden while he had his pleasure and the hotel owner's wife taught me the names for flowers, sky, trees. She asked where Beryl was and I assured her she was taking a shower. Beryl said afterwards that Captain Pascual had kissed her in a way no one else had, but had not touched her otherwise. Later, when she was feeling good from eating rather a lot of paella on tick, she said he'd loved her breasts. He was delighted there were no hairs on her nipples. Apparently some women had hairs. How would he know that if he'd only kissed Beryl?

'He kissed me with my bra off.'

I wasn't jealous. I just wanted to know what it was like. She said she hadn't let him take off her knickers because she didn't want to get into trouble. She could, she thought, get into rather a lot of trouble with him. He was meeting her that night and bringing along a Durex and a friend for me. I think she was very pleased with herself.

Captain Pascual brought the friend but I can't recall anything about him. The four of us went to clubs and smooched on the dancefloor. It was all straight stuff because Captain Pascual was so old. I know we had lots to eat and felt so good we didn't want to leave where we were, but Captain Pascual drove back to the hotel in a determined way and somehow made available another room for Beryl. She woke me at three o'clock and said he'd given her a brooch and she was in love with him. It was unlikely she'd get to the south of Spain, leave alone Bohemia. She wanted to stay with Captain Pascual and marry him. I was very upset. Not only would I lose an inseparable friend but a marvellous travelling companion. I'd never been caressed by a man as old as twenty-four but obviously they had talents lacking in teenage boys.

Beryl washed her face and covered herself in Nivea cream. As usual she went to bed in her bra and pants. We'd never seen each other naked. Washing was something we did in private. A tremendous knock on the door made the shutters rattle. Of course we did not answer. Those kind of knocks heralded a quick exit out the window. But we'd done nothing wrong, I realized. Another knock.

'Police!'

'No one's coming in here,' said Beryl.

'We'll have to. It's the police. You've done nothing.'

'I don't care who they are. Don't open it.'

'Why not?'

'Because no one's seeing me without my make-up. We look terrible without make-up, both of us.'

The owner said we should open the door or the police would break it in. It occurred to me there might be bad news from

England. My mother was a strong possibility. Beryl made me turn off the light before I opened the door. Six policemen in three-cornered shiny black hats, all armed, filled the room. The owner and his wife had to stay in the passage. The light snapped on and the chief said plenty in Spanish. It seemed he was angry but his eyes, I noticed, glittered with approval as he looked at Beryl, who'd started giggling uncontrollably. Her cheap white cotton Dorothy Perkins bra was stuffed with cotton wool to make her breasts seem larger. Neither of us was exactly developed, unlike Beryl's sister who'd worn a size 36C bra at thirteen. We carried a chart of 'bust exercises' torn from a women's magazine and we did them ten times a day.

'Passport!'

He said it was illegal to be in Spain without family, under the age of sixteen. That made the nocturnal visit OK with the boys. So he dismissed them, then got down to real business with Beryl. She needed an escort, then everything would be legal. Who better than he? He'd call for her at midday and show her the sights. He left abruptly, not quite clicking his heels, and we fell across our beds howling with laughter. The owner said the police had come because there was a scandal. The army captain had entered the hotel with Beryl, an underage girl. The whole of Casteldefels was talking. But there wasn't anyone in Casteldefels. All that was Spanish for he was jealous. It was he who'd called the police. He'd misjudged Captain Pascual. That one was no fool. As soon as he'd done what he wanted he'd left by a window.

The owner's wife said we looked better without make-up.

An hour later the police chief called again, alone. He wanted to make sure we were all right. He looked under the beds, in the clothes cupboard.

The next morning the owner's wife made us tortilla for breakfast. You're too thin. Eat. You must eat. You'll be prettier if you're fat. Spanish girls! *Muy guapa!*

She asked about our parents, what they did. We lied about everything, an important defensive tactic that.

We sat in the shade of the palm trees and looked at everything, taking our time. We felt lucky. Then Beryl said she was going to hide. She couldn't be seen with a man as old and hideous as the police chief. She'd rather be dead. I was to get rid of him. How? She didn't know.

Of course, a fifteen-year-old's behaviour would be a mistake at any other age. Beryl's spontaneous visit to the army camp, because she was mad about Captain Pascual, was an example. Her heart was in the right place but she didn't have enough in her head. To walk into a man's private world, that of a man she hardly knew, invited trouble. For a start there was a Mrs Pascual the Captain had failed to mention. Captain Pascual was in the shit from the moment Beryl arrived, because the police chief was only minutes behind her. I think jealousy was the predominant emotion. Mrs Pascual threw in her share. Anyway, the commotion was such that Beryl and I ran to the hotel. It seemed the moment to leave. The owner and his wife couldn't agree more. They even helped us with our rucksacks.

'But we can't pay. We couldn't get any work.' In other words Casteldefels was not suitable for begging.

The woman smiled. 'We never thought you could. Don't worry about it. It was a pleasure to know you.'

By the time we'd first arrived in Casteldefels I'd long forgotten the man on the stairs in Gerona, even forgotten Gerona itself. Rule one – only the moment counted. Only the future lasted.

THREE

We arrived back in Albany Park half starved, penniless, a bit mad-looking, not having slept for two nights, completely forgetting the reason we'd given for going abroad. The sight of us caused instant domestic turmoil. Naturally they thought we were on drugs. We were, but not heavily. One of the tabloids had done an exposé on speed and it had aroused our parents' vengeance. People like Beryl and me ended up on speed and then we'd end up even worse. In the Far East. The sex-slave traffic took care of that. I don't know if it was a fear or a fantasy but it was shared by both sets of parents. The drug look was caused by our shadowed sombre eyes used to seeing only the new, the exotic, the unexpected. Our eyes were no longer used to seeing Albany Park. I've seen people look like we did when they've come back from India. Their eyes show that they've been through some change and are on another life level altogether. They have little to do any more with what's available through Western pleasures. Anyway, we did not look as though we'd just finished a French language course at a youth centre in Paris – my original lie. The shock of seeing Beryl gave her mother ulcerated colitis. My mother already had everything so there was nothing much I could add. She did say I'd brought shame to the street. My father said I could have waited so I arrived back after dark. He made it clear straight away that I wasn't going to live off him. Out to work and pay your share! So I had to go to the local employment agency the very next morning. Beryl was at least given a day to recover.

On the evening of our return there was an all-night rave-up at Cy Laurie's. We couldn't miss that and one more night without sleep wouldn't make that much difference – we'd missed so many.

Beryl's rope sandals were worn out, flapping with exhaustion, and her trousers were skin-tight thanks to a row of safety pins. We looked haunted, dishevelled and very pale, exactly right for a trad evening. Beryl's sandals fell to bits after the first dance and that's when we both discovered the joy of going barefoot. Not just dancing. It was a real pleasure walking at dawn through Soho. Barefoot – instant freedom, but my feet would have preferred a different surface – stones, old stones, and the memory of Gerona stirred. I'd caught Gerona, of course, like a bug that lies dormant then breaks out in a dangerous irrational way, bringing my life to a crisis.

Because I'd been to grammar school – I'd left a year early under a decided cloud – I was offered a job as assistant cashier at William Perring's, the furniture store, in Sidcup High Street. I think the weekly wage was three pounds but that bought a lot of make-up, records, film magazines and cinema tickets in those days. Three pounds was exactly half the price of a really marvellous coat – the sort Beryl's sister would wear. Although I was a loyal Bohemian and wore the obligatory extraordinary clothes and ghostly make-up I still appreciated beautiful clothes and would have worn them if I could have afforded to. I'd been brought up on Hollywood films and I went straight from the arty phase over to the glamorous. It had to be Hollywood, and once again it was overdone. But I loved all kinds of clothes and styles. I never got tired of looking at people. I loved their physical presence, their lives. What they did in the morning, how they got through the day, what make-up they chose, what they loved. Beautiful glamorous people made me feel safe, especially filmstars. When I was still at school the film

Gentlemen Prefer Blondes cheered me up so much that for a whole evening I completely obliterated my mother's breakdown.

Albany Park was the quickest route to Hollywood imaginable. Living in a simple-minded place like that where nothing unexpected could ever happen would naturally propel you towards glamour. You'd be starving, dying for the fabulous, the superlative. If Albany Park had had some spark you wouldn't need Hollywood. You could go to somewhere moderate like Brighton. But the place was a catapult holding me back and when it finally released me I went to Hollywood. I just took rather a long time getting there.

Albany Park – no description really fits that place, so housing estate will do. Most of it was pre-Second World War, a lot of bungalows, no flats. The streets were more or less the same except in length but they were given an assortment of titles. Avenues, drives, lanes running across roads and streets, then the occasional close or crescent. The railway station was the centre with frequent stopping trains to Charing Cross or Dartford in Kent. The local pub, the Albany, was opposite. Everybody was straight and there were no murders or scandals, except what Beryl and I provided with our appearances. In the days after I left school, when I took Hollywood very seriously, it was a place to get out of. The good thing about it was the woods. They began at the end of my road and led to meadows, the River Cray, crossed by the Five Arches Bridge, Jordans Wood. So the real Kent countryside began just past my house. On the other side the suburbs of London began, then the city itself, an innocent, optimistic place in those days.

I cycled to William Perring every morning, arriving at 8.45. Huge rolls of carpet were already propped rather untidily so that the three-piece suites could be seen. Carpet was the fastest seller so had to be easily available. I simply took cash, made out discounts, filled in credit books, made the tea. I cycled home to lunch, then back at two. The whole thing looked very normal. Down the road Beryl was doing a filing job at a food wholesaler for £2.19 a week. At five-thirty I added up the day's take, had it checked by the real cashier, then cycled back to Albany Park. The journey took fifteen minutes and I knew every crevice in the streets, every branch on the trees. I'd walked from Albany Park to Sidcup and back hundreds of times a year since I was three.

The manager of William Perring tried to make me look normal. That was to be expected. He didn't want my kind of face behind his cashier's window. It didn't inspire confidence in the customers. He had trouble being personal so just said, 'Tone it down. All of it.' So I left off my earrings and my hair streaks and black nail varnish and black stockings. It was like stripping off my skin.

As soon as I got home I had – I think it was called tea – not a long meal – my mother found no pleasure in the kitchen. Then I got it all on, my personality, and stepped out for a night of excitement. As I shut the front door it would be flung open immediately. My father spoke, not, 'Goodbye. Have a nice evening.' But, 'Don't bring trouble home with you. Don't bring a baby to this door. Men, they just want one thing.' I ran up the street howling with laughter.

The Dartford loop line to Charing Cross took forty minutes. Then Beryl and I would go into the station lavatory and put on more make-up then walk to Cy Laurie's in Windmill Street, arriving about eight-thirty. Or we'd go to Chris Barber's off Leicester Square or the 100 Club in Oxford Street. In the music breaks we'd have a drink at the French pub or the Greek café in Old Compton Street. There was a lot of hanging around and giggling and picking people up and being chatted up. We wanted the attention of the real artists. They had marvellous lives – they were real travellers but we were too young and they were accompanied by mistresses and models, voluptuous older girls with unbelievable Bohemian style. We used to translate some of it for Albany Park and got sneered at. At least we provoked some emotion. Essentially, we were barefoot in long black garb, with very straight hair. The residents said we looked like witches. We could handle the aggression. We'd had enough when we were Teddy girls of twelve.

The Soho artists were always returning from Paris or heading for Italy and I was filled with such desire just to go. Only the dancing shut up the urgency. I wanted to do more than travel. I needed to capture it, record the experience, but I didn't know how.

Meanwhile Beryl's sister would be out with a proper man at somewhere posh like the Lyceum, or sitting in one of the very dressed-up pubs you found around Sidcup in those days. She worked in an office in the Strand, also doing accounts. She tried to tell me that Beryl was upsetting their mother. Every new layer of Outdoor Girl block mascara meant another dose of kaolin and morphine. Beryl's mother vomited with worry and the disgrace of it all. Then the sister said you didn't need a lot of make-up to attract men. Well, she could speak for herself. We'd got her number. She did it, definitely. Went the whole way: 24, 25, 26. And then another number came up: 69. That one made us hysterical.

The jazzclubs closed at eleven and we'd go from the real darkness into the partial darkness of the summer night. A lot of places were opening up from Soho right down past Charing Cross to the Embankment. Coffee bars where guitarists entertained free. Skiffle was about to come in and the famous 2I's coffee bar in Old Compton Street, hang out of the mods and singers like Terry Dean and Tommy Steele. Damp with sweat from dancing we'd see what was around across the cultural frontier before getting the last train to Albany Park at 11.48.

Notes on the Authors

TONI CADE BAMBARA was born and brought up in Harlem, New York, the setting of many of her stories. A former Rutgers University professor, she now lives with her daughter Karma in Atlanta, Georgia, and lectures in the North-East and on the West Coast of America. Her publications include *Gorilla My Love* (1972), *Sea Birds Are Still Alive* (1977) and *The Salt Eaters* (1980).

BOX-CAR BERTHA (Bertha Thompson), a hobo by birth and vocation, was born in the shadows of a railway yard, the daughter of radical parents. By the age of fifteen she was already on the road. She travelled from one end of the United States to the other in box-cars, 'decking' passenger trains, and hitch-hiking. She was in turn one of a gang of shoplifters, an associate of socialists and anarchists, a prostitute in a Chicago brothel and a research worker for a New York social service bureau. She was also the mother of her child. Above all else, however, she was a 'sister of the road'. Her autobiography, *Sister of the Road: the Autobiography of Box-Car Bertha*, as told to Dr Ben L. Reitman, was published in 1937. It was filmed by Martin Scorsese in 1972.

ISABELLA BIRD (1831–1904) was born in Cheshire and moved to Edinburgh after her clergyman father's death. She journeyed to the Outer Hebrides, about which she wrote articles, but suffered constantly from ill-health, insomnia and depression. At the age of forty her life took a turn for the better. She went alone to the Antipodes in 1872 and in 1873, wearing Hawaiian riding dress, rode her horse through the American Wild West. Here she met Rocky Mountain Jim, her 'dear desperado', who helped her climb the 'American Matterhorn'. She continued travelling, to the Japanese island of Hokkaido and the Native States of Malaya. She married in 1881, but did not stay at home. She went to western Tibet and Ladakh, Persia, Kurdistan, the Korean peninsula and China. She wrote numerous novels and recorded her expeditions in her travel books, which include *A Lady's Life in the Rocky Mountains* (1879), *Unbeaten Tracks in Japan* (1880) and *Journeys in Persia and Kurdistan* (1891). While at home in Edinburgh she kept to her day bed, but abroad she had the 'appetite of a tiger and the digestion of an ostrich'. She made her final journey at the age of seventy: she visited Morocco, where she rode a thousand miles on a black stallion given to her by the Sultan.

ELIZABETH BOWEN (1899–1973) was born in Dublin of Anglo-Irish descent. At the age of seven she left Ireland, but spent her summers in the family's ancestral home, Bowen's Court in County Cork. She began writing at the age of nineteen and in her lifetime published more than seventy short stories, many around the themes of love, ghosts, childhood, London in the Blitz, and English middle-class life. She travelled a great deal but divided most of her time between Bowen's Court and London, where her house was a centre of literary life. She spent her old age in Oxford and then Hythe in Kent, but in the fifties and sixties she was a writer in residence at several American universities. She published ten novels, including *To the North* (1932), *The House in Paris* (1935) and *The Death of the Heart* (1938). Her last book was *Eva Trout* (1969). She also published a large amount of literary journalism and non-fiction, collected into *The Mulberry Tree* (1985).

WILLA CATHER (1873–1947) was born in Virginia, USA, where her family had farmed the land for generations. At the age of eight she was uprooted to the wild western prairies, then a frontier land of immigrant people. This move, her constant attachment to Europe, and the numerous journeys she made into the American South-West profoundly affected her writing. She published short stories throughout her life – the first collection was *The Troll Garden* (1905) – but her first novel, *Alexander's Bridge*, was not published until 1912. This was followed by eleven further novels, including *My Antonia* (1918), *A Lost Lady* (1923), *The Professor's House* (1925) and *Death Comes for the Archbishop* (1927). *The Stories of Willa Cather*, selected by Hermione Lee, was published in 1989. In her later years Willa Cather became increasingly disillusioned by modern life, and in her will she forbade the dramatization of any of her work.

PATRICE CHAPLIN grew up during the war in Albany Park, a grim London suburb from which she ran away in the 1950s at the age of fifteen. Her father was ex-Royal Navy; her mother was insane. With her best friend Beryl she hitch-hiked to Paris and then Gerona, on her way to Bohemia. Here she met José Tarres, a Catalan activist who became a lifelong obsession. After a year, during which she had a small part in a Cocteau film, she returned to London. She became a student at the Royal Academy of Dramatic Art and a showgirl in Beak Street, where she slept on a pile of rags belonging to the designer who dressed Diana Dors. She then lived in Chelsea with a group of Bohemians. She married Charlie Chaplin's son Michael, but in 1966, on holiday, her car broke down in Calella, Spain, and she encountered José leaning against a wall. As a result her marriage also broke down. In addition to seven novels she has published short stories and the first part of her autobiography, *Albany Park* (1986). A playwright and Hollywood scriptwriter, she divides her time between London and California.

COLETTE (1873–1954), a woman of infinite talents and disguises, was born in a Burgundian village, daughter of a tax collector. She inherited from her mother a love of books, children, flowers and cats. Educated at the local school, she married 'Willy', the music critic and confectioner of light novels who proceeded to lock her into her room in order to make her write. This resulted in the 'Claudine' sequence of novels which were published under his name. She left Willy in 1906, becoming an actress, music-hall dancer, mime artist, and lover of the Marquise de Belbeur ('Missy'). She also lectured, ran a beauty salon, and wrote novels – including *Chéri* – and newspaper articles. The only woman to be elected to the Goncourt Academy, she was denied a Catholic burial but given a state funeral. Her collected works run to fifteen volumes.

ISABELLE EBERHARDT (1877–1904) was born near Geneva, the illegitimate daughter of a general's wife from Tsar Alexander's army and an ex-pope of the Russian Orthodox Church. She had an eccentric upbringing. In 1897 she left the family home and went with her mother to North Africa, where both converted to the Muslim faith. After her mother's death that year she adopted male attire, named herself 'Si Mahmoud', gained admittance to the Kadrya, a religious confraternity, and began her desert wanderings. She believed in French rule in North Africa and worked as an agent for the Deuxième Bureau; in 1901 there was an attempt on her life. She was expelled from Algeria. During her North African years she travelled widely, often aimlessly, becoming ravaged by the effects of starvation, disease, *kif* and alcohol addiction. She married her long-time lover, Slimène Ehnni, but died in a flash flood on the Algerian–Moroccan border. She was twenty-seven. Her novel *Le Trimadeur* was published in 1923. Her journal was first published in Paris as 'Dans l'Ombre Chaude d'Islam' (1905), 'Notes de Route' (1908) and 'Pages d'Islam' (1920).

Notes on the Authors

LOUISE ERDRICH (1954–) was born in Little Falls, Minnesota, the eldest of seven children. Her father is of German–American descent; her mother is Turtle Mountain Chippewa. As an undergraduate at Dartmouth College in the early 1970s, she was part of the first group of women to be admitted to the college and also part of one of the first groups of Native Americans. She published a number of stories – one of which won the 1985 O'Henry Prize – and a collection of poetry, *Jacklight* (1984), before her first novel, *Love Medicine* (1984) appeared. It has been translated in fifteen countries. This was followed by her novels *The Beet Queen* (1986) and *Tracks* (1988). Her next novel, *American Horse*, will complete this quartet. Her story 'The Beet Queen' first appeared in the *Paris Review* in 1985. She is married to a novelist and has five children.

MILES FRANKLIN (1879–1954) was born into a pioneering family settled in the mountain valleys of the Australian Alps. She was brought up on her father's station 'Brindabella' with six younger siblings. She wrote *My Brilliant Career* when she was only sixteen; its publication brought her instant fame and unwelcome notoriety. In 1904 she moved to Sydney, working as a domestic servant and writing *My Career Goes Bung* (1946). She then went on to America, where for ten years she worked for the Women's Trade Union League in Chicago and published a novel, *Some Everyday Folk and Dawn* (1909). During the First World War she worked in slum nurseries in London before going to Salonika as part of the Scottish Women's Hospital Unit. Afterwards she worked in London for the National Housing Council, returning in 1933 to Australia, where she finally settled down and wrote a further ten books; some under her own name, some under the pseudonym 'Brent of Bin Bin'.

JESSIE KESSON (1915–) was born in Inverness. She spent her early childhood in Elgin, the illegitimate child of a sensitive, poverty-racked mother in a street of prostitutes. Together they dodged the Cruelty Inspector and the rent man, until her mother was finally pronounced unfit to bring up her child. Jessie was put in an orphanage in Skene, Aberdeenshire. At sixteen she was sent to work on a local farm. She had a nervous breakdown and spent a year in a mental hospital, and went to the Highlands to recuperate. Here she was known as the Patient and one of the few who would speak to her was Johnnie, a cottar who had fought on the Afghan front. They married when she was nineteen, and camped in a wood. Her writing career began when she met the author Nan Shephard, who encouraged her to enter a writing competition which she won. She began writing poetry, and plays for the BBC. She has also been a cinema cleaner, an artist's model and a social worker in London and Glasgow.

She has published three novels: *Glitter of Mica* (1963), and *The White Bird Passes* (1958) and *Another Time, Another Place* (1983) – both of which have been filmed by Michael Radford – and a volume of short stories, *Where the Apple Ripens* (1985). She lives in London and is writing her autobiography.

BERYL MARKHAM (1902–86) was born in Leicester, England, but was taken to East Africa as a child by her adventurer father. She grew up amongst the Nandi children, running wild, before being apprenticed to her father in the training and breeding of racehorses. At eighteen she was the first woman in Africa to be granted a racehorse trainer's licence. She was twenty-three when she trained the winner of the Kenya St Leger. In 1931 she turned to flying: she piloted mail for the East African Airways and invented big-game hunting by air. In September 1936 she made world headlines by becoming the first person to fly solo across the Atlantic from east to west. In 1942 she published her extraordinary memoir, *West with the Night*, but apart from her few short stories and this famous book, she spurned litera-ture. Married three times, she also had six Kenya Derbys to her credit. She was still an active horse trainer when she died at the age of eighty-three.

KATHERINE MANSFIELD (1888–1923) was born in Wellington, New Zealand, and came to London in 1908. Here she met Virginia Woolf, D. H. Law-rence and John Middleton Murry, whom she married in 1918. Despair and unhappiness always drove her to escape. Her 'Indiscreet Journey' was based on an impulsive excursion to join Francis Carco in north-eastern France. The adventure ended in fiasco and she returned to London and Murry. Out of a life of exiles came some of the finest short stories ever to have been written in the English language. Her collections include *In a German Pension* (1911), *Prelude* (1918), *The Garden Party* (1922) and *The Dove's Nest* (1923). Much of her short life was spent travelling around Europe, desperately seeking a cure for the tuberculosis which finally killed her. She died at the Gurdjieff Institute at Fontainebleau.

EDNA O'BRIEN (1932–) was born in County Clare, Ireland, and now lives in London. Convent educated, she was briefly a pharmacist before turning to writing. Her first novel, *The Country Girls* (1960), and its sequels, *The Girl With Green Eyes* (1962) and *Girls in Their Married Bliss* (1964), gave her immediate recognition. In her nine novels and five volumes of short stories she charts the pain of separation, guilt and disappointment with originality and lyricism. Her most recent novel, *The High Road*, was published in 1988.

ANNA MARIA ORTESE (1914–) was born in Rome. She has lived in Naples, Venice, Milan and Genoa; she now lives in Rapallo with her sister. She has worked as a journalist, on *L'Europeo* and then on *Il Mondo*, winning two

Saint-Vincent prizes. Her first work, *Angelici Dolori*, a collection of short stories, was published in 1937. This was followed by eleven further books including her novel *L'iguana* (1965) and, most recently, *Il treno russo*, published in 1983.

GRACE PALEY (1922–), described by Philip Roth as 'splendidly comic and unladylike', was born in New York, the daughter of Jewish parents who arrived from Russia at the turn of the century. She grew up in Manhattan's Lower East Side and now lives in Vermont and Greenwich Village, New York. She began writing short stories in the 1950s and has published three collections: *The Little Disturbances of Man* (1959), *Enormous Changes at the Last Minute* (1974) and *Later the Same Day* (1985). A teacher and political activist, she has devoted herself to anti-war movements and the campaign for nuclear disarmament. She has never written a novel, believing that 'Art is too long and life too short'.

DOROTHY PARKER (1893–1967), humorist, short-story writer and poet, was the daughter of a Jewish father and a Scottish mother. Her celebrated and deadly wit has somewhat overshadowed her brilliance as a portrayer of the empty places in the human heart. During her early career she worked for *Vogue* (writing the advertising caption 'Brevity is the soul of Lingerie'), *Vanity Fair* and the *New Yorker*. A supporter of suffrage, a drinker and chain-smoker, with a weakness for floppy hats and eccentric *haute couture*, she was the leader of the 'Algonquin Round Table'. Following her divorce from Mr Parker she twice married Alan Campbell, a young bisexual film actor. In the 1920s she tried suicide twice, in the thirties she worked against General Franco and in the fifties she was cited by the House of UnAmerican Activities Committee. Her books include the significantly named volume of poetry *Enough Rope* (1926) and short-story collections *Laments for the Living* (1930) and *Here Lies* (1939).

JEAN RHYS (1894?–1979) was born in the Windward Islands: her father was a Welsh doctor; her mother was a Creole. She left for England at the age of sixteen. A drifter, chorus girl, mannequin and artist's model, she began to write when the first of her three marriages broke up. She spent time in Paris, where she met Hemingway, James Joyce and Ford Madox Ford. She moved in with Ford and his mistress Stella Bowen with 'nothing but a cardboard suitcase and [an] astonishing manuscript', and had a liaison with him. Her first collection of stories, *The Left Bank*, was published in 1927. This was followed by her novels *Quartet* (1928), *After Leaving Mr Mackenzie* (1930), *Voyage in the Dark* (1934) and *Good Morning Midnight* (1939). After 1939 she almost literally disappeared: many thought she was dead. She made a sensational reappearance with *Wide Sargasso Sea* (1966), followed by two further collections of stories.

ELIZABETH TAYLOR (1912–75) was born in Reading, Berkshire, the daughter of an insurance inspector. She worked as a governess and librarian before marriage to a businessman, and motherhood. She lived nearly all her married life in the village of Penn in Buckinghamshire, frequently spending evenings alone in her local pub, listening to the villagers' conversations. Her sixteen novels include *At Mrs Lippincote's* (1945), *A Game of Hide and Seek* (1951), *Angel* (1957), *In a Summer Season* (1961), *The Wedding Group* (1968) and *Mrs Palfrey at the Claremont* (1971). She also wrote four volumes of short stories, including *The Devastating Boys* (1972).

LISA ST AUBIN DE TERÁN (1953–) was born and brought up in London. She is half Jersey and half South American. At sixteen she married and wandered around Italy for two years with a group of Venezuelan exiles. She then spent seven years in the Venezuelan Andes, managing a sugar plantation and avocado farm. In 1978 she returned to England, settling in Norfolk with her daughter. She has published five novels: *The Keepers of the House* (1982), *The Slow Train to Milan* (1983), *The Tiger* (1984), *The Bay of Silence* (1986) and *Black Idol* (1987). She has also published a volume of poetry, *The High Place* (1985); a collection of stories, *The Marble Mountain* (1988); and *Off the Rails: Memoirs of a Train Addict* (1988). Her sixth novel will be published by Virago in 1989. She is now married to the Scottish painter Robbie Duff-Scott and divides her time between Venice and Umbria in Italy.

SYLVIA TOWNSEND WARNER (1893–1978) was born in Harrow, the daughter of a school housemaster. A student of fifteenth- and sixteenth-century music, she turned to writing fiction in the 1920s, contributing short stories to the *New Yorker* for over forty years. In the thirties she was a member of the Executive Committee of the Association of Writers for Intellectual Liberty; in 1937 she was a representative for the Congress of Madrid. She lived most of her adult life with her companion Valentine Ackland. Although she rarely moved from Dorset, her fiction ranges from fourteenth-century Norfolk (*The Corner That Held Them*, 1948) to revolutionary Paris in 1848 (*Summer Will Show*, 1936); from nineteenth-century Essex (*The True Heart*, 1928) to a South Sea Island (*Mr Fortune's Maggot*, 1927) and nineteenth-century southern Spain (*After the Death of Don Juan*, 1938). Her collected stories were published in 1988. It has been said that Sylvia Townsend Warner 'could not write so much as a postcard without being individual'.

EUDORA WELTY (1909–) was born in Jackson, Mississippi, which has remained her home nearly all her life. When she returned there from college, she took a job as publicity agent with the Works Progress Administration, travelling all over the state, taking unusual photographs of the people she met. Eudora Welty has said that the fiction she went on to write is in some way close to her practice of photography. One of the great writers of the American South, she has published five novels including *Losing Battles* (1970) and *The Optimist's Daughter* (1972), and numerous short stories, now published in *The Collected Stories of Eudora Welty* (1981).

EDITH WHARTON (1862–1937) was born into old New York society and married a Boston socialite. She found freedom from these restraints through travel to Europe. In 1910 her relationship with America finally closed when she moved permanently to France; that with her husband ended in divorce in 1913. She published her first novel in 1902, and thereafter averaged more than a book a year for the rest of her life. These included *The House of Mirth* (1905), *The Reef* (1912) and *The Age of Innocence* (1920). The first woman to receive a Doctorate of Letters from Yale University, winner of two Pulitzer Prizes, she was awarded the Légion d'Honneur and Order of Leopold for her war work. She spent her summers in an eighteenth-century villa north of Paris, and her winters in a converted monastery on the Riviera. She owned a car and one of her greatest pleasures was motoring around France, often in the company of her friend Henry James.

MALACHI WHITAKER (1895–1975), described as 'the Bradford Chekhov', was the eighth of eleven children of a Bradford bookbinder. She published four books of stories in the 1920s and 1930s, and then declared herself written out. She also published a kind of autobiography, *And So Did I*, in 1939. In 1984 Carcanet reissued *The Crystal Cabinet and Other Stories*.

HARRIETTE WILSON (1789–1846), described by the *Dictionary of National Biography* as a 'woman of fashion', was the daughter of a Mayfair shopkeeper. She was brought up to speak English and French, both indifferently. She began her career as mistress to Lord Craven, followed by an intrigue with the Honourable Frederick Lamb. She then became the kept mistress of the Duke of Argyle. Scott remarked of her: 'She was far from beautiful, but a smart, saucy girl, with good eyes and dark hair, and the manners of a wild schoolboy.' After 1820 she lived mainly in Paris, where she had an affair with – amongst others – the Marquis of Worcester. Her memoirs appeared in four small volumes in 1825 as

Memoires of Harriette Wilson, written by Herself. Over thirty editions are said to have been printed in one year. It was denounced as 'disgusting and gross prostitution of the press'.

JEANETTE WINTERSON (1959–) was born in Lancashire and brought up a Pentecostal Evangelist. She lost her faith and left home, working as ice-cream van driver, make-up artist in a funeral parlour and domestic in a mental hospital before going to Oxford to read English. She has published three novels: *Oranges Are Not the Only Fruit* (1985) – winner of the Whitbread Prize for a first novel – *Boating for Beginners* (1985) and *The Passion* (1987). She lives in London.